UNSETTLED SHORES

ALSO BY KELSEY GIETL

HOPE OR HIGH WATER — OVER THE ATLANTIC
Across Oceans
Twisted River

HOPE OR HIGH WATER — WAR ACROSS WATERS
Broken Lines
Unsettled Shores

UNSETTLED SHORES

—

Kelsey Gietl

Purple Mask Publishing
St. Charles, Missouri

For my parents, Ken and Ruth,
I'm blessed to call you Dad and Mom.
Thank you for always believing in me.

PROLOGUE

June 14, 1917
London, England

LONDON SMELLED OF MISERY. The city always carried a putrid tang with the constant smog that covered its rooftops, but today it also carried the weight of crumbled buildings and bloodstained cobblestones. Of yesterday's unexpected air raid and a war which, after over three years of scuffle, felt like it would never end.

Josie Harrington peddled her bicycle through Piccadilly Circus, the wheels' constant *clickity-clack* keeping pace to the rhythm of her labored breaths. It wasn't that she couldn't manage the ride; she had ridden this same route every day for over a year. From Holborn through Piccadilly to each required stop, ending in Chiswick then making the return route before blackout was imposed.

No, today she simply couldn't stomach the Great War's destruction anymore, her lungs and emotions depleted from dust-filled streets, air raid whistles, and being once again thrust into remembering her father's last words:

"Soon, Joselyn. This is only goodbye for a short while. Until then, send me your dear words and sweet treats, a stitched glove or two if you can spare the yarn. I shall write you all my love and letters, sporting tales of your heroic Pop fending off the Jerries!" A hug, a laugh, then her playful shove towards the railway car. A vigorous wave as he stood between two other soldiers half his age, one strong arm thrown over each of their young shoulders.

The sound of London now buzzed in her ears from flower sellers'

1

begs, motorcar engines, and passing pedestrian shouts. Masons salvaging bricks from a crumbled office building. A shopkeep snapping dust from a rug as though there were any way to actually rid the fibers of filth. The city itself as loud as the drone of airplane propellers passing overhead on an otherwise unobtrusive Wednesday morning.

Yesterday when she heard them, she had slid her bicycle to a halt, one hand angled over her eyes as she stared into a clear blue sky, searching. The Germans had only ever used Zeppelins to bomb London prior; no one suspected what was to come when the Gotha planes swooped out of the sky in broad daylight, releasing their destruction over the city. It all happened so quickly, Josie hadn't even moved. She stood there, staring into the sky while everyone ran for the underground platforms and residence cellars, streaking in both directions. Their voices sounded a bit like laughter to her crazed mind, and she imagined her father tugging her along towards Piccadilly, wanting open space to see the airplanes.

After it was all over, she realized how disappointed he would have been to read her letter saying how she survived another air raid and didn't see a single plane, nary even a wingtip. She had never seen the Zeppelins either, except in plastered warning posters. She was always in the wrong place at the wrong time, never where the action happened to be, always in safety. Not until the following day would she pedal her bicycle once again, *clickety-clack*, and see what misery the Germans left behind them. Yesterday's raid felled 162, eighteen of them children from a single school.

Her father had gone to war to experience excitement. Josie remained home and wished she hadn't seen so much.

She turned her bicycle onto the road into Chiswick, leaving behind most of the filthy air as the city's confines eventually turned more rustic. The fresh air motivated her to push her legs harder, standing up on the pedals as the cobblestones transitioned to dirt. Finally, she slid her bicycle to a stop outside the front steps of Olmsted Manor, a peach-stoned four-story Tudor converted into a convalescent home for wounded soldiers. With its opulent sprawling gardens, visits to the manor made for a lovely distraction from the pressing reality of

Josie's other daily delivery stops. Even when she didn't have a delivery for the home, she took delight sitting for a spell in its gardens. Often, she would join a recovering soldier for a welcome chat, both of them as eager for non-war related discussion as the other. As the days collected since her father had gone, she wondered if one afternoon she would arrive to find him sitting on one of those garden benches or, more likely, sprawled across a chaise lounge on the veranda, its sunshade flapping overhead, him basking in the moment like a nobleman on holiday.

The Olmsteds' footman, Cartwright, opened the door, his position one of the few leftover from the pre-war days. Now what servants remained at the manor had dual purpose, serving the needs of their countrymen first and the needs of their household second. The Olmsteds had rearranged their personal quarters to accommodate the soldiers with their grown children also having taken roles to assist the war effort.

"Good afternoon, Miss Harrington," the footman nodded, holding the door wide for her to pass. "Matron will be relieved to see you arrived safely. We worried after you did not appear yesterday."

"Yes, thank you, Cartwright. I am quite well today." Although she was not well in the slightest. She unpinned her hat and gave her flattened brunette curls a habitual fluff, knowing nothing would spruce them back up after her spin through so many dozen dust clouds on the London streets.

Cartwright led her through the entryway, past the open atrium where several patients were seated around circular playing tables. Each glanced over as she passed, with several offering a nod or a smile which she returned in kind. Others' gazes merely traced the room's corners, unfocused eyes lost in memory. Between throw rugs, Josie's worn shoe soles landed hollowly against the marble tiles until the footman opened a door and directed her inside.

What once served as the manor's luxurious ballroom was now lined with rows of wrought iron beds, each covered in starched white sheets between which lay wounded soldiers in varying states of medical duress. Five voluntary aids, including the matron in charge, fluttered about the room checking vitals, rewrapping bandages, and

3

distributing medication. Some of the patients were able to sit up and read, one or two even smoked a cigarette, but the majority lay beneath their covers, either asleep, staring blankly at the ceiling, or muttering softly to themselves.

It was not a room Josie would have stepped foot in without the war's assistance, nor one she liked to linger in for too long. Nevertheless, she visited whether Matron was there or not. Visited every room in the manor in fact. Just in case her father appeared in one of those beds. After all these months, she still searched for him, even knowing he wouldn't be there. His British Expeditionary Force identification tags were threaded on a chain beneath her blouse, yet she still liked to imagine the joyous reunion that would never be.

Matron met Josie halfway across the room, the older woman's hands clasped tightly against her white apron-clad bosom and concern etched in every wrinkled feature. She released a sigh before quickly crossing herself, her starched veil fluttering with her fevered movements. "Oh, thank goodness, my dear," she cried. "We were all so very worried yesterday when you did not arrive. So terribly afraid you were caught in the thick of it. To see you here now..." She shook her clasped hands as though offering thankful prayers. "Why, I must say, I am so very relieved."

"Yes, I've arrived no worse for wear." Josie returned a reluctant smile. It was more difficult to lie to Matron than to Cartwright. Matron found it far easier to see through Josie's emotions and tended to mollycoddle as a result. She wondered if her own mother hadn't passed so soon in life if she would have been as perceptive.

Matron continued to examine her with silent interrogation, so Josie decided to complete her assignment and escape to the gardens while there was still opportunity.

"I have today's delivery." She reached into her shoulder bag, searching for the twine-tied stack of envelopes she knew were buried there. Normally the letters for Olmsted Manor were all that remained in her pack, making them easy to locate, but today she had bypassed all her other stops in favor of leaving the city as quickly as possible. She would deliver the others on the return, but that meant she now had to sort through her bag to locate the correct ones. "One moment.

I know they're here somewhere."

"Hush, child. Not yet."

"Oh, yes, forgive me," she said as her hand landed on the correct bundle. She had nearly forgotten the most important part of their delivery process. "I suppose I was so flustered I forgot to say, *Victores in—*"

"I said hush!" Matron snatched Josie's wrist, shaking the packet of letters back into the bag. "We have an audience."

Josie followed Matron's line of sight to a patient bedded two rows over near the window, his eyes watching them intently rather than the pleasant view of the garden. Clearly a young man still, probably no more than thirty, he was wrapped in bandages of one form or another practically from head to toe. Casting braced his right leg and swathes of white linen packaged his right hand, sitting limply at his side. His chest rose and fell in anxious breaths while his unbandaged hand lay splayed upon it, as though counting each breath to ensure another followed. The upper half of his head lay hidden behind a bandage so concealing, she couldn't tell what color his hair might be or if he even had any. What parts of his face that weren't bandaged were riddled in various states of bruising.

"Who is that soldier?" she asked Matron. Her wrist still lay in the older woman's grip but was no longer attempting to shake her off.

Matron gently released her, smoothing her apron and meticulously adjusting her puffed armbands. "I'm not certain of his name. We haven't heard a word from him since he arrived. I only know what was passed from his rescuers." She lowered her voice, edging closer until her shoulder pressed Josie's. "He's one of the special extracts they said, caught on the wrong side of the French front line. Trapped in an air raid in Le Clé, had a church topple right on top of him. They managed to get him out, but the journey over—tended to by farmers then bouncing in that wagon and the rocking waves from Calais— about did him in. We think he'll make it, the question is what shape he'll be in if he does. He certainly won't be able to return to the front. It's a hard blow for some of these men to receive. They feel as though they're not valid anymore. Yet, the things they have seen over there..."

Josie knew some of the things Matron spoke of, horrors the

soldiers mentioned in the manor's confidence. She thought of the letters from her father, tucked away in her stocking drawer. In between lines of black censorship, his words crippled her in bed, knees drawn up beneath the quilts as she imagined bullets pelting off the dirt like hailstones mere inches from her father's helmet. Both his arms cocked upright, the rifle butt pressed tight against his shoulder while he took out one Jerry after another. She remembered watching his brigade march through the streets, that same rifle propped against his shoulder, the smile he tossed her as bright as the sunlight glinting off the weapon's barrel. Although neither a rifle, a helmet, nor a world of good intentions had saved him in the end.

She refocused on the wounded soldier and pressed a hand to where her father's identification tags lay beneath her blouse. She splayed her fingers perfectly positioned to match the stranger's and felt her own breath move in then out. Her father would never come home. This man might not either. What family would he leave behind?

"Do you believe he'll survive?" she asked.

"There's a chance," said Matron. "He's healing relatively well considering what he's been through, but the body is influenced by the mind. He doesn't yet know the extent of his injuries. He still has his hand, but I'm afraid the fingers were too badly damaged. He'll keep them, but they'll never work as they should. As for his leg ... well, that's to be seen. He needs something to live for or he may not live at all."

Josie hesitated as the soldier's eyes once again tried to hold hers. His bandaged hand raised ever so slowly, then outward as though reaching for her, before returning to its lifeless position on the bed sheets. With a grimace, he finally turned his head away. Josie didn't.

Matron released a low sigh. "That's the most response we've seen since he arrived."

"How long ago was that?"

"Nearly two weeks."

Josie turned to her in surprise, breaking the young man's spell. "Not a word in all that time? Not even a simple hand gesture?"

Matron shook her head. "Not a one. When he arrived, he was

barely even conscious."

Weaving around the rows of beds, past men blinded from mustard gas or with missing limbs, Josie lowered herself to sit on the end of the soldier's mattress and settled her shoulder bag in her lap. "Good morning, sir. The summer sun is lovely, isn't it?"

Tilting his chin, he examined her with that same focused stare, analyzing, as though trying to reach into her mind and extract information. They had trained her not to reveal anything, not to give any indication that she was more than a simple courier. She focused on keeping her expression a blank slate, although her eyes analyzed him as much as he studied her.

Who was this soldier? What made him such a "special extract" as Matron had called him? *Caught on the wrong side of the front line,* she said. How had he arrived there?

It wasn't her place to ask those things. That was part of her training too. Deliver, but don't ask. She had done it a hundred times. A thousand times. Why did he make it so difficult to obey this time? He hadn't even said a word.

He attempted to clench his fingers into fists and winced as his right hand refused to cooperate within its wrappings. Instead, he lifted the damaged hand to his chest and folded his good hand over it. He looked from her to the bag on her lap, the one which held dozens of letters still requiring special delivery. There was no way he could know about those though.

His good hand lowered from his chest, reached across ... and she lifted the bag out of reach. She set it on the floor behind her where he couldn't see. His hand lingered in midair, fingers outstretched, waiting for something. Did he want her to take it? That would be quite improper. But what exactly was considered propriety in a time of war? He had lost his brigade, his hand, and perhaps more in one day. She had lost any sense of normalcy the day the prime minister declared conflict with Germany.

Still, she let the soldier's hand linger there between them, didn't take it, yet didn't move away. Her own sat primly folded in her lap, right there atop her pressed wool skirt, grey and somber like the endless war and dust particles floating through the city streets. She had been taught not to trust anyone too easily. Wasn't that what her father cautioned her in one of his final letters before the Somme? Anyone could betray another, any man, woman, or child. War had taken even a lighthearted man like Hunter Harrington and made him think twice about the world. That was why she took this job. To prove she wasn't like everyone else. That she could be selfless. To help the families whose fathers, brothers, husbands, and sons might still have a chance to come home.

"I'm Joselyn," she said softly. "Josie actually. Josie Harrington."

Slowly his lips parted. "Peter Müller. From Iowa."

She forced back the edge of a smile. His accent sounded American. The way he said his name was not. Her father always said America had been built on the dreams of immigrants. "Traitorous rebels too," he would say with a laugh, "but you mark my words, sweet Joselyn, those same rebellious dreamers will return one day to save us all."

Finally, perhaps one had.

Slowly, she unfolded her fingers, one by one. Allowed him to rest his palm atop hers. Their fingers didn't fold over one another, just remained palm to palm, the back of her hand cooled by the bed's white sheets. Her bag of letters lay on the floor, waiting for one more message. His message.

"Tell me your story, Peter," she said. "Help me send you home."

PART ONE

—

Unsettled

ONE

AMARA KISCH SNIFFLED BACK another round of tears, threatening to expand to full-on weeping if she didn't rein in her fragility right now. There were only so many days an infertile married woman could measure lovely miniature garments before she must politely excuse herself from the shop floor for a pitiful cry. Not the unfortunate ugly weeping of drenched handkerchiefs and scrunched facial muscles until one wondered if her eyesight would forever be blurred by tears. That sort of emotion was reserved for under the bedcovers, chest pressed to her pillow while her husband was still at work or away on some fabricated errand.

Rather, this was a polite cry, palms pressed to her eyes to stem the flow before they could leave any hint of their existence. She could not allow her customers or the head seamstress to think her unable to complete tasks she had perfected as far back as childhood. She needed to retain some sense of normalcy in a life turned on end by a world war, prejudice, and now her own womanly emotions.

Nearly three months she had lasted this time, all the way from the return to school demands in August. Middle and upper-crust mothers had swarmed Daisy Mahlandt's seamstress shop with all manner of little ones, from mewling infants to adolescent boys pushing their mothers away and complaining about why they needed to continue school at all. They wanted to be away at the war front, fighting off the terrible Huns. Their older brothers, cousins, or fathers were off in the fray; why couldn't they join up too? Seventeen was a truly terrible age to be when mere months separated you from legal enlistment.

Europe's great war had already stolen so much from her. Per their father, Jürgen Müller's insistence, her brother, Peter, left to join the German army without a return word to his safety in nine long months. Despite his directive for her to stay safe, horrific discrimination against her birthplace had battered her sails like a thunderstorm, with false accusations forcing her to leave her newfound life and true identity behind in St. Louis. The one bright light in so much darkness was her marriage.

Although their friendship began rather rocky, she fell in love with Emil despite his many flaws. When he offered to run away with her, to forget the world and live each moment as though they might "jump into a European trench tomorrow," she agreed. She had spent every day since trying to forget the circumstances behind their escape, when they witnessed a mob hang an innocent man for simply being German-born like them. Or how Emil's morality squad partner threatened to turn her in as a spy when Emil accidentally revealed her true heritage one night over a few drinks. Even so, she had forgiven him then and forgave him now and every day, because where would she be without him? No doubt strung up on that street lamp right alongside her countryman.

But there were still some things the war would never change, that she could never forget, no matter how many times she whispered to herself, *What if?*

That was why she was blotting tears before they dripped on her black Singer sewing machine. Not because she feared someone would drag her away for being an enemy spy. Not because she worried they would discover that her alias Amy Miller was really Amara Kisch with an entire family in the *Deutsches Heer* and a carefully fabricated life. But because of all the children leaving the shop hand-in-hand with their mothers, heading back to the family she feared she would never have.

She had thought the war would cause many to temper their pocketbooks. Ladies everywhere now pieced together items for the soldiers' care packages as part of their patriotism—dozens of knitted hats and socks and gloves. She had assumed that surely they would then request less stitching for themselves. Yet, the opposite seemed to be so. Amara would greet each mother and child with her signature smile, her demeanor all politeness as she measured, pinned, and cut off hems to the correct length. All the while, it crushed her heart a little more each time.

It wasn't as though she hadn't had time to come to terms with what simply was. She had known for over five years now that her womb wasn't built for labor pains, and it certainly wasn't that she hadn't dealt with children in her infertile state. While living in Iowa, she had sewn plenty of children's garments for Mrs. Wilson's seamstress shop while Peter worked his self-made feed store with their cousin, Siegfried.

Or rather Zeke, she thought in disgust. He had stripped his given name the second he stepped foot off the ship from Germany. It was at his insistence that Amara received the detrimental health examination whose infertility result destroyed their engagement and revealed the type of man he truly was. Because of that examination, she spent the next five years believing her worth lay in little more than his bruises and insults. Not until Emil did she believe that even her brokenness could be beautiful.

"Amy?" Daisy called. She pulled back the floor-to-ceiling curtain leading to the front of the seamstress shop, irritated lines creasing the edges of her lips.

Hurriedly, Amara swiped both palms across her eyes then patted her cheeks to restore their natural color. She forced a smile and rose from the sewing machine's chair. "Yes, Mrs. Mahlandt?"

"Did you find that blue muslin? The way you hurried out, I expected you knew right where you'd lain it. But here you sit and no muslin." Daisy eyed her up and down. "It's the last item Mrs. Gibbons needs to be measured for her daughter." *But she won't pay the deposit until she sees the fabric is to her liking,* Amara finished silently. Of course, Daisy would never say that within earshot of the customer.

"Of course. I have it right here." Blinking, Amara snatched the blue bolt off the shelf beside her sewing machine table and tucked it beneath her arm, marching past Daisy as though she wasn't a mere four-foot-ten to the seamstress's five-foot-seven.

Hours later, Amara walked home alone from the seamstress shop, wishing Emil wasn't required to remain at work until long into the evening. A strong gust blew wayward autumn leaves from a tree as Amara passed under it, the swaying branches littering the sidewalk with orange and gold. With autumn settled in, the days had finally cooled, a welcome change. Since their arrival, it seemed like everything in New York City was only one temperature, horribly hot. The abundance of brick and stone skyscrapers packed its citizens in like a roaring oven. So many people stacked one beside the next, always shouting, never quiet, and the glances of blue sky far above were often blocked by factory soot. She had thought St. Louis to be rather stifling at times; however, it had been nothing compared to this. This was no place to be a newlywed. This was no place to plant roots and start a home.

The trouble was, she didn't know where home should be anymore or even what it should look like. Was it Oberammergau where she was raised, Iowa where she grew to womanhood, or St. Louis where she fell in love? Would she ever be able to return to any of those places? Or was this New York City with its noisy clatter and suffocating atmosphere to be her forever home now? Thank goodness she had Emil. Without him, she feared she would be completely lost.

She must remind herself that, all things considered, life was still good. She had plenty of food and clothes and a husband who loved her. She and Emil rented a small apartment, which although simplistic, was theirs to call their own until such time as they chose. They had both retained their good health and mental capabilities which was more than she could say for so many in this city, confined to living in tenements or facing the dangers of factory life. Her life was truly blessed. She had nearly all she could ask for in a marriage.

Except for one thing.

She found her feet directing her towards the nearby children's home exactly as they did every week. There were larger ones elsewhere in the city, but she preferred this one. Small and compact and rather insignificant from the outside, it reminded her a lot of herself. Petite and overlooked, never taken seriously due to her short stature and youthful features.

She never went inside, not even on the days she left a box of handsewn items on the front stoop. She merely watched from across the street, offering a quick prayer for what she hoped could be someday.

Worthless woman, you don't deserve such joy.

Her entire body jerked out of reflex as Zeke's words stomped through her mind. Insults she heard every day until he joined Peter in the German army. Degradations that usually accompanied his rough fingers around her upper arms or a shove against the kitchen table.

Peter never knew a single word spoken between them. He never saw a single bruise, so well hidden were Zeke's punishments. To this day, he still had no idea.

"You honestly believe I would prefer someone else's child when I can have one of my own?" Zeke had spat that April afternoon back in 1912. Mere days after she arrived in America prepared to marry him, he had thrown her to the sidewalk in anger, unwilling to accept that she could never bear him children. *"A secondhand son is like a secondhand coat, Amara. No one loves it; they tolerate it until they find a better one. Unfortunately for you, I'm not willing to."*

She laid light fingers to her ribs, remembering the fury in his eyes as he left her to bear her burden alone. How no one stopped to help. Only sixteen years old then, she had felt as though her life was gone.

Worthless woman, who will want you now?

Emil, she thought. Emil wanted her, brokenness and all. Emil would wait.

A little girl, perhaps five or six years old, appeared at the upstairs window to the children's home. Her tiny palms pressed flat against the glass, the crinkled curtain framing her blonde curls like a chapel veil. Curls that nearly matched Emil's platinum-blond locks. Amara raised a hand, waving to the child as a warm smile crossed her lips. The girl grinned back, her fingers waving back enthusiastically, each golden curl bouncing with the movement.

She could be ours, Amara thought suddenly. What would stop her, she wondered, from walking in and adopting that little girl right now?

That child surely needed a family as desperately as Amara wanted one. *She could be ours.*

"Evening edition!" shouted a newsboy from the street corner. "London suffers her third consecutive night of German bombings!"

Amara's enthusiasm vanished like a puff of smoke. As long as the war raged in Europe, they could never have that dream. It was simply too dangerous to bring a child into the middle of their mess. Right now, they had found a place of stillness in this new city, but that didn't mean their good fortune would last forever. She had seen a man hanged in this country because he bore the wrong surname. She would not expose her child to the possibility of that same fate. When the war was over and peace reigned again, when their future stood on more solid footing, then they could walk into that orphanage and make their dreams come true. Until then, she would hold onto the threads of her heart and pray they didn't unravel completely.

TWO

EMIL KISCH WORRIED ABOUT HIS WIFE. He worried about a great many things these days, but Amara most of all. How often she went to the children's home. How she knitted those orphans socks and hats as often as she knitted them for the soldiers overseas. He wished she would stop. He had politely asked her to stop. He could demand it, but he never would. If she needed that to help her through, he would let her. Even if he did think it ridiculous.

Wasn't it better to focus on what was right in front of them? Control the things that could be controlled, rather than grieving over a dream that sat frozen until the war ended? Truth be told, he was still bitter about losing his own dream to the war. All summer he read newspaper articles about the Yankees and missed his own Benton Park Brewmasters baseball team back home in St. Louis. He should have been playing ball this summer, preparing to try out for the majors, not tending drinks to the elite in Park Avenue's Forsythe Hotel. He ran a clean cloth around the rim of a lowball glass before filling it with amber fluid and handing it off to a waiting patron. Pouring whiskey rather than drinking it was a far cry from who he was before this war began.

Simply put, he had been a wreck back then. Horribly arrogant, life was focused on good times and the consequences of war weren't worth mulling over. He would imbibe worse than a fish tossed back in after a hook and never think twice about it. Until he met Amara, that

17

was. She made him reconsider every questionable decision. Even after he betrayed her to his morality squad partner, Jonathan Earhart, she still forgave him and, beyond reason, even married him.

Their New York life wasn't the one he had imagined for them—neither was their hasty escape from an unruly mob nor spontaneous country wedding—but what they had found satisfied him. They had a roof over their heads and jobs to pay the bills. They had found a peaceful church and welcoming neighbors to attend with. On Thursday nights, Amara attended the ladies' knitting group while he joined the men on the apartment roof for cigars and a few rounds of cards. The air clouded with factory soot and remained hot between the cement and mortar but in those moments, he could forget the war existed or that they held any personal tie to it.

Until someone called him Emmett or Mr. Miller and he remembered that his life wasn't quite his own. Not until the war ended.

It always came back to the war.

Two fingers tapped twice on the varnished bar top, drawing his attention to Alfred Hastings, a regular occupant of the Forsythe whenever he and his fellow businessmen needed a "change of pace." Lately, their paces had found them in the lounge several nights per week. Emil wiped another glass clean and set it on the bar top, tossing the drying cloth over his shoulder.

"Another of the same, Mr. Hastings?" He reached for a bottle of gin from the second shelf behind him.

Alfred gave his usual smooth smile. "Ah, my man, you know me too well. Where else can one find such superior service in this city?"

Tipping the last of the bottle into the lowball, Emil thumbed for the door. "I hear the Astoria treats their guests like the president-elect. It might be better suited to your—" He gave a half-smile. "Well, better suited to your fancy suit."

Alfred gave a mighty guffaw, far too boisterous for the poor joke Emil had presented. But he knew what his patrons enjoyed and once Mr. Hastings downed a few rounds of gin, he could be entertained by nearly anything. "Quite true!" he chortled. "Suit my fancy suit, it does! However, it doesn't have you, my man. You deserve an award for your service." He jostled his glass in Emil's direction. "Find another bottle. I'll return for seconds."

Fourths, actually. Emil watched Mr. Hastings and his hundred-dollar suit stride away through the smoky lounge, his laughter still echoing off the walnut-paneled walls. With a final chuckle, the man lowered himself onto one of several velvet-covered armchairs beside three other gentlemen with equal caliber attire. Emil didn't recognize them, but he had served Mr. Hastings long enough to hazard a guess as to the reason for their meeting.

Business was the name of the game at the Forsythe and based on the group's tight-lipped expressions, a deal was likely not far off. Being around these Wall Street types, Emil sometimes missed his time at Langdon's Saloon back home. Although the establishment had gotten him into more trouble than not, its clientele was far livelier. Here there was no gossip of extramarital affairs, no punches thrown in the back alleyway, and certainly not a factory-worker to be found. A rather bland atmosphere for a former morality squad officer, even if it was framed in gilded mirrors and glittering chandeliers. Emil was sure some of these men engaged in scandal elsewhere, but it certainly wasn't spoken of. Not unless one of those topics helped them get ahead in oil, railroad, or the market. And unless it directly affected their shipping practices, mention of war was akin to a bunch of boys playing battle with sharpened sticks. At least most of them, like Alfred Hastings, had a fair sense of humor and a heavy tipping hand to accompany their ignorance.

"What's got you so serious, brother? Bad case of indigestion?"

Emil started at the familiar feminine voice, certain he was imposing his personal memories onto whatever rude patron had decided to grace the lounge with her presence. He took in the young woman's meticulous makeup and bubbly blonde curls pinned into a stylish chignon above her olive suit. Then he performed a double-take as he recognized his sister's bright if not slightly mischievous smile and hadn't a rational clue why she would be here. She was smiling, so the visit couldn't mean bad news, could it?

"Winnie?" He glanced around the lounge, desperately hoping no one would return to the bar and request a drink from his alias,

Emmett Miller. That was all he needed, for his sister to question him in a highly public place and ruin his cover. He lowered his voice. "What are you doing here? How did you find me?"

Setting her valise on the cross-patterned carpet, she swung up onto the nearest barstool and casually leaned one elbow on the bar top. "Ulrich Klassen. You may have moved across the city, but I knew you'd leave word just in case. I begged his address from Reuben."

After their flight from St. Louis, Ulrich had been Emil and Amara's only contact in New York. The middle-aged man shared a cabin with Emil's best mate, Reuben Radford, on the trip over to the States. Known for his unsavory side, Ulrich hadn't been anyone's first choice of confidant, and given their current situation, Emil hadn't trusted him enough to remain living too nearby. He had, however, left the Forsythe's address in case his family needed to contact him quickly. Or in case the authorities came calling. If he or Amara disappeared without warning, at least someone would know their last known location.

Emil glanced down the bar top and finding its seats unoccupied, leaned in with a whisper, "First off, due to ... you know, what happened back in St. Louis ... folks here call me Emmett Miller, so please don't make a scene if someone does."

"A scene?" She fluttered her lashes innocently. "Honestly, when do I ever make a scene?"

He frowned. "I'm serious, Win. This is important."

"Oh, all right, I was only kidding with you."

"Well, your timing is poor. Where are Mum and Pop?" he asked, searching the lounge. At almost seventeen, his sister had never been much farther from their parents' home than school, the grocer's, and the Benton Park ball field.

She gave her curls a slight pat and threw a discreet glance over her shoulder. "They elected not to join me."

"And Fred?"

She sniffed. "That nit? I preferred to travel alone than listen to our brother's condescension the entire trip. Although he has been slightly more bearable to live with since you left."

"You're traveling unescorted? Is that wise?" Being an immature girl in such a large city so far from home must be a real treat. A treat that, due to her childish ignorance, would likely land her in trouble. Several lounge patrons were already openly staring, including Mr. Hastings, likely wondering which one of them she was connected to. Women hardly ever visited the lounge and when they did, they certainly weren't bright-eyed teenage blondes.

"Don't you think this is asking for trouble," she said instead, "working in a saloon? With your history? I'm surprised your wife agreed to it."

"Begrudgingly. Amy had the same thoughts you do, but I'm not like that anymore. I can say when I've had enough."

Winnie traced a nail over the bar's woodgrain and shrugged. "Very well. Seems like tempting fate to me."

"The only employment assistance I had in this miserable city was Ulrich. With his contacts, it was either this, a factory, or something far dodgier. At least alcohol is familiar. It's easy to blend in." He gestured to the carved paneling and decadent paintings on up to the coffered ceiling flickering with chandelier light. "And wouldn't you agree this type of *saloon* is better than most?"

Two taps on the counter turned both their heads. Three paces down, Willard Thompson, another regular patron, held his empty glass aloft and shook it lightly. "Another bourbon?"

"Of course, sir. I believe you were drinking the Oltrio, ten year?" With the man's nod, Emil selected the correct bottle and refilled his glass.

Mr. Thompson took a sip and sighed. "My thanks and do keep them coming. If you see me empty, bring another." He gave a side nod to a group of men seated near the fireplace. "There's business to do, and I'm afraid it may be a very long evening."

"Of course, Mr. Thompson. I'll keep a close watch."

Once he was seated back with his business partners, Emil returned to his conversation with Winnie. "You still haven't said why exactly you're here. Surely you didn't come just for a visit, especially not alone. Is something wrong back home? ... Oh no..." He felt a pain start somewhere at the base of his neck, creeping across his shoulders. "Did Earhart turn in his testimony? Did they come for our parents? Is that why they 'elected' not to come here with you? What of Fred?"

Winnie held up both hands then slowly lowered them to the bar top. "Whoa. Calm down. It was nothing like that. Mama and Papa are perfectly well. Last I heard, your rotten former squad partner was reprimanded for his poor behavior during the riot and forced to switch roles with Officer Lewis. He's now on front desk duty. Far as we suspect, it seems he's given up his endeavor to ruin you." She pegged him with a warning glare. "Course, I wouldn't suggest returning until the war ends either."

For months, Emil had felt a terrible nagging at leaving his family behind. As soon as Winnie began talking, though, all he felt was relief. When they left St. Louis, his former squad partner seemed dead set on reporting them to the authorities. He had even threatened them at gunpoint. They could only hope that a guilty conscience had changed Earhart's mind. However, Emil would take his sister's advice for once. He and Amara couldn't return to St. Louis yet, but at least it sounded like they weren't being tracked anymore. Tonight, they could breathe a little easier.

He grinned. "You have no idea how happy it makes me to hear that, Win. Then why are you here? I assume it's not only to see my charming face?"

She gave a light chuckle. "No. It was Uncle Sam, actually. You know, he's a terrible relation sometimes. When you see him on those posters, wagging that finger at you, he strikes me as a bit eccentric. The uncle you're always helping rearrange the furniture again because he's plumb crazy. Then you realize, he's still family and you have to keep him from destroying himself."

"What in Pete's name are you talking about?"

"Remember how we partook in that unfortunate incident back in June?"

"Yes, although I wouldn't say we partook in so much as ran from." How could he ever forget the man swinging from a street lamp simply because he was German-born? Or how he physically restrained his sister from charging into a mob of hundreds in an attempt to save him? She would have been killed and he would have lost another sibling. It had nearly destroyed their family after their brother,

Charles, died on *Titanic*. Their parents would never have recovered if their youngest child and only daughter was strung up like some offensive criminal.

"I know you thought I was foolish that night," she continued.

"You were."

She held up a hand. "Now let's not argue. I know I wasn't prepared to take on such a large task, but we still stood by while injustice happened. Well, I can't stand idle anymore. So, I enlisted."

"You joined the *army*?" Now the olive suit and the perfectly pinned hair made sense. He didn't even know women were allowed to join. More importantly, his sister *shouldn't* be allowed to join. "Have you completely lost your mind? You could be killed."

"I won't be doing anything too dangerous. They reserve those jobs for the men. I signed on to entertain the troops."

"Entertain? How exactly do you plan to *entertain* them?"

She gave him one gigantic eye roll. "Oh, do sweep your mind out of the gutter. You were clearly in that morality squad too long. It's going to be perfectly classy, nothing coarse. We ladies are simply there to serve meals, play games, distribute books, maybe perform a song or two. In short, keep the soldiers' spirits up. I'm not certain exactly which tasks I'll be assigned. I suppose I'll find out when I get there."

"Mum and Pop were accepting of this decision? How did you even join up anyway? You have to be eighteen, don't you?"

At least she had the decency to blush. "A little white lie on my application. Besides, I'll be eighteen in a little over a year, and I'm already as capable as any woman of age."

"That is a matter of opinion. And don't think you're getting out of answering my first question. Our parents don't approve of this, do they?" He raised both eyebrows. "Or do they not even know?"

"Of course, they know, but I had already signed the papers when I told them I was leaving. They couldn't exactly argue once the decision had been made." She looked down at her gloved fingers. "Between us though, Papa shouted and Mama started crying. I never wanted to make Mama cry."

Emil placed one gentle hand over hers, giving her fingers a small squeeze before releasing them. "They're afraid. With Charles already gone and me so far away, they don't want to lose you too. This is a war, you know. It isn't like your usual flight of fancy, acting out by trimming your hair short or sneaking off to some suffragette rally. People are dying over there, Win."

Her eyes shot back up to his, their vivid blue icy. "People are dying over here too. If not on street lamps, then slowly dying in their hearts. The Schneiders' uncle was sent to an internment camp three weeks ago, and Papa's shop has suffered even more for it. If I go overseas and serve, it'll not only help the war effort but also prove our patriotism. It will help all the German-Americans."

Emil had to admit she had a point. Although he and Fred had both registered for the draft, neither were currently serving, and Emil's quick departure probably made it seem to many as though he was avoiding the possibility of conscription altogether. If at least one of the Kisch children actively participated, it would certainly prove advantageous to their father's struggling business. He didn't have to like the way Winnie went about it though.

Before he could speak, however, Winnie extracted an envelope from her inner jacket pocket and set it on the bar top between them. She turned it so her brother could see the address. "This is the other reason I needed to see you before I left for France."

"For Amy?" he asked in surprise. His wife's name was scrawled upon the envelope followed by the words *Care of Maggie Frye, St. Louis, Missouri.* There was no postmark, no other markings of any kind. "Where did this come from?"

"Her brother."

"Peter?" Emil scanned the lounge, but the nearest patron sat well away. Everyone was too involved in their conversations and drinks to pay much attention. "Peter's supposed to be in France," he whispered. Even if an injury had sent Peter away from the front, he still fought for the Germans. The *Deutsches Heer* certainly wouldn't send him into enemy territory for medical care, which meant he must have been taken prisoner or worse, turned enemy spy.

Emil opened the letter, reading its contents. Shocked, he looked back at Winnie. "Have you read this?" The seal was already broken so someone had.

She nodded. "We all have. Maggie thought we shouldn't worry you about it. It was our parents who insisted I bring it straight away."

"Our parents?"

"Yes. Papa thought it only fair that you knew."

He stared at the letter a moment longer until the swirling script began to blur under the yellow bar lights. Then he returned it to the envelope and tucked it in his jacket pocket. "We need to get this to Amy."

"You have work to finish here though, don't you?"

Emil muttered a curse under his breath. Even though they were slow on a Tuesday evening, he still had three hours to go. "Would you be willing to wait? You can stay at our apartment tonight."

"Certainly." She stood, retrieving her valise from the floor, and searched the room for an empty armchair. Mr. Hastings gave her a welcoming smile from across the room, and she smirked in Emil's direction. "Perhaps I'll find myself a beau here and there'll be no need to bring one back from overseas."

Frowning, he pointed at the door. "There's a library down the hall."

THREE

November 6, 1917 –
New York City

IT WAS ANOTHER EVENING ALONE in the two-room apartment while Amara waited for Emil to return. Cozied on the sofa with a quilt tucked around her legs and surrounded by sewing baskets, her clicking knitting needles and the clock's ticking hand were her only company. She had already eaten dinner, read the evening news, and finished the dishes and scrubbing before turning to more caps and booties for the children's home. Winter would be upon them soon and she wanted to make sure those children were well cared for. Come the first snow, perhaps she would even leave a batch of scarves. With a last tie of the yarn and snip of the scissors, she laid her latest creation aside.

Half-past eleven. Emil would be home soon.

She still loathed how they fought for weeks after he told her he would be working at a saloon. No matter how elegant and refined he claimed it to be, the position still tasted sour to her, although it did make sense given his background as both a former morality squad officer and what he liked to call an "alcohol enthusiast." He didn't have to learn a new trade, which made it easy to earn money without drawing suspicion. From the first day, he promised to never come home intoxicated, and he never had, but that didn't mean she didn't worry whenever he was gone.

Usually, she was in bed by this time, but tonight she couldn't sleep. The cool autumn air blew through the solitary kitchen window and she thought of Peter over in Europe, preparing for winter in the trenches. Would he be warm enough? Would there be illness, frostbite, and hypothermia in addition to bullets and bombs? Maybe he was already dead and she should be praying for the repose of his soul, rather than the health of his body.

With a loud exhale, she dragged herself off the sofa and into the kitchen, setting a kettle of water on to boil. In another few steps, she set the percolator to brewing, certain Emil would want coffee when he arrived home. He would down the energy-inducing beverage and then somehow still fall straight into bed, curling up against her until his breathing slowed. Her eyes would pop open in the darkness, thoughts running until somehow, she found herself waking to morning's light.

She wished she could at least send her brother a care package, even an anonymous one. Hopefully, her mother or sisters had thought to do so. Back in Oberammergau, they would be helping their father bring in the autumn harvest; she could nearly hear the squeals of her nieces and nephews and see them racing from the wagon. Between her four sisters, she wondered how many more babies might be on the way by now. Nearly a year had passed since she had corresponded with either of her parents, the last letter from Papa demanding that Peter and Zeke return home to fight. Of course, she had left Germany under the assumption that she was unlikely to return, but she still wished she could share news of her marriage with them. Perhaps after the war. It was always "after the war" these days.

The kettle whistled and she quickly removed it from the fire. Pouring steaming water over tea leaves, she savored the warmth drifting across her face in contrast to the chilly breeze at her back. Like nearly all their other belongings, they had purchased the cups from a small church outside the city where possessions were dropped that no one wanted. Emil had broken the handle off one of the cups only two days in, now requiring Amara to carry her teacup to the kitchen table wrapped in a dishtowel. Thankfully, their unadorned apartment had come with a few furnished staples, not requiring them to transport and maneuver heavy pieces up three flights of stairs.

When she heard the front door open at exactly 11:52 p.m., she hurried towards it, expecting to be greeted by Emil's usual cheeky half-smile that she so adored. Except that when he entered, she saw he was not alone. At first, her heart stuttered to see a woman in their apartment, but then she took in the woman's blonde curls and ecstatic smile and her heart nearly stopped altogether.

"Oh, this is delightful!" Winnie declared. She glanced around the small apartment with a nod of approval, her eyes making a slow circuit from floor to ceiling. "How I would love to have a cozy place like this all my own."

Emil shrugged out of his jacket, tossing it over the sofa arm. "Though under different circumstances, I hope." He took a deep sniff of the air. "Made me coffee? Such a good wife."

"Ye-yes," Amara stammered, still amazed to have a visitor of any sort, much less family. "It's in the percolator."

Suddenly seeming to notice her sister-in-law standing there, Winnie dropped her valise to the floorboards and with a girlish squeal, ran to throw her arms around Amara. "Oh, Amy, it's been forever! How I've missed you!" She pulled back with a frown, her grip firm on her sister-in-law's shoulders from nearly six inches above. "Do you know how awful it's been back home, stuck there while you're out here having an adventure? Although I suppose I should feel sorry for *you*. You are here with my brother." She contorted her face and Amara couldn't stifle her giggle. Winnie always had been capable of diffusing a tense situation, even if it was often at inappropriate times. She and her brother had that in common.

Crossing behind them to the kitchen, Emil poured coffee from the percolator into a mug, wafting fresh waves of the bold brew's scent through the apartment. "I wouldn't call it an adventure, Win," he called. "Why don't you cut to the point and tell her why you're here?"

"Not until we girls have a chance to do some planning. Ooh, these pins are dreadful!" Winnie grimaced as she yanked one hairpin then another out until her blonde locks fell in loose curls at her shoulders. She fluffed them up with her free hand and grinned. "Much better. Now what should we decide first? You must show me around New York while I'm here. Did you make tea?" She peered around Amara and took off for the kitchen table, tossing the pins down with a clatter in order to pour herself a steaming cup.

"Did you feed her straight sugar?" Amara whispered to Emil as he sidled up and slid his free arm around her waist. "She's acting like all of the Frye children after cake at a birthday party."

"I made her wait for me in the hotel library, but all the ladies were elsewhere for the evening. She grew rather bored sitting alone for three hours." He bent low to press another kiss to his wife's cheek. "Would it be too much trouble for her to stay here for a few days? She showed up at the hotel out of the blue; otherwise, I would have asked you first. I know we only have the sofa—"

"Think nothing of it. She's family. I've missed having family with us." Amara stood on toe to kiss him once more while Winnie continued to blather on about the dazzling sites of New York. Amara didn't care much for the city they currently resided in, but she thought she could be happy just about anywhere as long as she had Emil with her.

Together. That was what they had promised.

"I heard New York has the best shopping," Winnie said, finally twisting in her chair to engage them. "I can't really take anything with me, but I can look in the windows and we'll pick you out something gorgeous for yourself, shall we? What about the Met?" Wide fluttery eyes turned up at her brother. "Emil, do you think we'd have time for a visit to see the art?"

"I very much doubt it. Not if you're shipping out in three days."

Amara turned to him in surprise. "Shipping out? Where is she going? Why is she here?" She extracted herself from Emil's arm to take the seat beside Winnie, hundreds of horrible outcomes flashing across her mind. "Is it your parents? Maggie?" she gasped. One hand lifted to cover her lips. "Is it Reuben and Tena's baby?" After losing four babies, her friends had finally thought their latest pregnancy might endure. She couldn't even know what to think if they had a stillbirth after making it nearly to the end. What sort of comfort could she offer when she couldn't even so much as post a letter?

"Oh, goodness, no," Winnie said. Her curls bounced against her neck in rhythm with her words. "I'm going overseas to entertain the troops. Lots of ladies are going, so you needn't worry. I'll be perfectly safe."

Entertain the troops, thought Amara. Winnie was going overseas to serve, which explained the olive-colored suit she wore. Amara should have understood that the instant her sister-in-law walked in, but she supposed the shock of the visit clouded all else. Although she was surprised to hear of Winnie's plans to support the war, she was also pleased that her sister-in-law was invested in a noble cause rather than her usual dramatic episodes. It was such a relief to know she was headed somewhere responsible rather than fleeing false accusations as they had done.

Jumping up, Winnie retrieved her valise and extracted several photographs of their family and friends, laying them out across the tabletop. "Hugo made sure I had some photos to take with me." She pointed to one of a baby with round cheeks and dark hair. "This is little Benjamin Raphael. Born August tenth. Reuben and Tena think he's the most perfect child in the world." She chuckled. "Don't tell Maggie that though. She'll insist hers are the most precious. Another war was nearly declared over it."

"Benjamin Raphael," Amara whispered, allowing her fingertips to hover slightly above the photograph. Raphael meant "God has healed." A perfect name after so much despair. Was there a chance God might heal her too someday, like the woman in the gospels with the hemorrhage? If she only had enough faith, enough hope, maybe someday ...

She slid the photographs back to Winnie and smiled. "He is indeed perfect. I could not be happier. You will tell Reuben and Tena I said so when you write?"

"Of course, and speaking of the goings-on back home ..." Then Winnie proceeded to fill her in on everything that had been discussed at the Forsythe. Amara breathed more easily once she explained how they believed Earhart had since relented on his threat to accuse them of spying.

"That certainly is a relief. I agree though that we shouldn't assume too much. We'll remain here, at least until after the war."

"A solid plan," Emil agreed and she was rewarded with his signature half-smile, the same one that set her insides to dancing from the day they met.

"What about that boy you were seeing?" Amara asked Winnie. "How does he feel about your leaving?"

"You mean Harold?" Winnie sniffed. She took a dainty sip of tea and shrugged as though bored. "It doesn't rightly matter how he feels because I told him things were through. Honestly, he wasn't the marrying type. Far too dull."

"Oh, I am sorry." Although inside Amara was glad Winnie was leaving for Europe unattached. She had never cared for the way her friend treated Harold, especially after she admitted once that she "only kept him around for the kissing."

"Yes, well, that's enough about me," Winnie said. She lifted her teacup with a nod to her brother. "Emil, don't you think it's about time you showed her the letter? Honestly, what are you waiting for?"

He sighed. "Always on your timing, isn't it, Win?"

She smiled around her teacup. "Always."

Retrieving his jacket from the sofa, he extracted a single envelope from its inner pocket and set it on the table in front of Amara. Surprisingly, there were no postal markings or return address, only her name and previous location. "It seems," he said slowly, "that we've received correspondence from your brother."

Amara gawked up at him, her eyes only returning to the envelope when he reclaimed his seat beside her. "My brother?" she managed, her voice emerging slightly strangled. "Where is he? Is he well?"

"We're not sure. The letter doesn't say."

As much as she had longed for news of Peter these many months, now she almost didn't want to open it. What if it said that he was hurt? Or dead? But if he was dead, how could he have possibly written? Which meant that, at least for this moment, he must be alive.

She ripped the letter from the envelope, hungrily taking in its words. Although the handwriting was not familiar, the cadence sounded like Peter's. She could almost hear his voice beside her. Perhaps he had hurt his hand, forcing him to write with the other. Or maybe he had dictated the letter to someone else. Or it could be impossible to find a level surface in the trenches, affecting his penmanship. There could be any number of reasons for the alteration. What mattered is that the words were his.

14th June 1917
Dear Amy,

I beg your forgiveness. I wanted to offer you an easy way out of the turmoil, a husband to hide behind rather than share a life with. But war isn't a time to make foolhardy decisions. I forgot my own mantra: nothing that lasts is built on ease.

You are strong. You are beautiful, and you are brave. Stay safe, but live your own life. I pray I may share in it again one day.

Peter

All this time worrying over her brother's health, wondering if he was dead or alive, and now here was the proof. He was alive. He was making peace with her, and he was praying for the possibility that they might be together again. Tears ran down Amara's cheeks for the second time that day, only now it was with happiness and relief. Peter wasn't home yet and she didn't know exactly where he was, but at least she knew he hadn't yet perished.

She reached for Winnie's hand. "This is beautiful. Thank you so much for bringing it. When did you receive it?" If she knew that, at least she could have a grasp on the last date Peter had been seen.

"Nearly three months ago," Winnie admitted. "Maggie waited a while to tell any of us. She thought sending it to you would only cause undue worry."

She felt her annoyance flare. Maggie had always had a propensity to treat Amara like one of her children, rather than trust her to make adult decisions. Even from hundreds of miles away, she was apparently still doing it. "I don't understand. She knows how much I've hoped for news of Peter. Why would she keep this from me?"

Winnie bit her lip, her cheeks flushing as she reached into her jacket pocket and extracted a second envelope. "Because that isn't the only letter."

FOUR

July 25, 1917 – Three Months Earlier
London, England

LONDON STILL SMELLED OF MISERY, each and every day Josie rode through it. The Germans had continued their aerial terrorization tactics with daylight air raids pelting from London to Stoke Newington. Her fellow city dwellers were afraid to leave their homes or be too far from shelter, lest they find themselves out in the open air with nowhere to hide.

She continued to ride her usual route from Holborn through Piccadilly down to Chiswick, carrying new letters for London's waiting people, sometimes arriving from America, sometimes from France, twice from Spain, only once from Belgium. With the entire Belgian people under German occupation, it was becoming increasingly difficult to smuggle anything across their country's lines. When a letter did arrive, it was usually written hastily on a scrap of newsprint or butcher paper, slipped within something inconspicuous like a pack of cigarettes. Rarely did those letters land in her lap anyway. Too often letters bound for Belgium went unanswered.

Josie finished her route as quickly as time could spare, wisely choosing to spend peak bombing hours at Olmsted Manor in order to return home under near darkness. Her boarding house wasn't near enough to any of the appropriate shelters to provide safety from the daylight air raids.

She felt terrible admitting it, but every night her bedtime prayers consisted of only one request—that Peter Müller be released, so she needn't wonder about him. She had already caught his eye too many times when delivering letters, so often in fact that Matron finally insisted they exchange the post in her private office near the kitchens.

"You're drawing excess attention to yourself," she scolded. "That private's time at the manor will end, but your task will remain as long as the war does. In service to all the soldiers, Miss Harrington, not merely one." Her expression softened, one hand placed gingerly on Josie's forearm. "Your place is here. Let him return to his American life unencumbered."

Matron was right, she supposed. Josie had taken an oath to the war effort—an unbiased oath—and Private Müller was swaying her neutrality. She had already composed a letter for him to the mysterious Amy. That was all she was obligated to do. If they never spoke again, she could put the situation to rest and move on with her life.

Besides, beyond the words which composed his letter, his lips had sealed, quite clearly unwilling to speak about his time on the continent. That was just as well. It would only make her consider again what her father must have endured before the end. How he was now buried in the French countryside with no marker, how even if they had located his body, it would likely have been unidentifiable. That's what the lieutenant explained when he knocked on her door nearly one year ago:

"Our condolences, miss, but he couldn't be located. He marched out to the Somme and that was the last we heard." He had laid a set of military identification tags in her open palm, her father's name staring up at her. "These were all we found."

She had felt herself nod, felt her fingers grip the doorway, felt herself smile and thank the officer like she was someone else. "Hunter Harrington was a good man," he said, "and an honorable soldier. You should be proud to be his daughter."

She had smiled again, nodded again, reached out to shake the lieutenant's hand and exchanged it for the official telegram. The door closed and she stared at the Union Jack on the wall beside her father's military photograph. Red, white, blue, red, white, blue, crossing over one another. The same colors as the Americans. Her father had promised they were coming. Every letter he wrote. She had never even spoken to an American until Peter, and now she couldn't remove him from her mind.

She was handing her winter overcoat and hat off to Cartwright when a call came from the manor's main staircase. Swinging her bag back onto her shoulder, she turned to find William Olmsted, the Lord and Lady's only son, jogging down the stairs towards her. With his shaggy almond hair, lack of suit jacket or tie, and shirt sleeves rolled to his elbows, very little about him spoke of being the heir to a substantial fortune. He had been granted an exemption from military service due to some technicality or another; however, despite his frivolous appearance, had proven a surprising asset on the domestic front.

Both arms outstretched, he wrapped her in an embrace which would have felt far too familiar if it had been offered by anyone except him. Once you earned Bill's trust, you were considered family and should be treated as such. "What an absolute delight!" he crowed. "Just the lady I was searching for."

"You were looking for me, Master William?"

He frowned. "I do wish you would stop with the formalities. The name's Bill."

"Too American," she argued. "William is a fine English name. If you must shorten it, might I suggest Will?"

"You might and I believe you have. It simply doesn't suit me. How would you respond if I suggested shortening your name to Jo?"

Her face scrunched involuntarily in disgust. "Not well. You had best not start calling me that either."

"Then we're agreed. Now, I have today's deliveries, so let's bypass the matronly middleman, shall we?" Reaching behind him, he revealed a small packet of twine-tied envelopes tucked in his waistband. "*Victores in bello non sunt,*" he whispered rather seriously.

"*Vince malum bono,*" she returned, "and your family's residence or no, you should carry more discretion. Packs of letters in your trousers only affords us unwanted attention." She handed him her stack of similar envelopes then dropped his into her shoulder bag before shrugging it to the other arm. "Would you care to join me in the garden? Offer afternoon greetings to the patients?"

"That does sound delightful, however, no. I have a more critical mission for you upstairs." Both her brows popped upward and he gave a sly grin. "A certain handsome private has been asking for you."

"Oh? Who is that?" She attempted to keep her expression neutral but knew she was terrible at playing coy, and although her interactions with Bill were few and far between, he saw through her as much as Matron did.

Bill jabbed his chin towards the staircase and started upward without waiting to see if she followed, although obviously knowing she would. Goodness, was she that transparent?

"He's improved a lot since you last saw him," he told her as they crossed the second-floor gallery. "I jostled Matron into seeing him moved to a private room up near my quarters."

"Did you? That was quite kind."

"It wasn't out of kindness." He glanced back at her, his smile vanished, as they made their way down the corridor towards the rear of the manor. He stopped at a closed door and turned his back to it, staring her down. "This fellow knows about our covert operations."

Josie restrained herself from rolling her eyes. For as frivolous as he kept his attire, Bill was also famous for treating what they did like a division of England's Secret Service Bureau. "What did he say?" she asked.

"Doesn't say much honestly, sleeps most of the days away, but every so often he gets a burst of energy and asks Matron when the next letter delivery will be. She knew he wasn't inquiring about the daily post. That arrives like clockwork. All the patients know that. He's interested in the special post."

"How could he know about that?" When she transcribed Private Müller's letter, she had explained her deed as a kindness to him, one she would have offered to any soldier without full use of his dominant hand. Not once had she mentioned how it wouldn't be delivered through standard channels. Their distribution system may not be an international spy ring, but they certainly didn't need anyone leaking word that they had devised a way to circumvent the official postal censors. Soldiers deserved to send letters to their loved ones unaltered, no matter who they were or where they came from.

"Don't know how he knows, but he knows. I told him he was confused from the concussion and all, but he insisted. Said a priest in France told him about it, ways to get word out on either side, but the air raid hit before he could send his letter." Bill paused, appearing disturbed. "Thing is, I know the priest he's referring to. The reverend is our contact in Le Clé. What I don't understand is why Father Ferdinand would tell this man anything to begin with. He even taught him our secret code phrases."

Again with the absurdity of the spy-speak, she thought. It wasn't unusual for a priest to accept letters for their distribution system. Especially when the soldier fought on one side of the front and their loved ones were situated on the other. What was odd was that the priest shared their distribution phrases. Those were to remain sacred, shared only between the letter carriers, only between those they could trust.

"Did you tell him anything else?" she asked Bill.

"Only that you would return when the time was right. After working on his letter for three days with a busted hand, he didn't much care for that response." He stepped to the side of the door. "I need you to find out what his angle is. If he needs to be neutralized."

"Oh, goodness, please stop." She brushed past him, closing the door behind her before he could mutter another word of his dramatics. Neutralizing people? Honestly. Perhaps he should join the Bureau. That aristocratic man had entirely too much time on his hands.

Peter looked up when she entered, tucked underneath the convalescent home's usual starched white sheets, his leg cast propped up on a pillow and his right hand still bandaged and useless in his lap. The wrappings had been removed from his head and face, revealing the rather handsome now-unbruised face of a man in his late twenties, his sandy-blond hair in need of a trim. A lit cigarette was tucked between his lips, smoke curls rising towards the ceiling.

Of the many items they had been forced to ration in the prior years, cigarettes still arrived in regular supply, even being included in the soldiers' assigned ration packs. The government considered them a necessary mercy, relieving the tension of war and providing a reminder of the normalcy of home. It only made sense to provide them to soldiers in recovery as well.

She strode to his bedside with a warm smile. "Why, look at you, Private Müller. You're recovering quite nicely, aren't you? Matron will have you up and walking the gardens in no time."

He removed the cigarette from his mouth, although he didn't return her smile. "It's inappropriate for us to be alone together," he said huskily.

She glanced at the closed door. Although privacy was necessary due to the sensitive nature of their impending conversation, it also could lead to questions on the subject of propriety between them. She would sit in the armchair across the room, holding their conversation from a distance. That way if anyone barged in, they could assume nothing untoward had occurred. "It's necessary," she replied.

He nodded, as though he understood why that would be, then gestured with his cigarette to the appointed corner wingback. "Pull that over here and join me. I need your help with something." She just stared at him, remaining where she was, wondering what he could possibly need help with in such proximity to one another. She had sat on the end of his bed the night they met, held his hand even, but they had been in a room with forty other men, five voluntary aids, and Matron watching.

"Another letter," he explained. He raised his bandaged right hand with a hard grimace before tucking it back under the covers. "I've tried writing for days and I can't get my left hand to resemble anything legible. You did such a fine job the last time, I hoped you would help me again."

There was no flirtation in his tone, no attempts to charm her over, unlike so many of the unmarried soldiers after months or years out on the front without suitable female companionship. Those men she always turned down, although it certainly was flattering to receive such attentions. Perhaps Matron had been wrong about Peter's interest in her. Perhaps his continued pursuit was related solely to her ability to write and deliver his letters.

"Do you already have paper and pencil?" she asked. When he pulled them from a drawer in the bedside table, she dragged the upholstered wingback across the room and settled herself on its edge beside him. She extended a hand for the parchment he offered her and paused, suddenly uncertain.

It felt like a violation, hearing more of his private correspondence. She wasn't supposed to read the letters. She was supposed to hand them off to the next carrier and move on. It was one thing when he could barely move and his life was still in question, but his recovery was now a certainty. The worst of his injuries were behind him. His dominant hand may have been rendered useless, but he was not without resources. The top sheet he handed her contained the first few lines of his latest failed attempt and although the handwriting was choppy, it was still surprisingly legible. It wouldn't be the prettiest letter ever written, but with a slow and steady hand, he could write it on his own.

He leaned back against the headboard, closing his eyes and exhaling deeply. He took another puff of his cigarette and exhaled again. She could tell it relieved him not to work on the letter anymore and telling him she refused to write it would likely only upset him. Asking him how he knew about their letter delivery system could send him over the edge. Best to ease him into the conversation with something more innocuous.

"What did you do before the war?" he asked suddenly. He didn't open his eyes. "Before you delivered letters for *Fides et Spes*?"

So much for being innocuous. "How do you know that name?"

He blew out another ring of smoke. "I know a lot of things."

Fides et Spes. Faith and Hope. The name of their clandestine letter delivery organization. Never written down. Rarely even spoken out loud. And never shared with outsiders until they were properly vetted and welcomed in. Why would this Father Ferdinand trust a common soldier with such vital information? In the wrong hands, such knowledge could land them all in a world of trouble.

"You need to write your own letter."

His eyes popped open, the cigarette dangling from his fingertips.

He jerked upright. "But I can't. My hand—"

"Still functions," she snapped. "You're so confident about spouting confidential information; you can find a way to be just as confident about writing a letter with your other hand. Be glad you still have a hand at all. Do you know how many amputees have made their way through this manor? Or how many are blind or barely breathing from mustard gas?"

He crushed his cigarette into the bedside tray beside a dozen others and picked up the pencil that she had tossed onto his lap. He examined it like it held answers. "Yes, I know how lucky I am." Lowering the pencil, he looked back at her, contrite. "I'm sorry. I can't help what I know."

"Perhaps not, but please keep it to yourself from now on." She nodded to the parchment. "Now write."

She watched him fumble the pencil lead across the page, wayward scratches forming lines then letters. *Dear Amy ...* She angled her chair away, her back to him and face to the open window, so she wouldn't be tempted to read any more. He had written to Amy in his first letter as well but hadn't told Josie about their relationship. Probably a lover back home waiting for him to return. All the more reason for her to forget him.

"Amy's my sister." Peter chuckled behind her and she shifted, folding her arm over the chair to look at him with what she hoped was an innocent wide-eyed expression. Judging from his, it wasn't, but she loved the way his face brightened, the morose clouds lifting a little with his subtle laugh.

"Your sister?"

"Yes, I'm asking her to come bring me home."

Well, color her foolish. "The army should facilitate that for you. They'll see to your travel, make certain you arrive where you need to be. You've served our country, let them make the pains to see you home."

Peter shook his head, his amusement deflating as he turned back to his letter. He scratched the lead awkwardly against the paper. "I lost all my identification in France. All they have is my word on who I am. I need my sister to bring me reissued papers so I don't have to fight my way out."

So, that was why the interest in *Fides et Spes*. He needed their help to contact his sister without the official censors discovering that he lost his identification papers and had been snuck into England via the resistance or as Bill would likely say, "covert means." Father Ferdinand had been rather foolish to share so much with this man; however, she believed his intentions were honorable.

"You must miss your sister."

"Yes." His brow furrowed and she couldn't decipher if it was from her comment or attempting to write a particularly difficult word. He set the pencil down and wiggled his fingers, circling his wrist twice before retrieving the instrument again. One careful letter at a time into a word then another.

"I never had siblings," she told him. "Before the war, it was only me and Papa. My mum passed when I was born and our flatmates cared for me while Papa went to the factory. Twenty years he worked in that factory until they called him up. Before he left, my job was simply to care for him. After, well, I spent a lot of time in church."

Peter's hand paused again. Unspoken considerations marched behind his eyes. "Which church?" he asked.

"St. Etheldreda's. I spent so much time there, the priest asked me to be their matron. Completing tasks, cleaning, visiting the market. All those little things men need women to do for them."

"And deliver letters?"

"Yes, and deliver letters. Although that wasn't until much later." She paused, not sure if she should pile on to his misery. But she hadn't had a true friend to speak honestly with since it all began. When she sat in the garden with the other soldiers or pushed their wheelchairs down the stone walk, they were the ones who spoke and she who listened. That was her task. The war had good people on both sides, innocents trapped in the middle. All their stories were more important than her own.

Peter returned to writing, his words coming so furiously that she wasn't sure if what he wrote would be legible after all. Several times he fisted the pencil and muttered outrages under his breath, but continued at it until he reached the final line. Then he folded the parchment, creased the edges, and slipped it into the envelope Matron had provided. Josie helped him seal it, then slipped it into her shoulder bag beside the others.

Dragging the armchair back to the corner, she offered him a light smile. "You did wonderful today, Private Müller. Be proud of your accomplishments. It could take over a month to receive a return message, so don't be discouraged if you need to remain here a while longer than expected."

"Understood. Thank you, Miss Harrington." He reached into the side table drawer for another cigarette and the lighter, noting an end to the conversation. Like so many other soldiers, he would sink into a cigarette smoke cloud and his private thoughts, waiting for her to depart so he could wallow. She wouldn't stay to see it. No man wanted his intimate miseries watched. Nor any woman.

But surprisingly, he wasn't finished. She could smell the first puff of smoke when the cigarette took and heard his voice scratch when exhaling that same breath.

"It's lonely for you too."

Such a simple statement, not a question in the slightest. An observation from one who saw what he was feeling reflected back. Smoke encircled his face, his eyes staring out through the fog. He knew how she felt, to be surrounded by people and still alone. He *knew*. Slowly, she nodded.

"Will you come see me more often?" he asked. "Only until my sister arrives. If it's not too much trouble. I know you have letters to deliver."

She could almost hear Matron's voice in reply. *"It'll bring trouble for you, Miss Harrington. Remember your place and leave the waters of his mind unmuddied."*

It wasn't her place to take such a direct interest in one soldier. Then again, if not for the war, it wouldn't be his place to take an interest either. It had been quite a while since she had called anyone a friend, let alone one as handsome as he. It was only a temporary arrangement anyway, wasn't it? Or was it? Perhaps there was more possibility here than met the eye.

She pressed a finger to her chin with a coy smile, purposely knowing he would see through it, and laughing when he did. "Why, yes, Private Müller. You did write your own letter. Such perseverance deserves to be rewarded."

"Tomorrow?" he asked.

"Yes, tomorrow. I'll be here."

Bill waited for her out in the corridor, leaning against the opposite wall with a cold stare. "Well? Do we need to worry about him or not?"

She waved him away like one might shoo a pesky fly. "No," she said. "We don't have to worry about a thing. He's one of us."

He pushed away from the wall, eyeing Peter's door warily. "One of us?"

She could be risking them all if she was wrong. *Dear Lord*, she prayed, *may your angels fly to save us if I am*. Slowly, she nodded. "Yes. One of us."

—

25th July 1917
Dear Amy,

First, I am still alive. Second, I need your help. My identification was lost, and I cannot return to the U.S. without it. I need you to bring new papers to London. I know this is a tall order, but I trust you. Will you help me?

Take your answer to the nearest Catholic church, addressed to St. Etheldreda's. Tell the priest, "Victores in bello non sunt." He will reply with "Vince malum bono." If he doesn't, try the next church. One will understand. One will help you find a way to me.

Please make haste.

Stay safe,
Peter

FIVE

November 6, 1917 – Three Months Later
New York City

"OUT OF THE QUESTION. Absolutely not."

"But you lived there for years!" Amara pleaded with Emil. "You can guide us. It will be perfectly safe."

Her husband continued to sip his coffee with the same firm expression. "I never lived in London. I've never even set foot in London. I wouldn't know the first thing about how to navigate that city."

"You would certainly know more than I would," she argued. She would convince him to go to London if it was the last thing she did. After so long with no word from Peter and now she was only an ocean away from finding him ... well, she wasn't about to allow that opportunity to slip through her fingers.

She held Peter's first letter up, pointing to the words scribbled there. "Read the letters again. He apologized for leaving me behind when he went to fight. He says I'm beautiful and brave, but I'm doing nothing more here than knitting socks and gloves. I have to go. I have to."

"I wouldn't call the work of a seamstress or a housewife nothing," Emil sighed, his hands still clasped around his now-empty coffee cup. "Your brother left you behind to stay safe. Following a mysterious summons—which could be from anyone using his name—isn't staying safe. Why would a German soldier be in England? Wouldn't he be with his own men or, if captured, held in a prisoner of war camp?"

"Wouldn't he have mentioned if he was in prison? If we bring him home quickly enough, we can protect him. No one will need to know which side he truly fought for. He didn't even want to go in the first place."

Relinquishing his coffee cup, Emil picked up both envelopes, flipping them over several times. "There isn't even postage or a return address; how did these get here? And what is the purpose of the Latin phrases? He wants us to simply hop from church to church until we find someone who may or may not understand what we're talking about? This whole letter is suspicious." He turned to his sister who had for once been quietly sipping her tea. "Who delivered these?"

Winnie set her teacup down and patted her lips with a napkin. "I don't know her name. She was young, perhaps twenty-five or so, and had a toddler boy with her. Carried a satchel that she pulled the letter from, but that was all. She never mentioned how the letter came to be with her and none of us thought to ask." She tapped a finger to her lips for a second then pointed in comprehension. "Although now that I think on it, she didn't wear the standard postal uniform."

"Doesn't that strike you as strange?" Emil tilted his chin towards Amara, concern etched into every handsome facial feature. "Why should we throw ourselves into more danger after what happened to us already? People accept us here. We have jobs and purpose. No one's chasing us now. We can finally settle down and be happy for once. Wouldn't you like to finally be happy?"

"I would. You know I would."

"And don't I make you happy?"

"Of course." He was guilting her. It was true, but not fair all the same. Settling down meant having a family and adopting a child. It was all she wanted. But when she pictured that life, she pictured Peter there. She wanted her child, if she were blessed with one, to know at least one member of the Müller family, since it was unlikely he or she would ever meet any of the others.

"Peter decided to fight for Germany," Emil was saying. "He knew what he was doing. He could have stayed here."

"Not when our father asked him to go. Family loyalty—"

"Don't lecture me on loyalty. He had his own mind. America was his home for ten years; he didn't have to go. He's over there killing his own people, Amara. Before America was in the war, it was bad enough, but now it's personal."

"Then you would condemn him to never return home again? Without papers, how will he ever get back?"

"I don't know, but I reiterate—that isn't our problem. It's Peter's. He left you behind and you chose to stay. Besides, how are we even supposed to obtain new papers for him? Do we waltz into the Department of Immigration and say, 'Ah, yes, my brother's trapped in England. Do be a good chap and draw him up some new citizenship papers.'" He tossed his hands up. "No one will do that without some sort of official request or reasonable explanation, of which we have none. The truth will only get us tossed in jail for fraudulent dealings."

Winnie's eyes lit up. "That's it! That's the answer."

Emil stared at her. "What's the answer?"

"Fraudulent dealings. There's no need for the government to become involved. We'll find someone to forge new papers for us."

"Oh, no, *no*, and I repeat, lest you missed the first two, no." Emil held up both hands, palms outstretched, and rose from the sofa. Crossing the room, he poured himself another cup of black coffee and turned to look at the two women like they were both stark raving mad. "I'm not going to jail for someone who may or may not have betrayed his country."

"You don't know that he betrayed us," Winnie said. "He may have defected and that's why he's now in England."

"Well, I'm not taking such a colossal risk for a 'may have.'"

"It could work," Amara said softly. She stared out the window into the blackest night, where she now saw a world of possibilities in the glass pane. "Didn't you tell me that Ulrich Klassen was involved with some unsavory characters? I would bet one of them could help us."

"Or one of them could steal everything we have or worse. I'm not taking two women—who look rather young, mind you—into a wolf's den. Don't ask me to be so unchivalrous."

Amara swung her full attention back to her husband, her good sense all that kept her from lunging across the table and striking the coffee mug out of his hand. "Don't you dare do that, Emil," she spat. "Don't you treat us like we're children. All my life people have seen my short stature and treated me like I couldn't possibly understand. You never treated me that way and don't you dare start now."

"I'm not," he said calmly. "I'm being logical. I used to be a police officer. I know what happens when innocent women go into questionable parts of town."

"Then be a gentleman and go alone," Winnie sniffed. "It is her brother, Emil. If there was a chance to get Charles back, wouldn't you take it?"

"That's uncalled for. Charles would never want me to do something like this. He would never even ask."

"Because he knew if he asked, you would go."

"Stop it, Winifred." His fingers were clenched around the coffee mug so tightly his white knuckles were outlined in red. "Charles died five years ago. You can't guilt me into something dangerous with hypothetical decisions." He downed the rest of his coffee, although his grip didn't loosen around the ceramic. "You could have just forwarded the letter on. Or kept it until we returned. Or burned it. You didn't need to bring it here. So, stay out of it, would you? This is between me and my wife."

"So, you think you know it all now, do you?" Winnie mocked. "My big brother has this entire little situation figured out?"

"I doubt it. I'm sure in another five years, I'll look back on today and realize I still didn't know anything." Emil sighed, his expression and iron grip finally easing. "Fine. We'll get Peter's papers and send them back to St. Etheldreda's. But we stay here. I'll help Peter, but I won't endanger our lives."

Amara shook her head. "No, this is too important to trust the papers with a courier. I have to take them myself."

"I understand your concern," Emil sighed, "but even if we did want to go, we don't have the money for steamship fare."

Winnie's face burst into a wide grin. She wrapped her hands around her teacup, rolling her fingertips across the china, each nail tapping one after another. She gave a slight giggle and bounced lightly in her seat, golden curls swaying with the movement.

"Goodness Moses, what is the matter with you?" Emil snapped. He reached behind him to pour yet another cup of coffee. Given the frequency with which he was downing it, Amara could tell he wanted a much stronger intoxicant than what coffee could provide. Back when they first met, he would have likely used such a stressful situation to drink himself under the table and not crawl out until morning. She was supremely glad they weren't having this conversation at the Forsythe, surrounded by liquor. He did not need a reason to accidentally fall off the wagon.

Looking to defuse the tense situation she had created, she offered her hand to Emil and he took it. Gently she tugged him towards her until he relented and lowered himself into the next chair over, clasping her fingers in one hand and the coffee cup in the other.

"Winnie," Amara chided. "Whatever else you are planning, I must remind you that Emil and I are partners. We'll do this together, whatever we decide."

"Noted, dear sister!" Winnie leapt from her chair, sending its four legs rocking, and it nearly toppled before settling to stillness. She ran for her valise still sitting by the entry door and extracted yet another envelope which she placed on the table with a flourish. "There!" she exclaimed. "All your worries solved."

"Another one?" Emil cried. "Seriously, Win, how many of these are you carrying?"

"This is the last one, I promise, but it's also the best. Open it."

Emil carefully lifted the envelope with both hands, holding it away from him as though it would explode on contact. There was no address, return or otherwise, and no postage. Nothing to offer a clue as to what could be inside. Slowly, he opened it and slid out two steamship vouchers. His eyes shot to Winnie's with a glare so severe, Amara wondered if it would melt his sister's feet to the floor. "What the devil is this?"

"Two third-class steamship vouchers to London!" She clapped her hands together with glee.

Amara squeezed Emil's hand hard before he could lash out against his sister again. She had done a good deed, in Amara's opinion. A deed rather presumptuous and out of line, but a good deed

48

nonetheless. If they were able to forge Peter's travel papers, there would be no other obstacles between Amara and her brother.

"Where did the money come from?" she asked. "Did your parents offer it?"

Winnie shook her head. "No. Mama and Papa encouraged me to bring the letters, but there wasn't enough extra from the tobacconist. Fred said he had already given you some from the safe when you left and another withdrawal would have depleted the assets. I couldn't bring myself to ask Reuben and Tena or Hugo and Maggie—they have their own families to care for. So, Harold and I took up a collection around town from the other German-American folks. They didn't hear the true story of course, but were very sympathetic to the one I fed them."

"I thought you ended things with Harold," Emil griped. "Or'd you use him to do your bidding and then drop him?"

"I ended things before. He offered to knock on doors all on his own." She rolled her eyes. "He clearly can't understand when something is over."

Emil took a long swig of his coffee, downing the remainder and setting the mug down hard. "When are you going to learn? I have to pay those folks back now. My position pays well, but not enough to batch out extra funds to strangers."

"They don't expect to be repaid," Winnie said. She finally returned to her chair in a more somber state. "Sometimes folks simply want to do something nice for a neighbor ... or for their brother."

Amara stood then, her hand still in her husband's, so she could meet him eye to eye. With the sixteen-inch height difference between them, she could still barely make it even. Gently, she leaned forward to kiss him, her free hand cupping his cheek with tenderness. When she pulled away, she could see the uncertainty in his eyes, but she also knew that he loved her. He had fled his hometown for her protection and he would do this for her too. "For too long we've been hidden away here, waiting until the war ends to truly start our lives. We pretend for the sake of our happiness, but why? We can't leave our happiness up to other people anymore. I want to go to St. Etheldreda's, bring my brother home, and then I want to—" She paused, her final statement caught in her throat. Could she really say it when she had already convinced herself that until the war ended, it could never be?

"We've only been married a few months," Emil had soothed her on more than one occasion. *"Be patient. We have our entire lives to adopt a child."*

Patient she was not, and no number of assurances of their many future years together could ease the ache inside. What if their life eventually grew so comfortable that it was easier not to change what they had? They wouldn't always have the war to hide behind, but there would be other reasons. Lack of space in their small apartment, lack of finances, lack of security, lack of confidence in themselves to keep a child healthy, wealthy, and wise. There would always be another reason if they found one, another wall masking their insecurities.

Emil and Winnie were watching her, the latter with curiosity and the former with deep interest. The fury had seeped from his expression and he gave her a small half-smile, the one she loved so much that she couldn't help but offer the same in return. She shifted their entwined hands so they rested against her stomach. "As soon as we return, I want to adopt a baby. We need to stop waiting for an armistice that may never come."

"And if this is a mistake?" he asked. "If they find out what we're doing and arrest us all? There will be no baby, Amara. Ever. We may not even live to see 1918."

"Then at least I can say I remained beside you for the firing squad."

SIX

EMIL WASN'T READY TO GO before a firing squad. He wasn't comfortable with Amara's plans and was perfectly happy to forget the entire ordeal. Still, he hated to tell Amara no, especially since his own poor decisions were to blame for living in New York when they should be in St. Louis near family. Although he didn't trust this lead, if there could be a chance of bringing her brother home alive, he reluctantly admitted they should cautiously follow it. Bringing Peter home would make Amara happy and hopefully her happiness would lead to fewer downcast visits to the children's home and less talk of adoption. She may have said that she wanted a baby right away, but they both knew it wasn't a wise decision. There was simply no place for a child in the midst of a war. Perhaps seeing the realities of life overseas would help her understand that.

It took three attempts, but they finally located a priest in New York who understood what they needed. The priest, however, had been less than accommodating with adequate information; every inquiry towards the origin of the mysterious letter or the strange Latin phrases was met with silence. Having been forced to learn a good deal of Latin in order to keep up with Sunday Mass, Emil had been able to translate their literal meaning, but couldn't understand how the phrases fit into Peter's association with St. Etheldreda's.

Victores in bello non sunt. There are no victors in war.

Vince malum bono. Overcome evil with good.

51

Obviously, they were some sort of code phrases, meant to decipher if one was able to be trusted. But who was at the other end of that trust? He was becoming more uncomfortable with the entire situation the further they pressed. Especially as he now followed directions scribbled on the paper tacked to his steering wheel, seeking out an acquaintance of Ulrich Klassen's in what was likely to be one of the dodgiest parts of the city. Although, he hadn't honestly expected a talented forger to live on 5th Avenue, had he?

The sun had barely risen above the horizon when he set out in his Model T Runabout, driving uptown until he left the city and headed into more rural areas. Amara had agreed to let him go alone as she needed to finish some final stitching for Mrs. Mahlandt, and Winnie was only too happy to spend the entire day strolling the Metropolitan Museum of Art.

"Perhaps I'll meet some young bohemian and he'll agree to paint me," Winnie suggested flirtatiously. "After the war, we can run away to his Parisian flat and live fabulously."

Emil had met her eyes and replied seriously, "Assuming there's anything left of Paris by then."

He now felt the miles passing by, wondering how much farther. Ulrich hadn't—or rather wouldn't—give any indication as to distance or even the name of Emil's contact. When the city was long behind and he crossed the border into Connecticut, however, he mostly wondered if Ulrich was in cahoots with this "contact" and Emil was being lured away to be robbed and left for dead. Just as he debated turning around and calling off the entire affair, the trees opened, revealing the blue-grey waters of Long Island Sound. Shortly after, a wooden sign welcomed him to Bridgeport. It was here that he finally wove his way to the Haversham Hotel.

The three-story sunshine-yellow corner colonial was definitely not what Emil had been expecting. When Reuben first suggested he make friends with Ulrich, he told Emil to "offer enough cigarettes and cheap liquor and you two will get along just fine." Little had Emil known that while Ulrich might reside in a rundown boarding house, some of his acquaintances lived on fine wine and sparkling champagne. Emil had no doubt that the guests of the Haversham would fit right in at the Forsythe, whereas Ulrich would be tossed back into the street by the doorman before he crossed the threshold.

The tinkle of piano keys guided him into the hotel's breakfast room, its floor to ceiling windows allowing sunlight to filter through white organza curtains. Waiters bustled between intimate café tables, serving all manner of hotel guests from married couples to elderly ladies in broad-brimmed hats to one particularly raucous group of four giggling youths, every single girl with bobbed curls and too-short hemlines. They reminded him of Winnie and her suffragette defiance, now taking her right into the heart of danger. While he approved of women's right to vote and applauded their desire to support the war effort, he also wondered how far their risky behavior would eventually take them.

Rather than dwell over that conundrum along with everything else, he allowed himself to be seated at the last available table and ordered a black coffee. While he waited, he pretended to read a worn copy of *The Adventures of Tom Sawyer* which Ulrich had literally thrown at his face, stating that it would be the contact's way of recognizing him. An hour later, however, as the breakfast room began to clear and the giggling girls no longer offered entertainment, he stopped pretending and started reading, passing the next hour with Tom, Huck, and four more cups of jitter-inducing coffee.

"Excuse me, but isn't Mark Twain rather provincial for a place like this?"

Startled at the interruption, Emil looked up from the story, mid-sip of his coffee, expecting to find a waiter urging him to order something more substantial or hit the bricks. Instead, a woman waited, dressed in a fancy day suit with gold buttons down her front and a parasol in her black-gloved hand. It was however impossible to tell her age as her hat contained a tulle half-veil, covering her eyes and nose but leaving her slight smile free.

"Pardon?" Emil asked. "May I help you?"

Her free hand gestured to the open book. "I said isn't Mark Twain rather provincial for a place like this?"

It took him another second of her silence to remember what his purpose was in coming here, which was certainly not reading a book he would have otherwise never picked up. At long last, his contact had arrived.

Closing the book, he stood and pulled out the chair beside him, repeating his own instructed phrases. "Yes, indeed. The Mississippi flows through the country. Would you care to join me so we may discuss it further?"

"It seems suitable." Leaning her parasol against the table edge, she accepted the seat and nodded for him to return to his. The waiter took her order and shortly returned with a piping pot of tea. "My thanks," the woman told him. "Now please leave us undisturbed."

"Of course, ma'am." The waiter gave a small bow then hurried off.

Emil folded both hands on the table and raised both eyebrows, fully immersing himself in morality squad interrogation mode. How ironic it was that if he were still actually on the squad, catching a confirmed forger would have awarded him Officer of the Month.

"Did we really need to come so far as Bridgeport?" he asked. "There are at least twenty-five decent hotels back in the city."

Placing a hand to the teapot lid, she poured a stream of amber tea into her cup and returned the pot to the table. Steam curls rose between them. "My acquaintances know me in the city. It would have been far too risky. Also, I needed to know how important the risk was to you. Traveling over fifty miles is no small task. You must truly be in need to come so far."

Not wanting to reveal the complete severity of the situation, he simply said, "There is need enough."

"Ah." She stirred her tea, letting the rivulets drain from the spoon before setting it gently on the saucer. "Who then is the woman?" she asked as she lifted it to her lips.

"Pardon? Woman?"

She smiled. One perfectly manicured white nail traced the teacup's side. "Young man, there is always a woman. Your girlfriend? Your wife? Perhaps a mistress your physical urges cannot allow to leave your side?"

He remained static, not shifting so much as an inch, rather than give anything else away. He was once again glad Amara and Winnie agreed to let him complete this task alone. "I'm here of my own accord. Mr. Klassen said he informed you of the situation and what I required."

"Mr. Klassen?" She chuckled lightly, lifting her tea for another sip. "Well, aren't you generous? I have never granted him the honor of such a salutation. Since the day we met, he has always been Ulrich."

Emil wondered what happened the day they met to grant him such familiarity, but seeing as he could gather a fairly good idea, let the matter go without comment. He extracted the envelope from his overcoat pocket containing her payment. Setting it on the table in front of him, he unfolded the lip just enough for her to see the slightly crumpled notes. "It's exactly as requested." When she reached for it, he shook his head. "Not until I know you have what I requested. As we established, I wouldn't have come so far for nothing."

"Perhaps not, but you're going to leave with nothing."

Emil's fingers wrapped possessively around the envelope. "That wasn't the bargain."

"You didn't make the bargain. I did. With *Mr. Klassen*. Now, you will hand me what is due. Only then will I inform you where to find what you seek."

He didn't trust her, but what else could he do? They needed those papers or there was absolutely no point in going to London. Of course, if she refused, it did provide him the perfect excuse to cancel the entire trip. He didn't want to go anyway. He could simply stand up and walk away and Amara would be none the wiser.

Except then he would have to lie to her about it for the rest of his life. If her brother died or was imprisoned, the guilt would eat him up, and he didn't know if he could keep that inside forever.

He tossed the envelope to the opposite side of the table where it knocked the salt and pepper shakers together with a clank. The woman smiled. "Very good." Tucking the envelope into her handbag, she removed a familiar-looking brass key and slid it over to him. "Time for you to head back to the city. When you arrive at work, visit room 143. When you have what you need, leave the key on the bureau."

That's why the key looked familiar. It was the same as the rows jingling behind the front desk at the Forsythe. He stared at her in alarm. "How do you know where I work?"

"When you are in a profession such as mine, you make it a point to know about all your friends." She returned that same sly smile again and he really hated that he couldn't see her eyes through all that tulle. He wondered if her irises were scarlet. "That way," she said softly, "they will never think of crossing you."

—

Two hours later, Emil slid the brass key into the lock for room 143 with shaking hands. Upon entering, he closed the door behind him, bracing his back against it with a sigh. No one had seen him, of that much he was certain. Not even a maid had been on this floor when he exited the stairwell.

There was nothing special about the room. Double bed, bureau, writing desk, washstand with a shared bath through the adjoining door to room 141. Seeing nothing obvious on the bed, he crossed to the bureau, opening each drawer in turn. Still finding nothing, he ran his fingers along the underside of the bureau, his nails finally snagging against a rectangular file.

Dislodging it, he sat on the bed and opened the file, one by one removing three sets of falsified papers. He hadn't asked for three, but when he read them, it became clear why Ulrich included them. There in plain ink was Emil's alias, *Emmett Miller*, then Amara's, *Amy Miller*, and finally Peter's, although only his last name had been changed from Müller to Miller.

Emil had hoped they would be able to use their own names while traveling as those were the names on their legal paperwork. However, after inspecting these new forged documents, he realized the flaw in that plan. A flaw that someone knowledgeable in underworld dealings, like Ulrich, probably noticed right off, and someone with time on the morality squad, like him, probably should have. Both his and Amara's legal citizenship papers listed their birth country as Germany. Based on the current temperature towards German-Americans right now, there was a likely chance they would not be allowed to board any ship overseas. Therefore Ulrich had requested them three sets of falsified traveling papers: for Peter Miller, Amy

Miller, and Emmett Miller, now born and raised in the United States.

Returning the papers to their file, he placed the key on the bureau and after a quick check that the hall was empty, let himself out of the room. In all his years of poor decision making, he never thought he would reach a new low.

SEVEN

November 7, 1917 –
New York City

THAT EVENING, AMARA SAT AWAKE in bed, looking over their forged documents again. Next to them were their own legal copies and she couldn't tell the difference. The forgery was so precise, she couldn't believe an upstanding member of society had created them. Perhaps that was why they continued to get away with the deceit. No one suspected the upper class to commit such a crime, much less a woman to be the one holding the pen.

But here they were in plain black and white. This was actually happening. Tomorrow they would be on their way to London.

She hadn't been on a ship since immigrating to America over five years ago. She had come to the States a child and would leave a woman in every sense of the word. What would Peter think of her when they met again? Would he approve of the life she had built for herself? Would he approve of Emil?

She spun her wedding band around her finger, praying that he would. Praying that if nothing else, she would at least find him alive and well.

When a knock sounded at the bedroom door, she looked up expectantly, hoping it was Emil, although knowing it wouldn't be. He still had a few more hours' work at the Forsythe, his last night tending bar for, what Amara hoped would be, forever. When he told the hotel manager that he needed to travel to London on a family emergency, he had been graciously offered one month to return or the position would be filled. Although the manager acknowledged it could very well be unavailable anyway. Someone would be hired temporarily. If that man proved more useful to the task, he would be in and Emil out. When Amara asked Daisy Mahlandt for the same arrangement, she had told Amara not to bother coming back. What if they didn't find Peter? They would have lost their jobs for nothing and returned worse off than before.

Winnie stepped into the room, her dressing gown tied tightly around her. "I wondered if we might talk a minute before bed?"

"Of course." Amara gestured to the foot of the bed and Winnie ran over, plopping down cross-legged beside her.

"Thank you for allowing me to stay. I've missed having my sister at home." She tucked her dressing gown under her bare feet, toying with its edge. The hem was worn and slightly stained, likely from many nights sneaking outside to meet Harold if Amara had to guess. She did hope that her sister-in-law wouldn't find more trouble than war while overseas. She had already lied about her age. She didn't need to be taken advantage of due to her naivete.

"You will come back to St. Louis after the war, won't you?" Winnie asked quietly, almost as though she was afraid to do so. Or perhaps more afraid to hear the answer.

"Yes," Amara assured her. "After the war, things will be different then." She looked again at the forged papers, then carefully folded and returned them to the envelope. Lifting back the bedcovers, she padded across the room to store them in her traveling case, clicking the latches closed with a sense of finality. No turning back now that the law had been broken.

"Are you afraid?" she asked Winnie. "To be so close to the war front? Don't you worry about the things you'll see?"

Winnie bit her lip for a moment then shrugged. "No, not much. Maybe a little, but I try not to think about it. I think about what will happen after the war. When I'm finally old enough to do all the things I've longed for."

Amara returned to the bed, stretching her legs back out under the blankets. She thought of all the things she herself longed for and how, even though she was five years older than Winnie, so many of them were still out of her grasp. "What is it you long for most?" she asked.

Winnie's cheeks blushed crimson, all the more noticeable beside her blonde locks. She lowered her eyes to stare at the envelope that had suddenly appeared in her hands, and Amara missed the next words out of her sister-in-law's mouth. Another letter? Her fingers clenched within the blankets. Where had it come from?

"So," Winnie was saying, "to make a long story rather short, I believe I would like to be an artist."

"Is that another letter?" Amara squeaked over her.

Winnie startled as though she had suddenly forgotten she was even holding anything. Slowly, her eyes rolled back up to meet Amara's and she held out the envelope. "Yes. It's the last one. You should read it alone." She stood abruptly and practically flew to the door.

"Wait. Don't you want to know what it says?"

Winnie twisted to glance at Amara over her shoulder. "Oh, I know what it says. Let's meet for Mass at six tomorrow morning. Maybe after a few hours of prayer and a douse of holy water, you'll be able to decide, because trust me, this one is a doozy."

How could it be worse? she thought. They were already leaving the country. Did this letter say that Peter was actually imprisoned or dead? Why wouldn't Winnie have mentioned that three days ago? All she asked, however, was, "Why wait until the morning? When Emil comes home tonight, we can read it together and decide then."

Winnie frowned. "I don't think that's the best idea."

"Why not?"

"Because once you read the letter, I doubt you'll want him to know."

EIGHT

September 27, 1917 – Six Weeks Earlier
London, England

JOSIE STEPPED OUT OF THE MANOR'S drawing room doors onto the garden veranda, the night breeze chilled with the first strains of autumn. Despite the blooming season being months past, thankfully the frost had not yet arrived, leaving remarkable blush and crimson roses against the lush green foliage. Buttoning her jacket against the chill, she located Peter and Bill, each entertaining a cigarette apiece, the box and lighter settled on the wrought iron table between them. Although he rarely used it now, Peter's walking cane rested against the chair beside him; he would leave it behind completely when he departed the manor on Monday.

According to Matron, his recovery had been incredibly quick considering his serious state upon arrival and his initial care provided by men trained only in animal husbandry. Despite being bounced around in a wagon for days with a broken limb, he now walked with only a slight limp, and that was due only to having the bone incorrectly set at the beginning. Another few weeks and he may even be able to perform an uneven sprint. He was far luckier than most of the men who arrived carrying similar injuries, with over half leaving either dead or without a limb at all.

As for Peter's hand, there had been no restoring it. The fingers would remain gnarled and only half-capable for the rest of his days. However, he had become surprisingly adept with his left hand in a short time. When one was motivated, one could accomplish incredible feats. And it seemed to Josie that few were more motivated than Peter Müller.

Both men stood as she approached, but she waved them back down. She dropped her shoulder bag to the ground and stole the chair between them.

"You're just in time," Bill told her. He held his cigarette out to the side so as to not send the smoke in her direction. "I was about to tell Peter about the job I found for us, exchanging letters on the docks in Dover."

Peter sat up straighter, his own cigarette dangling from his hand in astonishment. Quickly, he tapped the ashes in the tray before they fell in his lap. "Are you serious?" he exclaimed.

"Course," Bill laughed. "I'm tired of sulking about the manor and attending worthless company meetings like it's business as usual. We'll be of better use out there in the thick of it." He stabbed his cigarette in Peter's direction. "Also, it's high time we got your lazy bones out and about."

"Pfft, no joke about that." Peter took a drag on his cigarette and exhaled in the opposite direction. "I'm tired of sitting around here doing nothing all day." He transferred the cigarette to his mangled right hand and extended his left across the table to offer Bill a hearty shake. "Thanks, Bill. This is perfect."

Josie squelched the immediate pang of rejection that tapped in her chest. Why did he wish to go so far as Dover? Hadn't she been providing good company these many months? *Nonsense*, she scolded herself. *He's been planning to return to America all this time. That's much farther than Dover. You should be thrilled that he's chosen to remain in the same country as you.* Then why didn't she feel thrilled?

Perhaps because she always knew this situation wasn't forever. One day his sister would come for him. Perhaps not now, perhaps not until the war was over, but she couldn't believe Peter would choose to make his life here permanently. Not based on the stories he told her about his family. Eventually, Amy would come or the war would end and Peter would leave without hassle and without her.

"What about going home?" she asked him. "What about your sister coming to get you?"

Peter and Bill exchanged a look. "It's been months," Bill offered, "and we can use someone like him down in Dover now. No sense waiting around here. If she was coming, we would have heard."

"Not necessarily," Josie argued. "Sometimes letters take a long time to arrive, and sometimes they're lost altogether. You know that quite as well as I. We should send another."

Peter jammed his cigarette butt into the ashtray, grinding it down thoroughly. He reached for the pack. "I don't think it would make a difference. I sent her to an unfamiliar city and ordered her to marry a stranger all in the name of protection. I hoped my letter of apology would be enough for her to forgive me, but her silence clearly indicates otherwise." He tapped out another cigarette into his right hand and tossed the pack across to Bill whose own was nearly a stub. Picking up the lighter with his left, he flicked the end, sparking the flame to life.

Josie placed her own fingers over Peter's injured hand, hindering the cigarette's ascent to his lips. "Your parents then. You said they're still living. Or your other sisters. When the war is over, one of them will want you to return. Send them a letter and ask."

He stared down at her fingers, his own jutting out from beneath them at odd angles. Across the table, Bill tapped the cigarette pack repeatedly against the iron table edge, making sure they hadn't forgotten him.

"Josie, please stop," Peter said low, yet firm. "No one is coming. My parents probably think I'm dead, and perhaps that's as it should be. My other sisters won't know any different either. Amy and I didn't part under the best circumstances, but my father and I parted under the worst ones. Killed in action brings me back into his good graces. He can tell his friends how I died a hero."

"Then go home to Amy instead. If she's the only one who knows you're still alive, perhaps she can facilitate a reunion with your father later on. Once she sees you, I'm sure she'll forgive you. Besides, it's safer there. You've already fought for your life, why put yourself at more risk? America has more food and less threat of air raids."

Peter released a sigh and shifted in his chair. "What would I do in America? I will never regain full use of my hand or my leg, certainly not enough to perform any extreme labor, but I can deliver letters in Dover. With all the men out to war, I can be of use here. Besides, England is rather pleasant at times." He gave a wry smile, his fingers managing to just snake around the edge of her hand. "Gardens and fresh air and lilting British accents? I've become too fond to give it up entirely."

Josie released his hand and sat back in her chair with a huff. "Have another cig, won't you? Most of our days here are damp and rainy and London city is nothing but smog. There's rations on everything and I haven't had a cup of tea with proper sugar since before I can remember. And a new dress or pair of shoes?" She raised her foot to show well-worn and patched boots. "Well, you get the idea. Once you leave the manor and have your fill of our city—not to mention those crowded fish-smelt docks—you'll be glad to go home to your Iowan cornfields."

"But you're not there, Miss Josie," Bill injected with a smirk. Josie gaped and Peter glared and their friend just grinned from ear to ear. He pocketed his cigarette pack and lighter then slapped his thighs and stood. "Well, I suppose now's the time to retire, eh? Have a pleasant evening, you two." With a wink, he pushed his chair back under the table, swung his jacket over his shoulder, and headed inside, the veranda door clipping closed behind him.

Peter and Josie sat in silence. She didn't know if he suddenly noticed their close proximity to one another, but for her, it felt like his nearness positively radiated. He rolled the unlit cigarette back and forth on the table, now unable to smoke it with Bill having taken the lighter. When she met his eyes, his expression was serious. Too serious.

"Why are you trying so hard to get rid of me?" he asked. No, asked wasn't the word. *Accused* fit better for the tone he spit at her.

"I'm not trying to get rid of you."

"Yes, Josie, you are. You've given me every possible reason to go as far away as I can. America isn't exactly a day's ride, you know that, right? If I leave, you understand I'm not coming back?"

"I know."

He flicked the cigarette up from the tabletop into his fingers, holding it between the second and third digits. He glanced over his shoulder towards the drawing room doors then back again. "I understand what you're trying to do, but I can't go home as though the last nine months never happened. This guilt I still feel over the things I did in France—it rubs like a raw wound."

"Your other wounds have healed," she said gently. "This one will too."

"I don't think it can, not until—"

"Quiet." She wanted to take his hands between hers, to offer him some sort of comfort like she had the night they met. But they were now alone in the garden under the cover of darkness. It would appear unseemly if Matron or any of the voluntary aids were to walk by the window. Instead, she demurely folded her hands in her lap and said calmly, "All that is behind you now."

He shook his head, crushing the cigarette between his mangled fingers. He clenched his fist awkwardly on the tabletop. "It's not. Not yet. It can't be. That's why I agreed to join *Fides et Spes* and why I want to go to Dover. To make it right."

"You've already made it right, Peter. My father always said the Americans would come to save us. That's why God brought you here, why you lived through all you did. To save us." She smiled. "I think especially to save me." She hadn't realized how true the words were until she said them. Before Peter came along, she had been lonely, but she hadn't needed saving. Not really. She had never *needed* a man to take care of her. She and her father always took care of themselves as much as they took care of each other. Since his death, she had been able to navigate the air-raided streets of life all on her own. She had never *needed* saving, and she still didn't. But that didn't mean she couldn't embrace it when it came along.

She took a breath and exhaled. She had never been more ready to say what she was about to and never more certain that she should. No timing could be more perfect. "Peter, if I said that I'm pushing you back to America because I love you, would you think me ridiculous?"

She assumed he would let her down gently, tell her he never felt that way; however, she was such a nice girl, someone someday would come along that would. He was too compassionate to laugh at her confession and too kind-hearted to limp away without a word. Still, she could hope for a different outcome, just as every day she hoped for the return to a life without blackout restrictions and running for the underground. She could barely recall a life like that anymore.

Peter grinned then, lips wide and teeth dazzling and eyes more brilliantly blue in the moonlight than Josie had ever seen at noon. She had never seen him smile like that, especially not at her.

He extended his good hand palm up as though he were a gentleman requesting a dance. "If I told you that makes me want to kiss you right now, would you think me ridiculous?"

It only took her quick assent for him to scoot her chair a foot closer and press his lips to hers. A breeze swept from inside the rose garden, carrying sweet floral fragrance around them, and Josie shivered. Peter wrapped his arm around her back, his mangled hand drawing her nearer, his opposite fingers tangled within her curls. It was an extraordinary sensation, the way they embraced, the way his kiss stole her breath and also made her feel like she had never once choked on London's soot-soaked air.

He eased back to meet her eyes. "I love you too, Josie."

"*Ahem.*" The garden door shut rather abruptly and they both reddened as Matron stared down at them from the veranda, her expression more riled than any of the army lieutenants in their beds. "Nearly nine, Private Müller. We're about to turn down the lamps." She nodded to Josie. "Miss Harrington, John Simms is finishing up a letter. Local delivery. He's informing his wife up in Wembley that he's due to be home next week." Her brows rose. "That is, if you can spare a moment."

"Of course, Matron." Maneuvering herself from her chair, still only inches away from Peter, Josie headed towards the veranda. She heard him rise behind her, the moderate *shuffle-step-knock* of his altered gait and cane following her to meet Matron at the drawing room doors. "It is about time we had some good news, indeed," she told Matron. "I am most delighted for Mr. Simms."

She turned to Peter then, her back full to Matron to conceal the smile which was impossible to hide. "Goodnight, Private Müller. Do sleep well, won't you?"

Peter's expression didn't seem to register hers, suddenly diving back into seriousness. "And you as well, Miss Harrington. Also, speaking of letters, would you mind delivering one more?" He reached into his jacket pocket and produced a small envelope addressed to his sister. He offered it to her with both hands, his damaged fingers barely managing to clutch the edge of the paper. "Please see it sent first thing. It's highly important."

"Of course. Is everything well?" His demeanor had swung to a cloud in the last minute and she was uncertain how they arrived there.

"I worry for her safety. Perhaps I wasn't thinking clearly after my injuries." He looked away, obviously embarrassed at the conversation in front of Matron. "But I'm thinking clearly now."

"The war *will* end, Peter. Your sister will want you to come home."

He reached for her hand and raised it to his lips with a grim smile. "Goodnight, Josie. Tomorrow we speak of Dover."

Matron ushered him through the drawing room doors and out into the corridor, leaving Josie alone on the garden veranda. She examined Peter's uneven script on the envelope she held. *Tomorrow we speak of Dover.* What was there to say? Did he want her to go with him? Or did he want to reject the position and stay in London with her? If their discussion held good news, why had he suddenly become so somber?

She gazed up into the night sky, at the stars and the heavens then back through the drawing room doors. She let the evening chill seep into her skin, watched as the upstairs windows darkened one by one. Saw Matron draw the curtains directly above her and move on to the next room. Then she tore open the letter.

26th September 1917
Amara,

I don't know if you've received my letters, but if you have and plan to listen, I beg you not to. The situation has changed. It's no longer safe for you to be with me. Do. Not. Come. I wish I could explain more, but

Josie stopped reading. Not once since joining *Fides et Spes* had she ever opened someone else's letter, and she shouldn't have opened this one. It was an invasion of trust, especially against someone she had declared her love to only minutes before. Censoring letters was the work of the government, of the military, not *Fides et Spes*. Pass it along, no matter what. That was the rule.

No longer safe, he had written. *The situation has changed.* What situation? He wrote this before he kissed her. Nothing had yet changed. Bill hadn't even informed him of the role in Dover. Josie had spoken to Father Ignatius weeks ago about temporary lodging for him and his sister when and if she should arrive. Everything was set. But now ...

His sister's name was actually Amara. Was Amy a pet name then ... or another lie?

Send it on, Joselyn, she scolded. *Don't ask. Don't question. Send it on. That's the job they assigned you to do.*

The next morning, she placed Peter's letter in a fresh envelope and handed it with a stack of other letters to the next carrier then walked away exactly as she did every time before. Then she rode the miles to Olmsted Manor without divergence from her normal route. She sat at that same garden table across from Peter exactly as they had so many mornings, afternoons, and evenings. Nothing was any different. Except that everything was.

It would never be the same again.

NINE

WORRY OVER PETER'S FINAL WORDS kept Amara awake most of the night before their departure for England. His message had been more than clear. Another directive, another order, another missive to stay safe exactly like the one he gave when he left America for the war. The same one he later admitted to be an unfair request.

Do. Not. Come. What had happened to make him send such a command? How had the situation altered? What was she to do now with this information? She couldn't imagine abandoning her brother when he clearly needed her, but she didn't know how she could ask Emil to join her willingly. He would tell her it was too dangerous. He would say that he was clearly correct all along. Peter must be up to something nefarious and Amara had placed too much trust in him.

"What do I do?" she whispered to Winnie. The two women were seated in the last pew of Holy Cross Church as the final members of the congregation filed out around them. Sunrise filtered through the stained-glass windows, pale daylight striping the wooden pews. Behind the elaborate altar, candlelight flickered over three enormous paintings: Christ's crucifixion flanked by "The Vision of Constantine" and "The Finding of the True Cross." Amara reached up to finger the hem of her black chapel veil, its delicate lace draped against her shoulders, and prayed again for wisdom.

She listened for the slight swish of the narthex door closing before she spoke again. "I love your brother, Winnie. I promised him my life.

But how can I possibly confide in him about this? If I tell him about the letter, it will ruin everything, but if I don't, I fear ... well, I fear it will still ruin everything."

Winnie continued to stare at the altar, her hands folded primly upon her olive skirt. "My parents taught me that deceit is for the wicked," she said, "but I'm afraid I never listened very well."

Deceit is for the wicked. Amara had never thought herself wicked before. Most of her childhood she did as she was told. When Zeke battered her arms and called her worthless, she took it all quietly, never breathing a word lest her brother send her away for her safety. When Peter asked her to stay behind while he traveled overseas, she did so. When he asked her to marry an American, she questioned it, but ultimately did as he asked. And when he asked her to forge citizenship papers and bring them to London, she did without batting an eye. Now he was asking her to listen again. To stay behind, to leave him to whatever trouble and whatever fate he had gotten himself into.

How could she though? This was her brother. The only sibling who might return home to her. She already feared she had lost the rest of her family in the war; to return to Germany would never be an option again. She did not want to lose Peter too. *Could not* lose Peter.

"I can't tell Emil, can I?" she repeated even as she prayed for another way. They had promised to weather any storm together. How could she take the only umbrella and leave him to feel the rain?

Winnie finally turned her gaze from the altar. There was sympathy in her eyes, but determination too. "You said you would do anything to help your brother, did you not?"

"Yes, of course."

"Then how can you tell mine? Emil used to be a morality squad detective. Despite his abuse of the badge back then, the want to protect others is in his blood. Especially when it comes to you. My brother may be a colossal idiot sometimes, but I do believe he loves you. He has made many, many mistakes and that is unlikely to change, but I don't think you were one of them. Fred would probably even agree with me on that."

Amara didn't know how to respond. Fred, within all his condescension, might actually believe his brother had done one thing right. And that one thing was her.

Winnie must have noticed the emotion on her face, because she gave a self-conscious pat to her chapel veil. "This is the age of sister suffragette, Amy. Your life is your own, exactly as Peter said in his first letter. If you tell Emil, he will insist you stay here for your protection. Are you prepared to go to London without your husband in order to save your brother?"

No, she thought. She didn't want to make this journey alone. Peter said she was brave; however, few actions in her life had proven that to be true. She hadn't fought against any of the abuses or demands that had been placed upon her in the past. She hadn't stepped forward when she watched an innocent man hang from a street lamp in St. Louis. Instead, she had fled and panicked and ended up fainting on the living room rug. Then she hid in New York, pretending to be 100% American while her allegiance continued to be split down the middle. She knitted scarves and caps and gloves for the soldiers, purchased liberty bonds, and attended victory rallies while every day her heart bled for the family who fought against them. Peter's letter said, "You are beautiful, and you are brave," but she was not. She was full of fear and cowardice and would rather lie than openly defy her husband.

"I thought you said deceit is for the wicked," she whispered, "and we are in church."

"Even in church, sometimes you have to overturn a few tables to prove a point. Don't let Emil hold you back from what you know is right."

What was right? Was a lie of omission the same severity as a lie of deceit? Especially if that lie helped someone?

"Did your parents really ask you to bring the letters?" Amara asked instead. "Was that the truth? Or did you steal them?"

Winnie stared down at her for a minute as though considering whether Amara could handle the truth. Finally, she said, "Would your parents agree if they knew what you were planning?"

Amara pictured her strong father, Jürgen, and remembered the demands he wrote in his letter, ordering them to return to Germany. For Peter to do his duty and serve without question. There were risks to military service, risks her father would be well aware of, having four sons-in-law already away at war. While he loved his son, he would accept the possibility of death or imprisonment. He would be willing to grieve his son if it meant Peter died with honor in a German uniform. She very much doubted he would allow Amara to save him, to help him flee his duty and return home a coward to their people. And he would never approve of her doing so behind her husband's back.

"No," she said. "They would never approve."

Winnie returned a grim smile. "Then I believe you have your answer."

TEN

November 19, 1917 – Ten Days Later
London, England

EMIL AND AMARA SAID GOODBYE to Winnie at New York City's Grand Central Station before riding the rail across to the Hoboken piers. As soon as they arrived, it was immediately obvious why their steamship hadn't been recommissioned as a hospital ship or soldier transport. Simply put, the *S.S. Ledbetter* was a dump.

Her scuffed black hull required a new paint job and the interior was little better, although at least relatively clean. The third class accommodations were noisy and far too warm, with hundreds of passengers cramped eight to a room. To top it off, the food was meager and bland and Emil couldn't tell if the unsatisfactory dining experience was a result of war rationing or if that was simply the usual accommodation. Either way, he thought fondly of the private second class cabin his family shared on their passage to America those many years ago. By the time he and Amara stepped off the ship ten days later, he wished for nothing more than a filling meal and a hot bath.

Emil assumed the steamship would dock directly in the heart of London. The reality, however, was quite the opposite. While sailing ships were allowed access to the Royal Docks, steamships were required to disembark farther downriver at Tilbury due to their more substantial size. Passengers were then forced to travel the additional miles into the city by either rail or rented carriage.

Lugging their belongings to the nearest railway station, Emil paid for the cheapest tickets available and learned that due to government railway requisitions, the next passenger carriage wouldn't arrive for over two hours. Ever aware of his rumbling stomach and unlaundered outfit, he claimed a bench for them inside the station to wait.

As much as he didn't want to be here, he supposed he had hoped this trip would be an opportunity for him and Amara to create some new memories. He would like to visit Fontaine, his second hometown after his family moved to England from Oberammergau. He could take her to dinner and walk arm in arm through the center of the square. Maybe even see the row house his family used to own. He had so many fond memories there from before Charles died.

Unfortunately, it would have to wait. He wanted to locate Peter and return to New York as quickly as possible. If the Central Powers overtook London, he and Amara didn't need to be anywhere near it.

When the train arrived, barely a soul spoke or acknowledged one another, their expressions as somber as the atmosphere outside. The miles swept by in a blur of stone cottages and barren tree limbs, waving their branches across a grey and dreary sky. As they chugged into the heart of London, low-hanging clouds mixed with the soot-filled air until it was difficult to decipher where one ended and the other began. A light drizzle began to fall against the train windows and by the time they slowed at the station, the late afternoon light appeared as evening and heavy droplets pelted through the swoosh of steam along the platform.

Collecting their belongings, Emil and Amara followed the other passengers from the train car and down the platform, their winter overcoats offering inadequate protection from the storm. Water sloshed off Emil's hat and into his collar, sending waves of chills down his spine. Equally weather-beaten, Amara hustled beside him, her skirts and close-fitted cap providing even less comfort.

Rows of war propaganda posters bombarded them inside the station, many portraying a military officer with a bushy mustache, pointing one long finger and declaring, "Britain wants you! Join the army!" It was astoundingly similar to the posters of star-spangled Uncle Sam plastered to every other street corner in New York City.

Not wanting to stand under the poster's accusing watch any longer than necessary, Emil rushed Amara out the station's front doors into the drizzle to locate the nearest source of nourishment. Due to rationing, however, even the advertised "stew made like mother's" arrived as a source of disappointment. It was not at all comparable to Elsa Kisch's hardy German fare.

Swallowing the last bites of stew, they headed back out into the rain, Emil's toes uncomfortable in damp socks and fingers numb against the traveling case handles. Although he was certain Amara felt the same, she didn't complain, so he kept his grumblings to himself.

The taxi ride through the obviously air-raided city failed to cheer his spirits. Children climbed over the remains of a bombed-out house and he wondered where their parents were. Didn't they know what their children did was dangerous? The debris could collapse at any minute, burying them alive. With a sickening wrench to his gut, he realized they might not have parents anymore. Like so many others, this war may have already left them orphans. When he glanced at Amara, he could tell she was thinking the same thing and remembered her earlier request.

As soon as we return, I want to adopt a baby. We need to stop waiting for an armistice that may never come.

The queasy feeling in his stomach only intensified until he felt like he might be sick. Thankfully, a minute later the driver announced their arrival and Emil leapt from the vehicle, unloading their cases in record time. They raced down Ely Place, splashing through puddles in their haste to St. Etheldreda's. Rain dribbled down the centuries old stone façade as he pulled open the church's heavy wooden door.

Well, wouldn't you know it, he thought as they climbed the interior stairs and stepped inside the unoccupied sanctuary. *Even the church is dark and depressing.*

With the storm outside and no electric lighting inside, the church's details remained tucked in deep shadows broken only by minimal candlelight. He assumed the original architect hadn't intended to be morose but then again, the approach to worship was far different in the Middle Ages. Perhaps the intent had been for the congregation to focus on the negative.

As they walked down the church's single aisle and observed its special touches up close—saint statues along the stone walls and magnificent nearly floor-to-ceiling arched stained glass windows—he could tell that in the sunlight, the effect would be more impressive. At the very least they were out of the storm.

"Where do you think we'll find the priest?" Amara whispered. Her fingers clenched around her handbag, eyes wide as she stared up at the stained glass.

"Perhaps the rectory," Emil suggested. "We'll try there first."

They both spun as the sanctuary door closed behind them. A slender priest strode down the aisle, hands folded across his middle, his long black cassock floating slightly behind him. As he approached, the elderly man offered a smile that lit his face even in the dark sanctuary. "Good evening. I'm Father Ignatius, the pastor at St. Etheldreda's." He eyed their wet clothes with sympathy. "Looks like you were caught in the storm. My apologies that our church does not offer more in the way of warmth."

"Thank you, truly, but it's no matter," Amara said, even as she shivered beneath her wet coat, belying the truth of her statement. She glanced up at the stained glass behind the altar, the candlelight flickering over its lower half. "You have a lovely church, Father."

Father Ignatius followed her gaze. "Yes, such a rich history here as well. Did you know that our parish is the oldest Catholic church in all of England?"

"I did not," she replied, "and while that is rather fascinating, we are actually here searching for a young man, Peter Müller. Do you know him?" The priest tilted his head as though confused and Emil wondered if perhaps Peter had used a fake name. After all, he had instructed Amara to use one.

She extracted the letter from her handbag and held it out. "I received this letter from him instructing me to come here. You see, he's lost his papers—"

"Oh, ho!" The priest exclaimed. He pressed a hand to his forehead in disbelief. "You're his sister, Amy, aren't you?"

"Why yes! I'm Amy Miller and this is my husband, Emmett."

Emil flinched inwardly at the pseudonym, just as he did every time he had to introduce himself with the wrong name. The priest gifted them a broad smile, shaking each of their hands in both of his. "It is a pleasure to meet you both. Peter is a fine lad. He speaks of his dear sister often."

"You know where he is then?" she asked excitedly.

He nodded. "Come, your room is all set. I'll let you stow your belongings and then we can speak more freely."

"My room?"

"Yes. Your brother arranged everything for your arrival."

When the priest turned back down the aisle, Amara held Emil back. "Should we follow?" she whispered once the priest was through the narthex doors. "Do you think it's safe?"

He raised both eyebrows. "We have to in order to find your brother, which is after all, what we came for. You heard him, our room is all set, and frankly, I would love to get out of these wet clothes and take a nap. At least that way, if we die a grisly death later, I'll be well rested."

"Not funny." With a light smack to his arm, she marched after the priest. Emil followed, chuckling all the way down the aisle.

Hands tucked together under the front of his robe, the priest led them out the front entrance. Thankfully, the rain had stopped, and the clouds were beginning to part as suddenly as they had gathered. Several U.S. soldiers walked the church path towards them, all in pressed olive uniforms similar to the one Winnie had worn.

"Good evening, men," the priest acknowledged. "The Lord's blessings. England thanks you for your service."

"It is our pleasure to serve," one said. The others stood back to allow them to pass by, tipping their hats with nods of "Good evening."

"We've seen many American soldiers since your country joined the war," Father Ignatius said as he directed Emil and Amara around puddles along Ely Place and towards the main thoroughfare. "The Catholic Chapel of America's West Point Military Academy was modeled on St Etheldreda's, so our church brings a piece of home to this foreign soil. We are honored to have the United States join the Allied efforts. Miss Harrington has always said the Americans would come to save us."

Emil thought that a pretty bold statement, but he kept his opinions to himself. "Who is Miss Harrington?" he asked.

The priest smiled. "A fine worker, I must say. She assists the priests with all manner of errands in addition to her letter deliveries. She helped deliver the very letter you hold in your possession."

Amara took one of the traveling cases from Emil, so they each only carried one, and wrapped her opposite arm through his. Although the gesture didn't actually ease his burdens or add any real warmth, he appreciated her thoughtfulness all the same.

A few blocks farther they stopped outside a red brick tenement situated between a row of similar buildings. More recruitment posters plastered the brick up and down the street, several faded or with peeling edges as though they were posted much earlier in the war. The priest opened the tenement's main door into a cramped entryway then led them up three flights of even narrower stairs to a door centered within the corridor. The one room flat inside contained only a thin bed, aged wardrobe, and small writing desk. The bed sagged low in the middle, and he wondered if it would be safer to toss the mattress onto the floor. It would certainly be better than waking with a broken spring through his side.

"You'll have to excuse the rudimentary nature of the room," Father Ignatius apologized. "We were not certain as to the date of your arrival and could not afford to keep a better room for such a length. There is a washroom and kitchen on the lower level available to all the tenants and a bathhouse at the end of the street. You are welcome to remain for the duration of your visit, free of cost."

"For free? To both of us?" Emil asked. Taking Amara's traveling case from her, he set both cases at the foot of the bed.

"Why, of course. Neither Miss Harrington nor Mr. Müller mentioned you; however, if your wife shall claim for you, you are welcome to stay." He raised a brow at Amara.

"Of course, I claim for him. We are here together. You said you knew where Peter is," she pressed.

"Ah, yes, you can find him convalescing at Olmsted Manor. Last I heard, he was recovering quite well."

Amara gasped. "Recovering? What happened to him?"

"He was caught in an air raid in France. Trapped under a church which nearly killed him. I believe being in a place of holiness saved his life." The priest took her hand, giving it a slight pat. "There is no need for worry."

"I worry less for him than ourselves," Emil muttered. "Can you please provide us directions to this manor? I want to be away from London as soon as possible. No offense to you of course, Father."

"No, no, young man, no offense at all." Father Ignatius appeared weary, as though he had gained ten years within the span of his last sentence. He gestured to them to follow him from the room and when Amara immediately did so, Emil hastened out behind her. The priest locked the door then handed the key to Emil. "Come, come, I shall ring you a taxi."

ELEVEN

November 19, 1917 –
London, England

ALTHOUGH THERE WAS A FAIR amount of traffic within the city, the number of vehicles thinned as they traveled farther out, so that the trip to Olmsted Manor did not seem to take long at all. Before they knew it, the taxi turned onto a dirt drive, rumbling through two iron gates and towards a sizable peach-stone Tudor, the likes of which Emil hadn't seen since leaving England over five years ago.

Although cloud cover from the earlier storm had vanished, the sun had nearly set when a footman showed them into the foyer, offering to take their overcoats and Emil's hat; however, they politely declined. He wanted to spend as little time here as possible and the sentiment only grew as they moved into the open atrium.

Soldiers silently stared from around playing tables in the center of the room. Their eyes followed as the footman directed Emil and Amara through a door into what appeared to have once been a rather grand ballroom. Under different circumstances, Emil's memories might have returned to the night he and Amara danced under the stars in the skeleton of Wood-Smith Castle, the night she finally invited him into her life and won his heart. That had been a fantastical evening, however, this ballroom was anything but.

The first thing he noticed was the smell. The air was pungent with a mixture of antiseptic, sickness, and something he could only describe as the stench of tortured minds. Nurses skittered about between rows of wrought iron beds, their pinned white veils waving as they tended to their patients. Several of the wounded soldiers had bandages over their eyes, others cradled an arm half-missing, although most either sat in bed reading or lay under the sheets, still and silent. All had seen the front lines and been a part of battle. Peter had been one of them, sending bullets into Emil's countrymen. Only an act of God—quite literally as a church had exploded on top of him—had been enough to stop Peter's course.

Emil's eyes swung from one side of the room to the other and back again, not sure whom he was even looking for. He had never met Amara's brother and never seen a photograph either. She had described some of his general features, but it wasn't much to go off of now. There were at least a dozen other soldiers with features matching "sandy-blond hair and a thin-yet-attractive face."

"Do you see him?" he whispered, as though they were in church rather than a hospital. With so many men in the midst of recovery, it felt like hallowed ground.

Amara peered into the room, squinting to see those farther back near the full-length windows. Beyond that, a double set of doors led out to a veranda with stairs down to what he assumed were gardens. With the storm now passed, a few other men in wheelchairs sat outside, but none matched Peter's description.

"No," she said, sullenly. "He's not here."

"Perhaps in another room then." They turned to follow the footman back out the door, but stopped at a deep feminine call.

"Excuse me. For whom are you looking?"

A plump woman all in white approached them from where she had been speaking quietly with another young nurse in blue. Her skirts swished right to left in perfect time with her gait, wrinkled fingers folded primly upon her middle. She stopped when there was still a stride's space between them and nodded, although there was no welcome in her expression.

"Good evening to you both. It isn't often we receive visitors at this late hour." Her eyes shifted momentarily to the darkened windows, the November sun having finished the last legs of its descent only minutes before. "I am the matron in charge here at Olmsted Manor. How may I assist you this evening?"

"I'm searching for my brother, Peter Müller," Amara told her, using the correct pronunciation as the priest had also done so. It seemed curious to Emil that Peter would give his real name, but he supposed Müller might be a more common surname here than in the States. He and Amara would stick to their pseudonyms though. Müller might not raise any red flags, but Kisch would certainly make the Brits look twice.

"We received a message that he was recovering here," Amara explained. "We would like to see him if we may."

Both of Matron's thick brown eyebrows rose once then dropped. "That message must have been severely delayed as Private Müller was released from our care seven weeks ago. I'm afraid he left no forwarding address; however, he has been in close contact with the pastor of St. Etheldreda's. It's possible information may have been left there."

"We've already been to the church," Amara said. "The priest directed us here. He made no mention of Peter being released."

"Well, I assure you he was. Now, you must excuse me. There are patients to attend to." Matron turned away, her shoes soft against the hardwood as though she was a ghost gliding over each floorboard. She accepted a full wash basin from another nurse's hands. Sitting beside a patient, she placed the bowl on her lap and began unwrapping long white bandages from around the soldier's wrist.

Amara scanned the room again as though she had missed something the first time, her breath quickening. "Perhaps Matron was mistaken. He can't have left. If he's left, how will we ever find him?"

It went against Emil's better judgement to lengthen their time here. It would be so very simple to accept that all leads had ceased and return home immediately. Except that all leads hadn't ceased and that fact would weigh more heavily if Amara realized it when they were halfway across the Atlantic.

Slipping her hand into his, he directed her around the rows of beds, trying to ignore the fevered groans and erratic coughing beneath the starched white sheets. He wondered how many of these men would never leave this room.

The image of a newspaper photograph flashed in his mind—a Nova

Scotia curling club turned temporary morgue where they laid out *Titanic* victims for identification. His family had never visited as they knew Charles wouldn't be there. The body too disfigured to identify by sight, it had been the belongings in his pockets which confirmed Charles to be the man lifted from the ocean and subsequently buried at sea. Emil had known his brother wasn't one of the white-shrouded figures in the photograph, but the image still encouraged him to down half a bottle of his mother's cooking wine as a result.

Emil walked between the convalescent home's perfectly laid bed rows, white sheet after white sheet covering disfigured limbs and battered faces. So many of them barely even moved when he passed, and he felt as though he actually had stepped into that makeshift morgue in Nova Scotia. He stopped himself from searching for his brother's dishwater-blond hair and bright blue eyes, the same eyes as every other member of their family. He didn't want to see any resemblance which might cause him to backslide into a grief he had only recently recovered from.

When he marched up to Matron and said, "*Victores in bello non sunt,*" she spun around so quickly that the wash basin slid to the floor, landing with a porcelain crash that easily woke every man in the room. Several jolted upright, their attention darting about, looking for the source of the disturbance. The soldier Matron had been tending held his injured arm against his chest, his eyes full of alarm as water puddled across the floor.

"They've found us!" someone shouted. A convalescent barely old enough to enlist flattened his back against the wall, hands splayed upon the wallpaper. He stared out the window, observing the darkness before sliding to the floor, his hands moving to cover his face. "I won't go back," he wept. "Sister, do not let them take me."

Matron rose to her full height, her chin tilted to meet Emil's stare with abject fury. "I do not know what you are playing at, sir; however, you have upset my patients, which I cannot abide. It is time for you and your wife to leave." Gripping both their arms, she marched them between rows of concerned soldiers, while the boy's painful weeping engulfed a now otherwise silent room. A nurse with tightly pinned brunette curls hastened to quell his cries. She took his arm, attempting to lead him back to bed.

"Miss Clark!" Matron shouted at another young nurse standing at the end of the row, her hands full of clean wrappings. "Tend to Sergeant Moore, please. Then see that the floor is cleaned."

"Yes, Matron." The nurse gave a small curtsy and rushed to the bedside of the man with the injured hand.

Amara looked to the crying boy as the brunette nurse finally managed to settle him. "He won't be sent back to the front, will he?"

Matron closed the ballroom door behind them, shutting out the commotion and the boy's weeping. She released them both with a deep frown. "Likely, yes, he will."

"But he's ill!" Amara gasped. "Surely, you can see that."

"T'won't matter what I see. Physically, he has recovered. I assure you, they will send him back." Matron's face flushed, her lips pressing together when she noticed the atrium patients staring. Steaming, she pointed at the front door. "Out to the drive. We shall speak there. Mr. Cartwright?" she addressed the footman. He nodded, purposefully avoiding Amara and Emil's stares. "Please ring a taxi for our visitors and see that we are not disturbed until they have departed."

"Yes, Matron." With another nod, the footman left, his heels clicking towards the rear of the manor.

Matron did not speak again until the three of them were out on the damp drive, their muddy footprints illuminated only by coach lights on either side of the entrance. She stood with her back to the entry door, one flat hand to either pudgy hip like a white-clad sentinel. "How do you know that phrase you spoke?" she demanded.

"It's Latin," Emil said. "We're Catholic. I'll let you add those sums."

Her expression didn't soften. "I do not wish for your cheek. I need to know, why have you really come? Are we in danger?"

"Danger?" Emil laughed. "Why don't you tell us? We have no idea what's even going on. Peter sent us a letter to come to London. For some absurd reason, we followed. End of story."

"May I see this letter?"

Amara nodded and removed the letter from her handbag, offering it over. The matron's eyes scanned back and forth, taking in the urgency of the message. Finally, she folded it carefully and returned it to its envelope with barely a change in her expression. She handed it back with a quick exhale. "I suppose there's no avoiding the truth then. Your brother is a member of the organization, *Fides et Spes*."

"*Fides et Spes*," Amara repeated.

"Yes. It means Faith and Hope."

A fine name, Emil thought, especially during a time when so few people had much of either. "What is its purpose?" he asked.

"We receive letters from the soldiers and deliver them uncensored to their loved ones. Then we return news from the home front back to the frontline. Our organization is undocumented on any government records. One only finds us if they are brought in by another member."

"Why use Latin?"

"It is the universal language of the Catholic Church, yet also the universal language of no one else. It is unlikely to find a member of the laity who speaks it outside of Mass or daily prayer. Those specific phrases doubly so. Letters are passed from church to church by our carriers until being placed in the hands of their recipients. Those phrases are how we determine who is in our trust."

"But why deliver them at all?" Amara asked. "Why not receive the letters from the front, certify them, and send them through the regular postal service the rest of the way?"

"Is your head in the clouds, miss? Have you not heard of the censors? They watch all correspondence with an eagle eye, blacking out any news of the war front and confiscating those that may contain too much intelligence. If we send them through the post at any stage, they will be reviewed. Do you honestly believe they would allow your brother, a German soldier, to send a letter to you, an American?" She snorted. "Do not be so daft."

"You know about my brother serving Germany?"

"Of course. Being a part of *Fides et Spes* means you know what others don't."

"And that didn't bother you?" Emil said. "Being British, don't you side with the Allies? Hasn't the War Office asked citizens to report on possible German spies?"

She snorted again. "Of course, but we do not report on our own. If

Peter is a spy, I haven't the foggiest notion. As long as our members promise to remain true to our goals, their political views are not discussed. *Fides et Spes* doesn't choose sides. We send information where it needs to go, simple as that. If the occasional piece of intelligence happens to be contained, we are none the wiser. Unlike the War Office, we aren't in the habit of reading the mail we deliver."

How interesting, Emil thought. The ability to not choose a side was a luxury they hadn't yet been able to afford. With Amara's family still in Germany and his in the States, it had been difficult to choose, even though his own personal preferences leaned heavily in favor of the Allies. Despite the unwelcome riot last June, he still believed that America was the land of opportunity and the Central Powers stood in the way of all she stood for. Without the Germans' continued antagonism and the newspapers' constant colorful references to the barbaric "Huns" who lived there, he firmly believed they could have lived peaceably enough.

But the world was the way it was, at least for now.

"You honestly haven't heard any news since Peter left?" Amara pleaded.

"Last I heard he found work on the docks in Dover. The port is still open and accepting ships, so someone there may be able to direct you."

"Where is Dover?" Amara asked at the same time Emil stuttered, "Go to Dover? That's right across the channel from the Front!"

Matron appeared truly apologetic then. "I am sorry, but that's all the advice I can provide. You're welcome to stay a bout before heading back to the city. We don't have much in the way of refreshment, but I can have the kitchen toss something together."

"No, thank you," Emil said. "It's growing late. I'd rather head back straight away."

"Of course. Blackout makes these roads so terribly distressing to navigate." Matron offered them each a nod, her hands rising to rest upon her middle again. "Best of luck finding your brother. He was a kind man and I was relieved to assist in his recovery. I am sorry I could not help further."

As soon as she disappeared through the manor's entry door,

Amara immediately burst into tears. "What will we do now? If the church was her only contact, we have nothing else to go on except Dover."

Emil balked. "You're not seriously considering that we go to Dover?"

"What other choice do we have? Peter needs us. He only went to Dover because he couldn't come home. He had to work, otherwise he would be on the streets. Please, Emil, we have the papers. We can still bring him back with us."

"What if he isn't there anymore or he never was? How do we know Matron told us the truth?"

Her words were barely comprehensible through her tears. "I ... I can't leave without trying. You lost a brother, Emil. Do you really want to see me lose mine?"

She was trying to guilt him with Charles's death, which wasn't fair, but it did make him more level-headed. "Of course not," he said gently. He pulled her into his chest, gently circling her back with his palm. "But Amara, let's approach this logically. The pieces of the puzzle don't match up. Why would Peter ask you to come to London and then leave? Maybe your brother's missive isn't all that it seems."

"What do you mean?"

"This mysterious underground postal service claims to be for all people, but everyone has their alliances. Even the neutral countries slant one way or another in this war; they just aren't as vocal about it." He shook his head. "Peter could actually be on Germany's side. Have you even considered that? He could be using this letter delivery team to the Kaiser's benefit. Working on the docks would be a perfect opportunity to sneak British intelligence onto the continent."

Amara's chin tilted to glare at him. She jerked away from his embrace. "No. Peter is not a spy." She turned her back to him, her shoes squelching on the dirt drive. She peered towards the iron gates, her arms folded resolutely.

Emil remained where he stood, determined not to give in to her absurd tantrum. "We need to go home while we can still get there. What if they close the routes back to the States? It's already dangerous enough with the U-boats and the battleships. I do not want to be stuck in England."

"You used to live here. I thought you told me you had a good childhood."

"I did. A grand childhood, actually. I liked living here, but I like America much more. For one, my family's there—"

She spun on her heel, mud flicking up against her ankles. "Yes, they are, but my family's not. If Peter's asked for my help, it means he can't ask our parents for it. You can go home, but I'm going to Dover."

Emil could nearly feel his nerves crackling with the anxiety of it all. He rolled his shoulders and tried to level his emotions, but it was nearly impossible while feeling the heat from his wife's back. Her refusal to face him was like a slap to his ego. He had always wanted them to be equals, but she had also made that promise. Having her run off to an unfamiliar city without him did not factor into that equation, and he was growing tired of her taking advantage of his graciousness.

"What about Miss Harrington?" he suggested. Thankfully, it was enough to at least turn her cheek, her eyebrows raised in silent question. "If she delivered Peter's letters, she must have spoken with him at least once. We can return to the church and ask Father Ignatius for her address. We could visit her flat."

Without another second's hesitation, she surged forward, wrapping her arms around him to rest her head against his chest. He could hear the smile in her voice. "Oh, Emil, what a wonderful idea! You see, all is not lost. Miss Harrington will know where to find him."

"And if she doesn't?"

"Then the answer is simple. We go to Dover."

"And if he is not there either?"

"We keep searching. Perhaps the dock workers will know where to find him. Maybe another soldier he convalesced with. There must be someone who knows where he is."

She drew him closer, her slight fingers splayed against his back, her cheek nuzzled into his overcoat, as though a warm embrace would make him forget the magnitude of the situation.

The abrupt swing shocked his senses. His arms dropped to his sides, baffled by their current situation. A few weeks ago, his wife had been terrified of being accused of treason and carted off to an internment camp. She had sat behind her false persona and spent all her time knitting baby booties and soldiers' gloves. Rarely had she even spoken of Peter since they left St. Louis. And now, one summons had caused her to throw all caution to the wind.

This is never going to end, he thought in horror. She would probably travel all the way to Germany to have a piece of her family back.

He unfurled her arms from around him and placed her at arm's length. "Amara Kisch," he said firmly. "I'm putting my foot down and asserting my authority as your husband. If Miss Harrington cannot help, we are not going to Dover. We will be on the next passage from London to New York, whether we locate your brother or not. Understood?"

Amara stood slack-jawed, so much disbelief in her moist eyes. He had never spoken to her that way. Never demanded that she do something simply because he was the man in their marriage and could legally do so. But he didn't know any other way to make her see reason. She had always been the sensible one and yet her brother's letters had sent her on a whirlwind of self-destruction. This situation was out of control and if he let it continue unchecked, they were both liable to end up in a predicament no one could help them out of.

"I can't believe you just said that to me," she whispered. Slowly her eyes lowered to the ground, soft tears rolling down her wind-swept cheeks, and he felt like a lousy cad. But then she spoke again and he decided that he wasn't quite so sorry after all.

"That's exactly what Zeke would have said."

"Zeke?" he spat. "You're going to compare me to that louse?" He felt his hands start shaking, jitters rolling their way up his arms like he hadn't eaten in a while. She would *not* compare him to her jackwagon of a former fiancé. She would *not* place him anywhere near the same circles that man walked in.

The grind of a motorcar sounded from the darkness, becoming louder as a black Model T taxi rumbled up the drive towards them. Both of its headlamps were painted black, allowing only a sliver of light to show through, likely another result of blackout restrictions.

The thin beams swept over them and around the drive, stopping mere feet away. The taxi driver stepped from the motorcar, circling to open the rear door.

He tipped his cap. "Good evening, sir, miss. Would you be the ones who rang about a lift?"

Amara stepped forward. "Yes, that would be us." She took the driver's hand and placed one foot onto the running board, sliding into the rear seat.

Emil opened his mouth, about to say that they weren't finished with their discussion, but Amara cut in again before he could speak. "I would strongly advise against asserting your authority again at this moment. Please get in the auto and we can discuss this in the morning."

"Fine," he shot back. He folded himself into the seat beside her. "But you can bet we *will* discuss it."

TWELVE

November 19, 1917 –
London, England

THE REMAINDER OF THE TAXI RIDE passed in cold uncomfortable silence. Emil stared out his window and Amara stared out hers; they could have been in separate vehicles for all the acknowledgement they gave one another. Their uncharacteristic behavior was exactly long enough for him to realize how much he hated being at odds with his wife.

He still thought it was a poor decision for them to go to Dover, but he admitted that he could have handled the situation differently. If he had been on the other side of the coin and Winnie was the one missing and in trouble, he wouldn't have been any less dedicated to getting her back. And he would bet Amara would have handled the situation with far more grace and understanding. He would apologize as soon as they returned to their rented room and were out of earshot of the taxi driver.

But as they climbed the three flights of tenement stairs, he realized that a simple apology wasn't enough. Better yet, he should go to the church and question the priest. He would find out where Miss Harrington was and beg the information out of her towards Peter's whereabouts. If she was in *Fides et Spes*, he already knew which code phrases to say to get her to trust him, and his questioning was certain to be more successful if he didn't have Amara's currently erratic decision making in the way. He didn't want to say anything else that would pit them at odds with one another. This was the perfect solution.

"I'm going to take a walk," he told her once they were safely alone in their room.

"Now? It's rather late for a stroll."

He cast his gaze to the floor, attempting to appear deeply apologetic. "I'd like to clear my head before we continue our discussion."

"That's probably wise. Please don't wake me if I'm asleep when you return." With her back to him, she flipped the latches on her traveling case and began sifting through it.

Bending to press a quick kiss to her cheek, he hurried from the tenament, somehow managing to find his way back to St. Etheldreda's even in the dark. Upon entering, he noticed that the space was empty except for a man exiting the confessional.

Well, that certainly made it easy to locate the priest.

Allowing the other man to pass, Emil entered the confessional and eased the wooden door closed, immediately feeling trapped in the dark space. Thin curls of light slipped through the grate between him and Father Ignatius, and he hung back so the divided wall masked any sight of him. Why had he come in here? He could have waited until the priest left the confessional.

"Are you there, my child?" Father Ignatius asked gently. "I know it can be difficult to admit one's shortcomings; however, whatever you confess within this space will remain between us and the Lord."

Emil hadn't intended to confess his sins tonight, but maybe he should. There was so much weighing him down these days, and he had added one more grievance to the list tonight.

Making the Sign of the Cross, he lowered himself to the kneeler, propping his elbows on the rail and lacing his fingers beneath his chin. He stared at the grate, the curled light now swirling across his forearms.

"Bless me, Father, for I have sinned. It has been …" He paused, uncertain if he should tell the truth or not. It probably wasn't advisable to lie while in the midst of confession. Then he would have to confess that too. "Well, let's just say it's been a really long time since my last confession. Years." He paused, but when the priest didn't reply, figured he should jump right into it. "My wife and I had an argument. I said some things I wish I hadn't, but I fear there's just no reasoning with her. She's too emotional about the topic."

A long silence followed where he could hear his own nervous breathing and the more even tempo of the priest's. He knew Father Ignatius expected him to confess more as was traditionally done, especially if one had built up years' worth of sins. Emil didn't really want to delve too far into his past with this stranger though. He was on a mission to find Miss Harrington, the same as any number of missions he had undertaken during his time on the morality squad. Get in, get out, be done.

"I suppose that's all, Father. What's my penance?"

"That's all, is it?" The priest's tone was dubious. "Your admission did not bear much repentance."

"Are you judging the quality of my confession?"

The priest's voice remained steady, neither insulted nor irritated. "You say you said things you regret; however, it sounds as though you place the blame for your actions solely upon your wife. The confessional is not here to lay blame upon another. This time is for reflection on oneself. 'Why do you notice the splinter in your brother's eye, but do not perceive the wooden beam in your own?'"

A wooden beam in his eye, Emil thought. He could probably build Amara a house with the amount of lumber rattling around inside him. Even though he had moved forward from most of it, he still felt it there—the splinters, the planks, the nails, and the hammer that drove them. The war had made certain of that. Every day when he woke up hidden away in their New York apartment, he thought about his betrayal to Earhart that brought them there. When he stood behind the bar at the Forsythe, pouring drink after drink after blimey delicious looking drink, he thought about all those nights he got flash-blind drunk just to make himself feel better. When he saw the propaganda posters, plastering German hatred on every city block, he thought about that man hanged from a street lamp and how Emil had turned away from him. And when Winnie showed up ready to go into a war zone to improve their family's name, he thought about the guilt of leaving them all behind to save his wife and save himself. His life in

New York had been quiet and peaceful ... except for that it wasn't.

That's when it all came out. The entire sordid shameful story of the past five years. Every insult he ever flung at his father, every time he cared more about himself than his friends, how his brother's death made him an egotistical horror, and how Amara saved him from himself. Every lie he told, every rule he broke, every person he arrested on the morality squad for doing exactly what he did on an average Friday night.

When he finished speaking, he felt surprisingly better although rather emotionally spent. He rolled his shoulders and exhaled. Now he would be able to face his wife with a clean conscience.

After another moment of silence, Father Ignatius said, "Is that all, child?"

Emil's lips parted. "Isn't that enough?"

"I only wished to make certain you were ready for your penance."

"Yes, serve me my punishment."

Surprisingly, the priest gave a light chuckle. "This isn't the morality squad. I do not dole out punishments here. Tonight, I would like you to return to your wife. Make peace with her first and foremost then together pray for one another and your families. Pray for your happiness and pray for strength. Pray that you may follow God's will and help your children to follow it."

Emil's elbows slid off the kneeler, his clasped palms hitting the wooden rail. He hadn't mentioned anything to the priest about Amara's infertility. That wasn't anyone's sin or anyone's fault. It just was what was. "My wife can't have children," he said quietly. "We had hoped to adopt, but I don't know if that will actually happen."

"Why not?"

"Because ... well, look at the world, Father. It's falling to pieces. How can I bring a child into such madness?"

"Those children you hope to adopt have already been brought into this world. They will experience it either way. Whether that experience is built on love is the unknown. You ask how you can raise a child in a world such as this? My question is, how can you not?"

How could he not? he thought as he recited the Act of Contrition and the priest offered a prayer of absolution. He had never considered that it might really be as easy as that.

Then Father Ignatius was telling him to go in peace and Emil stood to leave. The grate slid shut, blocking out the tendrils of light and he then remembered why he was there in the first place.

"Wait!" he said rather too loudly and wondered if anyone was standing outside to hear. Returning to the kneeler, he leaned forward to speak through the confessional wall. "My apologies, Father, but I need one more moment of your time."

"You have more to confess?"

"No. I was hoping you could tell me where to find Miss Harrington. It's a matter of utmost importance."

There was a long pause where he heard the priest shift in his chair. The grate re-opened. "Emmett Miller? Is that you?"

He froze. Brilliant, he thought, now the priest knew exactly who had confessed all those terrible things. He hoped he never had to meet the man face-to-face again.

Just as before, rather than lie and be struck by lightning inside a confessional, he said, "Yeah, it's me. Do you know where Miss Harrington is?"

Another long pause. A suspiciously long pause, in fact, that all of Emil's former police training told him meant the man was formulating a response likely to be false. However, Father Ignatius was a Catholic priest seated in a confessional. Emil doubted he would flat out lie, but he might not provide all the information either.

"I'm sorry, Mr. Miller, but I have not seen Miss Harrington in several days. I cannot say when she is apt to return and she is unlikely to wish her address disclosed to a stranger."

His response was pretty much what Emil expected, which irritated him. Clearly the priest knew where the woman was. Why did he need to make everything so difficult?

"Thank you, Father. You will send word if she returns?

"Yes, of course. Good evening, Mr. Miller."

Emil closed the confessional door behind him with a heavy sigh, knowing he had nothing better to bring Amara than another dead end. He stared up at the crucifix. "You have a strange sense of humor. You forgive my sins and then leave me without answers?"

Silence was the only reply he was apparently going to get.

As he turned to leave, he noticed a young woman seated in the last pew waiting for the confessional. Her eyes viewed him with interest from beneath her black chapel veil. He nodded to her. "My apologies, miss. I'm having a rather rough night."

"Was the priest unable to help?"

"Not with everything. My wife and I had a terrible argument. She's back at our flat and I came here."

"That must have indeed been dreadful to require immediate confession." She gestured to the empty stretch of pew beside her. "Would you care to talk about it?"

"I already told the priest everything."

She smiled. "Another turn couldn't hurt, could it?"

"Aren't you here for confession?"

"My sins can wait a little longer." She gestured to the pew again. "Come sit."

Walking to the opposite end of the aisle, Emil slid into the pew, making sure to remain several feet away for propriety's sake. How much should he tell this stranger? The basics were probably best. "My wife received word that her brother returned to London after being injured at the front. Unfortunately, no one seems to have seen him for some time. Father Ignatius was our last reasonable lead to locate him."

"Your last reasonable lead?" she asked. "Does that mean you have an unreasonable one?"

"Yes. It isn't one I'm enthusiastic to follow."

"But your wife is."

"Yes." He sighed. He noticed two bits of blue thread braided around her left ring finger. He had heard of women selling their jewelry to make ends meet while their husbands were away at the front. It was a shame that she had been forced to sell the most important piece of jewelry she owned. "Do you and your husband ever have such problems in your marriage?" he asked her.

"Oh, I'm not married." She folded her right hand over her left, concealing the thread. "I was engaged, but the situation was terribly complicated."

"Because of the war?" That was the standard answer for everything these days, so he didn't know why her response would be any different. Frankly, he was exhausted from hearing the same old excuses. "What about after the war ends?"

"Even then, there are complications. So many complications. Who knows where we'll be then?" She shrugged. "*C'est la vie*, I suppose. I'm sorry, I didn't catch your name."

"I didn't catch yours either."

She smiled innocently, but said nothing and neither did he. Finally, she glanced at the confessional doors and said, "It's rather late. I would like to say my evening prayers and return home."

"Of course. Sorry to have kept you. Have a good evening."

Emil was almost to the wooden entry doors when a screeching whistle blasted from the other side, followed shortly thereafter by shouting impossible to decipher through the doors' thickness. Another whistle came soon after, then another shout. He hefted the church door open, the cold night wafting over him. Out on the sidewalk, people hustled past, all in the same direction down Ely Place. He could now make out the shout that had been behind the whistle: "Take cover! Take cover!"

Suddenly, the church woman was beside him. "Not that way!" she cautioned. Yanking him back inside by the coat sleeve, she pushed the door closed. She pointed at a set of stone stairs leading down to another set of heavy wooden doors. "This way."

Emil snatched her arm, tethering her from descending the stairs. "What's happening?"

"Air raid." Father Ignatius shuffled up behind them. "She's right, you know. The crypt's the best place to be."

"The crypt?" Emil exclaimed. "Isn't that where you keep the dead?" It sounded like a rather bad omen to him.

"Not anymore," the priest assured him. He started down the stairs. "The shelters will be swamped with people, but few think to come here. None of the other bombings have taken the church and I doubt this one will. We'll stay until the danger passes."

Emil looked towards the door that would take him back to Amara. She was still in the apartment waiting for him, likely asleep and unaware of what was happening. "I have to get my wife. We'll meet you back here."

"There isn't time," the woman insisted. "You won't make it to her then back in time."

He released her arm in disgust. "I can't leave her! What kind of man leaves his wife alone in an unfamiliar country during a war? Gah, I'm such a blimey idiot." Pulling open the church door, he sprinted in the direction of the tenement, shoving aside pedestrians in his wake.

Sardonically, all he could think was if he died, at least he had already made his last confession.

THIRTEEN

November 19, 1917 –
London, England

AMARA HAD BARELY DOZED OFF when a shrill whistle knocked her back awake. The tweet sounded in several sharp blasts followed by a shout she couldn't make out in her muddled state. Then the whistle again, closer now with the same call, this time discernible as the heralder passed under her window. "Take cover! Take cover!" The voice dampened again as it continued down the street on the other side.

Tossing off the bedcovers, she hurried to the window and swept back the curtains. From the top floor apartment, she was just in time to witness three white rockets flare above the buildings followed by shouts from the surrounding houses. Although every street lamp remained extinguished, she could still make out figures beginning to exit their homes. They merged into groups, all hurrying down the sidewalk in the same direction.

Across the street, a man fumbled to lock his front door, while his wife clutched the hands of two small children. Their expressions were impossible to discern in the darkened street. Amara lifted the window sash, leaning out. "Pardon me," she called to the couple. "Do you know what's happening?"

The man turned at her voice, pocketing his key before raising a hand of acknowledgement. Placing the same hand to his wife's back, he led her across the street to Amara's window and looked up. "Another air raid, I'm afraid."

"Air raid? What do we do?"

He gestured in the direction of the crowd. "Get to the Tube." Beside him, his little girl started to cry, her thumb stuck between her wailing gums. When he lifted her to his chest, her tears dampened his shoulder.

"What's the Tube?" Amara asked, feeling more alarmed by the minute.

"Why, the London Underground, of course!" his wife exclaimed. She clutched her other child's hand and peered up into the sky. "Nearest station's at Chancery Lane. Come, Richard." Then she took her husband's arm and pulled him off into the crowd.

Amara closed the window and sat back on the bed. What should she do now? She had read newspaper articles of the bombings over London but having lived in America, never thought she would experience them first-hand. She peered around their dim room, her cold feet petrified to the carpeting.

She and Emil had parted terribly and foolishly, and the reasons seemed so trivial now. She shouldn't have let him leave like that. No matter how angry she had been, he was still her husband.

Would he come back for her or would he head for this "Tube" the couple spoke of, assuming she would too? She could follow the crowd to Chancery Lane and hope to find him there. But what if he wasn't? She had no idea which direction he had headed; he could very well be in an entirely different part of the city. What if he returned to the apartment and found her missing? Should she remain here, huddle under the bed covers, and pray for survival?

A dull thud sounded from somewhere outside like a tree felling a long way off. Rising from the bed, she returned to the window, craning her neck out in either direction. Nothing unusual had occurred on the street or above the rooftops. The sound, however, repeated a few minutes later, a little louder this time. When the third sounded louder even still, she understood. Bombs were falling on London and they were coming towards her, not away.

She shoved her arms into her overcoat sleeves as quickly as she could and buttoned it over her nightgown. Likely, Emil had followed the crowd in the direction of the Tube. That was where she would head too. Grabbing her handbag, she closed the apartment door and realized that Emil had the key. *Does it matter whether the door is locked*, she thought, *if the entire building ends up in ruins?*

Making a split-second decision she dearly hoped wasn't an extra second she would need later, she ran back into the room and threw the latches up on her traveling case. She withdrew all three sets of forged citizenship papers and shoved them into her handbag before racing back out the door. It was possibly a foolish risk to bring them, but it would do her no good to see them burned to bits.

The apartment staircase was crowded, fellow residents jostling her down all three flights of stairs, but once she stepped onto the sidewalk, movement became less restrictive. Due to blackout laws, the moon was their only source of light and at this time of the month, it was but a sliver. Another thud sounded behind her and this time she didn't look back.

Keep going, she thought. *Keep going towards Emil. Don't stop.*

A loud roar tore through the sky, and her hands pressed to her ears as a biplane passed low overhead. Its propellers whirling, it streaked away into the night and thankfully left her unscathed. Perhaps it had already unloaded all its ammunition? She wouldn't wait to find out.

A moment later a brilliant flash lit the night sky and she heard a child say, "Ooh, it's pretty. Mummy, look at the sunrise."

Amara started running then, blindly following those in front of her, not knowing how much farther to the shelter, and every step felt like a thousand. Hundreds of shoe soles clattered across the cobblestones and her chest hurt with the exertion, a deep pain creeping into her side along with her ankles. She wasn't accustomed to running such a distance, or really running at all. There hadn't been any need since the night of the riot in St. Louis and rarely any occasion before that. Not since she was a child and would engage in foot races with Peter and Siegfried. She clutched at her ribs, her feet slowing as she neared the next cross street, her breath falling in deep gasps until she wanted to retch.

When she heard her name, she thought she must be hallucinating and likely about to faint. A tall figure ran towards her out of the darkness. "Amara!" he called. "Amara, is that you?"

Emil snatched her up in his arms, his lips moving, but the roar of another plane drowned out the words. "Oh, Emil," she cried. She clutched his coat sleeves. "I'm so sorry for what I said. You're not like Zeke; you're not. I thought I might never see you again."

He pressed a quick kiss to her lips. "I'm sorry too, but right now we have far greater concerns." Taking her hand, he led her back into the darkness of the side street and away from the fleeing crowds. He pushed her into a narrow alleyway between two buildings. "This way. We need to get inside."

Amara glanced over her shoulder. "I believe the shelter's back that way though."

"It is, but I know a better place."

Emil pushed their way through the thickening crowd and only when he turned onto Ely Place, did Amara recognize where they were. They rushed through St. Etheldreda's main entrance and down a short staircase where he banged on another set of wooden doors.

"Father Ignatius!" he called. "It's Emmett Miller, and my wife. Please let us in." He pounded on the door again, but there was no response. "Father!" He banged harder. Still nothing except silence. "Blast," he muttered. "They said they would be here."

"They?"

"Father Ignatius and some woman I met in the church." He sat on the stairs and stared at the locked door. "They were heading down here when I left. They said it was the safest place."

"You came back to the church tonight?" she said, astonished. "Why?"

He met her eyes again. "To find Miss Harrington. I wanted to be done with it all."

"And did you find her?"

"No."

They both looked up as another bright flash of light blazed across the front windows and the glass panes rattled. Cursing, Emil launched himself off the stairs and his shoulder straight into the door, groaning when it didn't budge. Backing up, he slammed his entire weight against the jam instead, which only resulted in another curse and him rubbing his bicep. "Who blimey made this? Why did they have to be such capable carpenters?"

He wiped the back of his hand across his brow, now beaded with sweat. "Should I go out front and break a window? Do you think God would smite me for that?"

"We're in an air raid," she said, her voice soft. "Perhaps God's smiting us now."

She had barely released the words when the door opened, and a young woman yanked her into the dimly lit corridor. With a squeak, she grabbed onto Emil's fingers, pulling him in along with her. He slammed the door behind them.

"Quickly!" the woman urged, her voice echoing off the stone walls. With every stride, the sleeve of her grey overcoat scratched Amara's skin from where she held her, and her light brunette curls, carefully pinned back on both sides, swayed against her shoulders. Likely no more than mid-twenties, she carried a confidence Amara hadn't seen in too many of London's residents.

The woman led them into a dank room built partially into the ground with round stone pillars and several stained glass windows high on either side. Five short wooden pews sat on either side of a short aisle leading up to a simple altar. Only three candles were lit: the red tabernacle lamp and two white, one now being held by the woman and the other by Father Ignatius seated in the first pew. If not for war conservations made on candles, every votive rack beneath the windows would likely have also been stocked and set ablaze.

"Good to see you both again, Mr. and Mrs. Miller," the priest greeted them. He nodded to the pew opposite. "Do have a seat. You're safe here."

"What took you so long to answer the door?" Emil asked. "We could have been blown away."

As though in response, another flight of planes swooped overhead, their engines vanishing as quickly as they had come. The woman pointed upward to the sound. "They make it difficult to discern knocking from the general chaos. Now sit." She pointed to the pew the priest indicated then deposited herself in the pew behind Father Ignatius. Emil directed Amara into the pew, wrapping his arm around her shoulders so she could meld against his side.

They remained in stillness for several minutes, four separate people listening for the next explosion to sound. Wondering if it would land directly upon them. *What type of person would bomb a church?* Amara thought, then realized that it would be the same type of person who exploded one on top of her brother.

She listened to the planes overhead and the bombs falling, wondering if Peter had the same experience she was now. The church which crushed him was probably little different from this one. Had he huddled against the wall or stood tall? Had there been anyone with him in those moments? She had Emil at least. Who had been there for Peter?

Tears dripped from her eyes and she leaned closer to her husband. She let herself cry quietly into his side while he held her and stroked her hair and told her that everything would be fine. Knowing that it might not be. Two hours ago, they had been at each other's throats. Now, none of that mattered.

"We'll go home," she promised, finally managing to rein in her emotions enough to speak clearly. She eased away to swipe a palm over each eye. "If we live through tonight, we'll leave England whenever you wish. You're my husband. You're the man I should follow."

He stared at her. "You would do that for me?"

"I would."

Emil's chin dropped, his sweat-soaked hair falling partially across his forehead. The crackle in his voice confirmed that his blue eyes held unshed tears that matched her own. He lifted her hand to his lips, pressing a soft kiss to her palm. "I made so many mistakes before we married that it's a wonder you agreed to marry me. But I sure am glad you did."

She expected him to say something arrogant then to lessen the intensity of the situation. To call attention to what an amazing specimen of humanity he was, or some other such malarky. That was typically how he masked his emotions. Only this time he didn't.

He kissed her palm again and gripped her fingers tightly. "I can't believe I'm about to say this, but if you need to chase this feeling, if you need to find your brother to be at peace, then I'll help you. I love every piece of you, and I never want you to feel like you face anything alone."

She felt tears slide down her cheeks again, so many she was sure she would drown in them. She didn't care that two strangers sat ten feet away. All she cared about was this one singular moment with her husband. "I wish I could give you babies," she said softly.

"You will." Heedless to their viewers or the chapel's reverent atmosphere, he lifted her up for a kiss, holding her to him like a soldier's final breath on the edge of battle.

"We'll find Peter," he said when he finally drew away. "We'll bring him home."

"You're right, we will." The young woman stood beside their pew, the candlelight flickering over her features, her curls casting rings of shadow across her expressionless face.

"I'm Josie Harrington," she said, "and I can tell you exactly where your brother is."

FOURTEEN

September 29, 1917 – Seven Weeks Prior
London, England

LONG AFTER THE SOLDIERS' USUAL BEDTIME, Josie and Peter remained in Olmsted Manor's open atrium, enjoying a fourth game of Snap and light conversation. Only two nights stood between them and separation and although neither said it, they were glad Matron had, for once, decided to turn a blind eye to their blatant disregard for curfew.

Every time Peter laughed, his excitement turned Josie's belly into mush with lovely butterflies. She adored the quirk of his lips, the crinkle at the corners of his eyes when he smiled. Hearing him laugh at something so simple as her British peculiarities was enough to wish the war to a hurried end. If only that were tonight; he wouldn't ever need to leave for Dover and they could be together now. No more secret letter deliveries. No more postings of dead soldiers and black mourning armbands. She wanted something to celebrate. To put on her nicest dress and walk arm in arm with him through Kensington Garden. She wanted Peter to kiss her again. More than almost anything she wanted that, and she had never considered herself silly enough to be struck stupid by love. If he asked her to return to America with him, she would gladly go.

A pair of threes fell from their hands and she slapped her palm on the deck, watching him purposely move a second too slowly. Letting her win again. She knew it was only to keep her there a few minutes longer, so she let him do it and never let on that she had him figured.

When she had arrived that afternoon, Peter had been so relieved to see her safe and she him, that they didn't even speak for the first full hour, simply sat beside the fire and one another in silence. Unable to add to his worries, she decided not to mention his last letter to Amara or ask about what might have changed. Their silence eventually turned to small talk and when their small talk became painful, she suggested Snap and an exchange of favorite childhood stories. That's where they were when the air raid warning came for the second time in two nights.

Matron ran the length of the gallery and down the stairs, calling to the voluntary aids, to the nurses, the servants, and the patients. "Another raid! To the kitchens! Get to the kitchens!" Built of sturdy stone blocks, the kitchen was located on the bottom level of the manor with three sides built into the ground. It was well situated for roaring oven fires and equally suited for defense against Gotha bombers.

At her words, Peter leapt from his chair, something he wouldn't have been able to do a few weeks before. He grabbed Josie's hand and pulled her towards the servants' stairwell where the nurses were directing the rest of the patients. Down the stairs, their feet clomped to the basement stones below. They herded into the kitchen, sidling up against one another with hushed whispers. It wasn't the first air raid any of them had endured, and they certainly didn't want it to end with a different outcome than the others.

Last night, Josie had sheltered on an underground railway platform with a hundred other people, her back pressed against a brick wall while five feet away, a mother shushed her crying child. Over their heads was only silence, while fears pummeled her mind like the German bombs must surely be pummeling some part of her forlorn city. She could only imagine Peter's fear. Even though she still questioned his mysterious letter to Amara, she prayed beyond her own safety to his. What did it matter why he wrote that letter steering his sister away? The situation *had* changed. It *was* no longer safe. At any moment a bomb could shatter through the parlor wall.

Down in the manor kitchen, Peter practically pushed Josie into the farthest corner, her back forced against a wall, shoulders touching the edge of a cupboard on one side and a potato bin on the other. He placed himself in front of her, his back to her front like a human shield. With blackout restrictions enforced, no one but her could feel how his trembling belied his soldier's stance.

When the first bomb dropped, it could barely be heard. The second was equally far away. When the third sounded, Josie breathed easier. They were moving into the city rather than outward towards the manor. Even with the gentle rattle of window panes, the distance must have been miles; they had faced far closer calls than this.

As the impacts continued to distance themselves, a low chatter arose to ease the discomfort within the confined space. Peter, however, remained inches in front of her, steadfast in his protection while continuing to tremble. During the other air raids, Matron had given him a tincture to sedate him, but he was to be released from the manor in two days' time. Pronounced with a clean bill of health. There was no reason to give an otherwise healthy man a sedative, especially when others needed it more.

Knowing they were hidden in the dark, Josie slid both her arms around his waist to lace her fingers over his stomach. She rested her cheek against his tense back muscles and felt his shallow breaths beneath the shirt's smooth fabric. Tentatively, he laid a hand over hers. "Don't pity me," he said in a strained whisper.

"I don't. It's not shameful to be afraid." She paused and when the only response was another rattle of window panes, whispered, "I'm frightened too."

He turned then in her arms, welcoming her down to sit beside him on the cold stone, shoulder-to-shoulder. He cradled her hand in his, his crippled joints pinching where they attempted to clumsily lace through her fingers. She didn't mind. She would accept the intimate gesture even if he only had a stump to offer.

It was incredible how much one simple kiss could change one's longing for another. How one dire life-or-death situation could make you never want to be apart. "I am sorry I wasn't here for last night's raid," she said softly.

"It was terrible," he admitted. "Every time they come, I remember

France. The sound of mortars landing fifteen feet away, gas and gun smoke clogging my nostrils. I'm thankful we can't hear the airplanes this far out because their whine is something you will not forget."

"I have heard them."

Even in the near darkness, she could tell her answer caught him off guard. Outside of that first night when Matron told her how he was injured, they had never spoken in depth about the air raids. He had no idea she ever experienced one up close. It simply wasn't something he wanted to relive and she had respected that. But tonight was different. Tonight, they had crossed that threshold. Tonight, they were in this together.

"The day before we met, there was a raid, the worst I ever saw. They swooped down in broad daylight. Too many were injured, so many buildings destroyed." She ran her thumb across a jagged scar along his own, finally faded to pink rather than the puckered ragged red it used to be. "Children died that day," she whispered. "An entire schoolroom of infants."

She inched closer until their arms pressed flush together, offering a bit of warmth against the chilly stone floor upon her ankles. Peter acted like she hadn't even moved. With the rigid way he stared at her, she wondered if he had forgotten she was even there. "Peter?"

Suddenly, he stood, pulling her up before she could think. He edged his way out from the cupboard nook, nodding excuses as he elbowed between patients and nurses, dragging her along behind him. When they reached the stairs leading to the kitchen's exterior door, Matron threw up a warning hand from across the room, barely discernible in the low moonlight. Josie allowed herself to be ushered up the stairs and through the servants' entrance before her brain triggered that they were outside during an air raid.

"Peter, where are we going?"

He led her across the drive, their foot falls loud in the otherwise silent night. The breeze stilled which would allow them to hear any Gothas which might pass overhead, although it would also likely be the last thing they ever heard. There would be no time to return to the kitchens before their bodies were littered in tiny pieces across the manor grounds.

"Peter?" she edged again as they passed through the slight servants' gate and practically jogged down the dirt path towards the stables. Halfway there, he finally stopped, panting slightly, his hand now moist against hers. A quarter mile in the distance, she could make out the edge of the stable roof against the night sky, its lanterns extinguished. A quarter mile behind the same could be seen of the manor's main house.

"Peter, what is it?" she demanded, her voice entirely too pronounced in the empty air. She lowered her tone. "Have you forgotten there's an air raid on? We must return to the kitchens."

"I helped murder those children."

He said it so quietly, she wondered if she made up the terrible words in her head. But what sort of twisted mind would she have to have to imagine that the man she loved would admit to murdering innocents?

"Pardon, but *what*?"

Peter released her hand to fold his arms over his chest. He tilted his head back and stared up at the moon. "I tried to tell you in the garden, but then we kissed and ... well, the situation changed."

She felt her throat closing. "I won't believe you were involved in anything so vile. The day before it happened, you were already at the manor, barely even conscious."

"Maybe I didn't plan the mission or drop the bombs, but I did fight for the people who did. I wore their uniform and stood in their trenches. That might make you hate me, but I would rather have you hate me for the truth than love me for a lie. I thought if I told enough people I was an Allied soldier, maybe I would actually feel like I was one. But your story about the children made me realize that I can't just paint over my choices with someone else's life."

"But you can." She laid a hand on his arm, expecting him to throw her off, but he didn't even acknowledge the gesture. She had seen this reaction from other soldiers in the home. Stress from a prior war trauma—in Peter's case, the air raid that buried him—caused them to temporarily take responsibility for the entire war.

"I suspected you might not be all you seemed when you arrived," she explained. "Matron called you a 'special extract', 'trapped on the wrong side of the line.' In my line of work, there are only a few things that could mean."

"That didn't bother you?" he gaped. "I'm the enemy."

"In *Fides et Spes*, we accept everyone, no matter their political cause. We sacrifice our own allegiances to ensure that no family lives without word of their loved ones. It means that I don't have the luxury to mind who you were before."

"That sounds like a spoon-fed response, straight from *Fides et Spes'* rule book."

"Perhaps it is, but it's also true. I don't mind who you fought with before. What matters is that you don't side with them now." She paused, doubt creeping in for the first time. "You *don't* side with them anymore, do you?"

"No. I don't favor Germany's cause, never did. I only fought for them because my father asked me to. My sisters' husbands were all in the *Deutsches Heer* and America hadn't yet joined the Allies. I had no justifiable reason to side against my family."

"You left Amy behind. She's your family too, isn't she?"

"She's different. My other sisters are married; they already chose their path. Amy has no one to protect her except me. I could never ask her to knowingly follow me into danger. Just like I could never ask you."

Is that why you told her not to come? Josie wanted to ask, although that would be admitting to a major break in his confidence, not to mention a violation of one of *Fides et Spes'* cardinal rules.

She jumped as a bugle sounded somewhere to the east—the signal for all clear. Time to return to the manor. If they didn't, Matron would come searching or send Bill which would be worse. She stepped towards the house, then paused when Peter didn't immediately move to join her. "Aren't you coming?" she asked.

"Not yet. We're alone here, but we won't be there." He stared at her for a long moment, waiting for the bugle to silence. Then he continued speaking as though nothing had interrupted them.

"I used to run a feed store in Iowa. Built it with my cousin from the ground up. We were supposed to sell people grain and tack and attend church on Sundays and grow old surrounded by our families and our horses and a couple corn fields. That's what I was supposed to do. All I wanted was to be a normal American." A deep breath followed by a longer exhale. "Instead, I climbed into a trench and killed fourteen men. Probably more. Back in Iowa, I didn't even own a gun."

Josie reeled at his defeated posture and the hollow hopeless sound of his voice. Even with this news, how much she still loved him. How she wanted to remove his pain but couldn't! There was nothing she could say to change what had been done. In all these months, she had never thought about the lives he must have silenced or those her father must have also taken down. Never once had she lingered over what it actually required for any of the convalescents to be a soldier and achieve victory. If her father had lived only a little longer, he may have been Peter's fifteenth kill. Or Peter may have been her father's ... how many? It was too awful to imagine her carefree father looking into another man's eyes and pulling the trigger even once. She stared down the road towards the stables and imagined those dead men marching up the path to meet them.

"I gave them names," Peter told her. "Each and every man I shot. I prayed for their souls inside the very church that crushed me. I chose to become an American; I should have been on their side. Instead, I killed them." He looked at her then and with his final words, she wished he hadn't. "I betrayed my country, Josie. Heaven knows I deserved to have a church bury me for it."

FIFTEEN

"YOU KNOW WHERE MY BROTHER IS?" Amara leapt from the chapel pew, standing nearly toe-to-toe with Josie. "Tell me! Is he well? Is he safe?"

"I know where he is, but I don't know if he's safe." Her eyes raised sadly to Amara's. "I'm afraid I likely don't have the answers to most of your questions."

"Then what can you tell us?" Emil demanded. He rose beside his wife, easily matching the woman's height and then some. "How do we know we can trust you?"

Josie let the candle in her hands flicker between them for a moment before answering. "A valid question. How do I know I can trust *you*?"

Narrowed eyes turned on one another, she and Emil locked in a standoff that neither one seemed willing to concede. Likely, it would have continued all evening if Father Ignatius didn't decide to immediately intervene. "Why not ask him the code phrase, Miss Harrington?"

She continued to eye Emil warily. "I don't know to what you refer."

"I would bet you do," he countered, "and you seem clever, so let's save time, shall we? You say, '*Victores in bello non sunt.*' I reply with '*Vince malum bono.*' Then I show you Peter's letters and you tell us where he is."

Amara to handed them over and watched Josie's eyes sweep across the handwriting, her expression revealing nothing. Did Josie know about the final letter ordering them not to come? If she mentioned it, Emil would know that Amara kept it from him. They had only reconciled minutes before; she didn't need everything to crash down around them now. Especially if Josie's information only led them straight back to America.

Slowly, the woman folded the letters and offered them back to Amara, who returned them to her handbag. "That proves nothing," she said. "Your brother served in the German army, did he not? How do I know your alliances are not of a similar nature?"

"I thought *Fides et Spes* was neutral," Emil said. "Why should our alliances matter?"

"Then you *are* for the Kaiser?"

"No," Amara said quickly, lest her husband's sharp tongue land them in any more trouble or help Josie recall the letter Amara hoped she hadn't even seen. "I am for my brother and my husband. As a married woman, surely you can understand that at least."

"I'm not married," Josie said, but two bits of blue thread braided around her left ring finger implied otherwise. Apparently struck with the same thought, Emil pointed at her hand.

"Your attachment to that thread betrays you, Miss Harrington. You already told me in the church that you were engaged. What you didn't reveal is that you're engaged to Peter."

Amara nearly slid from the pew in disbelief. How had she not even considered that her brother might have found love while overseas? That was why he asked her not to come, why he said the situation had altered. He had fallen in love and planned to marry, but their relationship was too complicated to explain in a letter. Surely, he planned to tell her more once there was more to tell. It both pained and pleased her that Peter found someone to share his life with. She was ever so happy for him, yet felt her heart ache at the thought of him living so far away.

"It would have been difficult," Emil continued, "for Peter to purchase an engagement ring without any money. Dover was the only place he could find a position, so he left, intending to return once he made his way. You have your own position in *Fides et Spes* and he

114

would never ask you to abandon it, so you remained here." He leaned back in the pew and grinned. "I do applaud you, Miss Harrington, for your ability to keep us off the trail. The search nearly drove us mad."

Josie, however, wasn't smiling. "Peter and I are engaged; however, your assumptions are missing several crucial details."

Amara wasn't interested in the details anymore. Not when she had a clear path to her brother. She reached for Emil's hand, squeezing it with a smile she hadn't managed in a long time. "I know it's far, but could we go to Dover? Only for a quick visit, then I promise we'll go home. If Peter plans to live here, who knows when I'll have this chance again?"

Emil smiled back at her. "Of course, we can go. We'll visit your brother and then return home."

Josie interrupted then, her expression grimmer than they had yet seen. "You need to listen. Peter's not in Dover anymore."

The chapel went silent and it was then that Amara noticed all outside had been quiet for a while. No more windows rattling or explosions in the distance. The air raid must be over.

"Oh, ho!" Father Ignatius declared. "I do believe the bombings have stopped." He shuffled out of the pew and offered a low bow to the tabernacle. Rising, he turned to the three of them. "Best for me to go above and see if we've suffered any damage. Miss Harrington, do ensure our guests return home safely, will you?"

She nodded. "Of course, Father. I shall return in the morning to assist with any cleanup."

"Only once you've rested. It seems your night may be longer than most." Then he disappeared down the aisle and into the stairwell corridor, his legs taking one careful step at a time.

Emil continued to watch the empty doorway long after the priest disappeared. His brow furrowed. "Father Ignatius knows Peter's whereabouts, doesn't he? He sent us on a circular mission for nothing."

"Not for nothing," Josie quickly assured him. "You are not part of our organization. You don't understand how important it is for our secrecy to be maintained. How was he to know if you spoke the truth about your identities? What if Peter's letters had been intercepted by the wrong sort of people?" Her hands went to her hips. "After Peter left, we had no way to identify you for certain. Matron and Father agreed that when you arrived—if you arrived—I alone would decide if you could be trusted with Peter's whereabouts."

"It's no coincidence that we all ended up here tonight though, is it?"

"Not entirely," she admitted. "I was at the manor this evening when you spoke with Matron. She came to me at once to inform me that Peter's sister and her husband had arrived and were tossing confidential information around. She mentioned that you visited Father Ignatius, so I left immediately and came here. I wanted to know what he told you. Based on Matron's description, it was obvious who you were when we met."

"Wait," said Emil. "If you knew who I was all along, why didn't you interrogate me then? When I asked for your name, why didn't you provide it? You let me run off and never once mentioned a thing."

"I needed to know that I could trust you. When you chose to find your wife rather than save your own life, you proved to me that I could." She focused on Amara then. "You were right about one thing though. When I met Peter, I only intended to help him get home to you, but life had other plans. He couldn't afford a ring so I made my own." There was nothing joyful in the announcement. "Peter proposed to me September 30th, the day after he told me he deserted Germany. The day before he returned to France."

Amara felt her heart, her soul, everything drop away. She felt like she was floating and only Emil's hand kept her grounded. Peter returned to France. He had escaped and then willingly placed himself back in mortal danger. Heat pricked the edges of her eyelids, stinging to the tips of her fingers. Her entire body felt hot to the point of pain. *How could he?* she seethed inwardly. *How could he do something so utterly foolish?*

"Where?" she asked. "Where is he?"

"Near Le Clé. It's where he was injured. Another member of our organization, Bill Olmsted, went with him."

"Why?" she choked. "Why would he go back there?"

"He had his reasons."

When Josie didn't volunteer any further information, Emil sighed. "Well, then I suppose we'll have to ask him those reasons when we get to France."

Amara was sure she must have heard him wrong. "We're going to France?"

He gave a solemn nod and she wished they were alone. She wanted to hold this moment, this memory, the way his lips formed his next words. How beautiful it sounded when he said, "We're going to France. Together."

"Together?" she asked. "Truly?"

Josie placed her hand atop Amara's, the blue thread ring golden in the candlelight. "Together."

SIXTEEN

November 20, 1917 –
London, England

HAVING FINISHED PACKING THE last of her belongings into a single traveling case, Josie now toyed with the frayed strings of her makeshift engagement ring. Peter hadn't had a proper one to give her; his proposal had been so spontaneous. Maybe he had intended to return to France all along, or perhaps his fancy began when he believed Amara wasn't coming for him, but Josie had been the one to seal his conviction. Her story about the infants in the air raid had been his undoing. He blamed himself and no amount of local letter deliveries would stave off that guilt. The job Bill lined up on the docks quickly turned to working a vessel across the Channel.

They had parted ways with him swearing to return and she expecting never to see him again. He was returning to war-torn France, to *German-occupied* war-torn France. Everyone in *Fides et Spes* knew what that meant. Their organization had lost many a good carrier to gunfire, bombs, gas—name anything and it had probably taken the life of at least one.

Her own position was comfortable, now that she thought on it. Even with the constant threat of London air raids, her daily tasks were little risk compared to what others experienced on the continent. Unlike most of *Fides et Spes*'s carriers who were recruited, she had stumbled over it nearly by chance. She had just stepped from the confessional of St. Etheldreda's when she heard two voices speaking in hushed whispers. The woman was crying, the man firm in his replies.

"We must find someone to take her place," the woman wept.

"But who? Who could possibly replace her?"

That was when they noticed Josie. She had fit the bill. Right physical type, discreet looks and figure. Already both her parents passed on. If she was to throw herself into peril, no family would be left mother- or childless. No husband out on the battlefield to grieve her loss.

She carried letters to each stop from St. Etheldreda to Olmsted Manor, handed them off to the next carrier, and accepted the batch handed to her. The same route every day. Father Ignatius handed her coins each week to run church errands, another slight stack at week's end as payment for herself. She never asked where the money came from. He never told her. On and on it went, day after day, wondering if the war would ever end. If the blackout orders would cease, if her ears would stop ringing from the air raid whistles, if one day she could take tea with spoonfuls of sugar and cream. Cakes with icing swirls. All sorts of lovely decadence.

Her father had loved cake. Perhaps it was good that he never made it home from the Somme. He would have been disappointed with the way she left their flat. How she sold it to move closer to St. Etheldreda's, into the heart of danger, to make it easier to travel her assigned route. She had a tiny room beside many other girls with equally tiny rooms, a shared bathhouse down the street, and a community kitchen. Her roommate, Viola, was a scant girl who worked fifteen-hour days at the factory, churning out sets of polished uniform buttons, one beside the next, every effort made to help the Tommies beat the Jerries. At week's end, she dropped her earned pence in a jar on her bedside table, never afraid that Josie would steal them. There weren't that many anyway.

Josie held the small bag that contained her earned coins, so many more than Viola would ever have. Maybe they were from an anonymous donor eager to help the war effort. Maybe the priest pulled them from the donation plate. Or maybe Bill picked them off unsuspecting passengers at the Royal Docks.

She would return them all for one more day in that convalescent home with Peter, one more day before that last day.

"Wait for me," he said that final morning. "I'll return for you."

"Why must you go to France at all?" she asked. "Look where you're headed, where you came from. It nearly killed you." She clutched his arms, his rough overcoat material catching between her fingers. "Be sensible. Stay here with me or have us both go home to your sister. We'll find somewhere safe for all of us."

"There is no safety anywhere. At least in Le Clé, I'm working for the good of something."

She dropped her hands to her sides, affronted. "And by remaining here, I'm not?"

"That wasn't what I meant. You know that any work for *Fides et Spes* is work worth doing."

"Then we've circled round again. Why go to France when you have equal purpose here?"

"Because it *isn't* equal, Josie." He shouldered his pack, staring out the bedroom window into the gardens they had frequented so many times before and never would again. "Because London hasn't felt my sins."

She laid a hand upon his back, sliding her arm around to embrace his side. She rested her cheek upon his bicep, wishing, wishing. *He's a good man*, she thought. An honorable man. She would accept him even with his sins. "Is being crushed beneath a church and losing full control of your hand not atonement enough? You told me you never wanted to be part of the killing. Not even when you wore the uniform."

"It doesn't matter what I wanted. It matters what I actually did. *Vince malum bono*. Overcome evil with good, right? I'm going to Le Clé to find Father Ferdinand. He saved my life once. I need to return the favor." He turned into her arms, drawing her against his chest. "Then I'm going to come back and take you to America."

It had already been seven weeks since he said those words. In terms of the war, seven weeks was no time at all, but to her worried heart, it had already been years.

Dropping twelve quid into Viola's jar, she said a final goodbye to her London life and closed the door.

PART TWO

—

Uncertain

SEVENTEEN

November 26, 1917 – Six Days Later
Brindille, France

BY THE TIME THEY ARRIVED in Brindille, the last French village before the front line, Amara, Emil, and Josie were beyond exhausted both physically and mentally. After five days bumped about in *Fides et Spes* carriers' wagons or walking for miles after little sleep and inadequate food, all they wanted was to find Peter and Bill, set a roof over their heads, and settle down for the night. There would be another uncomfortable return journey ahead of them. So, when Julien, their latest of many *Fides et Spes* contacts, pulled the wagon to a stop beside the darkened form of Saint Sebastian's Catholic Church, they couldn't have been more relieved.

Rather than lead them to the church's front doors, however, Julien directed them through the adjoining cemetery to a small thatched-roof cottage on the property's southwest corner. Smoke trailed from one of its twin chimneys into the failing twilight and blackout curtains were already drawn on every window.

"Is this the rectory?" Josie asked.

Julien knocked on the front door and nodded. "*Was* the rectory," he corrected. He knocked twice more followed by a ten second pause, then a third knock. "France doesn't offer military dispensation for the clergy. No matter their moral objections, if they are of fighting age, they're required to enlist. When Father Jean left in '15, Monsieur Thoreau became Saint Sebastien's appointed steward. He occupies the rectory now."

From inside came a shuffling followed by the sound of something large being pushed out of the way, its edge scraping across the floor. Then the deadlock slid over and the latch clicked. The door opened a sliver and the distinct scent of extinguished candle sulfur drifted through. "Julien?" came a gruff voice. "*C'est toi?*"

"*Oui,*" Julien replied. "*C'est moi. Victores in bello non sunt.*"

"*Vince malum bono,*" came the expected reply. Julien removed a stack of letters from his satchel, sliding his hand into the darkness of the door. When it emerged again, he held a different stack, tied with twine, which he returned to his satchel.

The men exchanged a few more stiff lines in French before the door swung fully open, revealing a grizzled man dressed in drab trousers and a worn Henley shirt, all three buttons undone. He studied them from behind dark eyes set in a worn expression, his close-cropped hair seemingly the only refined part about him. "I am called Quentin Thoreau," he said in stilted English. "You search Peter and Bill?"

Amara stepped forward, even as Emil placed a wary arm to ease her progression. "Yes, I am Peter's sister with my husband and Peter's fiancée. He asked us to come."

The lantern light sank Quentin's dark eyes even farther into his skull, reminding her of a wrinkled jack-o-lantern. "Sister?" he asked. She nodded and then so did he. "I take you to him. Three miles to farm. We walk all the night." Turning on his heel, he disappeared back into the darkness of the rectory and bolted the door. They could hear him rummaging through the house, clattering about who knew where.

"More walking?" Josie searched Amara and Emil's weary eyes, landing on Julien last. "Might we trouble you to take us a bit farther, Monsieur?"

Even before he spoke, Amara knew what his answer would be. Appearing apologetic, Julien shook his head, quickly backing down the walkway. "I am sorry, but I must be back. May God go with you." He was off like a shot, weaving through the gravestones, the glow of his lantern swinging through the darkness until it too vanished.

Quentin emerged from the rectory bundled in a patched overcoat and wool stocking cap. A lit lantern hung in one hand and a bulging khaki haversack swung over his opposite shoulder. After locking the rectory door, he afforded them a brief glance, dark brows knit together in annoyance. "We go. You fall behind, I leave behind." He stomped past to the narrow street without waiting to see if they would follow.

"Pleasant chap, isn't he?" Emil grumbled. "He had better not be wasting our time."

—

Amara quickly learned that their guide was not the conversationalist sort. On their three-mile trek through the French countryside, surrounded by mysterious nightlife cries and legs nearly frozen from damp air soaking through their stockings, Quentin Thoreau spoke little more than a few words to any of them. It wasn't that he was silent, however. Often he would grunt and exhale loudly. He had complained several times in French using words that Emil's minimal French skills either couldn't or wouldn't translate. When Amara dared to ask, "How much farther?" Quentin glared at her and continued walking.

When the farmhouse finally came into view, she released Emil's hand and ran towards it, her traveling case slapping against her thigh and heart pounding with anticipation. The moon was nearly full, bathing the single-story wooden structure in a swath of cool blue light. It was of a decent size, obviously well cared for, although slightly smaller than her father's farmhouse in Germany. Past the house, the dirt drive curved to a moderately-sized mud-and-stone built barn and behind that, a mile of substantial fields swept to a darkened tree line. Every one of the farmhouse's blackout curtains were drawn tight.

Quentin yanked Amara's arm back before she could knock on the door. Holding her wrist up in front of her face, he shook his head, the lantern in his opposite hand swinging shadows across the front wall. "*Non.* I to knock."

Emil barged his way onto the stoop between them, positioning himself in such a way that Quentin had no choice but to release her arm. "Please don't touch my wife," he said slowly. Amara nearly burst out laughing at the calmness of his request, as though asking a favor from a friend, when inside she was certain he was seething.

Quentin muttered something, likely profane, to himself in French then gave a sharp rap on the farmhouse door. "Madame Clermont!" he shouted. When no reply came, he shouted again, "Solange!"

Less than a minute later, the door flew open to a woman's startled expression, her long black lashes fluttering and dark brunette hair flowing over her dressing gown. She would be completely lovely if not for her too-slender figure, the slight paunch against her hips the only evidence of still receiving adequate nutrition—or perhaps only a leftover effect of prior child bearing. Her weary expression held a significant amount of trepidation as she viewed the unexpected strangers outside her home. Upon her right hip, a tow-headed toddler boy bounced energetically, assuaging any guilt Amara had over the possibility that they had awoken her. Obviously, the tyke was the initial reason for her late night wanderings.

She eyed Amara, Emil, and Josie quizzically, holding the toddler tighter to her side. "Monsieur Thoreau?" she addressed Quentin. "*C'est la nuit. Qu'est-ce qui ne va pas?*"

Quentin removed his cap and pressed it to his chest. "*Je suis désolé. J'ai amené la sœur de Peter.*"

Madame Clermont's eyes visibly widened even in the dim lantern light. "You are Peter's sister, Amara?" she asked, this time in perfect English, and Amara was certain she must have learned the language, if not in America itself, then at least from an American. She had heard those syllables too many times back in New York to doubt it. Solange Clermont was the first person here with any connection to home and Amara could have wept with relief.

"Yes," she said. "That is me." Quickly, she made the same introductions to Emil and Josie as when they met Quentin at the rectory. "Do you know where my brother is?"

"Do come in and I shall tell you all you wish to know." Solange ushered their group into a small front sitting room, swathed in near darkness due to the drawn curtains. Once the door was closed and bolted, she headed for the low fireplace at the room's opposite end.

"Please take a seat. Once I light the fire, I'll tend to refreshments. There isn't much, but I'm certain I can find something."

Josie was quick to speak for them. "We don't need anything, truly," she said, although Amara knew the woman's stomach must be aching as much as her own. However, they had been informed several times on their journey that French rations were thin. It would be more polite to swallow their hunger until breakfast. Surely, their uninvited presence had already inconvenienced the poor woman enough.

Solange hustled about the room, lighting stick candles on the coffee table between two worn sofas, then juggling wood from the box into the hearth ashes. When she bent to light the fire, the child in her arms squirmed and kicked, pushing against his mother's chest with repeated whines. She expertly shifted him to her other hip while managing to strike a match and set the tinder to light.

After hanging their coats on several wall pegs, Amara allowed Emil to guide her to a seat on the sofa between himself and Josie, their traveling cases placed end to end on the floor in front of them. She could now see that the sitting room's cushions and wall hangings were cozy with warm autumn colors, their hues made more pronounced as the fire gained strength. Two additional traveling cases sat near the end of either sofa, a patched quilt folded over each one. One of those was Peter's, she thought excitedly. It was real. He was actually here!

"When do you expect Peter back?" she asked.

"Quite soon." Solange drew the blackout curtains away from one of the front windows, tying them back before lighting another stick candle on the sill. "To help light the way home," she explained. "I forgot to set it before, and they will expect to see it." She continued to speak in English, although Amara knew it was only for their benefit. Quentin made no pretense of being an expert in the language or of his preference for his native tongue. He released a grunt and flopped himself backwards into a wooden chair at the tea table, his frame far too large for the dainty piece of furniture.

Amara ignored him. "I must ask, Madame Clermont, where did you learn English? Your accent reminds me of some of the ladies back home."

"I don't think that's really important right now, Amara," Emil interrupted. He folded his arms and sank back into the corner of the sofa. "What we should be asking is why we've arrived at yet another location where your brother is not. I'm tired of this chase."

"I assure you he will be here." Solange claimed her place on the sofa opposite and laid the toddler down beside her, easing his head onto her lap. The child would have none of it, however, popping right back up to bounce his bottom against the cushions. "If not for *Fides et Spes*, many Frenchmen would have long given up hope," she said while he bounced happily. "When Bill and Peter arrived, searching for a safe house near the front lines, I couldn't refuse them."

Emil's expression didn't alter. If anything, he was now staring at Solange like she was completely mad. "The front is a fluid thing though, with both sides advancing and retreating all the time. Aren't you worried the Germans will take control of your farm and you'll be a prisoner with the rest of Le Clé?"

"Cease interrogating her," Josie scolded. She tugged at the blue string around her finger repeatedly. "None of this is taken lightly, despite what you may believe."

"*La Liberté guidant le peuple*," Quentin gruffed out from his corner. He had lounged back, both muddy boots propped up on the opposite chair.

"Liberty of the people?" Emil translated. "What does that mean?"

"No, not 'liberty of the people,'" Solange said. "Liberty *Leading* the People. It's the title of a well-known painting. Remy, *arête*." She placed a firm hand on her son's shoulder to cease his bouncing, although his legs still kicked in rapid motion. She turned back to Emil. "The painting depicts a half-clad woman holding the French flag aloft, leading our revolutionary soldiers to victory over bodies of the fallen. When my family first saw it at the Louvre, my father found it distasteful and forbade my sister and I from ever visiting the museum again. Once was enough though to remain with us. We did not gain victory in the revolutions for our freedoms to be stolen from us now. I believe the fight for liberty is an American ideal as much as a French one, is it not?"

Emil remained silent. There was no rebuttal to such a statement. The French had gifted the United States with Lady Liberty for that exact reason.

"To answer your first question," Solange addressed Amara, "I was born in Paris, but my mother was from Rhode Island. Being American, she insisted my sister and I learn English amongst all those other ladylike endeavors. Our parents were less than delighted when Colette married a penniless artist and I ran away with a farmer."

"Is your sister still in Paris?" Amara asked.

"No. She and her husband have both recently passed on." Amara didn't need to ask where Solange's husband was. From her comment, the answer was obvious. A third casualty of war.

Josie stood suddenly. "Madame Clermont, may I have a glass of water? I'm afraid I feel rather warm."

"Certainly. There's a pump out back and glasses in the kitchen, second cabinet." She indicated the doorway to the kitchen and Josie hastened through it before Emil or Amara could say a word.

Wrapping an arm around the toddler's middle, Solange hefted him onto her lap where he continued to squirm and whine in incoherent French. Or at least, Amara assumed it was French. Toddler language was difficult enough to decipher without adding another barrier. Solange raised one hand to her forehead. "My apologies. He is the only one who refuses to rest."

"You have other children?" Amara asked gently, hoping the answer wouldn't involve more death and devastation.

Thankfully, their host seemed to brighten at the question. She lowered her hand from her forehead. "Yes. Lucien is ten and Maël, five. Remy is not yet two, and he has much to show for it."

When he continued to squirm, she set him to his feet, where he immediately toddled over to Emil, raised his arms, and cried, "*Haut!*" Emil merely looked at the boy with an expression of extreme discomfort. He probably saw any interest in the Clermont family as his approval to extend their stay longer than necessary.

Remy clenched his tiny fingers around Emil's knee and swung one leg up to rest across his thighs. He hung there, half of him across

Emil, the rest swinging above the floor, all while still shouting, "*Haut! Haut!*" Amara let out a giggle.

"*Haut* means 'high' in French," Solange explained. "He wants you to hold him." Except for one chipped tooth, her smile was as lovely as the rest of her.

Apparently resigned to the situation, Emil lifted Remy to sit on his lap, but the little boy flopped himself over to kneel instead, reaching up to pat Emil's wispy cheeks. A layer of light growth had accumulated during the travel from London to Brindille and Remy ran his hands back and forth over it, seemingly delighted with the sensation.

"You remind him of his father," Solange said quietly. "He always wore his beard thick before the war."

Without warning, Remy grabbed both sides of Emil's face, planting a giant sloppy kiss right on his new friend's lips before howling out a boisterous laugh. He bounced on his knees, continuing to pat Emil's cheeks, and with each pat, Amara watched Emil's expression transform. A slow grin graced his lips and then he began laughing himself, releasing a rather uncouth snort when Remy pinched his nose. The sound made the toddler fall across their laps in fresh peals of glee and Amara felt her heart constrict with the same familiar ache.

It was remarkable how similar the boy's blond locks were to her husband's, just as the orphan girl's curls had been at the children's home in New York. She knew Remy would likely outgrow the color, his hair darkening as most boys' did, but for that moment she couldn't catch her breath. All those days staring at the orphanage windows and not once had a boy stared back at her. She would give anything to provide Emil with a child of his own blood who shared all the same features.

Soon, she thought. *Soon we'll adopt one. Emil and I. As soon as we find Peter, we can return to New York and I'll be a mother.*

"Where is my brother?" she blurted far too loudly, nearly shouting in the poor Frenchwoman's face. Both Emil and Remy's laughter instantly ceased. Even Quentin raised a brow in surprise, slapping his boots off the table to the floor.

"I'm sorry," she said more quietly. "It is only that my husband is right. We have obligations back in the States and the sooner we locate Peter, the sooner we can take him home."

Solange and Quentin shared a wary look. *"Tu sais qu'il ne partira pas,"* he told her pointedly.

"What do you mean Peter won't leave?" Emil demanded. He stood up, Remy still in his arms, his face afury. He took two long strides towards Quentin and the resulting breeze caused one candle to flicker and die. "What man with his full senses would be taken to relative safety then volunteer to return to harm, all to deliver a few letters to people he doesn't even know? If he planned to remain here indefinitely, he could have at least had the decency to tell us not to come."

Amara felt her face flush and hoped if Emil noticed, he would assume it was from the heated conversation or the nearby fire. Within the confines of her consciousness, the words of Peter's final letter burned just as warm.

Solange rose and took Remy from Emil's arms, allowing the child to nuzzle himself into her neck. He rubbed a fist against his eye, then rested his head upon his mother's shoulder and closed his eyes. "I can't speak for Peter's reasons," she said, "but he did not make this decision lightly. The journey he and Bill regularly undertake is not easy, and I do use the word journey correctly. It's a grueling five miles to Le Clé then five back again. It's the chance of being captured, tortured, or killed while he's there. Or sent ..." She paused, looking away. "Sent to the prisons out east. He does it all while not being whole himself. Did he write to you of his injuries?"

"No. Miss Harrington told us."

"You will see soon enough. It's impressive that he goes anyway, but to go with an impairment? Many would call him ... what is the proper English word?"

"Blighty barmy?" Josie re-entered the room, a glass of water in hand. She walked to the front window and stared into the night, the lone candle beneath her dripping wax upon the sill. "Have they made any progress with extracting Father Ferdinand?" she asked.

"Non," Quentin shook his head. *"Non."*

"All other deliveries have however been successful," Solange was quick to interject. "Bill had suggested they recruit a few more men in order to take shifts with the traveling to Le Clé. Two or three sets of two, trying to lower the overall risk. Peter refused. He insists on going every time. Takes only a day or two to rest, then he's out there again. He will not let anything slow him down—not injuries, not people, not even the continued air raids. Once I saw his determination, I wondered why he waited so long to return. I suppose you're the answer to that wonderment though. Are you a letter carrier as well, Miss Harrington?"

Josie's eyes flipped away from the window. Even in the dim candlelight, her surprise was apparent. "Yes, I've delivered letters nearly a year now. Surely, Peter must have mentioned it."

Quentin replied with a gruff laugh, muttering something in French that no one bothered to translate. It was Solange's turn to look sheepish. "I'm sorry, Miss Harrington, but I'm afraid Peter never mentioned you at all."

EIGHTEEN

ONE MORE MILE AND Peter would be able to rest. He pushed aside another tree branch and despite the full moon, tripped over a root that nearly sent him sprawling. Bill paused behind him, his normal stride silencing as Peter dislodged his boot and flexed his ankle. It was becoming more difficult to carry on this way, pretending his limp wasn't affecting his ability to achieve a successful run, acting like his right hip and lower back didn't now scream in agony from compensating with his opposite side.

Two days between runs was no longer adequate to rejuvenate his broken parts.

He wished they could use the Clermonts' workhorses for these trips over the line, but knew it was too risky. Horses required food, water, and rest. They made too much noise and could spook far too easily, giving away their position at the worst moments. The second they trotted into town, the mares would be requisitioned for the "German good" and Solange would be required to work the fields with a hand plow and a shovel. Their farm had already been picked over by the French army; only their continued ability to produce food for the soldiers and citizens had allowed them to retain their remaining two mares.

Peter slapped another branch out of the way, trying to muffle the sound of his *shuffle-step* through the leaves, which only made his hip ache more. He couldn't rest now. This entire endeavor had been his idea. Sure, Bill gladly went along with it, but Peter had been the one steering the reins.

They called him crazy, the dockers who hired him and Bill to work the tender back to France. They didn't care that Peter didn't hold a single sheet of proper documentation. After all, what sort of idiot volunteered to go to a war-torn country? Once Bill mentioned that Peter was concussed in battle, the dockers assumed the blow to his head had affected his thinking as well.

They stayed in Calais for a week, earning their way, Peter doing all he could despite the fact that his right hip ached from sleeping on the floor of a warehouse with only a thin blanket to cover him. But the more he worked, the stronger he felt. The longer he could move, the easier it became to push away the discomfort, until he felt new muscles form beneath his skin. It wasn't until they had run from Brindille to Le Clé over fifteen times that the effort began to take a toll.

He wondered if Amara ever got his letters.

Distracted in his thoughts, his knee twisted, sending him palms first into the moist and rotting leaves. Without any way to support his weight, his mangled fingers collapsed upon themselves, his elbow and forearm driving hard into the packed earth. He fell onto his side, the forest's scent pungent in his nostrils as he inadvertently shouted a German curse that his father probably wouldn't even use.

"Shut up, would you?" Bill hissed. He grabbed Peter's good hand and yanked him to his feet. In the darkness, he apparently couldn't see Peter wince or chose to ignore it. "German, man, really? You know that language is like poison around here."

"Lay off me, Bill. I didn't mean to use it. It just came out." Peter shuffled away as fast as his legs would take him, a line of pain now slicing from his right knee to hip with every step. He felt like two months in France had tripled his only twenty-eight years, and made him an old man barely able to walk or grip a pencil. But he knew he had been through worse and that's what kept his legs moving. Only a half mile more.

When that air raid had collapsed a church on him, Peter assumed he was going to die. He remembered lying under a mound of rubble, dust in his eyes, in his hair, staring through a small pinprick of light between the debris. The only evidence that life existed somewhere else. He remembered praying. Not for life, but for a quick end. To be taken without any more pain, to be spared the punishment.

But he had not been spared. When Father Ferdinand first smuggled him out with the letter carriers, he was in so much pain he figured he would die before he even reached the tender from Calais to London. At times, he wept so violently from the torture that he wanted to roll off the carrier's wagon and let himself be crushed under the next passing cart. It was only the thought of his family that kept him going. He had to get word to Amara. If he died in the middle of France wearing no identification, she would never know what happened to him. They would be safer together, rather than apart.

Then he met Josie. He knew she was a member of the secret letter resistance from the moment he laid eyes on her. He saw her from across the manor's convalescent room, watched her try to hand the stack of envelopes to Matron, then discreetly glance his way when Matron noticed him staring. At the time he hadn't noticed her lovely light brunette curls, the delicate sweep of her hips, or how her eyes sparkled every time she laughed. He wouldn't notice those things until later. Back then, all he thought was that he could finally send a letter home to Amara. He could finally warn her against the path he set her on and save her from a bleak secretive future.

He hadn't planned to fall in love with Josie. Hadn't understood that he did until one morning when he rolled out of bed and noticed that his fingers didn't hurt. He stared at them in disbelief, wiggling them over and over and realizing he was healed. He could walk, although still with a limp, the bruises on his face were gone, and now the last piece put back together. No, he would never regain full mobility. His fingers were poorly shaped and his joints popped and clicked in protest with every movement. There was still an ache in every joint, but not pain like there once was. An ache was manageable. An ache he could carry with him back to France. But in France he would experience an entirely different kind of ache. An ache in his heart. The ache of losing Josie.

Stomping on through the woods, he ran both hands through his mussed hair, fingers coming back grimier than they already were. Despite his exhaustion, he didn't want to drop onto Solange's sofa covered in filth. He would regret laying in it tomorrow morning and she wouldn't appreciate washing the blanket out again. Besides, the cold creek water might do his tender muscles some good. It couldn't possibly be worse than standing ankle deep in icy trench mud.

"Hey, Bill," he said when the tree line finally came into sight, "I think I'll take a dip in the creek real quick before bed. Get all this grime off of me." Silence. He turned around. "Bill?"

His friend stared past him to the farmhouse. "Quiet, candle's lit."

Due to the war, candles had become something of a commodity. There was no telling when they might be able to purchase more and crafting them took time. When they did manage to locate some, they took at least half to Father Ferdinand for distribution throughout Le Clé. As a result, they usually ate dinner by the hearth fire. Ever since leaving London, Peter had greatly missed electricity and running water. Steaming cups of tea, no matter how bland they were. Freshly pressed sheets and three meals a day, even if they were rationed beyond reason. And Josie. Especially Josie. Only Josie. He would gladly leave the rest of it behind forever.

That wasn't important right now. The blackout curtains were open in the front window, a single lit candle flicking on its sill. That was their agreed upon warning signal. Something was wrong.

It wasn't until he eased open the farmhouse door, however, his boots tracking mud onto the worn wooden planking, that he understood exactly how terribly wrong everything was. And how terribly right.

Josie stood by the window, that same single candle casting brightness across her perfect lovely features. He stepped toward her, but then her attention shifted and his knees wanted to buckle again.

"Hello, Peter," Amara said. "I got your letters."

NINETEEN

November 26, 1917 –
Clermont Farm, France

AMARA DIDN'T KNOW HOW to regard the stranger staring at her like he was seeing an apparition. She knew he was her brother; he held all the familiarity from the wrinkle on his brow to the mop of sandy-blond hair, although it now hung longer with a patch of mud clinging to the base of his neck. That same mud cascaded down his right side, a dark smear of filth from the hem of his overcoat clear up across his cheek. Had he fallen somewhere along the way? Was he pushed? Had they been chased? All the possibilities of his demise that she feared during those long months apart came flooding back, worry cascading over her like the cold rainfall they rode through three days ago.

This man looked like her brother in all the usual ways, but she could tell that this was not the man who left her on Hoboken pier nearly a year ago. That Peter had been afraid and uncertain. This Peter held a grimace on his lips and hardened emotion in his eyes.

Still, it could not stop her wide grin or tears from falling down her cheeks and wetting her loose hair. She leapt from the sofa like a girl on Christmas morning and ran to throw her arms around her brother's neck. He gasped, wrapping his left arm around her as they tripped backwards against the door frame.

"Peter, I'm so glad you're safe!" she cried, her cheek against his, not caring that the dirt from his skin was flaking about hers and likely down the collar of her dress. She already looked a sight from their days on the road; what was a bit more to contend with?

She could feel his muscles flex, awkwardly embracing her almost as though he didn't know how to perform the action anymore. It was likely from shock of seeing her in a foreign country, especially after he told her to stay away. Even with his injuries, she could tell he had become even stronger than in his days hauling feed bags and saddles. She couldn't believe that after nearly a year apart, they were finally back in the same room together.

Solange gasped behind her. "Bill, why are you both so mussed? You're not usually this filthy."

The man Peter had entered with—the man Amara now assumed to be Bill—stripped off his overcoat, his sweater and trousers underneath nearly as rumpled as his outer layer. "We had a close call," he told her. "Had to duck behind some crates for entirely too long until the Jerries passed. Peter's leg's been acting up from the cramped quarters."

Amara eased away from her brother, stepping back to examine both his legs. They appeared fine, at least from what she could observe from his trousers. "Josie said your leg had healed, Peter. Why would you return to France if you were still injured?"

"It isn't injured," Peter told her, his voice the same as she remembered, but with a gruff edge she did not. "Like Bill said, it just acts up from time to time." He took a step around her and winced, his right hand moving to awkwardly clench his thigh. Amara noticed the way his fingers bent in on themselves, their movements no longer natural. Almost gnarled like tree branches. Josie had cautioned her on what to expect, but she never imagined this ... the shape of his fingers was like something from a Gothic novel.

Catching her staring, he used the deformed hand to unbutton his overcoat with surprising quickness and moved to hang it on the overcrowded pegs. It was only then that Amara noticed his altered gait, placing more weight on his left leg than his right, his steps more crooked than they should have been. Limping around her, he practically fell onto the empty sofa seat beside Solange, who now held a finally sleeping Remy. He nodded at Emil. "Who's this?"

Amara scurried over to reclaim her seat beside her husband. Reaching for his hand, she managed to smile even though her heart thudded like a marching band drum. She had pictured this day for so long, to introduce her brother to her husband and listen to his glowing words of approval. But in all her mental images, she had never encountered the scowl now aimed in her direction or the frustrated growl low in her brother's throat. "Peter," she said gently, "this is my husband, Emil."

"Your husband?" Peter gawked. "Apparently, you didn't listen to any of my letters then." He pushed on before she could say anything, his seething tone becoming darker by the moment. "You shouldn't be here. None of you."

He shot out of his seat, but immediately fell back to the sofa, his right hand twitching against his knee. He gritted his teeth and Amara wondered how much pain he must be in to be acting this way. Peter had rarely yelled before. As her guardian, he had made demands and reprimands, but raising his voice was a rarity. It was one parental tactic he had borrowed from their father.

He leaned back against the sofa cushion, his focus directed at the ceiling while his breath hissed through clenched teeth. Amara cast a glance to where Josie remained near the window, her face washed of all color, her expression a mask of concern. Amara knew her new friend wanted to run to her fiancé, to care for him and accept all his pain. She knew it because she had felt it so often before in regards to Emil. She wondered why the woman didn't swell forward or why Peter sat stiffly pretending Josie wasn't even in the room.

"Peter?" Bill said carefully. He straddled the sofa arm and attempted to rest a hand on his friend's shoulder. "Perhaps you should rest and we'll continue this in the morning."

"I'm fine, Bill." Peter edged away, swinging his gaze back to his sister. "I told you not to come in my last letter. I told you things had changed." He glared at Emil. "If you're her husband, why did you bring her? Have you no sense at all?"

The instant he spoke the words, Amara knew she was in trouble. Peter's final letter called to her from the depths of her handbag like an air raid whistle, mocking her with incoming destruction. She should have burned it, or trashed it, but she hadn't, although she couldn't exactly explain why. As such, she had always known this day would find them, yet had never devised a suitable response. She supposed she had hoped lightning wouldn't strike until they returned home with a baby to distract them.

Emil's focus slowly met hers, his eyes narrowing the minutest amount. "What letter? We didn't receive another letter." He paused, offering her every opportunity to set the record straight. "Did we?"

She heard Winnie's words, *Deceit is for the wicked*, and ignored them. "It must have arrived after we left."

There was another ten seconds of silence where he didn't speak, only analyzed her like she suspected he would analyze a prisoner during a morality squad interrogation. It was only ten seconds, but ten seconds is an eternity when you're the one in the cinderblock room.

Finally, he turned back to Peter. "I apologize. We were under the assumption that your first request still stood, for us to bring your papers and return you home. Now we've done as you asked. We brought the papers. Pack your things for tomorrow we leave."

Peter shook his head. "Thank you for bringing them, but I can't return home yet. Not until I convince Father Ferdinand to come with me."

"He's a priest though," Emil argued. "Devoted to his flock. He's not going to leave them."

Peter massaged his knee, wincing every time he slid his thumb along the bone. "Then I'll wait until the Germans have moved on from Le Clé. They've abandoned occupied towns before, they probably will again. All we need is for the Allies to drive them back past the town."

Emil didn't appear convinced. "Who says the line won't move farther into France? It's a game they play, isn't it? One side advances then the other. A never ending tug of war until someone calls truce or obliterates the other side."

"'*Fides et Spes* stands until the white flag flies,'" Peter quoted. "That's what Bill told me when I joined. 'The white flag flies or the last one dies.' Eventually, the white flag will fly, but I won't let Father Ferdinand die before it happens."

"Then let us help you," Amara practically begged, praying he wouldn't lash out at her again. She only wanted to help, to keep him safe. Couldn't he see that? "In your letter, you said I was brave. Let me prove it to you. Let us join *Fides et Spes*."

"Amara!" Emil snapped. He gave a curt shake of his head, *no*. She knew he didn't approve of this change of plan and was barely restraining himself over "asserting his authority" again. After all, she had promised him that they would bring Peter his citizenship papers and return straight home. But she couldn't leave now. She was finally face-to-face with Peter after nearly a year of worrying whether he was alive or dead. He was part of something far bigger than himself, helping others, working against injustice. She couldn't help but think what Winnie would probably say:

"They're doing something good, Amy. Something grand. Something folks will remember 'till our grandchildren tell their grandchildren stories. It's time for us women to do something we'll be remembered for. Something beyond just having babies."

However, having babies was something Amara would never be known for.

"Please, Peter," she said. "Let us stay. Let us help you. I don't have to deliver letters. I can stay right here on the farm where it's safe." She switched to German, her eyes pleading as much as her voice, hoping that their childhood language would sway him. *"Bitte lass mich nicht wieder zurück."* Please do not leave me behind again.

For several moments, his stance remained the same and she assumed he would dismiss her, but then his eyes softened. "Perhaps," he said gently. "Perhaps I could allow *you* to stay, but you must understand. I don't know anything about this man you're with. I don't know if he presents a threat."

"I promise he doesn't."

"That's for me to decide." He addressed Emil. "Sir, where are you from?"

"St. Louis, Missouri. I'm a sort of relation to her friend, Maggie."

"No. I meant, which country are you from?"

Emil offered Peter his signature smirk, and Amara suspected that this conversation was about to get unnecessarily complicated. "Time for you to learn a bit more geography, mate. Missouri's in America."

Peter frowned. He finally removed his hand from his knee and folded his arms. "I know where Missouri is, but you don't sound American to me."

"It's a land of many unique dialects. I've picked up a little of this, a little of that. I like to hold true to our melting pot philosophy."

"Then you were born there?"

Emil scooted forward to the edge of the sofa, folding his arms in a mirror of Peter's. "Listen, Pete, I used to be a morality squad officer, so I see what you're up to here. Let's cease the interrogation now, shall we? You told your sister to marry an American. She did that. You handed her off to a stranger and when you did so, you gave up your place to protect her. That's my job now."

"You have a sister then?"

"I do. Five years younger."

"If your sister made a mistake, wouldn't you want to protect her?"

"Course I would, but sometimes we have to make mistakes to know when we're not making them. My sister's volunteered to go off and serve the soldiers. I don't like it. I think it's a mistake. Her foolishness could get her killed. But I can only hope that a little bit of life might make her an adult, instead of simply thinking she's one."

Peter's stance didn't waiver. "Where were you born?" he repeated. "Are you Allied or for the other side?"

Emil stood then, stepping forward to peer down his nose at Peter still seated on the sofa, knowing full well that the other man wouldn't rise to meet him. "I suppose I should pose the same question to you, shouldn't I? I was told your little organization here is neutral, but I also heard wind your personal allegiances are a little foggy, Peter. Or should I call you Jerry?"

"That's enough!" Bill shouted. Without an injury to restrain him, he shoved Emil who jerked backwards, but managed to retain his balance. Bill stepped forward, both fists clenched, at the same moment Remy woke with a scream.

"Oberammergau!" Amara shouted over him. Leaping up, she reached out to push Bill back. With her slight stance, it didn't so much as move him an inch; however, it was enough to force both him and Peter to look at her. "Oberammergau," she repeated, directing all her attention to her brother's incensed gaze. "That's where Emil was

142

born. Same as us. Our mothers served together at the church. We're exactly the same."

Her brother's eyes swiveled to Emil then back to her, steam in his gaze. "You married a *German*?"

"No, Peter. I married an American. Exactly as you asked me to."

Her comment left everyone frozen except for Remy, who was now shrieking his little blond head off and pummeling his mother's chest with his fists. With a sigh, Solange stood him on the floor and he bounced over to wrap his arms around Emil's leg, shouting "*Haut!*" With a sigh, Emil lifted the child to his hip where Remy rested against his shoulder, spinning the buttons on his shirt.

"What if we allowed them to stay on a temporary basis?" Solange suggested. "A few weeks even? We could use the extra help around the farm."

Peter appeared as though he wanted to do anything except that, but he leaned into the sofa cushions and huffed. "Fine. They can stay for now. They're not to be consulted about our business or assist on runs to Le Clé. Understood?"

Amara enthusiastically nodded agreement. She was simply glad he had agreed to let them stay at all. When Emil didn't so much as move, she nudged his side with her elbow. He glared at her, but finally nodded. Nods followed all around the room.

She wondered how Peter had arrived in this obvious position of power after being in *Fides et Spes* for such a short period of time. Although he had co-owned his feed store back in Iowa, it was always Zeke with the iron fist. Their customers loved Peter for his kindness and caring attitude, especially when working out deals with those of limited means. Zeke had been the controlling partner, so how had Peter so swiftly climbed the ladder now?

Bill clapped his hands together. "Good! Then that's settled. Solange, how shall we divide the sleeping arrangements?"

The French woman smiled, lifting herself from the sofa and likely glad for a change of conversation. "The house may be small, but there's room for everyone. I'll make pallets for Lucien and Maël in my room and—" She nodded to Emil and Amara. "—our newlyweds shall have the boys' room. Bill and Peter remain in the sitting room and

Quentin can take the hayloft. Miss Harrington, you may share with me."

"Oh, no," Josie spoke up. "I couldn't possibly. You need privacy with your boys."

"Nonsense. I've had plenty of privacy for years and far too much time alone with my thoughts. It will be welcome to have someone to share the darkness with." She chuckled. "My, I am sorry, that sounded dreadful. This is why I am glad to have you here. Left on my own, it is difficult to keep sight of the sunshine."

Josie ducked her chin with a sad smile. "I lost my father last year to the Somme, and it's been quite lonely since. Until Peter, at least." She turned her smile towards him and Amara thought the corners of his lips may have turned up ever so slightly. Then he looked down at his hands, chipping the side of his disfigured thumb nail with the other.

"I need some cool air," he said suddenly. "Quentin, you take the sofa. I'm going to sleep in the barn tonight." He struggled to lift himself from the sofa, averting his face so they wouldn't witness him grimace from the effort. Turning abruptly, he shuffle-stepped to snatch his overcoat from the rack, his boots clipping loudly through the sitting room. The slap of the front door punctuated his departure.

"A smoke first," Quentin said. "I be out back." He sauntered in the opposite direction through the kitchen door.

Even though her brother hadn't spoken one word to Josie, Amara knew he wouldn't return tonight. The barn was his safe haven, just as it had been in Oberammergau or Iowa. When the world of men became too much, he always sought shelter with the horses. Horses were easy to understand; they had few needs that couldn't be fixed by a farmer's loving hand. It was people who were difficult to make sense of.

After Bill helped relocate Lucien, Maël, and Josie into the main bedroom, Solange led Emil and Amara to the only other. A beautifully stitched blue and white quilt covered the full-size bed with a single trundle tucked away underneath. Emil deposited their traveling cases on the floor beside the chest of drawers. "Married in the middle of a war," Solange said wistfully. "What a way to begin a life."

Amara smiled at Emil. "It's a good life though. I'm glad we didn't wait."

"Me neither." He returned her smile, although it didn't reach his eyes. Solange didn't seem to notice, though. She removed an extra blanket from the bottom chest drawer, setting it on the bed before returning to the doorway. "We all pull our weight around here. If you work hard and prove your worth, I believe your brother will be more than accommodating. Don't let him fool you. He's missed you something fierce."

"I hope so," Amara said. "I've missed him too."

Solange gave them the last few pieces of information: meal times, the outhouse location, and directions to the cellar if there should be an air raid.

"There are warnings out here then?" Emil asked. "We experienced a raid back in London. Without the whistles and 'take cover' warnings, we might not have made it."

"Oh, mercy, no," Solange said incredulously. "There are no warnings here."

Amara thought about her brother, how he had been nearly killed in the last raid only a few miles from here. "Then how do you know when to hide? What did you do when they bombed Le Clé?"

"We heard the planes."

"What if we don't hear the planes next time? If they strike during the night?"

"Then I suggest you make peace with the Almighty every time you close your eyes."

TWENTY

November 26, 1917 –
Clermont Farm, France

EMIL CLOSED THE BEDROOM DOOR behind Solange with a sense of ominous finality. Now came the most burdensome part: arguing with his wife yet again. Since Winnie showed up at the Forsythe, it seemed like that was all they ever did. Blimey, had it really only been three weeks since then? It felt like ages.

"Well," Amara said, "that was certainly cheery. Now I'll be wondering if we'll be blown to bits while we sleep."

"We're miles from town," he assured her. "We'll be fine." *Fine from an air raid*, he thought, *but not from each other.*

He tossed his overcoat into the corner with the traveling cases then bent to unlace his boots. They landed on the floorboards with a thud. "Amara," he said slowly, knowing what was coming, knowing the row that was about to ensue. "I know Peter's your brother, but we don't belong here. He even said so." Standing, Emil folded his arms and leaned back against the chest of drawers. "Where's the last letter?"

He had expected her to deny it, to hold to her earlier story that it arrived after they left. But she simply reached into her handbag and handed the envelope to him. Here lay her lie in plain black ink. Even before they left New York, she was thoroughly aware that Peter didn't want them to come.

"How could you not tell me?" he asked. He needed to stay calm, because the second he raised his voice even a little bit, he would start railing on her like there was no tomorrow.

He had known they would have it out eventually. Long before Winnie showed up with the fateful letters, they had been ignoring their problems, but they hadn't gone away. In fact, he was pretty sure the silence had only compounded them. Just having these thoughts made his chest tight.

"What about the money for our passage?" he continued, still staring at the letter rather than her. Those dark lead lines could have saved them a world of hassle and worry. "It wouldn't be past Winnie to lie about the neighbors funding our tickets. You and her are so chummy, she probably told you the truth rather than her own brother, didn't she?"

"Yes," Amara said softly. "And no, I don't believe she lied about the money. Although, I also believe your parents aren't aware Winnie brought us the letters."

"Did she steal them then? That sounds like something my wild sister would do." He handed the letter back to her and watched as she returned it to her handbag. "She's rubbed off on you, you know."

Amara tossed him an incensed expression that was entirely too Winnie-esqe. "What is that supposed to mean?"

"It means we're supposed to be a team. Teams make major life decisions together. We promised that we wouldn't let this war separate us, but it's starting to feel like a one-sided promise. Why did you want a husband if you're only going to do whatever suits your flight of fancy anyway? That's hardly different than Winnie stringing Harold along with no promise."

"It's entirely different," she huffed, "and you are well aware of that fact. We are a team, but I didn't tell you because I knew you would be upset. Showing you this letter would have been one more reason for you to not even consider coming. You would say it was too dangerous."

"I said that anyway!" *Calm down,* he ordered himself. *Calm down, calm down.* He couldn't calm down. It had just caught up to his brain that they were in war-torn France, only five miles from the line of German occupation after nearly being blown to bits in an air raid. After days jumping from wagon to wagon, he was tired and dirty and emotionally exhausted. There was a pain in the center of his chest, threatening to strangle him, and the only person who could stop it was the one making it worse.

"You never wanted to go," Amara told him. "You never even wanted to try. My brother needed my help and that letter would have sealed his fate. You're still my husband; I would never defy you to go alone."

"So, instead you completely deceived me? You know, I thought I had a wife who wanted what was best for all of us, not only her brother and herself. When Earhart thought you were a German spy, I could have handed you over—it certainly would have been easier—but instead I left my job, my family, *everything* and went to smelly, closed in, and congested New York to protect *you*. What more do you want from me, blood?" He sat on the bed, forearms propped on his knees, and tried not to heave. The room was spinning and not in the "I've had just enough drinks to feel bloomin' marvelous" sort of way either. He wanted to cry. He wanted to throw up. He wanted his wife. For pity's sake, he wanted *his wife*! "We've only been married five months and look at us. We're a wreck."

He wanted her to contradict him. He expected her to, so when she didn't, it about broke him. Since there wouldn't be any decent alcohol due to rationing, he considered storming to the kitchen for the cooking sherry, then drinking the entire blasted bottle like he was an immature kid of seventeen again. He wanted to, but he didn't.

"You were always the cautious one, Amara. I didn't need to stop you from doing dumb, foolish things like I did. I was the screw up drunk and you would keep me in line. Now the tables have turned and I don't care for it."

"What is it you don't care for? Actually having to be responsible?"

"No." He finally looked up at her. "I don't like you not being who I thought I married. I loved your spunk, always did, but I loved your intelligence too. Running out and throwing us in harm's way isn't the wisdom I saw in you."

Her tone quieted significantly. "Perhaps I'm not the woman you married, Emil. Perhaps you're not the man I married either. Those people likely ran away the night we did, and we may never be able to bring them back." She turned from him. "Maybe we'll just have to accept that."

"And if we can't?"

"Then maybe we really are the wreck you say we are."

A painful silence spread between them until it filled the room and swam in his ears. Was this how their marriage died a slow and painful death? In a cold and crowded French farmhouse with soldiers killing each other on the other side of the ridge?

Never. It was never supposed to be that way for them. He wouldn't let it. She was still his wife; she was here. They would get through this.

"Emil—" Amara began, but he cut her off with an outstretched hand.

"Don't say it. I don't want to fight anymore." Drawing her to him, he grazed his fingertips up her jaw to glide through her tousled hair, gently massaging her scalp until his heart rate descended. With each tender motion, the tightness in his chest began to subside.

She closed her eyes and focused on the pull of his hands. "You're avoiding," she breathed.

"I am." His hands slid around to her back, fumbling with the buttons on her dress. "You know, we never had a real honeymoon, and I've been told France is one of the most romantic places on Earth."

Her eyes popped open at his suggestion. Those bright blue irises stared back at him so sweetly, the same way he found himself completely lost in them the night they met. There were certainly more than a few things he would rather do right now than argue and none of them involved words.

"I have heard that," she said. Snatching her waist, he swung her onto his lap, but then held up one finger seriously. "Afterwards though, we return to our discussion."

Wriggling away from him, she crossed the room and locked the door. "Somehow, my husband, I seriously doubt it."

TWENTY-ONE

November 26, 1917 –
Clermont Farm, France

JOSIE UNPACKED HER TRAVELING CASE while Solange's older boys slept, their soft snores floating brunette curls away from their eyes. Even though Solange offered to share the bed, Josie insisted that the boys should be with their mother. It was difficult enough having them relocated from their own room. She would sleep well enough taking a pallet on the floor.

While she folded each article into the dresser drawer, she finally allowed herself to ponder all the questions she had wondered since Peter limped through the Clermonts' front door. Why had she come? Did Peter even want her there? Had she made a mistake in following him? He hadn't even mentioned her existence to Solange, much less how he proposed mere hours before leaving London. He promised to return and marry her, to take her to America, yet had written but once and seemingly not bothered to carve her into any other part of his future plans. The day he left London, he kissed her like the world was about to end, yet tonight he barely met her eyes. She needed to know why.

Temporarily abandoning her unpacking, she made for the front sitting room, quietly closing the bedroom door so as not to wake the boys. Bill was stretched out across the sofa cushions, one arm folded under his head and his long-underwear-clad bottom thankfully covered by a thick quilt. He raised both eyebrows at her swift entrance. "Where's the fire, Miss Harrington?"

She flattened both palms against her sides. "Why didn't Peter tell anyone about me?" she asked outright. "Quentin and Solange didn't even know I existed."

Bill closed his eyes and said languidly, "You're a distraction. You were keeping him from his mission."

"His mission? Why must you insist on referring to our runs that way? We are neither soldiers nor spies and such inaccurate vocabulary makes you sound as though you're playing a bit of boyhood battle."

"Have you forgotten who you are?" Bill scoffed. His eyes didn't open, but his tone boded no argument. "You are a member of *Fides et Spes*. Until the war ends, that is all that is important. 'Until the white flag flies or the last one dies,' remember? You are here to serve the people, not your own interests or Peter's. He knows what he's doing. Do you?"

She stared at him open-mouthed, her anger simmering. "Of course, I do. I want to serve the people as much as you do."

"Do you?" he asked again. He smashed his pillow into a smaller ball beneath his head. "Did you even locate someone to replace your route before you flitted off like some empty-headed romance novel heroine?"

"Of course, I did. Father Ignatius told me he knew the perfect contact to take over."

Bill snorted.

"He did! I have always been responsible in my decisions, unlike you. How could you convince Peter to return to France? Five-mile runs in either direction, sneaking through enemy lines, his dominant hand unable to even grip a pistol? He isn't fit for that sort of exertion."

"I'm certain Peter will be pleased to know you consider him an invalid."

"I never meant—"

Bill held up a hand, shushing her with a hiss. His eyes opened with rare irritation. "I'm rather exhausted from my own five-mile trek sneaking through enemy lines, so let's circle back to my irresponsible decisions and be done, shall we?" He propped himself up on one arm and eyed her squarely. "First of all, Peter came to me about this mission. He wanted to return to Le Clé and asked me how he could enter undetected. I knew about the Clermont farm, that Quentin was already in Brindille and Solange was sympathetic to the cause. This is where Father Ferdinand first brought Peter after the air raid."

"What about the job on the docks in Dover?"

"That was only ever temporary. The end goal was always France. He wanted to go alone, but I couldn't let him have all the excitement, could I? Mother kept me living at the manor so I'd stay safe, because I'm heir to the estate. If she knew Matron and I were involved in *Fides et Spes*, she'd have locked me in the attic. That's why I posted her a letter from Dover about ten minutes before I stepped on the tender. Do you know whose idea that was? Peter's. He's the ringleader here, he planned this entire thing. He's not going to rest until he's convinced Father Ferdinand to leave Le Clé.

"Second, you were the one who invited him into our organization in the first place. Father Ferdinand may have told him about us but you confirmed it all. You drank in his charm, consequences be forgotten."

"It isn't as though I sought him out," Josie argued. "You asked me to speak to him."

"I also told you he was suspicious. I moved him upstairs so we could keep an eye on him and asked you to put him off the trail. Instead, you gave up all our secrets, then came racing to France after you told his sister and her husband everything. Very foolish, if you ask me. We could have our entire organization found out by the censors and shut down because you can't keep your emotions in check."

She wanted to tell him that he was far from correct, that she only wanted what was best for all of them, but he cut her off with another raise of his hand. "If you want Peter to give you your castle-in-the-sky happily ever after, you'd better find a way to steal that priest out of Le Clé. Because I've met the man and he takes his vows seriously. Nothing Peter does will convince him. If you ask for my opinion, I'm glad of that. Peter's more determined to set wrongs right than anyone I know. Call me selfish, and perhaps I am, but I don't want him to return home yet. What use is he there with everyone pitying his impairments? You know that isn't the life he deserves. Now please leave me to sleep." Sinking back into the sofa cushions, he rolled away from her and yanked the quilt up to his neck. The action uncovered his feet and he shivered, drawing his knees up awkwardly against a manly frame too large for the sofa.

The fire was dying in the hearth, down to nothing except a slight flame and glowing embers. Josie stole another few logs from the box and arranged them on top, tossing a bit of dry kindling to light. Within minutes, the fresh tinder caught, the room crackling with renewed warmth.

"Have you ever been in love, Bill?" she asked.

He twisted his neck around to squint at her. "What?"

"I asked if you've ever been in love. If you had maybe you would understand how I feel."

"Yeah, I was once, except she was nothing like you. She wanted me to join the military. The day the war started, she asked me to register, so I did."

"I thought you were granted an exception, weren't you?"

"That didn't matter. She still handed me a white feather and called me a coward. Told me she never wanted to see me again. I haven't seen her since." Closing his eyes, he turned back over. "It's ironic though. I still ended up in France with a pistol strapped to my side. At least if they capture me, they can't get to her. When you're alone, you have no one to risk but yourself. Peter knows that too."

I am being ridiculous, aren't I? Josie thought suddenly. Their organization kept so many things a secret; it was likely wise not to display your personal associations when there was risk of capture and painful interrogations on the line. Peter had done no less than what they taught him and likely done so to protect *her*. Whereas she had recently broken so many of *Fides et Spes'* rules and possibly put them all in danger.

"I have to speak with him." She grabbed her overcoat off the peg and turned for the door.

"Here, take this." Reaching into his satchel, Bill tossed her a black box flashlight.

She turned the torch over in her hands. "Where did you get this?"

"Le Clé. Those pesky Germans leave all sorts of things lying around."

—

Josie walked past the untilled fields towards the barn, her torch beam slicing its way across the moonlit night. Overhead a thousand stars glittered like the Olmsteds' ballroom chandeliers with no London smog to block their beauty. She wished to be back in the manor's gardens, sitting beside Peter at that tea table, free of all the mess that surrounded them now. What would life be like without a war to hold them together? Without *Fides et Spes* and the need to deliver letters and engage in secrecy? Would they still be compatible then? Would Peter love her if she was merely Joselyn Harrington, the girl from Piccadilly?

Cheer up, Josie, she reprimanded herself. *You had far more purpose before you were a fiancée and you retain more purpose as a letter carrier than a wife. Fides et Spes is your family. Your loyalty to it remains whether Peter wants you or not.*

Except that for the first time in her life, she wanted to be a wife far more than she wanted anything else.

She imagined him stepping from the barn onto the frozen dirt, meeting her when she was still ten paces away, and sweeping her into his arms. Holding her against his chest and whispering all the words she longed to hear. Rather, he met her at the door and said nothing, nothing at all, his empty words billowing like smoke in the frosty air between them.

His leg still bothered him, even after six months since the raid. She had seen it in his eyes, in his stance, in every painful step across the sitting room floor. She knew it had become more than a minor inconvenience. He had been able to walk more than ten feet at the convalescent home without a grimace on his lips. The day he departed, he had rid himself of the cane and practically swayed through the corridors with barely a limp. Matron never would have released him in the distress Josie witnessed tonight.

She would never mention it, though. He didn't want to be treated as feeble and she didn't wish to view him as such. Bill was right. For now, this was where Peter belonged.

She waited for him to step forward, to kiss her, tell her he still loved her. Something other than this wretched silence between them. The torch hung limp at her side, her fingers clenching ever more around it with each white breath from her lungs.

"You're pleased to see me, aren't you?" she asked finally. "I know I'm certainly pleased to see you." She laid a gentle hand against his arm and his eyes dropped to the pool of light at their feet, exhaling through his nose. "It's been awful without you these past months. I should have come with you right from the beginning."

Peter shook his head, "No, you shouldn't have. You had purpose in London. That was your place."

"My place is beside you. Wherever you are, that's where I belong. Your sister taught me that and during an air raid of all places. Why did you propose to me if you didn't plan to share this part of your life with me?"

"I think you know why."

"I do. It's the same reason I'm here now."

He cupped her free hand between his, fingers still dirty from the road, and she likely appeared no less worn from her own journey. They were a matched set, as strange a set as their circumstances allowed. She loved the feel of his brokenness, how his damaged fingers caressed her skin in their own unique way, a way no one else ever could. He had run from her and she chased the miles to find the other beat of her heart.

"My body is failing me, Josie. My leg, my hand. They won't do what I need them to. But I can't leave yet. I can't." Tears she knew he couldn't bear to cry caught in his throat. He stared at the hollow of her neck, the rounded space right where her coat collar met her skin. He didn't look up until her fingers gently nudged his chin.

She knew she could try to dissuade him from any more "missions" to Le Clé. Now that she was here face-to-face in his misery, she might even be able to persuade him to return home. But that wasn't her decision to make.

She offered him a gentle smile. "Come back to the house. I'll mix you a tincture to ease the pain."

He shook his head. "I don't need a tincture. I only need you."

He kissed her slowly then, allowing his lips to linger, and she tumbled into his affection, allowing them for one moment to just be.

TWENTY-TWO

November 26, 1917 –
Clermont Farm, France

AMARA FELT THE NIGHTMARE'S draw as soon as she closed her eyes. She had suspected one might visit her tonight. Stress had a way of reminding her subconscious that her worst days were not necessarily behind her.

In the dreams, she always lost her sense of self. Dream Amara forgot that she wasn't in immediate danger. She forgot that she had a husband who loved her, who would protect her, and that Zeke's slaps and tobacco-laced insults were now half a world away. That was all the nightmares ever were. Zeke's sneer, Zeke's fists. With no way to stop it. She was trapped in a misery of her own design. There was nothing outside of it. She didn't even know she was dreaming until she awoke.

In Iowa, when she had suffered at Zeke's hands, she would run out to the edge of the cornfields and stare to the horizon. Tears on her cheeks, she would always pray the same prayers, asking God for deliverance. In life, He had answered. In sleep, there was nowhere to run.

The dreams were never exactly the same twice, the room she stood in always different. Tonight, it was a dim bedroom with green papered walls and a bay of windows overlooking the river. Outside a storm raged, hail raining down into the street. It bounced upon the cobblestones and ricocheted against the house. The roof leaked, a steady *drip-drip-drip* upon the floorboards.

Then she saw him. Standing in the open doorway with his twisted smile, his intention clear before he ever entered the room. Shadows sprang along the wallpaper with each rumble of thunder, Zeke tearing toward her while lightning snaked across the sky. She ran for the bed, dove beneath it in a dash to reach the other side, but too slowly. He had her by the ankles, yanked her back across the floor. Clutching both her arms, he hauled her to her feet.

"Please," she begged. "Have mercy. You loved me once."

She felt his nails dig into her muscles, saw the victory in his eyes. "Once was a very long time ago."

In another crackle of thunder, Emil appeared and she realized that for the first time, she recognized another person in her nightmares. This was her husband! He would help her!

She reached out, one arm stretching beneath her cousin's. "Emil!"

Zeke slapped a hand over her mouth, inching her back against the wall until she drew up on her tiptoes against it. He spun his words towards Emil, but his attention remained directly on Amara. "Stay out of this, Kisch," he sneered. "She isn't good for you. She's nothing but a liar."

"Oh, I know that," Emil replied dismissively. He practically peered straight through her then, more attention offered to the wall than his wife.

Her heart pounded as the air seemed to slow. Lightning flashed and thunder cracked and she heard none of it for the utter indifference in her husband's eyes.

"You know you deserve this," he said. Then he stepped away as Zeke stepped forward, drew back his hand, and slapped her.

—

Amara jerked awake, her breath expelling in heavy gasps. Flat on her back, she stared at the dark ceiling as the bed seemed to tilt beneath her. She covered her face with shaky hands, her palms warm and clammy, the imagined sting of Zeke's palm still upon her cheek. Gulping the cold bedroom air, silent sobs crushed her chest, her body heaving from the weight of her nightmare. Beside her, Emil breathed evenly, oblivious to her fear.

She knew that hadn't been him. She knew he would never allow it; he would defend her every time. *He loves me*, she kept repeating in her head. *He loves me*. But it had seemed so real. Everything about his dream counterpart looked the same; his voice had been no different than the one she heard every day. She was torn between wrapping her arms around him for comfort or fleeing the room. Perhaps some air, a quick walk around the farmhouse perimeter would clear her mind and calm her heart. Help her forget the terror of her nightmare. Then she could come back to bed and embrace her husband without hesitation.

Somehow managing to find a steady breath, she slipped silently from bed, buttoning her coat over her nightgown as she tiptoed from the room. Once outside the farmhouse, winter bit at the remainder of her exposed skin, filling her with a burst of sense and recognition. She was in France at the Clermont farm. Zeke wasn't here and would never be. For the first time in nearly a year, Peter was only paces away.

Waking at this dead hour could be a sign, the perfect time for them to speak alone and without interruption.

She opened the barn door and stepped into the darkness, allowing her eyes to adjust to the dim moonlight through the window grills high above on either end. The heady scent of hay and horses met her nostrils as she walked the aisle, reminding her of Peter's feed store in Iowa and their father's barn in Oberammergau many years before. It was a pleasant memory at last and calmed her wired senses.

A bay mare angled its head out from one of two occupied stalls, snorting a visible breath and stamping its hoof into the hay. In the next stall over, another mare of similar coloring showed its blanketed hindquarters, likely asleep or simply not wanting to be bothered. Amara stepped forward, hand outstretched, when a low whistle came from above. Her brother sat in the open hayloft window, his figure half draped in moonlight. "Amy," he called. "Up here."

The mare gave a whinny of protest, shaking its head and stomping its hoof again. Amara gave his muzzle a quick rub. "That will need to satisfy you for now," she soothed. "I promise to bring you a treat tomorrow." With another warm snuff to Amara's hand, the mare allowed her to step away without protest.

She climbed the loft ladder one careful rung at a time, hay scratching through her stockings as she lifted herself onto the loft's wooden floor. "You always ended up in the loft back home when you couldn't sleep," she noted as she brushed errant hay bits from her nightgown.

"Or when I was frustrated or angry, and I'm all of those."

She looked up at his disheartened tone. He sat with his back to the window frame, legs stretched across the sill's broad ledge, the open satchel beside him revealing a stack of cream-colored envelopes. In his misshapen right hand, he held a single sheet of parchment and in the other hand, a smoking cigarette. *A cigarette?* she thought. Her brother? Surely not.

"You know how dangerous that is, Peter, to have fire in a hayloft. All those years in Father's stables should have taught you better."

He frowned up at her, blowing a wisp of smoke from between his teeth. "Don't worry about me. I've never burned the barn down before."

"You never used to smoke either. You said it was a wasteful habit."

"Yes, well …" He took a long drag and released it slowly. "There were a lot of things I never used to do before I joined the *Deutsches Heer.*"

She settled herself on the hay across from him, allowing a moment of silence to pass. Smoke curled from his lips, up around eyes staring outward but not truly seeing her. There was an entire world there that she had never experienced and worried she would never truly know.

She nodded to the paper in his hand. "What's that?"

He crumpled it awkwardly into his fist and shoved it in his satchel. He flipped the flap, concealing the other envelopes. "Correspondence from one of our contacts. They've heard some reports of additional German movements near the Le Clé border. Means we'll have to take another way in next time. Likely the Brindille Bridge."

"Are the bridges not being monitored?"

"They are. Germans don't let anyone past without a fight."

"Then isn't that dangerous?"

"Considerably." He flicked a bit of ash out the window, the

particles immediately stolen away on the wind. "Bill will warn me against it and if I manage to return alive, Josie will probably murder me on the spot."

His chin turned minutely, barely enough for a normal person to make anything of, but Amara was his sister. Even after a year apart, she still knew him better than most. She followed the direction of his subconscious attention across the farmyard to the dark and quiet house where his fiancée slept. "Oh ... Peter ..." she breathed.

He exhaled a thick stream of smoke into the night. For a moment, it hovered about his face like a visible cloud of irritation. "Why did you bring her, Amara? I understand why you came, because I asked you to, but Josie? She shouldn't be dragged into this."

"You want her here though." Not a question, a fact. "I saw how you reacted when you first saw her in the sitting room. When you thought it was only her here, you were pleased. It's my presence that upsets you, not hers. Tell me the truth, Peter."

He sucked on the cigarette with a fierce intensity, drawing breath after breath, until the roll was nearly down to ash and he had to turn away to cough into his elbow. The motion shifted his weight onto his right hip and he stifled a groan, his unoccupied hand clasping his thigh while he grunted through clenched teeth.

"If your leg hurts this badly, how did you even manage to climb the ladder?"

"The same way I manage to do everything else in my life," he shot back, his voice husky. "One step at a time." He immediately ceased massaging his leg and leaned back against the window frame, even though she could tell it caused him pain. He lifted his opposite boot to grind the remainder of his cigarette on the sole and wiped the ash from his hands.

"It isn't your presence which upsets me, Amara. What upsets me is that you don't believe I have a reason to be upset. *Fides et Spes* isn't a secret club like we had with Zeke when we were children. There are lives at stake and many more than mine."

"I know that."

"I don't think you do. If you did, you wouldn't have brought your husband."

So, that was it, she thought. He was angry with her for bringing Emil even though it was Peter who originally ordered her to take a husband. Peter told her that was the only way to stay safe from anti-German discrimination. Of course, he rescinded his command in his letter, but at that point it had already been too late. What was she to have done, being already married? Was she to have abandoned her husband as Winnie suggested? No, Peter would have had her not come at all. Whatever he may say with his words, he didn't want her here. Coming all this way was a mistake if she couldn't convince him to trust her.

"Emil is a good man," she said. "He can be trusted to protect me and trusted to protect *Fides et Spes'* secrets. In many ways, he reminds me of ... you." She let the sentence trail, refusing to add "*who you were before.*" She drew her legs up under her nightgown and wrapped her arms around her knees, although the gesture did little to ward off the chill.

"You're cold," Peter said, as though that was the appropriate response.

"I'm not." She continued to peer out the window, pretending as though she and Emil weren't five miles from the epicenter of an enemy occupation and her brother wasn't the one responsible for it. Like he wasn't responsible for all of this. She didn't want to be irritated with him. She had only just gotten him back. Her thoughts turned inward, her eyes drawing closed, and she saw Zeke's palm rising behind her lids, coming forward ... She opened her eyes before the nightmare could resurface fully, shuddering.

"You are," Peter argued again. "And you're annoyed with me." Searching his coat pockets, he located a fresh pack of cigarettes. Tapping one into his palm, he stuck it between his lips and the pack between his thighs, obviously not intending this to be his final smoke of the evening.

She hated seeing him with a cigarette and enjoying the effects. It reminded her too much of Zeke who was rarely without a smoke, whose breath always smelled of tobacco and whose fingers were stained from the tar. Emil would also have the occasional cigar, but he kept it to a moderate level, and rarely indulged in her presence.

"Should you really be smoking so much?" she asked.

Peter flicked the lighter, its flame glowing eerily against his skin. "I'd like to see you shoot fourteen men and not smoke like a train engine after." Her face paled and he paused midway to touching the cigarette tip to light. His expression softened minutely. "I'm sorry, Amara. Being out there ..." He waved his unlit cigarette haphazardly towards the tree line. "I know you expected to find someone else in me than who you see."

"I did," she said, her voice little louder than a whisper. "Except I've seen things too. Probably not as terrible as you, but I'll never shake them from my memory. Back in St. Louis, it all happened as you feared. We were chased out of town on accusation and there was a man ... a German man ... who they hanged from a street lamp." The memory slashed across her vision. Those brown trouser-clad legs dangling above her, the man's eyes searching the mob for salvation and then searching no more. She would never forget the sight. It had haunted her ever since.

She pushed the thoughts away, focusing instead on her brother's face, now as hard as the frozen ground thirty feet below. "I prayed every day for your safety, Peter. I always wanted you to return. It never mattered to me how I found you as long as it was alive."

He had to flick the lighter four times before he managed to retain the flame. He set the cigarette to light and inhaled slowly. He exhaled again just as slowly.

"Peter?' she edged.

"I was going to come home," he said. "That's why I asked you to bring new papers. When I first arrived at Olmsted Manor, I thought I was going to die. Then, I learned I would live with a deformity and all I wanted was to get back to the States. But then you never replied to my letters and the situation changed."

"Josie," she said simply.

"No, not Josie, although she was part of it. I knew I needed to find a way back to France in order to set things right for Father Ferdinand. After all he did for me, I had to return the favor. He called me foolish." Peter granted her a smile then. "I think you're foolish to come too, but I will admit, I am honestly glad to see you. It's been a long year without my favorite sister."

She smiled back, enjoying a moment of levity rather than the frustration she had witnessed until that point. "Do you remember when we decided to style Hochburg's mane?" she asked.

He laughed, lightly coughing on the smoke he had just inhaled. He blew it back out and chuckled. "I do. We tied those ribbons in so tight, it took Papa's knife to get them out again. Hochburg barely had any mane left at all when we were through with him."

Amara laughed then too, recalling the easy days of their youth when one Sunday she had the grand idea to make their father's favorite stallion as pretty as she in her church clothes. If not for Peter's exceptional knot tying, they would have gotten away with the lark. Instead, they had to reveal a half-sheared horse to their father. It took months for his mane to grow back. They were in hot water even longer.

She shook her head, still chuckling. "Papa was so angry."

"Yeah, he was." Suddenly, Peter sobered. He stared at his cigarette like he was going to be sick. "He never forgave me for leaving you behind. I know he would never forgive me for deserting. In his eyes, what I'm doing would probably be the same as if I joined the Allied army instead." He flicked ash out the window. "It's good he believes I'm dead."

"Peter, you know Papa wouldn't want you dead."

He sighed. "I don't know that. Maybe after the war is over, I'll find the courage to tell him the truth behind it all."

After the war. The words should be branded on her brain for how often she heard them.

"What is the truth, Peter?"

"The truth is, Amara, that I wanted him to see me as a hero, to see that I still respected him, even though I disobeyed him. That's what our family does. It's what we've always done."

"You could have made your way back to them. Your impairments would have granted you an honorable discharge. You could have returned home a hero."

"Do not fool yourself. There was nothing heroic about the things I did in the *Deutsches Heer*."

164

"Is that why you deserted to join *Fides et Spes?*"

He didn't even pause, didn't blink. He launched into the story as though he had been preparing every day for this moment. Likely, he had been.

"The day of the air raid that nearly killed me, I fell in the street while we were fleeing town. Despite being in a German uniform, it was a French woman who reached out to help me. The *Deutsches Heer* had taken over the town, probably taken her husband and sons, harmed her daughters, and requisitioned her belongings. We stole her livelihood and she still showed me kindness. I now know how this world treats us, and it matters little which nationality we hail from. It hurts us equally. We each lose in our own way. We each carry our burdens and shoulder our pains. Life doesn't discriminate, why should we?"

"*Fides et Spes* truly is neutral then?"

"That is the philosophy they espouse, yes."

She found she could breathe a little easier with his statement. Ever since Emil had suggested Peter might be a spy, a part of her had worried that it might be true.

"What about Josie?" she asked carefully. "Where does she fit into your plans?"

He smiled, but this time there was an underlying sadness. An apprehension. "She's everything, Josie is. Once I rescued Father Ferdinand, I had planned to marry her."

"But now you don't?"

"I want to, but when I met Solange, I wondered if I would even have the opportunity. Her husband, Simon, was in Le Clé the day the Germans rounded up all the able-bodied men. They just marched in and took them east. To the work camps or the prisons, no one knows. More likely he's dead. Even with *Fides et Spes'* contacts, we haven't been able to locate him." His gnarled hand flexed in stilted motions upon his knee while the cigarette smoked from where it hung limp between his good fingers. "I don't want to be captured on a run and leave Josie waiting three years, wondering like Solange has."

"Three years?" Amara sputtered. Such a long time without knowing if your husband was alive or dead or would ever return. So terrible for Solange's sons to grow up without a father just as Amara's sisters' children were growing with their fathers away in the trenches. At least her sisters had their parents and each other to provide emotional support. How much more difficult for Solange to raise three boys alone, one of whom had barely begun to talk ...

"Wait," she said. "If Monsieur Clermont has been missing for three years, then Remy couldn't be ..." She let the thought trail away into the night. "I'm sorry. It isn't polite to assume such things." *Even if they are obviously true*, she finished.

Peter turned to exhale before facing her again. "It isn't as you think. Remy is Solange's nephew, the son of her sister, Colette. Remy's parents were both killed about six months ago, she in a Paris air raid and he at the front. Remy was on the side of their house that didn't collapse."

"How awful. I'm sorry I thought ..."

"You're not the first to assume Solange's unfaithfulness, and few would blame her for seeking comforts. Even Bill and Quentin have mentioned it. They consider her husband to be dead anyway."

The way Peter said it, so aloof, so matter of fact. Simply, this is how it is now, this way of life. As though it was perfectly normal for men to be dragged off to unknown lands and women to be crushed within their own homes. A house should be a place of safety. One shouldn't need to wonder if it could fall down around them at any time.

We should have stayed in America, she thought. When their father asked Peter to go fight for Germany, he should have stayed with her. She would spare Zeke no hard feelings for leaving, but her brother should have stayed. Perhaps they would both be in a better place now.

Of course, that meant they would also still be living in Iowa. She would not be married. Emil would have no place in her life at all. Despite their many arguments lately and her troubling nightmare, being without him was nearly impossible to consider.

"It's been trying for the Clermonts without a husband and father to lead them," Peter continued, unaware of her inner thoughts. "We help her with the farming and the housework, trips into Brindille for whatever meager food and supplies are available. I only hope as her boys grow, they'll be able to rise to the challenge. If her husband doesn't return, she'll likely need to take another once the war is through." He drew in again on his cigarette. "Who knows how many men will even be left by then."

"After you rescue Father Ferdinand, will you return to America?" Amara asked. She twisted at her wedding band. "Or will you marry Josie and live in England?"

He wouldn't look at her then. "I don't know. The end of the war seems a long way off. How can I think about the future, when every day I wonder if I'll even make it to tomorrow?"

TWENTY-THREE

November 26, 1917 –
Clermont Farm, France

PETER LIT UP ANOTHER CIGARETTE as he watched Amara walk back to the farmhouse. He had never smoked before the *Deutsches Heer*. Never smoked a day in his life. Never wanted to. Then he landed in the trenches and men were killing other men and he was surrounded by rats, lice, and rotting flesh from every angle. So, when Zeke offered him one, he tried it. Coughed and sputtered and hated it at first, but after a few more, he began to notice that it did relax him a little. Not enough to forget why they were there or that only a few hundred yards away lay dead men that he had shot to the ground. But it did make their situation seem more normal, almost as though he and Zeke were standing in front of their feed store while his cousin stuck another smoke between his lips.

He understood why Amara was disappointed in him, but his sister would never understand what he had been through. Nor would she understand the position she had placed him in by her presence here. The two women he loved most in the world were only miles from an unimaginable threat. How could he do his duty to *Fides et Spes* and protect them both? He couldn't.

He needed to find a way to trust this Emil character. He supposed he should trust Amara to have chosen a worthy husband, but did she know enough of the world yet to choose one? What if her husband wasn't trustworthy? What if he was a spy? What if he would turn in *Fides et Spes* to the French or German authorities? Their entire system, everything they worked so hard for, would be dismantled in a moment, leaving thousands of innocents with no way to send letters across the line. And him with no chance of saving Father Ferdinand.

Keep your friends close, he thought, *and your enemies closer*. Until he determined which Emil was, he would need to hold his brother-in-law tightly in his sights. He would speak privately with Bill on the matter in the morning.

Closing the hayloft window, he limped across the wooden floorboards, practically dragging his right leg so he wouldn't need to bend it. Succumbing to exhaustion, he stumbled and fell onto his makeshift bed, one blanket between him and the hay, the other draped over himself. He lay on his back, pulling smoke into his lungs and silently back out through his lips, and somehow managed to keep himself from drifting asleep and setting the barn ablaze. He considered if dying in a fire would hurt worse than having a stone church collapse on him.

Smoke in, smoke out. Breathe in, breathe out.

Josie had been the one to help him climb into the loft tonight. She had encouraged him one agonizing ladder rung at a time until he sat at the top panting from the exertion. His body hadn't hurt this much since the early days at the convalescent home. She had taken his mangled fingers between hers, kissing each one in turn, and her tenderness filled his heart. He wanted a home with her. A life. To have all of her and she to have all of him. But a stranger's farm was not the place to make a home nor a hayloft the proper place to take a marriage bed.

He had eased her hair back and placed a gentle kiss on her neck, telling her to return to the house so he could rest. He wrapped her in his arms one final time, determined that if there was an "after the war" for him, he would never let her go.

TWENTY-FOUR

November 27, 1917 –
Clermont Farm, France

EMIL WOKE WITH AN EMOTIONAL HANGOVER in an empty bed. Amara's side of the sheets was already cold, yet when he glanced at the window, the sky above the trees contained only the first glimmer of sunrise.

He laid back and rubbed his face with his palms, groaning. As nice as their post-argument intimacy had been last night, the truth was that they had resolved nothing. Amara had still lied to him about Peter's warning to stay away, proving he had been right to dissuade her in the first place. Now that they were here, though, it sounded as though it would be far from easy to convince her brother to leave, especially if they failed to extract Father Ferdinand.

Emil wanted to be back in St. Louis and home with his family. He missed every one of them, even Fred. No matter how much of a clod he could be, Fred had been integral in helping Emil and Amara escape from Earhart's threats. He had put his own life and reputation on the line and for that Emil would forever be grateful.

He would send a letter back with Quentin to let his parents know that he and Amara were well, at least for now. Although they would worry considerably over his current location, they deserved the truth. If anything happened to him, he didn't want his parents to be left wondering. No parent deserved that.

—

Four hours later, Emil's completed letter was tucked inside his winter overcoat while he maneuvered another wooden fence post into place, nearly completing the stretch assigned him after their meager breakfast. It wasn't his forte—manual labor—but he figured if they were going to be consuming Solange's precious food rations, he may as well earn her hospitality. Thankfully, she had sent her two sons to help him with the task, although Maël, being only five, spent more time climbing the fences and chasing after red squirrels than actually assisting.

Even in the cold, a trickle of sweat slid down his collar, leaving him both warm and chilled with each passing breeze. He wiped the moisture away with a gloved hand, watching the Clermonts' two mares trot across the open pasture. Blankets secured over their backs, they tossed their heads and whinnied proudly. White steam rising from their nostrils mirrored the thin layer of fog which covered the fields at sunrise.

"You're not done yet, Monsieur Kisch," Lucien reprimanded in French, his lips pressed into a firm line. The boy had done little but berate Emil since they began their task, becoming increasingly frustrated with Emil's lack of French fluency. What exactly was anyone to expect, though, when his conversational skills had been ingested during his time on the morality squad? He had never needed translations for words like fencepost or crossbeam.

He struck another rail out of position with his hammer, hefting the cracked beam onto the pile with the others. Pointing to the new beam, he wordlessly directed Lucien to lift the other end. Once it was in place, he set to the task of nailing the posts together. Lucien told him that nails weren't necessary as the slats fit together well enough, but Simon Clermont had always desired a secondary assurance. A weak point increased the possibility of a broken fence later on. If the horses ran free or were attacked by local wildlife, it meant a loss to their farm and their family.

Strictly speaking, Emil supposed that Lucien was now considered the man of the household. Such responsibility would be a load for any child to bear, but especially tiresome for one barely ten years old.

"Why aren't you fighting in the war?" the boy asked. He handed

Emil a nail from the leather pouch he held. "Maman said a lot of papas are gone like mine. Are you here because you're not a father yet?"

That gave Emil pause. He glanced towards the house where Amara was, wondering if she would afford him a warmer reception at dinner than their nearly silent breakfast. "Not only fathers go to war," he explained. "Monsieur Müller fought and he isn't a father either." He struck the nail into the wood, splitting the fibers. He sighed, gesturing for another, this time taking more careful aim. This time, the nail struck straight, the wood intact.

He held his hand out for another nail and noticed Lucien staring at him with accusation. "Why aren't you fighting then?" he asked. He handed over two more nails, the last needed to complete their project.

Emil drove them into place, feeling sweat again coat his neck as though under the morality squad's interrogation lamps. "The army didn't call my name."

That didn't seem to appease the boy. He yanked the hammer from Emil's hand and rested the handle over his shoulder with a scowl. "My Papa didn't go right away either. I think that's why the Germans took him. You'd better be careful or they'll take you too." With that, he called for Maël and the two boys headed back to the house and through the kitchen door.

Emil let out a breath, the air fogging around him like the cigar smoke he used to share with his father. Amara should be glad they didn't have children yet. No one else to question their difficult decisions besides themselves.

Bending, he secured his arms around the first batch of dilapidated beams and with much struggle, managed to lift them across his shoulder. They would soon be chopped for kindling, probably his task for this afternoon. He carried them across the farmyard and kicked at the barn door, waiting for someone to let him in. Peter and Bill were supposed to be inside discussing their latest run or having a "debriefing" as Bill called it.

Instead, Quentin answered, a dense cloud of cigarette smoke accompanying him. Inside, Peter and Bill lounged against the barn wall, their own personal cigarette smoke haze floating through the air.

A number of papers were spread across the floor in front of them surrounding a map covered in pencil markings. When they spotted Emil standing there, they quickly shuffled the papers together, folding one over another.

"No need to stop your conversation on my account," Emil huffed. "I've got another few loads, then I'll be out of your way." Grunting, he dropped the pile of timber against the barn's far wall and turned back for the door.

"Hold up, mate," Bill called after him.

He paused just inside the door where Quentin still stood, hand on the latch, ready to close him out the moment he finished his task. Peter was scowling. "This isn't any of his business, Bill. He isn't part of our team."

"Well, why the devil isn't he?" Bill asked. "He seems like a trustworthy soul. Married your sister. He fixed that fence, didn't he?"

"A fence isn't La Clé, Bill."

Quentin slid the barn door shut with a clatter, throwing the thick wooden latch across the brace. "We discuss over a drink, *oui*?" He snapped his fingers at Bill who immediately dug into the haversack beside him, extracting a squat round bottle of brandy. Prying the cork out, he took a long swallow straight from the bottle.

Emil stared. "Where did you get that? Surely, the Germans aren't giving their liquor away."

Quentin sidled past him and took the bottle from Bill for a taste of his own. He handed it back and wiped his mouth on his coat shoulder. "All we can spare is snuck into Le Clé. Once or twice they sneak something back."

Bill grinned. "Swiped it from a German locker. Some dumb bloke left his door unlocked, so I waltzed in and took it."

"Some dumb bloke?" Peter muttered. "I think the fool was you more than him for sneaking into a soldier's quarters." He accepted the bottle from Bill, sniffed it, and made a face. "Yes, definitely you. That is revolting. Not even worth it." He held the bottle out to Emil who moved forward and accepted a draw without thinking. He would have to give the Germans credit; it smelled awful, but the taste was worth it. He admired how it warmed his chest down to his stomach, while remembering how not so long ago, he used to do more than sip. He used to chug, glug, wash himself under the rug more nights of the week than not. He used to shoot high-end whiskey and love the feeling. He would let the liquor go to his head rather than his stomach, making one insensible decision after another. Then he met Amara and all that changed. She was the only one who could convince him that there might be more than one outlet for his grief and frustration.

Yet, he had still traveled to war-torn France without an ounce of alcohol to blame.

He handed the bottle back to Bill. "I should get the last of those rails moved. I promised Solange I would finish before dinner." But Quentin stood in his way, rubbing his thumb and forefinger across the dark stubble on his chin. He nodded to the others. "You do not leave yet. We must finish discussion first."

"What discussion?"

"Your recruitment," Bill said simply.

Emil turned back, gawking at him. "*Recruitment*? I'm not joining your crew. I plan on getting away from here as soon as possible."

"See," Peter said. "I told you. Married men have no place in *Fides et Spes*."

"As though you're not two steps away from the altar yourself," Bill said dryly. He pointed the brandy bottle at his friend. "Marital status aside, you've been killing yourself by taking every mission. You need a break or you'll slip up and get yourself killed and likely the rest of us too."

Peter took a long draw on his cigarette, slowly releasing the smoke up into the barn rafters. He stared at the loft window and said nothing.

"You know I'm right, Pete. We've shown our faces too many times in that town. The Jerries are going to start noticing that we're not on any of the census records. Especially with injuries as noticeable as yours."

"We'll be more careful. I'll grow a beard. We can have Quentin take a shift or two."

"*Non*," Quentin puffed, sucking his cigarette like a train stack. "I do not cross border. I take letters to Brindille. I hand them off. I bring new ones back. I bring you food. Supplies. I do not go to danger." More puffs encircled his face and he frowned when the cigarette became a stub between his fingers. He dashed it to the barn's dirt floor. "I already go to war. Was injured. Will not go back."

"Quentin shouldn't go," Bill agreed, "but frankly, I'm plum tired of putting my own life on the line all the time. And yours. Let someone else hold his toes over the fire for a change."

Peter looked like he wanted to reach over and punch him. "What did you think we would be doing when I asked you to join me? Throwing one of those fancy dinners your family enjoys so much? There aren't any white glove affairs here, Bill."

"I didn't think that. I just didn't think it would be, well..." He waved his hand around the barn. "...This."

"Then go home," Peter seethed. He looked at each man in turn. "Last night, you agreed to stand on my word and I will hold you to it." He attempted to raise himself to standing, probably to storm out if Emil had to guess, but his leg seized, sending him back to the ground. Fingers clenched into fists, he gritted his teeth against the pain.

Bill handed him the liquor bottle and Peter took a swig. "See, Pete, you can barely walk across a barn. How do you plan to walk five miles to Le Clé and five back again? You'll fall behind and I'll have to drag you the rest of the way."

"You could leave him," Quentin suggested. Bill and Peter glared at him and he shrugged. "*Quoi*? It is a choice. A man who is foolish should be treated as a fool."

Emil was foolish to even still be listening to this conversation. He wished Quentin would get out of his way. "You know, I really should be getting those rails moved," he tried again, but Bill continued to talk over him like he wasn't even there.

"We're in France, Pete. When's the next time we'll come across someone who speaks German and also looks the spitting image of a Jerry? Even without a uniform, they'll likely still assume he's one of them."

"You want me to pretend to be a German soldier?" Emil admonished. "Just to sneak a few letters over the border?" This idea was insane. It was suicidal. No man in his right mind would agree to this.

"Not at first," Bill clarified. "You only have to act like a soldier if you get caught."

Quentin eyed Emil up and down. "*Oui.* He gets captured, he talks himself out."

"No," said Peter. Finally, he acknowledged Emil. "My sister would never forgive me if I took you to your death."

Well, thank goodness for that, Emil thought. He was tired of this conversation and wanted to be involved in as little of this as possible. He wouldn't sacrifice his life and leave Amara widowed just so they could avoid the censors. Innocent civilians deserved to send their loved ones letters, but he wasn't willing to die so they could.

"We should head back to the house. Lunch is likely ready." He would finish hauling the old fence posts later. He didn't want to venture back into this barn until he knew he could do so alone.

—

Extinguishing their cigarettes, Bill offered Peter a hand up which he begrudgingly accepted. He knew that he needed to rest and equally knew that the only way he could continue taking runs was to share the load with someone else. With Emil, they could accomplish much more than simply trading letters and leaving supplies with Father Ferdinand. Emil wouldn't have to stick to the shadows and duck in and out of doorways. He could walk straight down the street, carrying supplies in a satchel on his shoulder and a pistol at his hip without anyone giving him a second glance. And if they did question him, he seemed like the type of man who could smooth talk himself out of trouble.

Keep your friends close and your enemies closer.

Emil would prove himself worthy of Peter's trust or Peter wouldn't hesitate to show his sister exactly what type of man she married.

He watched his brother-in-law slide the barn door open and take off for the house with the urgency of someone fleeing a crime scene.

TWENTY-FIVE

November 27, 1917 –
Clermont Farm, France

JOSIE STACKED ANOTHER LOG in the cast iron stove, already filling the small kitchen with a pleasant warmth. She had quickly figured out that even with the sitting room fireplace lit, the kitchen was still the warmest place to be. Surprisingly, the barn was second. Thoughts of her time alone in the loft with Peter the night before brought even more warmth to her cheeks.

One more log went into the stove and she latched the door, extracting her hand from the warm mitt. It was good her fiancé sent her from the barn before they could engage in more than a few kisses. She very well might have stayed all night if he asked and likely would have regretted it after. She eagerly anticipated the fire that would burn between them once they married.

If we marry, she thought sullenly, then immediately pushed the thought away. She wasn't the type to cry and moan over a man's promises; there had been no man before Peter, after all. In *Fides et Spes*, one must be certain of every choice. There was no room for doubt, not even when it came to romantic interests. Especially not then.

"What has you so flustered?" Amara asked. She sat at the kitchen table mixing a batch of "war biscuits," a terrible concoction of rationed ingredients that hardly resembled pre-war bread. Josie had suffered a version of it back in London, but rationing was tighter here and with Brindille being so near the occupation line, supplies were

177

more scarce. Solange said it made for some creative culinary decisions, ones her upper-class Parisian parents would no doubt cringe at if they were still living.

"I'm not flustered." Josie wiped her warm brow with the edge of her sleeve, embarrassed that her friend caught her lost in daydreams. "It's rather hot being so close to the fire."

"It certainly is," Amara agreed. "Far warmer than cooking with gas, but I prefer it to the cold outside."

Josie thought of Peter, Bill, and Quentin out in the barn, bundled up in their winter overcoats and stocking hats, discussing plans for their next run and tactics to enter Le Clé unnoticed. They were a well-oiled machine, wrenched together bolt by bolt months before she arrived. They didn't even know how she could fit into their plan now. A member of *Fides et Spes*, but not qualified to participate in such dangerous games.

"What was Peter like before the war?" she asked. "Back when you lived in Iowa?"

Amara stirred the batter, breaking apart lumps when they rose to the surface. "The way he was before the war probably wouldn't tell you much about who he is now."

"Was he as accomplished at his feed store as he claims?"

"Probably more. Peter never took the credit he was due. He was always too modest for that. Not the man in command like you see now." She stared into the batter, wistful. "He never smoked. He rarely raised his voice. He was the kindest man I knew, although overly protective of me."

"He is still kind," Josie assured her. "Don't be upset about someone willing to protect you. That's what you allow Emil to do, isn't it?"

Her hand stilled on the spoon handle. "Yes ..."

"Peter spoke of you often in the convalescent home. He wanted few things more than to be reunited with you. He wanted life to go back to the way it was."

"We all wish for that."

Amara moved the mixing bowl from table to counter, then began scooping the gloopy mixture into rows across a greased tin tray. Josie stepped around her in the small space, shimmying past the stove's heat to avoid singeing her backside. She dipped her finger into the batter for a taste, and Amara smacked her hand away with the spoon, a trail of batter slipping down Josie's wrist.

"That's your share of the biscuits right there on your hand," Amara reprimanded, although her lips turned up at the edges. "We don't have enough for you to waste it."

"I like to pretend it's slathered in heaps of marmalade and butter," Josie jested. She licked the excess from her hand. It was little better in liquid form than fully baked. "Can you imagine how wonderful it will all taste when the war ends? Real food and wine and no one telling us how much or how many we can have? I do suspect I'll be round as a globe from it all."

"Or round with a baby?" Amara suggested. She smiled, but there seemed to be an underlying coolness to her tone. Josie had seen her friend's gaze of longing towards Remy and guessed that she likely questioned why she and Emil had not yet been blessed. No doubt she was wondering if her brother, who was to be married after her, would reach parenthood before she did.

"Let me place your mind at ease," Josie said gently. "Your brother and I will not marry until the war ends. There is no sense in bearing a child when danger lurks at every turn." It was a humbling thought. When Peter first proposed back at Olmsted Manor, she had believed that if he managed to free Father Ferdinand, they would marry immediately after. Now she knew it had never been that simple. Even if Peter helped the priest, it would not dissolve the need for *Fides et Spes*. Their work would continue until the "white flag flies or the last one dies." How could she run from air raids or enemy fire if she was pregnant? Her extended stomach would only slow her down and make her an easier target.

"That's what I thought too," Amara said as though sensing Josie's thoughts. "I believed there was no space for a baby during a war, but now I know there was only space lacking within my fear. When we return to New York, Emil has promised to start our family."

She looked up through the flicker of dark lashes and this time when she smiled, it was without an ounce of jealousy or sadness. "It is all in God's timing," she said. "That is something I am trying to remember and to be content within the waiting."

"Yes," Josie agreed. "Although the waiting is so terribly difficult, isn't it?"

Amara released a slight sigh then a chuckle. "Impossible."

She spooned the last bit of batter onto the tin, the mixture not quite solidifying into round lumps as it should. Although they knew little about each other, it felt natural to be here performing such domestic work together. Josie was glad to have found such an instant camaraderie with her future sister-in-law. All her life, her family had consisted of only two people: her and her father. Very rarely had she entertained a schoolmate in their flat and not once had her father invited romantic interest into their lives. Only once had she ever asked him about it, a few years before the war began. She wanted to know if he ever planned to court again. If he was ever lonely.

"I have you, sweet Joselyn," he had said with a rumble of laugher, "and you have all the beauty of your mama. You make it feel as though she's still with me." He hugged her then. "As long as I have you, Joselyn, I shall never be lonely."

She had been glad for such simple moments, happy to have no worries beyond their small flat and the factory. But once her father enlisted and their flat remained empty evening after empty evening, she finally felt the loneliness her father spoke of. Only Peter and *Fides et Spes* had been able to fill the void his departure left behind.

Solange entered the kitchen, Remy attached to her hip and Maël tagging at her heels. She sat at the table and Remy immediately leapt from her arms to run circles around the kitchen table. "How can I help?" she asked, looking like she was about to drop.

Setting the mixing bowl aside, Amara scooped both arms under Remy before he ran headlong into the burning cast iron stove. His little legs whirled in the air, shins slapping against her thighs. He shoved her away with a whine, leaning backward at a nearly forty-five-degree angle.

"We told you we would take care of the meals," Amara told Solange while she held the boy at bay. "It's the least we can do to thank you for your hospitality."

Stars danced in their host's eyes. "That would be so lovely. I thank God that your group came to us." She gestured for Amara to let Remy down and gave a swat to his bum as he scampered into the sitting room. She looked back at her new friends, her weary eyes now red-rimmed. "Even with your help, the days are long and terribly difficult to bear. I love my husband, but every day he grows more distant from me. With the boys growing older, it would be nice ..." She let the words trail, as though ashamed to even think them, much less speak them aloud.

"To be allowed to move on?" Josie suggested gently.

"Yes."

"There's no shame in longing for companionship," Amara told her. "You know you can't give up on Simon though."

"I know. I only wish I could be certain he was still alive."

A tramping sounded from the back porch followed by Emil's swift entry through the kitchen door. Outside the window, Peter limped beside Bill, making his way from the barn careful step by careful step, his progress worse than his last day at the manor. He winced with each pained movement, fingers clenched against his hip where Bill couldn't see. Josie wanted to guide him back to the loft as she had last night. She wanted to sit beside him and take his hand like she did the day they met, when he was wrapped in bandages and little more than a ghost of a man.

If given the chance, she would marry him tomorrow and serve *Fides et Spes* with him forever. There was nothing else she was more certain of.

All he need do was ask.

TWENTY-SIX

November 27, 1917 –
Clermont Farm, France

AMARA ATTEMPTED TO STAY awake as long as she could that night, hoping that when she finally gave into exhaustion it would carry her through until morning. She even allowed Emil to snuggle up against her, hold her, and kiss her neck.

She wasn't aware of when she fell asleep or how long she lay there, but somehow, she was being shaken awake in a state of complete panic. Her eyes shot open, her breathing heavy. Emil knelt over her, gripping her upper arms, waves of blond hair falling across his concerned expression in the moonlight. His fingers lay exactly where Zeke used to grab her daily. He only needed to squeeze a little tighter...

Her hands struck out on instinct, shoving his chest away, attempting to move an impenetrable wall of bone and muscle. It had been another dream, she thought. Only a dream. Except this time, she couldn't remember it. She couldn't recall anything that happened tonight while she was asleep. Had Zeke been there? Had Emil? Or someone altogether different? Her limbs felt on fire and her heart was about to slash a hole in her chest.

"Let me go!" she screamed. "Emil, please, I beg you!"

Immediately, he did as she asked. He sat back on his knees and she scrambled backwards against the headboard. "Amara, what is it?" He spoke slowly, deliberately, staring at her like she might hang herself with the bedsheets.

That was it! Tonight's nightmare had concerned the German man who hanged from the street lamp last June, the one they watched die then walked away from. In the dream, he stared straight at her, his accusing gaze boring into her soul, more furious than even Zeke on his worst days. "This was your fault," the man said. Everything was her fault. It was because of her that they were all in danger.

She rolled out of bed and was across the room in the blink of an eye. Eyes still crusted with sleep, brain only half-aware, she managed to light the hand lamp. The flame flickered to life, casting the room in an eerie orange glow and the potent scent of kerosene. On the other side of the blackout curtains, the world lay still in darkness, not even a glimmer on the horizon. *Perfect timing*. She dragged her traveling case from under the bed and flipped up the latches. They could make their escape before anyone was the wiser.

A knock at the door halted her progress, Bill barging into the room without asking if he could, Josie and Solange directly behind him. They looked from Amara crouched on the floor to Emil on the bed. "What is going on in here?" Bill asked. In a rushed attempt at modesty, he had thrown a sweater on over his long johns, while the women were still belting their dressing gowns.

"We heard screams," Josie said in alarm. She knotted her belt as she looked to Emil. "One of those screams was your name."

"Amara had a nightmare," he explained. He stumbled off the bed, his long legs unable to find their waking stance yet. "Thanks for your concern, but we're perfectly fine." Raising both hands, he backed them into the hall, then shut the door and locked it. He turned to Amara, one hand still on the knob behind him.

She sat before the traveling case, all ten fingers clutching its contents, her hands buried within a pile of skirts and shirtwaists and chemises, stockings and underthings. Beneath all that wrapped in delicate paper were her pearls. Those perfect pearls Peter bought her the Christmas before he left to join the *Deutsches Heer*. She wore them the night she fell in love with Emil. She wore them at their wedding. She hadn't worn them since.

Gently, carefully, Emil sat beside her and reached an arm around to meld her against his side. In her confused state, it surprised her that she let him. She moved her right hand to grasp his. "This was a mistake," she whispered.

"What was?"

"Coming to France. Following my brother's letters. All of it. We have to get away from here before it ruins us." Already she was again comparing him to Zeke, remembering that slap, and wondering what was true and what was illusion. They had to return to New York, back to the world they knew.

"Amara, please look at me." She tilted her chin upward to that shining face watching her intently. There was fire and flame in the lantern behind him and part of her wondered if she was even awake at all. Perhaps this was still part of the nightmare. She wanted to be held in the safest arms she knew, except her lips still burned from the taste of liquor on his kiss when he returned from the barn that afternoon.

She hadn't mentioned it at the time, knowing it would only incite another argument, but his indulgence plagued her thoughts for the rest of the afternoon. Where had he even found the alcohol? He had led her to believe he hadn't sipped a drink in months, but now she wondered. Had he imbibed behind the bar of the Forsythe Hotel too? If he drank early enough in the evening, the evidence would easily be cleared by the time he returned home, and she would be none the wiser. Or was it only this place and being here that brought out his vices? If so, she truly was the cause of her own misery.

"Come back to bed," he said gently. "Being here is what you wanted. You'll remember that in the morning. So, come back to bed. I'll keep the nightmares away."

That was what she wanted too. He had promised her once that he would protect her, keep her safe from everything she feared. Except he couldn't dive into her unconscious mind and he couldn't stop a war. She feared that they would never convince Peter to return home and she would have to decide between her husband and her brother. During the air raid in London, she told Emil that he should be the one she followed and at the time, she believed it. She knew she should believe it still. Except that Peter hadn't been there then; she hadn't known if he was even still alive. The decision to follow Emil had seemed so easy. Now that she and Peter were reunited, it felt as though the London fog had descended, making it difficult to decipher head from tail.

Emil studied her. "There's more bothering you, isn't there? Did Peter tell you about what Bill asked me to do? You don't need to worry. I'm not going."

She abruptly sat back on her heels, dislodging his arm and causing him to fall forward. He caught himself on his bare palm. "Going where?" she asked. "Where did Bill ask you to go?"

He righted himself, propping one knee up and hooking his elbow around it. "He and Quentin want me to be part of the letter deliveries. They think I'll draw less attention since I look so German."

Another secret Peter was keeping from her. "What did you say?"

"I told them no, of course. It's too dangerous. Even Peter disagreed on account of us being married."

"So, if we weren't married, you would go?"

"No. If we weren't married, I wouldn't even be here."

"That's what you want. To not be here."

"Amara, please don't lapse into some feminine oddity about how this is your fault and we shouldn't even be married. It takes two to tap a waltz and I'm a rather fine dancer." He unhooked his arm to run a hand through his mussed hair. "I'm not going to have the same argument we've already had six times. It's like a skipping record and this place doesn't even have a player."

"Should we argue about something else then?"

He sighed. "I would rather go to sleep or make love to my wife, but since it sounds like those options are off the table, fire away."

She didn't understand why she was picking a fight at this dead hour. Pure exhaustion, she supposed. They had never fought so much in their marriage as during the weeks since they received Peter's letters. She always knew the accusations and resentment would need to be dealt with one day, but she had hoped it would be after the war, when life returned to normal and was on solid footing. If only they had stayed in New York. They would be warm and safe in their apartment. They might have even been signing adoption papers and bringing their baby home.

Instead, they were trapped in the bleary French countryside and the endless night was changing them. Perhaps beyond recognition.

"This afternoon when you were out at the barn, you were drinking. Where did you get the alcohol?"

His lips parted in surprise. "Who told you I was drinking?"

"You did. I could taste it on your kiss."

"Bill swiped it from a German locker when he was in town. I only had a swallow, absolutely harmless. It's not like I snuck off to drink it alone." He wanted her to believe him; she could see it in his eyes and hear it in his tone. "Amara, I haven't been full-tilt plastered since before we were engaged. I promised you I wouldn't go back to that again, but I never promised I wouldn't have a drink. *A drink*. One. Even two would have been fine. I know my limit. I know when I need to stop."

"That's what you said the night we met too, then you drowned yourself and couldn't even remember what happened the next day." She turned from him, wrapping her arms around herself. She was so cold. So very cold. "I'm afraid you're going to turn into him."

"Who?"

"Zeke."

She heard his sharp intake of breath and imagined his eyes round as dinner plates. She wished she could take it back.

"Zeke?" he spat. "You're comparing me to him *again*? Name one way that having one drink and not harming anyone even comes close to the way he treated you?"

She raised uncertain fingers to her cheek, hearing the sound of Zeke's goading laughter from her nightmares. She felt herself start to tremble, only she couldn't run this time. How could you run from a memory?

Somehow, she managed to pull herself together and return her hand to her side. *It wasn't real*, she thought. *In real life, Emil would have stopped Zeke, not joined him. He would never leave me alone.*

"I don't know," she said, backpedaling to find a reason without condemning him for deeds not done. "I think that in other circumstances, you and Zeke probably would have ended up the best of friends."

"In other circumstances?" he said slowly. "Do you mean in other circumstances before I met you, being who I was and what I liked to do? Or back when you were in love with him because he made stars dance across the sky? Maybe in those circumstances, we would have been bloomin' great together. Then again, given the nature of those circumstances, I believe so would he and you." Emil ran a hand through his hair, breathing heavy, then turned to look at the bed's rumpled sheets. It was difficult to believe they had shared intimacies there only one night ago; now, it felt like ages.

"Emil," she said gently, wanting to fix this. Her mind was in knots, her heart in turmoil. This man whom she loved and never feared before, tonight only compounded her uncertainty.

He tilted his chin to stare down at her, his gaze more wounded than angry. He reached for her hands, pulled them to his chest, and tugged her closer, eyes pleading. "I thought we left the past behind us. What will it take for you to forgive me?"

"Let me join *Fides et Spes*." The words were out before she planned them, but as soon as they were, she knew it was exactly what she always meant to say.

"*What?*"

"I want to go to Le Clé and deliver letters exactly as Bill and Peter asked you to do. I'm the perfect candidate for what they need. People have always viewed me as insignificant and childish; why would German soldiers suspect anything different? I can pass letters without notice."

He gripped her fingers. "Is that what you *want*?" he asked, then more quietly, "or is that the only way you believe Peter will return home? Will it always be me against another man in your life and failing every time? Surely, there's another way we can overcome our demons."

"It isn't only Zeke or Peter, Emil. It's everything coming together. Don't you ever think about the man we saw hanged? Don't you wonder if we could have done something to stop it?"

"Of course I do, but this isn't the answer."

Her husband was the most physically nonviolent person she knew and here she was asking him to let her go into a situation more dangerous than any he had encountered on the morality squad. He never once drew his pistol on someone then and she knew he wouldn't want either of them to now.

She didn't want to either.

But he had been right last night when he said that they were a wreck. They needed to fix themselves. They needed to find their way back to who they were before they left St. Louis, before the broken promises and doubts. She knew that they couldn't have helped the man on the street lamp, but he had still been a warning, the same as all the nightmares she couldn't escape and all the daydreams too. A warning to not sit idle lest everything they loved was slowly stripped away. It might be anyway.

"I want to join *Fides et Spes*," she repeated slowly, confidently, not a hint of question in her tone. "*Vince malum bono*, Emil. Overcome evil with good. That's what we're here for. That's what we need to do."

Emil nodded. Dropping her hands, he pushed himself up from the floor. Lifting the bedcovers, he slid between them. "Just remember, Amara, there's another part to their motto. *Victores in bello non sunt.* There are no victors in war. None."

"That phrase doesn't even make sense. If there were no victors in war, then it would continue forever. Someone has to win."

Emil stared towards the window where the blackout curtains hung straight. They both knew what was on the other side, five miles from where they sat. Rarely, could they hear the gunfire and never heard the villagers' oppressed cries, but occasionally French soldiers rode the distant road, reminding them of where they were. Surely, he must be considering whether there was another way to help without placing her directly in the heart of danger. If he devised another solution, she would gladly hear him out.

"I'll go," he said finally. He turned to her, his lip raised in that arrogant smirk she remembered from so long ago, and she knew she would lose this conversation without needing to say another word.

"I'm better suited to this sort of mission," he continued. "I appear more German than you do, I already know how to use a pistol from my time on the morality squad, and I've spent my entire life using wit to wheedle my way out of scrapes. Everyone knows how incredible I am, so logically I should be the one to go." He grinned, but his egotism didn't show in his eyes. If she hadn't known him so well, she might not have noticed, but she knew all his little quirks by now.

"I can't let you do that," she whispered. Tears burned her vision. "This was my idea."

"No, actually it was originally Bill and Peter's idea. Your idea was to keep your brother's last letter from me. I've gotten to make few decisions to this point, so I'm making this one. I'm going, not you, end of discussion."

"Are you asserting your authority again?"

"Why not? You already think I'm turning into Zeke. You might as well have a reason to." Then he reached over and blew out the lamp, plunging the room into darkness.

TWENTY~SEVEN

December 18, 1917 –
Clermont Farm, France

FOR THREE WEEKS, PETER AND BILL claimed the barn as their training facility, testing Emil on nuances of the German military and pouring over hand-drawn maps of Le Clé. Peter would seat himself against the stall doors, his bum leg stretched across the aisle to rest while they drilled Emil on every detail. His brother-in-law sat across the aisle, legs crossed as well as arms, somehow managing to accurately return every question. His unexpected competency wasn't making the decision to trust him any easier though.

"What's the full name of the Kaiser?" Peter asked.

"Wilhelm the second."

"And his wife?"

"Augusta Victoria of Schleswig-Holstein."

"And his chancellor?" Bill asked between cigarette puffs. He leaned against the stall beside Peter, blowing smoke rings across the aisle. Behind them one of the mares snorted, probably annoyed with their continued presence sans treats.

Emil hesitated a moment before saying, "Georg von Hertling."

Bill lowered his cigarette, frowning. "You faltered."

"No, I didn't."

"These answers need to come as easily as breathing. These are things anyone billeting in town would know."

"Why would they ask me any of this?" Emil argued. "Won't they

190

assume I already know?"

Bill shook his head as though the answer should have been obvious. "You'll be unfamiliar to them. If they don't recognize you, they'll instantly be suspicious and want to question you. Now, if you're encountered on the street, how do you address a German officer?"

Emil addressed Peter instead. "I thought you said we were sticking to the shadows? Stay to the outskirts, hand everything off to Father Ferdinand, and leave. Why would we even encounter a German officer?"

"Because," Peter explained, "sometimes they scout the countryside and look for signs of resistance. Not all Germans are stupid barbarians like those Hun posters make them out to be."

"I know that. Don't you think I know that?

"That's what we're trying to make ascertain." Bill let another smoke ring float languidly from his lips and watched it trace its way to the ceiling. "We have to consider every way the Jerries could hijack our mission and infiltrate our defenses."

"Thank you, Agent Olmsted," Peter muttered. Like Josie, he appreciated that their friend was so invested, but also like Josie, he thought Bill could take his spy intensity down a notch.

"Now, Emil," he continued, "let's review the occupation mandates. They'll be tacked up on every street corner but remember, actually stopping to read them would draw suspicion. You need to know the contents inside and out from memory."

"'Nine p.m. curfew for all French citizens except those at work for German wants. Any French home, property, or person may be requisitioned for German use at any time without notice." Emil rattled off each restriction like he was reading from a textbook. Peter knew he was tired of repeating the same information every day for a week, but this might be the only chance they had to test his competence on a run. It was their only way to make clear his loyalties which seemed to be rapidly leaning away from *Fides et Spes*'s neutral position.

"What about gatherings? Where would you attend church on Sunday?"

"I wouldn't. All French-organized gatherings, including religious services, are banned. Too many French in one place could lead to mass rebellion. Although to be honest," Emil argued, "Le Clé's citizens would be better off if they did rebel en masse. There are easily more of them than there are Germans."

"More women and children," Bill corrected, "but not men, and the majority of those remaining are unarmed. They wouldn't survive an uprising. It would be a bloodbath."

They both paused to see if Emil would counter any arguments, but he simply gave a roll of his eyes and flicked his wrist for them to continue. Peter really wondered sometimes what was going on in his mind. Did he approve of their role in the war? Did he really want to be a part of it or had Amara somehow persuaded him to join? He had seemed sincere when he accepted Bill's offer, yet to Peter the sudden change of opinion seemed unusual. Why would he put up such a fight only to acquiesce less than twenty-four hours later?

He hadn't brought his suspicions up to anyone though. Not even Josie or Amara. Especially not Amara. He knew he was no longer the key male figure in her life, which he supposed was as it ought to be, but that meant she would share more with her husband than Peter would prefer. Through a series of carefully placed questions and manufactured situations, he would have to make his own decision. Once Emil completed his first successful run, perhaps then he would bring his sister's opinion into the mix.

"Listen, because this is important," Bill said. "Since most of Le Clé's men, like Solange's husband, were rounded up and sent east, every house now has a census attached to the front door. Any Frenchman your age should have already been carted off; however, looking as you do, even not in uniform, the soldiers should assume you to be one of them. If you can't blend in, you give us away. You can't be nice to the French citizens. You have to hate them and you have to act like you mean it."

"It's a rotten lot," Emil muttered even as he nodded anyway. He returned Bill's challenged stare. "Regardless of my personal opinions, I believe I'm well equipped to handle whatever the Boche want to throw at me."

"We shall see, won't we?" Lifting his boot, Bill ground out the now burnt cigarette stub on the sole. He lowered his foot back to the ground and gestured for Emil to stand. "Let's work on your combat skills."

"I thought you were neutral and peaceful."

"We are. That doesn't mean everyone follows those rules."

Combat was the last training challenge Emil needed to complete and they had purposely left it for last. If he couldn't memorize the other information or prove his ability to read a map, there would have been no purpose in exerting effort on anything more taxing.

"First, we'll head down to the creek for some target practice," Bill said. He shoved a crate out of the way, revealing a wooden trap door crafted into the barn floor. Wedging his fingers into a crack between two planks, he pried the boards away from a shallow compartment just large enough for five pistols, a single rifle, and the supply haversack they carried on their run three weeks ago. He removed the rifle and two pistols, showing them to Emil. "These will be yours on the mission. G98, C96, and Browning 1910."

"Brownings are Allied weapons, aren't they?" Emil asked. "Shouldn't everything be German-based?"

"You certainly ask a lot of questions, don't you?"

"You wanted me to 'blend in', didn't you? Wouldn't someone in the *Deutsches Heer* be knowledgeable in their own firearms?"

A sly smile crossed Bill's lips. "That they would." He exchanged the Browning for a different pistol and held it up. "Luger P08. Now, the goal is that you won't need to use them. If you have a reason to draw, odds are your opponent won't give two pence which type of weapon you're waving in their face." He held out the C96. "Let's start with this one."

"I'd rather not. After experiencing that riot last June, even the thought of pulling the trigger leaves me with a sick taste in my mouth."

Both of Bill's eyebrows rose to his hairline. "Weren't you a bobby?"

"Yes, but I was in the morality squad. We never encountered anyone who required more aggression than a little roughing up and a couple firm words."

Nonplussed, Bill offered Emil the pistol again. "This is only one step above that. If you can learn how to slap a man with your words, you can learn to shoot him."

"I'm not sure that logic follows."

"You can't go without a weapon."

"I'll take the weapon when we go. I'm trained to shoot; I just don't want to unless I have to."

"Easy to say when there's no imminent danger." With a sniff, Bill dropped the guns back into the compartment and rose from the ground. He stepped toe-to-toe with Emil, although he still stood about two inches shorter. He lifted his fists, grinding his boot heel against the floor. "You need a good gut punch and you'll clear that thinking right up. Fight me."

"Bill," Peter reprimanded. "Enough." Pushing himself to stand, he cuffed Emil's arm with his mangled hand, making sure his brother-in-law noticed how the fingers couldn't quite curl all the way around. How they would never be able to do so again.

"Emil," he said slowly, "I know you think being in *Fides et Spes* isn't going to change you. Maybe it won't, but there's a better chance that it will. A man changes a lot in a time of war. None of us know where we're going until we're there."

Emil paused, staring at Peter's deformed fingers with that same unnerved glance Amara used the night she arrived at the farmhouse. It had caused an unease in Peter he wasn't sure he would ever get used to.

"He's going to freeze out there," Bill huffed. "He's going to get us killed."

"No, I won't." Emil's eyes snapped up to meet Bill's right before threw up his forearm, thrusting forward to ram it into the other man's chest. Taken off guard, Bill toppled. He fell into the open weapons compartment, landing hard against the barn floor.

Bill stared up at Emil in dismay. "I thought you didn't enjoy violence."

"I don't *enjoy* violence," Emil bit back. "That doesn't mean I can't defend myself given the need." He looked back at Peter, his heavy breaths steaming the frosty air even in the relative warmth of the barn. His expression begged Peter to challenge him again, but Peter knew better than to court a rabid dog.

Peter let the tension linger a moment longer before he said, "Let's take a break, shall we? Cool our tempers, then Emil will show us his aim with a pistol." He continued on before Emil could argue. "Only three shots required; no reason to waste bullets. You find your mark and tomorrow you'll make your first run, no further training required. Sound fair?"

"Fine," Emil said and strode from the barn.

Offering his good hand, Peter pulled Bill up and out of the weapons compartment. "This is a mistake, Pete," he said. "That guy's a liability."

"It's been three weeks since we completed a mission, Bill. We need to get back out there. The letters are piling up and Father Ferdinand probably thinks we both died."

"You don't really think Emil's ready though, do you?"

"As ready as he'll ever be."

"So, that means no, he isn't."

With a scowl, Bill returned the floorboards over the compartment then hefted the crate back into place. "I'll go with him. You know it should be me. You need to stay here and rest."

"I've rested for three weeks!" Peter snapped. "I'm tired of resting. My leg is fine."

"Fine enough to walk ten miles? To crouch behind corners and flee if you have to?"

"I guess we'll find out." The pain had reduced considerably over these weeks of convalescence. His hip no longer ached and his gait had returned to its usual slight limp, the one that would always be there, no matter how much rest he received. He knew there was a chance it would flare up again as soon as he pushed himself too hard, but that was a risk he needed to take. He had coerced Bill into supporting his scheme to bring a third carrier into *Fides et Spes*, so he needed to be the one to lead the mission.

He may not completely trust Emil yet, but Amara did. If Peter was going to send her husband into danger, he needed to be the one to lead him out again.

TWENTY-EIGHT

December 19, 1917 –
The French Countryside

OH, THE THINGS WE DO *out of stubborn idiocy*, Emil thought as he shifted the G98 rifle to his other shoulder. He didn't care for the feel of it, had never liked carrying a weapon at all, and thankfully had never needed to fire one even during his time on the morality squad.

This was different, though. There was a very real chance he would be forced to combat someone, whether that be with his fists or to shoot them outright. He didn't know if he was ready for that. It had been difficult enough to wallop Bill in the barn.

As promised, *Fides et Spes* had outfitted him with an arsenal. Besides the rifle, he carried the C69 pistol at his side and the Luger carefully concealed in a secondary holster against his back. The C69 would be readily available for quick action while the Lugar, primarily issued only to German officers, would remain out of sight, yet easy enough to retrieve. The way Bill geared him up, one would think he had indeed been trained for the Secret Service Bureau, rather than a group of citizen-led letter carriers.

Could he play the enemy's role? He had been born in Germany. He did know the language and looked the part. But he hadn't lived there in over fifteen years. He could barely remember his birth city and retained few traditions from his homeland. When it came to brass tacks, could he really pass for a boot-stomping Boche? His identity was so entwined with being an American now that, despite his agreement to remain neutral, it was impossible to squelch his desire

196

for the Allies to win. He hoped it didn't show.

This is just like when you were on the morality squad, he told himself. *The same as all those other times you pretended with Earhart in order to secure the arrest. You* can do this.

Yes, maybe he could, but should he have to? What were they truly accomplishing except for placing themselves at unnecessary risk? Exchanging a few letters would have little effect on the war's overall outcome; hopefully after this run, Amara would finally acknowledge that.

When she kissed him goodbye, she had laid a hand on the rifle at his shoulder and said, "It suits you." He wasn't sure if she meant it as a jab or a compliment, so all he said was, "I'll be back in two days. I love you."

Based on the warning correspondence from Peter's contact, they would need to cross the Brindille Bridge rather than their usual route along the southern roads. Although the town of Brindille lay on the Allied side of the front, the Brindille Bridge stood at its eastern-most corner and directly opposite the line of occupation, three and a half miles from Le Clé. As they neared, Peter directed Emil off the road where they crept through the trees one careful step at a time. To Emil's surprise, Peter managed incredibly well even with his limp. The weeks of rest must have actually done him good. He was surprisingly spry, maneuvering around the landscape with ease, while it sounded as though Emil's boots crunched every dead leaf and were liable to wake the forest.

About twenty feet inside the tree line, they crouched in the brush, waiting for their best opportunity to cross the bridge. A rudimentary shack had been erected on the far side where a German soldier stood bundled in his grey-green military-issued overcoat. With gloved fingers, he awkwardly turned a page of the book he held, seemingly oblivious to anything else, such as the watch he should be keeping. His rifle was propped against the shack wall beside him.

"This should be easy," Peter remarked in a mere whisper. "Clearly, this area hasn't seen much action or he would be alert and at attention. Likely he isn't the brightest fellow either which is why he received this assignment. Unintelligent men are quick casualties at the front."

"I don't care how stupid he is," Emil said. "He'll still notice if we waltz across the bridge in front of him. Not having me in uniform might work inside the town, but there's no logical reason for a German soldier to be out here in civilian clothing."

"True." Peter reached for Emil's rifle. "I could shoot him."

Emil swung the rifle away onto his opposite shoulder. "You try it and I'll kick your bum leg out from under you." Was his brother-in-law mad? Was that what he meant by the war changed people? Did it make them want to shoot anyone in an enemy uniform, even a non-threat?

He settled a hand on Peter's shoulder. "Is this what these runs are going to be like with you? Reckless impulsivity made manifest? Shoot first, ask later?"

Peter shook him off. He glared threateningly at the soldier beside the bridge. "I really hate the Germans."

"Then do you hate your sister? Do you hate yourself? You're supposed to be neutral, remember?"

"I could never hate my sister." He thumbed towards the bridge. "This is your first test. If you want to stay on our team, you need to get us past that guard."

"How?"

"Doesn't matter. My sister thinks you have a certain charm about you. Maybe you can convince him to let us pass. Or otherwise knock him senseless."

"Or maybe I won't go near him at all."

The answer was so obvious then, Emil couldn't hold back a grin. He led Peter quietly back the way they came, circling through the woods until he was certain the guard could not hear or see their approach. About a quarter mile down the river's bank, he dropped down onto the muddy bed and heard Peter follow lightly. They crouched there against the embankment, watching the guard shack downstream. From this angle, the soldier wasn't visible which hopefully meant neither were they.

Emil gestured to the frozen water, then set one boot atop its surface, testing its weight. It seemed to hold, not a crack underfoot.

He stood again and gestured for Peter to follow him across, but the other man shook his head and mouthed, "No."

"Yes," Emil mouthed back. He pointed across the river then up into the trees beyond. They would sneak past the back of the guard shack and off through the woods before the soldier finished his next chapter.

"Low," Peter whispered. He pushed his hands in a downward motion then lowered himself onto his belly and began to crawl slow and silently across the ice. The extra caution seemed unnecessary—and painfully slow—but Emil matched his position and followed, crossing up into the trees without detection.

"The ice would have cracked," Peter explained when they were finally far enough from the bridge to speak freely. "I could tell it wasn't thick enough. The second you reached the middle, you would have gone through."

A sudden burst of unexpected memory interrupted Emil's attention, filling his mind with thoughts of his sister-in-law, Tena, and the time she broke through the ice while they were sledding. The incident had been partially his fault and he would have never forgiven himself if she had drowned. Thankfully, her now-husband, Reuben, pulled her from the water no worse for wear.

Although it had been five years since then, he should have recalled that event and exercised more caution on the center of the river than on its edges.

"It would have made for a pretty pathetic mission if I died before we even made it there," he said with a light chuckle. Peter didn't return the humor and he knew that Amara wouldn't have either. She always hated it when he used inappropriate humor to lighten a situation. He shifted the rifle so it swung between them. "So, did they, uh, teach you that in the army?"

Peter shook his head. "No, I grew up near the Ammer River. It was one of the skills our father insisted we learn. Amara would have been able to tell the same." He pushed a tree branch out of the way without looking back. "Only another mile to Le Clé. That's where your second test begins."

"I thought we were going to the outskirts to see Father Ferdinand

and exchange letters."

"We are, but that comes later. First, we need to see if the Jerries will accept you as one of their own. You need to walk into the bar and order a glass of anything. Tell them you refuse to pay for it. Then leave and meet me back here."

Emil grabbed Peter's arm, forcing him to turn. "Order a drink?" he asked dubiously. Surely, he expected more of a challenge. "That's all?"

"Yes, that's all."

TWENTY-NINE

December 19, 1917 –
Le Clé, France

EMIL HAD NEVER SEEN so many soldiers in one place in all his life. The streets of Le Clé teemed with them and the bar Peter indicated contained no less than forty military-clad men. They sat around rectangular wooden tables, deep in their conversation, meals, and drinks, which may have been why no one seemed to give notice to his entrance.

Acting calmer than he felt, he sat at the far end of the unoccupied bar top and tried not to think about what his wife would say. Not all too long ago, he used to drink whiskey practically like water. Ever since he began work at the Forsythe and promised Amara he wouldn't drink hard liquor anymore, it had been nothing but cheap mediocre beer. Well, except for that splash of brandy in the barn three weeks ago, but that had been barely more than a swallow.

The bartender offered him a tight smile. A layer of grey speckle covered his low hanging jowls, standing out against thinning white hair across his scalp. He was clearly advancing in years, making him one of the few men not recruited for the French army or taken east by the Germans.

"What can I get you, *sir*?" The man spoke in French-accented German, the final word little more than spittle against his lips. Emil was sure he would prefer to expel it a bit farther and directly into his face. To make matters worse, he realized that he didn't know a single French drink to order and didn't want to ask what the choices were;

that would sound too suspicious. Thankfully, the bartender saved him by saying, "We have many German requests. The transports bring them on the regular; however, only soldiers may order them."

"A glass of *Glühwein* then," Emil demanded, barely restraining himself from adding "please" at the end. Served warm, the spiced wine had been a Christmas favorite of his parents back in England. The entire house would fill with the sweet scents of cinnamon and cloves, then his father would add a traditional splash of rum before toasting to the upcoming new year. It reminded Emil of better times, back when his brother Charles was still alive. Having the drink now, so far away from normalcy, would make him feel like he held a small piece of home.

The bartender nodded, rattling off a sum of French currency Emil couldn't tell was a fair price or not. In this case, it didn't matter. "I'm not paying that, *sir*," he spat back with venom. "I'm a soldier and that deserves respect. You'll mix me a glass without pay."

The bartender turned away, muttering in French, "Filthy German pig."

"Pardon me?" Emil replied, also in French this time.

Startled, the bartender dropped the glass. It broke into five large pieces on the floorboards and elicited a few casual responses from the other soldiers. The bartender's glower was so hostile, Emil wondered if the Frenchman would reach over the bar and knock him clean off the stool. Didn't he understand that such abject defiance could earn him at least a beating and at worst, a death sentence without reproach? What life were these people living that they no longer cared about the consequences?

Emil shifted his gaze to the soldiers who had quickly returned to their conversations and cigarettes, apparently believing he had things well in hand. He was playing the soldier's role, but he didn't feel it inside. Peter would probably tell him to remain stiff and hostile, except Peter wasn't here. Emil would accomplish this his own way.

Removing his cap, he smoothed his hair back then replaced it. Even in the winter weather, his brow lay damp with sweat. "Sorry," he muttered, still in French, the din of the room able to drown out his apology from anyone's ears except the bartender. "Do you have coffee instead? It's been a day like you wouldn't imagine."

The bartender's brows rose slowly, then just as slowly his frown eased. "There's no cream or sugar," he said.

"I prefer it black anyway." *I'm in a bar and I'm not drinking. I need it black.*

"Most of these soldiers don't bother with anything but spirits. I can make you a cup though in my private quarters."

"I would appreciate that. Thank you."

The bartender was about to leave when someone sat beside Emil, a soldier dressed in common uniform. Setting his military cap on the bar top, he ordered an ale—also with no mention of future payment—then turned to Emil with a grin. "Good day, friend," he said in jovial German. Accepting his glass from the bartender, he held it aloft to Emil. "To your health."

Sensing a break in the soldier's attention, the bartender disappeared down a side hallway into the back.

"Sorry, do I know you?" Emil asked the soldier, also in German and rather surprised that his disguise was continuing to fool.

"I don't believe so. You appeared a trifle lost, rather in need of a drinking partner. This your first time in Le Clé?"

"*Ja.* Just brought in from the front. Couldn't wait to have a breath away from the uniform." He had no idea when the last transport from the front had actually arrived, so he thought it best not to provide a specific date of his arrival.

The soldier laughed. "Don't spend too much time dressed like a civilian. The officers don't care for it. They think it dampens our authority." He held out a hand. "Albert Voss."

Emil smiled and gave the man's hand a firm shake. "Emmett Müller, and thanks for the advice. It seems I still have a lot to learn." Like how his former soldier brother-in-law apparently didn't know as much about the *Deutsches Heer* as he claimed.

"Where are you from, Emmett?" the soldier asked.

"München." The morality squad had taught him that a lie was more easily remembered when it was close to the truth. München was not too far from Oberammergau.

"I've always wanted to visit München," Albert said thoughtfully.

"Perhaps after the war." Emil tacked on the words that the man chose not to say: *If I survive.* It was, after all, the same sentiment all the soldiers likely ran through their minds daily.

He glanced towards the darkened doorway the bartender had disappeared into then back to Albert. The soldier studied him, two fingers tapping his glass rim, and Emil wished the bartender would be a little quicker with that coffee.

"Would you excuse me, Herr Voss? I need to visit the ..." Emil hesitated, wondering how soldiers discussed the necessity to relieve themselves. Were they vulgar? Polite? Did they mention it at all or simply stand and walk away? Was he causing more of an issue by debating such a mundane topic to begin with? Oh, the many, many things that Peter and Bill hadn't thought to tell him. Nor had he thought to ask.

Settling upon the middle road, he decided on the German word for toilet and followed it up with an unrefined joke. Thankfully, Albert chuckled and waved him on his way, downing the last of his ale as he did so. "There's an outhouse in back. Go through the Frenchie's quarters; he won't mind."

Emil nodded to the soldier and took off for the same darkened hallway the bartender had disappeared into. He wasn't going to the toilet. He wasn't going anywhere except to find Peter, deliver their letters to Father Ferdinand, and return straight back to the farmhouse.

Barely out of sight of Albert Voss, someone grabbed his arm and yanked him into a side room, aggressively wringing his overcoat sleeve in the process. The cramped area served as both kitchen and bedroom and was barely lit with a single candle and a tiny potbelly stove.

"Who are you?" the bartender growled. "You obviously don't belong here and you're going to give yourself away." The bartender's accent had changed from the French-accented German of the bar to a more natural sound, closer to that of a German native-born. It surprised Emil, but not enough to completely drop his cover.

He jerked his arm away. "Unhand me or I'll have you arrested."

Frowning, the bartender simply stepped around him and closed the door to the tiny apartment room. He turned, his eyes narrowed. "What German soldier says "Unhand me?" They aren't that kind to the French. If you were really one of them, you would have beaten me and called me some foul name." He moved back into the room, pacing around Emil to check the stove, then back again. "Coffee's almost done and you're wasting precious time. They're going to notice something's afoot."

"You dragged me in here. It seems *you're* the one wasting *my* time."

The man was glowering again. He breathed one syllable at a time from lips barely moving, words indiscernible if you weren't standing one foot away. If you didn't know what to listen for.

"Vic-tor-es in bel-lo non sunt."

It took all Emil's willpower and training not to lurch at the phrase. He had believed Father Ferdinand was their only ally in this village. Clearly, that was another account Peter had been mistaken on, or at least chosen not to tell him about.

"*Vince malum bono*," Emil whispered. "How do you know those words? You're not just a bartender, are you?"

"No. But you're not a soldier either."

Retrieving a coffee mug waiting on the counter, he offered it to Emil. Or Emil assumed it was filled with coffee, until he reached for the handle. Tucked inside was a scrap of tightly rolled parchment.

His eyes rolled up to the bartender.

"Take it and leave as though nothing's happened. Then you get that letter where it needs to go. I'll bring the coffee out. I'll act frustrated when I see you've left without drinking it. No one will be the wiser."

"If you make a scene, they could arrest you."

"It isn't about me. That message is important."

A round of commotion went up from the other side of the closed door followed by the sound of the bar door slamming. Another group of soldiers had likely entered the establishment, creating the perfect opportunity for Emil to exit without notice.

Quickly, he plucked the paper from the mug, slipping it up his sleeve cuff. He handed the mug back. "How did you know?" he asked.

"The most recent transport from the front was two new officers. You're not one of them." The bartender paused, letting his intention become clear. "They're billeting three doors down. Be careful." Emil only nodded in response.

He left the bar with a smile to Albert Voss and as normal of a pace as he could muster; however, he really shouldn't have bothered acting so nondescript. The second he stepped out the door, Peter barreled down the street towards him, waving his arms and shouting, "Go! Go!" in English, as though that wouldn't only gain more attention. Behind him a German soldier gave chase, the man's sandy-blond hair peeking out from under his officer's cap.

An officer? Emil thought. *Seriously?* He pulled his own cap closer to his eyes and raised his coat lapels, trying to make his six-foot-two-inch frame appear unnoticeable. How many blunders was Peter going to make on this run? If they survived this, there was no way he was taking on another.

Peter seized Emil's arm and spun him around, dragging him surprisingly well considering he was doing the dragging with his busted hand.

"Peter!" The officer yelled behind them. "Peter, stop! *Out of my way!*"

Glancing over his shoulder, Emil saw the officer shove through a group of Frenchwomen who had carelessly decided to linger in his path. One of them fell, causing the officer to trip over her and land hard in the dirt. It wasn't much of a delay, but enough for Emil and Peter to gain some additional distance. Swearing, the officer jolted back up and continued his pursuit.

"Stop watching him!" Peter ordered. He pulled Emil between two buildings, shoving him down a narrow alleyway barely large enough for one person to stride. When they emerged on the other end, they found themselves approaching the crumbling ruins of a stone church, its altar area and the Marian Chapel the only parts remaining erect.

Peter's haversack and rifle thumped against his back as they sprinted across the open area towards the rubble. Shattered stained glass fragments littered the entire area, creating a colorful artistic effect which reminded Emil of Winnie's more modernist paintings.

Climbing as carefully as they could, they stumbled their way over a mound of broken pews and collapsed pillars, dropping down behind the wall of what he assumed to have once been the Marian chapel. The statues had been removed, leaving a dusty kneeler and burnt candles as the only reminders.

A biplane rumbled by overhead, clearly visible through the nonexistent ceiling. Peter stared up at it, fear behind his eyes, his gnarled fingers clenching the haversack strap with white knuckles. In short order, the plane completed its pass and disappeared from sight. The sound of its engines faded into the winter wind and Peter released a long exhale.

"This is the same church, isn't it?" Emil asked. "The one you were buried beneath during the air raid."

Peter nodded. "See that pew?" He pointed towards the church's main nave where a pew lay overturned. Although caked in stone dust, it was one of the few left unbroken. "That pew is the reason I'm alive. It crushed my hand and my leg, but saved everything else. Father Ferdinand said life wasn't finished with me yet."

"Is that what you think?"

"I think it's no coincidence that I'm back where it all began."

They both quieted again, waiting, listening for shouts or footsteps or another plane to pass by. They couldn't remain in these ruins forever. Eventually they would have to take a chance and leave.

"Do you think he's still following us?" Emil finally asked. "Or did he go back for more men?"

"I couldn't even guess. He was in my regiment, but he wasn't a lieutenant back then. Surprising they would make him one now. Did you get that drink?"

Well, thought Emil, *I suppose that topic of conversation has reached its abrupt end.* He removed the bit of rolled parchment from his sleeve and handed it to Peter. "The drink and this. Did you know the bartender was on our side?"

Peter examined the roll for a second then pocketed it without opening it. "He had been on friendly terms with the Clermonts before Le Clé fell. I had a suspicion he could be involved."

"But you didn't know for sure?"

"I took a risk and it panned out. I would have checked it out long ago except that the bar is frequented by soldiers. Any one of them could have recognized me."

"Like that lieutenant back there?"

"Right."

Irritated, Emil raised on his knees to peer over the rubble and thankfully, didn't see anyone about—officer, soldier, or Frenchman. "I think we've lost him. Let's get to Father Ferdinand and over the border before you take another risk that rallies the guards."

THIRTY

December 20, 1917 –
Clermont Farm, France

PETER AND EMIL WERE LATE. They were supposed to have returned that morning after traveling through the night. Both Bill and Solange assured Amara that it wasn't unusual for runs to be waylaid, returning hours or even a full day off schedule. Father Ferdinand could have requested an additional errand or extra troops could be searching the woods, and Peter and Emil would hide until the danger passed. "Trust me," Bill told her. "Peter is very good at avoiding danger."

His words brought little reassurance though when she kept wondering if she made a grave mistake in allowing Emil to join the deliveries. What if the delay came as a result of his death or imprisonment? The guilt would sit squarely on her conscience.

Therefore, it caused her to literally leap from her chair, sending yarn and knitting needles scattering to the floor, when at nearly nine that night, Peter and Emil finally walked through the farmhouse door. "You've returned!" she cried at the same time Josie laughed from the neighboring seat, a delighted smile transforming her face.

Although her friend had the inhibition to stop a proper distance away from her fiancé, Amara felt no such restraint. Emil dropped his haversack to the floorboards and she rushed into his open arms, her body crushed against his. There were no thoughts of Zeke, only memories of the last two lonely nights in a cold bed sick with dread that her husband may never return. Together, they stood in silence, her cheek upon his chest, listening to the rhythm of his living heart and the feeling of his embrace around her.

"What happened?" she heard Josie ask. "What detained you?"

"We encountered an officer," Peter said. "He recognized me and gave chase."

Josie gasped, one hand splayed against her chest as though her lungs had frozen. Peter on the other hand appeared rather unaffected. "There's no need to worry. We managed to sneak away before the officer caught a second glance. Once he sleeps on it, he'll probably assume he mistook me for someone else. Someone whom he believes is actually living."

Both women looked to Emil for confirmation and he shrugged helplessly. "I honestly don't know if it will come to anything. After ten minutes in Le Clé, I was already convinced that I was an idiot for agreeing to do this and we were all in danger. I had planned to come right back and tell you we were leaving."

"But you're not now?" Josie asked.

He shrugged again. "I don't know how long we'll remain here. All I know is that it isn't yet time to go." He turned his attention to Amara, blue eyes bright with an excitement he hadn't exhibited since before they left New York. "I wish you could meet Father Ferdinand. He's unlike any priest I've ever met. There's such confidence to him, such ... belief in what we're doing. He told me how he says private Mass in order to avoid the restrictions. He prays with the people in cellars and attic spaces while soldiers march past the curtained windows, and he collects letters along the way."

Emil bent for the discarded haversack and eased it open to reveal dozens of letters. "I couldn't believe how many were willing to risk much in order to correspond with their families. Although, it wasn't until I opened one particular letter that I understood how important this all is." Handing the haversack to Peter, he slid a loosely rolled strip of parchment from his coat pocket and held it up. "This is what convinced me." He locked eyes with Solange, seated near the fire. "It's from your husband."

Her own knitting needles clattered to the floor, the attached ball of olive yarn bouncing along behind it. Bill stuck out a foot to stop its motion before it rolled straight into the burning logs.

"It's from Simon?" Solange said, her lips barely forming the words. They emerged like the whisper of the wind as it turns through a mountain pass, in a breathless whistle then silence.

"Yes. He's in prison, but he's alive." Grinning, Emil handed her the letter. She caressed it between her fingers as though it was rations made of gold. It was beautiful to witness as Solange's eyes brimmed over, gentle tears flowing down her cheeks and past her chin as she read. The note was short; unrolled, likely no longer than a few sentences. It wasn't what it said, however, that mattered. It was that Simon had been able to say anything at all.

Solange raised her tear-stained face to look at each of them in turn. "*Merci. Merci.* Oh, I cannot say it enough times! I am so grateful."

Josie crossed the room to sit beside her, enveloping her into a tight embrace. She brushed Solange's scattered curls from her face and ran a thumb across another tear as it escaped her eye. "He is alive," she whispered with a smile. It is a Christmas miracle."

Solange extended a hand to Bill who rose to join her on the other side. He accepted her reach and squeezed her fingers. "This is why you are here," she told him. "Why you are all here. You must not stop delivering letters. There are others like me out there, and they deserve to know."

"They will," Bill told her. "Nothing lasts forever nor will this. The work we're doing *will* make a difference."

"What about the boys?" Josie asked. "Should we wake them? Surely, they'll want to know."

Solange nodded, fresh tears emerging. She sniffed them back, wiping an already-damp sleeve cuff across her cheeks. "Let them rest. I don't want to get their hopes up, but they have waited so long for a letter from their father. I will show them in the morning." She grinned, another sob releasing with a laugh. "All hope is not lost."

With another squeeze to Josie and Bill's hands, she rose. "I will head to sleep now. For once, I believe I will rest easy. *Bonsoir.*"

There was another round of "good night" from all, then Solange made her way from the room, clutching Simon's letter to her heart.

"Can you believe it?" Josie said, her own voice crackling with emotion. She leaned into the sofa cushions and sighed. "We've delivered letters for so long, I wondered if we would ever see our work come to fruition."

"You saw men in the convalescent home read letters all the time," Bill told her. "Sometimes you read them to them."

"Sometimes even wrote them," Peter said quietly, so quietly that Amara believed she might have been the only one to hear him. When she turned to look at him, he was staring at his shoes.

"I know," Josie continued, "but it is never the same as this. This is bringing a dead man back to life, making a widow into a wife. We've given her the possibility of a future that isn't as bleak as it appeared."

"She's right," Emil said. His hands wrapped Amara's waist, drawing her back towards him. "I should have listened to you. As much as I loathe to be wrong, I'll admit I was viewing *Fides et Spes* too simplistically. Their motto isn't an either-or; it must be spoken together. There are no victors in war, therefore we must overcome evil with good. We needed to be a part of it, if for no other reason than to bring Simon's letter to Solange. If we help one person, then I think it was right for you to make me go." He bent to kiss her forehead gently. "I hope you know how much I love you."

He was filthy from the run, his blond hair sticking up every which way, mud caked in his beard, but to her, he was beautiful. She ran her fingers over a patch of stubble along his jaw and managed a smile. "I do. I know."

"I hope so, because there's one more thing I need to tell you." He took her hand and gently kissed her palm before placing it on his chest. "I received Simon's letter from a bartender."

"You were in a bar?"

"Yes, I was and although I initially ordered a drink, I decided to order coffee instead, and I hope you'll believe that."

Did she? She wanted to. She should probably be grateful that he had even admitted to it. She hated that her mind always leapt to the worst conclusions and knew her silence wasn't what Emil wanted. He wanted her to agree immediately and believe every word. He probably needed that assurance as much as wanted it. It was the way her parents had raised her, to be the dutiful wife. Most of the time she was and wanted to be. Then other times the past crept back in, too difficult to ignore.

He stepped away, leaving an abrupt coldness where he had embraced her. The fire's warmth rose at her back, although she still shivered. Then she shivered again when her husband extracted two pistols from beneath his overcoat and handed them off to Peter.

Emil bent low to kiss her. "I'm going to wash up then head to bed. I don't think I'll have any trouble sleeping either." He offered her a sly smile. "Don't keep me waiting too long."

He disappeared down the hallway while Amara stared after him dumbfounded. She felt Peter watching her out of the corner of her eye and didn't want to answer a slew of parental questions about the state of her marriage. She and Emil would be perfectly fine.

Thankfully, Peter shrugged the shoulder holding the haversack and said, "I need to offload our weapons. I'll be along in a while. Wait up for me?" he asked Josie. She nodded and he limped away towards the barn, an extra hitch in his step and Bill on his heels. Josie's worried brown eyes were instead locked on Amara.

"What's the matter?" she asked. She patted the sofa seat beside her and Amara dropped onto it, leaning into the corner of the sofa's arm with a sigh.

"I'm worried," she admitted.

"What could you have to be worried about? Your husband admitted you were right and he was wrong. I'm not married, but I know that doesn't happen every day."

"No, no, that's not what I'm worried over. I'm worried because Emil keeps surprising me."

Josie raised a brow. "And that's bad, is it?"

"One minute he's himself, then the next he's lapsed into this man I thought he had escaped. Now I'm afraid he's changed into some other person entirely. He'll never lose me, but I feel like I'm about to lose him."

"Perhaps he is changing. Change doesn't have to be a misery."

"Except for me it is. My former fiancé was a good man too, caring and kind, before he turned on me. I would have followed him anywhere and did, all the way to America. I always hoped he would come back to himself one day, except he never did. He only changed more and more, and that ended up changing me too." She waved her hand around them, encompassing the house and everything beyond. "What is all of this I'm choosing to embrace? All I ever wanted my entire life was to settle down with a family. Why didn't I stay in New York where I could have had exactly that?"

Josie waved her hand in the same direction Amara had. "Do you know what I see in 'all of this'? I do see a family. I see the men we love working beside us and Solange's three little boys finally having father figures again. Right now, she's enjoying hope of her husband's return after three years of having little. Most of all, I see you and me with bright and beautiful futures. For the first time, I believe my life may exist beyond the war." She looped her arm through Amara's and gifted her with a genuine smile. "This wasn't the life I imagined even six months ago. If this is the change you speak of, it looks rather fine to me."

There in the tender glow of firelight, Amara realized how blessed she was to have this woman for a future sister-in-law. Peter had chosen well. "There are no victors in war, so we must overcome evil with good?"

"Exactly right." Josie squeezed Amara's arm as they watched the fire dim to embers. "What we have here is very, very good. Don't you believe for an instant that God didn't intend this life for you. He meant you and Emil to be here with us exactly as you are."

Later, as Amara settled beneath the bedcovers beside her husband, he offered her a soft smile, which she couldn't help but return. Josie was right. God was very good. They really did have so much to be thankful for.

PART THREE

—

Unknown

THIRTY-ONE

December 25, 1917 – Five Days Later
Clermont Farm, France

THE WEEK BEFORE CHRISTMAS, Josie suggested that Amara send a letter to their landlord in New York, requesting that their personal belongings be boxed and shipped back to Maggie in St. Louis. A note went alongside the request: *My brother is worse off than expected. We will remain here to assist in his recovery.* Enclosed, Amara added enough payment for shipping their possessions. So as not to arouse suspicion, she attached postage to the envelope along with Olmsted Manor's return mailing address.

Josie now stood beside Solange at the kitchen counter, mixing the last of their meager Christmas peace pie while they listened to the others' merry-making waft across the threshold from the sitting room. Yesterday afternoon, Bill and Emil took to the woods in search of the perfect Christmas tree, returning with a balsam beauty that filled nearly half the sitting room. As the holiday's eve progressed, Solange's delicate baubles were hung, Lucien and Maël spinning the glass spheres to catch the firelight like sunshine off sea glass. Emil had lifted the younger brother up to settle his grandmother's heirloom angel upon the highest bough and then each member took turns leading their favorite carols. Renditions sounded in every language from traditional hymns like *Cantique de Noël* and *Stille Nacht* to more secular choices like *Jingle Bells*.

Unable to attend Midnight Mass—or any Mass due to the lack of available clergy—they finished the evening with Solange's lovely reading of the Annunciation and Nativity. The verses had all been in French, but even foreign words of the Savior's birth felt especially meaningful given their unusual circumstances. For the past two Christmases, Josie had celebrated with Father Ignatius and before that with her father. This year she was surrounded by a motley crew of British letter carriers, French resisters, German deserters, and American refugees. She supposed they were her family now. Had her father been alive to meet them, she believed Hunter Harrington would have approved.

Gingerly lifting the doughy crust atop her fingers, she settled it across the pie plate and teased the edges into plump waves. After so long consuming meager portions, her mouth watered with the thought of such deliciousness only a mere hour away. In order to have enough rations for a hearty luncheon, the entire house agreed to skip breakfast the previous week. Not entirely understanding why their already small meals had taken another division, Lucien and Maël complained tirelessly. At least until they returned to their bed pallets on Christmas Eve to discover a spectacular gift from Père Noël: a flat cracker topped with a dollop of berry preserves. Any complaints of missing breakfasts were thereafter erased from memory.

"Do you think this will be the last Christmas of the war?" Solange asked Josie. She portioned berry preserves into a wooden bowl as pie topping and waved her spoon in dismissal. "Oh, I know we think that every year. The first year the soldiers even held that holiday truce and we thought perhaps soon ..." She sluiced another spoonful of preserves from the jar. "After finally receiving news from Simon, I can't help but hope it means there will be peace soon. I cannot stop picturing him walking through that door."

Josie couldn't stop picturing what peace would mean for all of them. Solange would have her family back, her boys finally reunited with their father. Emil and Amara could return to America, free from threat. Bill would be back at Olmsted Manor, likely reneging on his entitlement in order to take on another foolhardy yet surprisingly honorable endeavor. And Josie? Well, she would never have her father return, but she would have Peter. Together they could make a home and begin a family of their own. Where they lived didn't matter much. What a wonder just to be able to leave the sleepless nights of *Fides et Spes* behind them.

"I hope so too," she told Solange sincerely. She reached for her friend's hand and offered a squeeze. "Simon will return. Now that you know he lives, you must not stop believing that."

"Right, right. Of course, you're right. His note was more than I could have asked for. It is enough just to know ... excuse me, I need something from the cellar." She waved her hand before her, spinning out the back door with preserves in hand.

Josie let her go. Some emotions were best dealt with in one's own silence. She remembered all too well the ache of searching the daily post for letters she knew would never come.

A peal of childish laughter rose from the sitting room, quickly followed by stampeding feet. Lucien flashed past the doorway, Maël on his heels, followed a second later by Remy toddling behind them. When Lucien streaked back in the other direction, the force of his slip-stream dislodged Remy's steps, sending the boy in a slow tumble onto his backside. Not to be deterred, the toddler flipped himself onto his knees and crawled away, blabbering vicious insults Josie knew she probably shouldn't laugh at, but did.

She followed the boys into the sitting room just as Emil reached out and snatched both Lucien and Maël's arms. He wrestled them onto the sofa where he and Maël proceeded to tickle Lucien mercilessly. "*Non!*" he cried, "*Arrêtez! Arrêtez!*" but his protests were clearly only for show. The eldest Clermont boy giggled as much as the rest of them.

"How is luncheon coming along?" Amara asked Josie. She sat at the tea table, having paused from her knitting to watch her husband's antics. She had truly seemed to come alive this past week, ever since their talk upon Emil and Peter's return from Le Clé. Josie hadn't known Amara long enough to judge, but it seemed as though her future sister and brother-in-law were finally in a state of rest with one another. Despite the still-lurking dangers, neither's expression held the static apprehension of the past month.

Unlike Peter who seemed to express nothing *except* an

apprehensive attitude. Josie had managed to draw a smile from him here or there, but otherwise he remained stoic. She wished he would invite her into his private thoughts or at least invite her into the barn where he spent the majority of his time alone. Although he acted untroubled by the German officer's recognition, she sensed that the event had set a more dangerous plan in motion. A plan she feared not even Bill would be invited into.

The Englishman lounged across the sofa opposite Emil with eyes closed, although she knew he wasn't sleeping. He never took a nap when others were present. If he did, he might miss a piece of information "useful to the cause."

"Luncheon is nearly ready," she told Amara. "I would guess another thirty minutes. The pie will finish while we eat."

"Lovely," Amara sighed, still watching her husband. The boys now settled, Emil flipped through the Clermonts' Bible in search of a story, the task made more difficult by Remy finagling his way onto his lap. He asked Lucien something in French to which the ten-year-old nodded and accepted the Bible.

Wanting to stay, yet knowing there was no time like the present, Josie tapped Bill's shoulder, which immediately opened his eyes. One brow lifted. "Pardon you, I was sleeping."

"You were not. Do you know where Peter is?"

"Out at the barn, I think. That's where he usually is, isn't he?"

"Almost always."

—

The smell of smoke met Josie at the barn door. She couldn't immediately tell what was burning, only that it wasn't from the home fires and it was too near to be attributed to a neighbor burning brush. The scent mixed sweet with sour, a tinge of cigarettes and something she couldn't place. Thankfully, the air in the barn's main room remained clear, meaning the fire had only recently started. Her nerves didn't sting quite as much with the realization.

"Peter!" No human response met her call, nor either mare's whinny. If the horses weren't disturbed, then the fire must be on the barn's opposite end in one of the unoccupied stalls.

However, when she ran in that direction, she found nothing. Rounding, she raced back again and stopped dead in her tracks beside the first mare's stall, her boots skidding. She braced a hand against the stall door for support. "Peter!" she cried. "What on earth are you doing?"

He spun from his place on the stable floor, knees and hands in the dirt, frantically attempting to sweep a pile of grey ash into his satchel. The ground was littered with envelopes, some clearly empty, the remainder obviously opened, although left intact. One lay to the side half burnt, its singed corners curling upwards.

His good hand lay palm-splayed in the dirt, his damaged one holding open the satchel flap. There was no denial in his eyes. He had been reading the letters. *Burning* the letters. What had come over him? It was against everything *Fides et Spes* stood for!

"Peter, what ... what are you doing?" she stammered. "We have to send every letter on. They belong to someone's father. Someone's son."

He remained silent, crumbling another envelope and letting the pieces fall to the floor from beneath his fingers. He appeared as though he had already said too much by saying nothing.

She knelt, one gentle hand resting on his arm. "Please, Peter, don't exclude me again. You close yourself off and it'll feel as though we have that English Channel between us again. You'll be hundreds of miles away and me wondering where you are."

He ran a furious hand through the ashes, sweeping them out across the aisle and sat back on his heels. "It isn't the same this time. I want to tell you, Josie. I wanted to all along. I was only afraid that if you knew I'd rejected our neutrality, you would want nothing more to do with me. Spying for the Allies and burning damaging intelligence wasn't part of our agreement."

"Then you assumed incorrectly. I love you, Peter. I know your intentions are pure. Even if they are not the same as mine, that does not mean we must be on separate paths."

"It doesn't?"

"Of course not. Your actions may have gone against *Fides et Spes*, but that doesn't mean they cannot be reconciled."

"Reconciled?"

"You need to return to what we stand for, helping the innocents on *both* sides."

He shook his head. "I'm sorry, Josie, but I can't do that."

"This war has treated us all the same. Why should you be allowed to treat it any differently?"

He gathered the remaining envelopes, shoving them back into the satchel as he spoke. Ash from his blackened fingertips stained the cream parchment and Josie thought how the recipients would imagine their loved ones writing in the midst of gun smoke and mortar strikes.

"At first I wanted the same things as you," he told her. "To help people, no matter who they were. Then Bill told me what it was really like, past the newspaper articles which only show part of the story. He's seen the good that can be done by trading more than love letters and family photos, and I wondered what I might be passing along unseen that could make all the difference."

Bill too? All this time she had believed him to be on her side. Then again, she had also believed that Peter shared those same beliefs as well.

"This isn't what *Fides et Spes* is supposed to be about," she argued. "You're risking too much, especially now that you've brought Emil into it. He doesn't even know what he's truly helping with, does he?"

"No."

If she had been a slapping sort of woman, she probably would have just then. "You have to stop him from distributing letters. For your sister's sake, don't place him in any more danger. After the war, you may never see the rest of your family, but don't break that bond you have with her. Let her keep her husband."

Peter flipped the satchel flap closed and stood, lifting the strap onto his shoulder with a scowl. "What about the husbands on the battlefield? Do you think most of them had a choice to stay home and be silent? They had to do their duty, plain and simple. I wish I would have stayed in Iowa, standing behind my feed store counter without a clue what was going on over here. I wish I didn't know. At least if I was ignorant, I could stay away without a guilty conscience. But I know. We all know, Josie. How can we sit by and do nothing when so many other men don't have that option? When at least fourteen other men won't come home because of me?"

She feared this side of him, the guilt that ate at him when she wasn't looking and jumped out to attack when she least expected it. Like the night of the air raid when he blamed himself for the room of children crushed beneath their school building. It haunted him.

"Peter," she said, her voice as calm as she could manage while peering into his untamed eyes. She reached a hand out to him, which thankfully he accepted and then held. "Emil isn't you. I know you feel like you have a debt to pay, but he doesn't. Don't put him in a situation where he has no choice at all. Don't inadvertently turn your sister's husband into a murderer."

"This is war, Josie. Sooner or later, one way or another, war makes murderers of us all." His tone wasn't depressed or filled with fury. It was complacent. Hollow. Worse than if he *had* screamed.

He drew her to her feet. "I'm going to hitch up the wagon. I need to take you somewhere."

"On Christmas?" *Was it really still Christmas?* Days seemed to have passed since she walked into the barn. "We have luncheon waiting for us. Everyone will worry if we disappear."

"Afterwards then. We have enough light to make it there and back. I promise it isn't far."

"Far to where?"

"The Somme battlefields."

Her head started to spin. *The Somme?* She had known it was nearby but had simply tried not to think on it. She didn't want to imagine for too long the place where her father died.

"Why would I need to go there?" she asked. "Why would I ever *want* to go there?"

"Because you need to see it. You need to know what I've lived through. It's the only way you'll ever truly understand."

THIRTY-TWO

December 25, 1917 –
Somme, France

SILENCE. NOT A WORD WAS SPOKEN for all the miles it took to travel through the Somme. The wind seemed to billow in every direction then still. It tugged at Josie's overcoat and stung her eyes then left her once again with an aching emptiness. As though it sensed they shouldn't be there, as though it knew nothing belonged in this desolate place.

She assumed they would find one singular battlefield, contained within easily identifiable boundaries and the rest of the land left unscathed. The truth was a ten-mile expanse of destruction with little sense of calm in between. Even a year after the final gunshots, little appeared to have changed. A landscape of mounds and crevices and abandoned trenches were left, some collapsed, others not. Every so often, Peter left the road to steer the wagon around mounds of debris or hazardous terrain either bombed out or washed away. Even the local fauna knew this to be a place of mourning. Birds flew overhead then seeing no adequate place for nesting, continued past.

She understood that it would not last forever. That wasn't how nature's bounty worked. Someday grass would grow again, green and lush. Someday trees would sprout from the destruction. One day, left to its own affairs, the Somme would be healed. Today, however, was not that day. Today, a broad-brimmed Brodie helmet sat atop a jagged stone as though forgotten when in reality, it marked a memorial to its owner's missing body. It was identical to the one her father had worn.

Josie's eyes stung and this time not due to the wind. She touched Peter's arm. "Please stop the wagon." When the mares paused, she climbed down and stepped carefully through the frozen mud until she lifted the steel helmet with both hands. Even through her gloves, she felt the metal's frigidity. There was no identification either outside or in. For all she knew, it could have been her father's.

She imagined Hunter Harrington standing in a trench here beside his fellow Tommies, likely telling a joke and taking bets on how quickly the battle would be won. He had always been able to win friends easily. It was a shame he hadn't received a command; his men likely would have followed him anywhere. *29 June 1916,* his final letter had read:

Dear Joselyn,

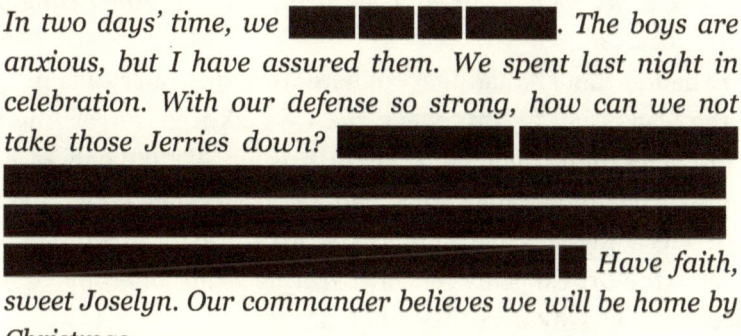

In two days' time, we ▆▆▆ ▆▆ ▆▆ ▆▆▆▆. The boys are anxious, but I have assured them. We spent last night in celebration. With our defense so strong, how can we not take those Jerries down? ▆▆▆▆▆▆▆ ▆▆▆▆▆▆▆▆▆ ▆▆▆ Have faith, sweet Joselyn. Our commander believes we will be home by Christmas.

With Love,
Your Papa

Except he wasn't home by Christmas and neither were 125,000 of his fellow British infantrymen taken in the Somme's battlefields. She hadn't received his correspondence until months later, long after learning of his death. In the commotion of war, the postal bag containing his last letter had been misplaced. By the time the censors had their way with it, there was little left. She thought it a pitiful disgrace, how they couldn't allow her those final words related to a battle now over and a man long gone. She had attempted to read through the black scratches many times over during those first months, holding the parchment up to the sunlight, electric light, and gas lamps, even so close to a candle the paper singed. The censors had been thorough with their job. Those brief lines she received were all she would ever have. Shortly after that, she had been recruited by *Fides et Spes* and pledged to deliver letters uncensored, so no spouse, parent, or child would ever be left wondering.

Now, however, she stood upon her father's burial ground, observing the sharp craters flooded with muddy water, the debris littering the landscape, and the general feeling of hopelessness that seeped from every corner, and she was overcome with fury. *This was where he died*, she thought. *This was the last place he ever saw. Not our home, not a hospital bed. Not me.* In his last moments, her father had experienced nothing but cruelty and devastation. Blown to bits by German mortars with nothing left to find.

You mark my words, Joselyn, he had said. *The Americans will come to save us all.*

They hadn't though, had they? Where were the Americans in 1914 when the war began or 1915 when the U-boats were terrorizing the channel? Why didn't they come in 1916 when her father was here trudging through the mud? She had seen the Doughboys parade through Piccadilly this past August of 1917, waving their flag and listening to the British people cheer. *The Americans will come to save us, Joselyn.* Then why were they still fighting?

Her fingers tightened around the Brodie helmet's rim. It wasn't only the Americans to blame though. Any of the neutral countries could have come to the Allies' aid. Didn't they see how the Central Powers rained terror on everything they touched? Germany had swallowed Belgium whole and taken control of a dozen or more French cities, even bombing some into obliteration. If the neutral countries joined the Allies, there could be a swift victory over the German plague. Instead, they sat silent, watching the front line draw closer and pretending like it wasn't moving.

"How are you?" Peter asked her gently. He was watching her from the wagon seat, allowing her space to consider.

"Not well," she said simply. She returned the helmet to its mockery of a gravestone. "How could anyone be well in a place like this? Why did you bring me here, Peter?"

"Because I wanted you to see what I've seen. You saw air raids, but I saw this. I saw men destroy each other, pieces of my friends' bodies flying through the air. Lice and rats and rotten toes from ice water freezing the skin to our boots. I saw a soldier climb over the top our first week in because he couldn't handle the terror." He paused, inhaling deeply, his expression apologetic, no doubt from whatever emotion he saw in hers.

"I know this isn't polite conversation for a woman," he continued, "and my fiancée no less, but I need you to understand. Being neutral won't end the war. It can't. Being neutral lets the horrors continue unchecked." He waved his hand across the battlefield. "How can you turn a blind eye once you've seen this?"

She faced back to the destruction, the wind swirling tendrils of brunette hair against her face. She tucked them behind her ear and heard the wagon bed creak as he stepped down beside her. The horses stamped the frozen mud and snorted into the silence, but she didn't turn, not even when he placed a gentle hand on the small of her back and drew her close.

"Please understand," he said. "I love you. I want what you want. I just want it a little differently than you do. The Allies are growing closer every day. We only need to find the right person, the right piece of intelligence, and we can help them end it."

Had she been wrong to join *Fides et Spes*? To remain neutral when her father fought and died so valiantly for the Allies? There was good and evil on both sides though, wasn't there? British and French troops killed Germans too, brave men like her father who only wanted to serve their country. German men with families of their own— children, wives, and sweethearts. Men like Peter who pledged loyalty, but longed for peace. A band of innocents caught in the middle. *Focus on the innocents, Josie.* It was the innocents she had always focused on, yet it had only brought them to this.

She laid a hand over the identification tags strung beneath her blouse. Their oval shape pressed against her sternum; their metal warmed against her skin. In July 1916, they were discovered somewhere on the land where she now stood. Right where the rest of her father would be forever buried, the story of his final moments silenced beneath the muck. All around the world, children mourned because soldiers like her father, like Peter, did their duty.

"What are you planning?" she whispered. "Tell me how I can help."

—

They rode back to the Clermonts' farm in silence, Josie's arm woven tightly through Peter's and his hands clutching the reins. Once again, the situation had changed between them. Had the normalcy she believed she saw on Christmas Eve been a phantom star, a trick of holiday cheer like Scrooge's ghosts?

They climbed from the wagon and returned to the farmhouse for the remainder of the festivities. They acted as though they had only been out for a romantic Christmas ride. That evening she climbed into bed and pretended to sleep, all the while waiting for the two o'clock bell to chime. Then she donned her dressing gown and walked towards the barn, boots crunching frozen earth. She climbed to the hayloft, kissed Peter goodbye, and returned to the house without a word.

THIRTY-THREE

December 26, 1917 –
Clermont Farm, France

EMIL HEARD THE FARMHOUSE'S front door close shortly after the two-o'clock bell, soft footsteps tapping down the hall and ending in Solange and Josie's room. It wasn't the front door or the footsteps which woke him though. The truth was he never fell asleep. He had lain awake since eleven, listening to the sound of his wife's soft steady breathing, thinking about what Josie told him after dinner. She had drawn him aside while Amara helped Solange ready the children for bed.

"Peter's being reckless," she had said.

Emil couldn't help but laugh. "No news there. He's always reckless." Josie, however, only returned a stony stare.

"He's been reading the villagers' letters and passing anything important back to the American War Department. Except he isn't considering the consequences to *Fides et Spes*. He's wearing blinders like a horse at the races and I'm afraid it will be our ruin."

"Why are you telling me this?"

"Because Peter's agenda doesn't match the one you agreed to. You shouldn't participate in another delivery without understanding exactly who you're helping."

Amara's sweet voice lighted from Solange's bedroom, wishing the boys a peaceful rest. Seeing as she couldn't speak a lick of French, her return would be imminent. They needed to finish their conversation before she heard him declare what he was about to.

He turned back to Josie, speaking quickly. "Listen, I agree that everyone deserves news from their loved ones, but in my heart, I'm more American than I ever was German and I want the Allies to win. I'm not going to condemn Peter for working towards an outcome I'm also rooting for." He tipped his chin, blanketing her with his best police interrogation stare. "You're from England. Isn't that what you want, too?"

Like a criminal with everything to hide, she avoided his persistence in exchange for a glance towards the drawn blackout curtains. "If only it were so simple," she said. "You should ask Peter about his other plans." She left him then, walked out of the house, and let the door slam behind her.

Emil hadn't told Amara any of this yet. She had been so happy these past few days, like a new person—like the intriguing woman he fell in love with—that he didn't want to ruin the wonder. Especially not on Christmas. In bed beside him, her gentle breaths fell warm against his shoulder. He wanted to stay here forever, close his eyes, and never breathe a word of what he knew. Let the water pass under the Brindille Bridge, so to speak. Whatever Peter was planning, he could manage on his own, couldn't he?

Except Josie's comments about Peter's recklessness kept tossing around Emil's mind. He knew he wouldn't help his marriage by allowing Peter to do some fool-headed thing which could possibly lead to an early demise. They had traveled all this way specifically to find him. If he perished now, they may as well have remained in New York. Best to get it all out in the open and let the dust settle before Emil faced his wife at dawn's early light.

Easing himself out of bed, he silently changed out of his night clothes, tugged on his boots, and exited the room, leaving the door slightly ajar rather than risk waking Amara when the latch caught. He tiptoed past Bill sprawled across the sitting room sofa, the opposite sofa empty as Emil expected it would be. Snatching his winter coat off the crowded wall pegs, he buttoned the front and walked across the chilled night towards the barn. Sure enough, a lantern flickered in the hayloft window. Peter was awake.

Low clouds whispered across the night sky with the promise of impending snow, their expanse blocking the moon and leaving the barn's interior indiscernible. He heard the mares prancing in their stalls, irritable, although from what he couldn't tell. Perhaps they knew Peter was up to something too? More likely, they heard Emil's entrance and wondered why they had received another unexpected visitor in the dead of night.

Rustling sounded from the loft above, although looking up, the lantern's slow flicker was the only movement he could see. He climbed the loft ladder one steady rung at a time, silently making his way to the top. If the rustling he heard was merely Peter rolling over in his sleep, there would be no need to disturb him. Emil would sneak back to the house and back into bed and for one more night, hope Josie's worry was for nothing.

Unfortunately, he had never been that lucky. Peter knelt in the hay, folding a pair of trousers which he then placed into the haversack beside him, the same haversack they used to carry supplies into Le Clé. He was going on a run? Now? Alone?

Emil hated to agree with Josie, but it appeared Peter was indeed treading dangerous waters.

"What are you doing?" he asked before he even finished drawing himself off the ladder. Startled, Peter spun, falling back onto his hip with a grunt. He rubbed his worn knee and frowned at Emil. "Are you a spy sneaking up like that?"

Emil pushed himself up to stand, stepping away from the loft edge while swiping bits of hay off his trousers. "I'm certain I'm not, but are you?"

Peter didn't even hesitate. "I deliver letters, you know that."

"Then what are you doing in the middle of the night packing a full sack of supplies?" Emil peered into the haversack. "You're either up to something or you're deserting us and the latter doesn't exactly seem your style."

Peter's frown deepened into a grimace. "Except I am a deserter." He returned to his bag, shoving in a crumpled shirt. "I deserted America to fight for Germany, then I deserted Germany to join *Fides et Spes*, then I deserted Josie and returned to France."

"So, now you're deserting everyone? Are you switching sides?"

"There are no sides to take in *Fides et Spes*."

Emil stepped carefully across the hay until he was practically right on top of his brother-in-law. *Keep the high stance.* That was one of the traits Captain Alberts taught him in morality squad training. *If you lower yourself to the criminal's level, they feel they hold the power.* Peter wasn't a criminal that he knew of; however, the same principle applied. "Josie told me you're spying for the Allies."

Peter half-turned, his grimace now replaced with a wry smile. It was an odd expression really, as though he was actually pleased Emil knew. "Does Amara know?" he asked.

"Not yet, but don't you think she should?"

"In time."

"What does that mean, 'in time'? Whatever you're up to, you need to trust her with it right now. I tried to hide things from her before, important things, and it brought us to where we are now."

"No," Peter corrected. "My letters brought you to where you are now." He finished rolling a blanket into the haversack and cinched the ties. He slung it over his shoulder and stood, meeting Emil's interrogation from several inches shorter. "Hopefully by tomorrow I can find the key that ends the war and then I'll tell her everything."

So, Emil thought, *there is more to all of this than simply saving a priest.* "It's too large a task," he reasoned. "No matter what you did out there on the battlefield, you can't make up for it by throwing yourself into danger. Putting your life on the line won't fix this."

"The sooner the war ends, the fewer people die. The fewer soldiers who go mad in the trenches. Fewer widows, fewer orphans. The sooner it ends, the sooner we find normal again. I can barely remember a time now when I didn't search the sky for Gothas, when I set food on the table and knew there would be some again tomorrow. By now the limp in my leg feels as regular as breathing." Peter clenched his gnarled fingers into a fist against his chest. "I don't want this life for my family, Emil. I want to marry Josie without fear that the world could take me tomorrow."

"It might. I didn't let that stop me from marrying Amara."

Peter's attention veered to the hayloft window and Emil realized he needed to get back to the point. He struck out and grabbed his brother-in-law's shoulder, forcing the man to pay attention.

"Look, Peter, I'm not going to stop you from spying. I applaud you for it, actually. However, don't be foolish enough to counter the Central Powers on your own and think you'll still live to marry Josie."

"I'm not."

Now Peter did smile, a wide, almost boyish grin. The grin Emil recognized from prisoners who thought they had finally pulled one over on the police. "Why do you think Josie told you I was being reckless? She did it because I asked her to. If you thought I was making another mistake, I knew you would come running to stop me."

Now Emil was really confused. "You want me to stop you?"

"No. I want you to help me. We only need to find the right person, the right piece of intelligence. If we find our way in, we can end this together. But if I asked for your help outright, you would have dragged my sister into it before we had our plans aligned. You wouldn't want to tell her until you had all the facts. Right, detective?"

Emil shook his head in amazement. "You *are* taking too many risks. How do you know I didn't lie before? Maybe Amara already knows everything."

"She doesn't." Peter turned away, kneeling to kick a foot over the side of the loft onto the ladder. He dropped the haversack to the barn floor where it landed with a thunk. "If you told her, she would have followed you. Grab the lantern on your way down, will you?" He started to descend the rungs far faster than Emil would have credited him for given his limp. He hopped down from the last rung, hoisting the haversack back to his shoulder, and waited for Emil to follow.

"What's the plan then?" Emil asked when he arrived at the bottom. The lantern created a thin pool of light around them, casting long shadows across the floor. "How do you plan to stop an army with a haversack and a few pistols?"

"By using my contacts. Nepotism isn't useful only in business. Remember the lieutenant who chased us through town? That was my cousin, Zeke Rohrbaugh. I think I can convince him to turn spy for the Allies."

"*What?*" It took everything in Emil not to let revulsion flood his expression and he thanked the low lantern light for concealing most of what he did reveal. That creep was here? Only ten miles away from where Amara slept? So, war hadn't dealt him the miserable death, or at least maiming, that he deserved after what he did. If Emil had known that the officer chasing them was responsible for the worst days of his wife's life, he would have thrown his peaceable nature aside and pummeled him. Zeke probably wouldn't mind if the entire Allied army burned so long as it earned him another promotion. And Emil cared very little whether Zeke simply burned.

Somehow, he managed to grit out, "What makes you think he will?"

"Zeke doesn't care who wins so long as it's the side he's on. He told me so. If we can convince him the tide has turned in favor of the Allies, I believe he'll decide to help us."

Peter had a point, Emil loathed to admit. If Zeke could pass enemy information to the Allies, he could be a substantial asset and possibly blow a hole in Germany's defenses on the Western Front. If he believed the Allies had a greater chance of victory, he would likely switch sides, if for no other reason than to save himself.

The plan was still playing with fire, though, and praying they didn't get burned. Peter didn't know about Zeke's cruel nature towards Amara, details Emil did know which made him question this plan's likelihood for success. But if he revealed how Zeke abused Amara for years right under her brother's nose, Peter would do one of two things: either shut down with guilt over it all and not even try, or more probable, rage straight after Zeke without giving rational thought to the repercussions. No, if they were going to attempt this, they needed to be level-headed. This plan required finesse and careful calculation from someone who could say all the right things and match Zeke's smarmy arrogance stroke for stroke. Obviously, the plan needed Emil.

"Very well, you've convinced me. I'll come with you." Emil headed for the hidden weapons compartment, taking the lantern and the light with him. "Alone this is a fool's mission. With me, it has a chance of success."

Setting the lantern on the floor, he shoved the barrel off the secret compartment and knelt to pry back the loose floorboards, trying to ignore the substantial wringing in his gut. He knew what needed to be done and also knew that he didn't want to do it. To succeed, he would have to play nice with a man he despised, which went against everything in his head and his heart.

He extracted two pistols and holsters from the compartment and held one of each out to Peter. "Here's what we're going to do. I've spent my life smooth-talking my way out of problems and chasing down criminals, so I'll be the one to meet with Zeke and gauge the situation. If he responds positively, then we'll bring you in to close the deal."

Accepting the pistol, Peter slid it into the specially designed holster and secured it around his middle. "Shouldn't it be me? He is my cousin after all."

"You deserted the German army and made him believe you to be dead. His opinion of you is likely sullied, hence the chasing. He hasn't formed an opinion of me yet."

Peter's brow furrowed, thick shadows made even darker in the lamplight. "My sister will hate me if I bring you."

"Well, mate, you should have thought of that before you asked."

"Maybe we *should* tell her before we go. Josie knows. It's only fair."

This plan just kept getting worse, Emil thought. If they told Amara, he worried she would be all too in agreement with the decision. Even after everything Zeke put her through, she still wanted to believe the best in him. That he could be turned back to the boy she knew as a child. Her hope for his soul remained, the desire for redemption of the man she once loved. It wasn't something she spoke of often, not nearly enough to justify the jealous pangs Emil had experienced lately. He knew she didn't love Zeke that way anymore. But sometimes he felt that she was simply waiting for him to mess up again, for him to fall off the wagon, roll through the mud, and drop into a ditch she wouldn't want to help him out of again. Even after traveling all this way together, proving himself to her time and again with barely a drink to calm his nerves, sometimes he felt his past betrayals would never be forgotten in her eyes. Just as sixteen years of fond memories related to Zeke sometimes blinded her to the reality of his cruel nature.

Fine. Emil would admit he felt threatened. Even though Amara married him, not Zeke, he felt like he was still competing to win her. He felt like nothing was ever enough for her lately, that she had swept him into the same dustpan as her abusive past relationship and expected him to be the same. He wanted to face his nemesis, if for no other reason than to kill the ghost which haunted them and prove once and for all that Zeke was a miserable louse with no hope for reform. If there might be a chance to return her cousin to their favor, it would only reaffirm her belief in his inner goodness and strengthen her need to retain it. If Emil told her their plans, she would insist on going with them and seeing her with *him* would only make Emil's inner demons run wild. What if Zeke struck her or insulted her? What if this time he killed her and Emil had to watch it happen?

Never.

He hadn't saved her from an unruly mob, sheltered her from imprisonment, traveled an ocean, and lived in a drafty room with meager food for months, only to allow her to run off and endanger them all.

He strapped on his own pistol and rolled his shoulders, rebuttoning his coat one painful clasp at a time. "We'll leave Amara a note. By the time she reads it, we'll be well away. You don't want her following us, do you?"

Peter nodded slowly. Emil, frankly, could barely believe they were doing this. Was he about to leave Amara widowed and his parents with only one son? He had only recently reconciled with his father. He was finally on decent speaking terms with his brother, Fred. He thought of their oldest brother, Charles, lost on *Titanic* almost six years ago. *Am I being a bloomin' fool?* He pictured Charles's expression, stark reality painted across his features, and Emil finished his own question. *Don't answer that.*

"What will I be doing while you're with Zeke?" Peter asked.

"Why, you'll be breaking into his room, gathering information." Emil gave an overconfident—and incredibly false—grin. "That way if I fail and your mangy cousin blows my brains out, well, at least we managed to steal everything that Jerry had."

—

Peter followed Emil to the edge of the Brindille Bridge, crossing the now fully frozen river without incident. There was no guard posted outside to spot them; another lucky pass. He doubted their luck would hold out forever though. With a sigh, he adjusted the haversack on his shoulder and reached into his coat pocket for a cigarette, thankful to fill his lungs with its soothing properties. It would be his last until they returned. Any closer to town and the smell would indicate human presence to any soldiers in the vicinity.

He was glad Bill didn't know about this particular run, or that he decided to bring a pack of smokes with him. He didn't need to hear *again* how he was taking too many risks. He knew he was.

Zeke had been furious with Peter when he sent Amara to St. Louis instead of bringing her with them to Germany. His cousin had literally shoved him into the street outside the Hoboken piers, Peter narrowly missing his end upon the hood of a motorcar. They barely spoke after that, even when they were positioned practically side by side in the trenches. While Peter hesitated with every pull of the trigger, Zeke shot seemingly without qualm. When Peter hid his tears until the cover of nightfall, Zeke leaned against the muddy walls, cigarette smoke leisurely curling from his lips up towards heaven. Peter hated every minute of his time as a soldier and it worried him how calm his cousin was towards a job with only one requirement—to kill. Only once had Peter asked him about it, one day when they happened to pass on a walk to opposite ends of the trench. The mud felt firmer underfoot, the stench of death and vermin only slightly less stifling than unbearable. Wooden slats once laid for makeshift floorboards now sank in a layer of crusted mud, providing a muted *thud-thud-thud* whenever someone crossed over them.

Peter asked Zeke if it bothered him that they could be firing at soldiers they used to call countrymen. "It was only a few months ago that we were Americans ourselves," he said. "Don't you ever consider if maybe we should be over there instead?"

"I don't really care who wins or loses," Zeke had replied. "Both sides are wrong, both sides are right. It's all in how you look at it. Yesterday, I was an American, today I'm not. In war, there are no heroes; only villains who make their villainy appear heroic. Don't think that would change if you fought under forty-eight stars rather than the imperial eagle. Germany has the best chance of winning. That's the only reason I'm not still in Iowa selling horse feed and saddle polish."

Peter had thought about those words often since, about whether right and wrong were nothing more than a matter of opinion, a matter of which side you happened to be on. He figured there had to be a line somewhere. He just wasn't sure yet where that was.

It had to end. That was all he was certain of right now. One way or another the fighting, the oppression—the killing—needed to end.

Zeke might not be the best chance to end it. But right now, he was the only chance they had.

—

The next morning, Amara woke to Emil missing from their bed. A small square note lay on his pillow, folded over only once. She saw Emil's familiar handwriting, his curling script forming the letters of her name, and she had no need to open it. She knew.

Tossing off the bedcovers, she ran in stockinged feet from the house, the front door banging back against the wall behind her.

"Amara!" Solange yelled as she passed. "Amara, your coat!"

She didn't turn back. The cold was barely with her as she entered the barn to find it empty. The loft as well. Hay poked through her stockings and scraped her skin from where she knelt upon it.

Josie breathlessly climbed the ladder after her. She held out Amara's winter coat, her own dangling open from her shoulders.

"It isn't a normal run this time, is it?" Amara asked quietly.

"You don't truly want that answer, do you?"

Outside the loft window, the sky was grey. Grey and dismal. "Yes, Josie," she said. "I think it's time you told me everything."

THIRTY-FOUR

December 26, 1917 –
Le Clé, France

PETER AND EMIL MOVED THROUGH Le Clé's alleyways and shadows, the sky grey above them. Grey and dismal. Within the next day it was certain to snow. The air smelled ripe with it. Peter only hoped the storm held off until they returned to the farm.

Le Clé wasn't decorated for Christmas. No evergreen wreaths, no holly. None of the usual cheer he missed from holidays past back home. Instead, any merriment had been exchanged for blackout curtains and armed soldiers in the street. One day was always the same as the next. To the villagers who remained, there were few reasons to celebrate anymore.

So as not to draw suspicion, they lurked in the church ruins until well after daybreak, when villagers and soldiers alike would wake and start their rounds. From Peter's few visits to the village during his enlistment, he recalled that the officers tended to take breakfast at their residence then depart for tactical meetings. Unfortunately, he couldn't recall the location of those meetings, which meant Emil would need to intercept Zeke between him leaving the residence and arriving at the next location. If they didn't time it right, they would have to wait until that evening to attempt negotiations.

They squatted beneath the kitchen window of the two-story officers' quarters, backs to the white-plaster wall, practically holding their breaths while they listened for the tell-tale signs of breakfast to end. After twenty minutes, Peter's right leg started to ache from the strain of one position. He debated if he could stretch it out beneath him when footsteps finally moved across the room above followed by the clatter of china. A woman's grumble followed and a cabinet closing. More racket and the back door opened, a gush of dishwater being thrown out into the alleyway, drops of mud splattering up onto both men's pants. Thankfully the door closed immediately after and Peter released a relieved breath.

"I think it's time," he whispered. One glance at his friend's face, however, told him that Emil didn't appear at all certain of his task. "You don't have to do this, you know," he told him. "I won't think less of you if you want to leave."

"I know, but I would think less of me." Emil eased upward, peeking through the window before he rose fully. "All clear now. Let's go." He turned the doorknob and found it eased inward. He closed it again. "Unlocked. That makes it easy for you. Head upstairs and I'll go around front to intercept Zeke."

Peter grabbed his friend's arm, holding him back. "What's your plan for convincing him?"

"Take him to the bar. Most men are willing to negotiate once they've had a couple drinks."

"The hour is still early and Zeke doesn't drink."

Emil frowned. "He doesn't?"

"No. He never cared much for the taste. Do you have another option?"

Emil's frown immediately flipped into a sly smile. "Of course. I had to coerce people into all sorts of things while on the morality squad. You leave everything to me."

He attempted to turn away again, but Peter kept a firm grasp. He kept remembering Emil's earlier comment about Zeke blowing his brains out. "You're sure?"

"Peter, please." Gingerly, he lifted Peter's hand away and dropped it to his side. He backed off down the alley with that same self-assured grin. "I'll take care of it. Now get upstairs and steal some intelligence."

With that, he jogged away down the alley and around the corner. Now that the plan was in motion, Peter needed to act quickly. He couldn't afford to be in an officer's quarters when his cousin returned.

Easing the door open, he allowed only a second to listen for footsteps then stepped silently through the kitchen. The stove's fire heated the small space, further moistening his neck already slick with nervousness. He swiped a hand across it and wiped the excess on his overcoat as he moved on toe across the room and peered around the corner. All clear.

Without hesitation, he hurried down the hallway and up the front staircase, managing to stay relatively silent all the while. Luck was with him as the upstairs hall also lay empty and he slipped into the first bedroom without notice. Right away he could tell he was in the right place. The personal belongings gave it away immediately. The washstand held his cousin's monogrammed shaving kit and on the floor beside it, a military-issue haversack stamped "S. Rohrbaugh." A deck of playing cards sat on the nightstand next to a recently used ashtray and two packs of cigarettes. The tang of tobacco hung in the air.

Zeke hadn't brought much with him the day they traveled to Berlin and hadn't acquired much since. Despite his often-gruff personality, his room back in Iowa had always been tidy. Careful not to disturb anything, Peter opened drawer after drawer, searching as quickly as he could with one ear directed towards possible movement at the door.

Sliding his hand under the mattress, he came across an unlabeled manilla file, stuffed full. *This has to be something!* he thought and would have opened it if not for a disturbance on the street below. Shouts rang out, shifting his attention fully to the window. Edging the curtain aside, he watched as a German soldier dragged a French girl down the street, his grip fierce on her arm as she struggled to free herself. With her tattered coat and sunken cheeks, it was difficult to place her age, but Peter thought it unlikely to be much older than nine. Even so, the few onlookers turned a blind eye, proceeding on to their respective locations, knowing that to interfere was inviting their own punishment.

All of them except for one.

From the front stoop directly below, he saw Emil step into the street. One hand rose to hover against the pistol hidden under his overcoat.

Peter felt torn between running down the stairs to help and screaming, *"Don't do it! This sort of injustice happens all the time!"* Ever since the *Deutsches Heer* took control of Le Clé, they had imposed on the French people from every angle. They forced new restrictions, took food from families who had little to begin with, and billeted in whomever's house they wished, bedding whomever's wife or daughter that they wished. Peter had never performed such atrocities and thankfully neither had the fellow soldiers he called friends, but he had heard first-hand accounts from those who did. Sometimes they brought a French family's hard-earned rations back to the trenches and Peter's stomach would turn over. He ate because he was hungry too, but it always sickened him.

Emil took another step forward, the hand opposite his pistol clenched into a fist. If he defended the girl, they would question him. Without proper identification, they would know he was an imposter and arrest him. Their mission would fail.

Shoving the folder into his haversack, Peter clomped down the stairs, heedless to the noise. The house was still empty for now, although he couldn't say where the other occupants currently were or when they would return. Zeke at least hadn't been among the crowd on the street.

Opening the front door, he stopped still on the stoop.

Two soldiers had Emil by both arms, restraining him as he tried to get to the soldier who contained the struggling French girl. A fourth soldier pressed his nose inches from Emil's, screaming such obscenities that Peter hoped his brother-in-law forgot how to translate his birth tongue. Then the soldier lifted one finger and demanded they take him to the cellar.

What cellar? Peter thought in a panic. Where was the cellar? What would happen to him there? Was that where they performed prisoner executions?

Emil lashed his foot out, striking the profane soldier in the knee with enough force to tumble him into the man holding Emil's right arm. The two soldiers drove him to his knees, yanking his arms backwards until he visibly winced. With the sickening sound of flesh against fabric, the profane soldier drove a punch to Emil's stomach and the French girl screamed, drowning out his resulting groan. With a swift motion, they were carted off in opposite directions.

Peter could only pursue one of them. Saving Emil would secure the mission, although there were a number of guards and only one of him. He would likely end up captured himself. If he followed the girl, he would only have one soldier to contend with, but what would he do with her once he rescued her? Should he wash his hands of the whole affair, chalk it up to the results of war, and sneak back to the farm he currently called home?

Josie's oft-repeated phrase chose that moment to cross his mind: "Focus on the innocents, Peter." She always had the right approach to *Fides et Spes*, passing letters for the good of families, rather than viewing it as a battle tactic. Of course, his approach wasn't necessarily bad—ending the war would save families too—but even if he did rescue Emil, there was still a chance that Zeke wouldn't follow. Was a hypothetical chance more important than the living girl right in front of him?

Emil and Josie would both tell him to save the girl.

Peter followed the sound of her screams, ducking into doorways whenever he caught sight of an approaching soldier. Even if the villagers noticed him tailing the girl, he knew they wouldn't interfere. He could still make out the girl's muffled cries of resistance as the soldier shoved her through the doorway of a rather ramshackle home.

Without any more thought, he opened the front door as though he belonged there, surveying the scene with disgust.

The soldier had the French girl pinned to the sofa, both of her thin arms restrained in one hand while he maneuvered open her overcoat buttons with amazing swiftness. When she saw Peter enter, her eyes widened in horror, no doubt assuming he planned to make her situation worse. "*Non!*" she screamed. She writhed beneath the soldier, attempting to kick her legs out from where they were trapped beneath him. She shouted a stream of French that only resulted in the German soldier slapping her full force.

Gripping the man's overcoat, Peter hauled the soldier off of her and onto the floorboards. Before the soldier could fully comprehend who had assaulted him, Peter held his hand out to the girl. "Hurry! I am here to help." Not knowing the translation in French, he said it in English and hoped she would understand. She gaped at the man on the floor in terror.

The soldier leapt at Peter's ankles, knocking him backwards into a side table. The fragile wood toppled, breaking into pieces as he landed atop of it. His knee twisted painfully to the side and he shouted out of instinct. Grasping the soldier by his lapels, he rolled and sent a punch to the other man's jaw that felt like his hand was breaking all over again. He had forgotten that his dominant hand was already busted and in no shape for a fist fight. Now those fingers hung limp, blood throbbing through every digit.

With his left, he pulled his pistol and aimed it at the soldier. His aim wasn't as good, but he suspected it would prove competent enough at close range. "Stay there!" he shouted in German. "If you move so much as an inch, you're dead." He saw the man's attention shift to where his rifle lay near the sofa. Only officers were typically issued pistols. Probably acknowledging his disadvantage, he remained where he was.

Without taking his eyes off the soldier, Peter directed his next question to the girl. "Do you have family here?" he asked in English. Silence. He tried again. "*Famille*? Maman? Papa?" At least he knew those few words from hearing Solange and her sons say them.

She shook her head, mussed hair flying. "*Non, pas de famille. Seulement moi.*"

Non meant *no*. He didn't need to know the rest. She had no other family and so much the better. He offered her his injured hand and cringed when she clasped it. Her grip was like a vice.

"You won't escape," the soldier spat. "My fellows are everywhere. They will apprehend you."

"They can try." Peter backed the girl behind him, momentarily releasing her hand to sling the soldier's rifle over his shoulder on the way to the door.

Hiding in the shadows, they maneuvered their way back to the forest, racing through the trees to place as much distance between them and the soldiers as they could. He helped her across the uneven terrain, clutching her small pale hand in his larger one, all while trying to soothe the girl's fears in a language she didn't recognize. When she began to cry, he gave up trying and swung her up onto his back, jostling the haversack and rifle across his front instead. His right leg protested with the effort, but thankfully, she secured her petite arms and legs around him, relieving some of the strain.

By the time they reached the Brindille Bridge, his entire right side was screaming, but he didn't allow himself to rest. Only when they were safely on the opposite side of the border, did he lower her down. She awkwardly slid from his shoulders and ran behind the shelter of some brush, the sound of sobbing heard shortly thereafter. He decided to allow her a minute to grieve. Not only had she suffered trauma, but could never return to her home.

He opened the file he had swiped from Zeke's room, the one that appeared so official at the time. Inside was nothing more than his cousin's personal transport papers, letters from his parents, and a flyer listing Le Clé's new German laws, the same as hundreds plastered around the village. A packet of inconsequential information.

He stared at the papers in his hands, his heart sinking lower than the frozen earth beneath his feet. He had taken Emil to his doom and had nothing to show for it. They were no closer to ending this war than when they began.

—

Josie didn't sleep that night. She couldn't. She and Amara lay side-by-side, awake and waiting. They watched the shadows creep across the room until near sunrise when Josie sensed a stillness followed by Amara's soft and steady breaths. Her friend had finally found some ease in her worries while she, rather, knew the risks much better and could not keep them from tromping through her mind unchecked.

Slight streaks of purple velvet had just graced the sky when a soft tap sounded at the bedroom door. *Could it be Peter and Emil?* she thought hopefully. Carefully, she slid herself out from under the bed covers, careful to tuck them back into place before the warmth could escape. Her toes, however, curled as soon as they hit the icy planks and she hurried to secure her dressing gown, although its material too was chilled.

Rushing to the door as quickly as her silent tiptoes would allow, she threw it open only to discover Bill waiting on the other side. Despite the early hour, he was already fully dressed, including boots laced tight. He greeted her with a wide stance and folded arms, and his expression held a heaviness that she had rarely seen.

She released an involuntary croak and stepped into the hallway, drawing the door closed silently behind her. "Bill?" she tried again, her voice no more composed than before. Something was dreadfully the matter. "Where is Peter?"

"In the sitting room. He's a bit battered, but otherwise well. There's a girl with him."

Josie stepped back. "A girl?"

"A child," Bill clarified. "Rescued while in Le Clé. Solange hasn't managed to extract her backstory as of yet."

Peter rescued a child? What were the circumstances that led to such an action? She shook her head. The why was irrelevant. He had returned. They could handle the child's story in due time.

She started for the sitting room, but Bill grasped her hand, holding her tethered. She met his eyes, their brown depths full of despair. He hadn't been appointed messenger because Peter was physically unable to walk to her room. He had been sent because Peter couldn't bring himself to deliver whatever news was next.

Bill squeezed her hand and that brief touch transported her back to a summer's day in Piccadilly, when an English lieutenant handed her a set of identification tags and explained how she was now the last of the Harrington family line.

"No," she whispered.

"I'm so sorry, Josie. It's Emil. We lost him."

THIRTY-FIVE

December 26, 1917 –
Le Clé, France

EMIL KNEW HE SHOULDN'T HAVE DONE IT. He should have stayed true to the mission and walked away from the little French girl. But how could he? This wasn't like during the riot in St. Louis when they turned from the man strung up on the street lamp, although that decision still haunted him. He had Winnie and Amara to protect then. This time he had no one to protect except for that French girl. She couldn't have been more than ten. She didn't deserve whatever had been about to happen to her. Correction, whatever now had happened to her. Try as he might, he hadn't saved her. She had been taken away by her assailant while he was dragged in the opposite direction.

The soldiers took him to a dark cellar, ironically only one door down from where Zeke billeted. So close to his goal. He had resisted of course, but it was little use when his weapons were confiscated and he fought five against one. The cellar's dank rectangle smelled of overripe potatoes and must. There were no windows, nothing to let the daylight in. From the flashlight one soldier carried, he could see shelves filled with food and barrels of unknown identity. He wondered where it had all come from with rations being what they were and rumors of import blockades against Berlin and several other German cities. Two soldiers shoved him flat against the wall while the others emptied the cellar's supplies with swift efficiency, carrying armloads of provisions up the stairs.

After the room had been reduced to a blank slate, one soldier faced him, pistol in hand. He was the one with a tongue that deserved a sound washing. The other two continued to restrain him, all waiting for answers. He offered none.

"Speak," the foul-mouthed soldier shouted in German. "Why did you interfere with one of your own?"

"She was only a child," Emil replied in the same language. "He was out of line."

"She was French. He could have done what he pleased."

"Are we all expected to be so degraded? Does the *Deutsches Heer* no longer maintain a code of ethics by which we should abide?" *It's despicable*, he thought. He had heard all the rumors of the German pestilence. Peter mentioned a few things and Solange too. He knew they were a heartless army, but he didn't want to believe they were completely without morals. Surely, there was an exception somewhere.

The soldier considered him, rubbing his thumb and forefinger together in thought. "Ethics are highly flexible in a time of war. Tell me your name, soldier. Whose command are you under?"

Well, shoot. Peter hadn't provided him that bit of information. They really hadn't thought this plan through, had they?

Emil panicked and gave the only name he knew was an officer. "Lieutenant Rohrbaugh. I'm in on leave from the trenches. Only just arrived."

"He's lying."

Emil turned to see the soldier from the bar, Albert Voss, stride into the room. He stepped into the circle of lantern light and peered at Emil with his chin cocked to one side. "I met you," he said. "In the bar a few weeks back. You told me then that you had only just arrived. How is it that you are arriving again? No one would receive two leaves in such short order."

"I was injured on the front." Emil pointed to his side in explanation. "They sent me back to convalesce."

The other soldiers looked to Albert for direction and Emil realized that this soldier must be of some importance. Not an officer, but still ranked above anyone else in the room. Therefore, he had the authority to call the next action.

Emil saw the man's fist heading for his gut, but there was nothing he could do to stop it. His arms were still restrained on either side with another soldier's pistol inches from his back. The punch slammed into him, knocking his breath away and doubling him over, his arms angled up behind him in the soldiers' grips. He stifled a groan.

"You are not a soldier," Albert spat. "If you were you would know that injured men are typically sent to casualty clearing stations to recover, not into town. Also, I had the honor of dining with Lieutenant Rohrbaugh's regiment over Christmas. You were not in attendance."

"That's because I wasn't invited." Emil attempted to quip, although his voice released in a slight wheeze. "The lieutenant was afraid my wit would outshine him."

And that smart remark earned him his second gut punch of the afternoon. Dropping to one knee, he released a tight exhale before immediately lifting himself back to standing. He couldn't be defeated this early in the game. He needed to figure a way out of this and toying with the armed guards wasn't going to work. Apparently, all his time on the morality squad didn't mean anything when you landed on the other side.

"An Allied spy, perhaps?" the soldier holding Emil's right arm suggested.

That caught Albert's attention. He rubbed his knuckles, eyeing Emil up again. "A likely suspicion. Their type does tend to be rather imbecile. Tell me, soldier, who is it that really sent you here?"

This time, Emil remained silent. He would never give up *Fides et Spes* or that he hadn't arrived alone or that Peter was Zeke's cousin or that the rest of their organization lay only ten miles from Le Clé. He thanked God that he and Peter didn't carry maps or identification on them. What little he did have couldn't betray anything.

Albert circled the room, striding somewhere behind Emil in the dark where he couldn't see. When he attempted to turn his neck, he felt a pistol jab painfully against his spine. He faced back around, staring at the glow from the stairwell doorway.

"Let me phrase this another way," Albert said slowly, still pacing behind him through the darkness. "Although you speak German well, I suspect you are not. I also assume you are not French. I do not know what you are, but you will tell me. You will tell me who sent you. You will tell me how to find them. You will tell me everything I wish to know or I will ensure your stay is really quite painful." The man rounded back to Emil with a conciliatory grin. "If you tell me now, I will ensure you are only sent to a work camp rather than executed. Although I suspect that will be little solace to your wife."

He stepped forward and examined Emil's eyes, shining the flashlight into them until he was forced to squint and look away. Footprints patterned the dirt floor, boot lines over boot lines marching away into the dark. If he caved, he would be marched away to a German work camp, trapped behind enemy lines exactly like Simon Clermont. Solange hadn't heard from her husband in three years and there was no guarantee he would return once the war was through. Emil assumed there were rules related to liberation, but that didn't mean the Germans would follow them. If he caved, he would not only be giving up his freedom, but that of his family and friends and possibly costing them their lives in the process. He couldn't. He would remain silent and he would find a way to escape. Or he would let them add his blood to countless others.

Goodness Moses, he was going to die here, wasn't he?

The realization made his gut clench painfully, allowing him to feel where each punched bruise would emerge tomorrow, assuming tomorrow even came. He felt anger against Peter for talking him into this, then at himself. But how could he let Amara lose her brother? He should be furious with her instead. She had insisted they follow Peter's letter. She had wanted to join the letter deliveries. If not for meeting his wife, he would still be in St. Louis, happily unmarried and drinking whiskey with Earhart every night. No, not happily. That life had made him miserable. He would still rather be in France married to Amara than anywhere else without her.

No one made him do anything. He had a choice every step of the way and he made each one of his own accord. He chose Amara even when she didn't choose him. He would choose her every time.

He remained quiet, tilting his chin to the side as though he couldn't understand the question. A full minute passed while he watched Albert's frown lengthen until the shadows of his face blended together into one horrific scowl. Finally, Emil cleared his throat. "I will only speak to Lieutenant Rohrbaugh. You bring him to me, alone, and I will tell him everything."

Albert shook his head. He stepped backwards out of the pool of lantern light, his silhouette dissolving into darkness. A minute later he reappeared in the stairwell doorway. "Prisoners do not dictate the terms of their imprisonment. You will speak or you will die in silence." He nodded to the men at Emil's sides. "He claims to be one of Rohrbaugh's soldiers. Make sure he understands the meaning of insubordination."

THIRTY - SIX

December 30, 1917 – Four Days Later
Clermont Farm, France

AMARA EXPECTED HER NIGHTMARES to wreak havoc within her sleep, but they didn't. Perhaps it was because she could barely think. She felt numb as the days passed by in a fog. She heard the others' conversation but couldn't chime in. It was exactly like the night of the St. Louis riot. She continued replaying that awful moment in her mind over and over again.

When she awoke to Josie's gentle hand upon her shoulder and grim tear streaks down her cheeks, she knew what must have happened even before she heard it. "Emil's been captured," Josie told her. "It all went horribly wrong."

Amara had turned over in bed, raised the blankets to her chin, and closed her eyes without reply. Josie sat beside her for several minutes then rose. "I'll be in the kitchen. Come out when you're ready." A pause. "I truly am sorry. If it is any consolation, Peter feels terribly about what's happened."

It wasn't any consolation. Piling more guilt onto her brother's shoulders did not lessen the grief now tumbling through her.

It would be a full day before her mind sobered enough to hear Peter's story and another two days of emptiness before any of them learned about the child he had rescued.

The young girl's name was Bernadette Marchand. Her parents were both resisters during the initial invasion of Le Clé, murdered when they attempted to stop German soldiers from requisitioning their home. Bernadette was taken up by her aunt, although not long after, her home too was requisitioned. From what they could gather through the girl's few words, her aunt then became intimately involved with Bernadette's assailant, all the while allowing him to treat her horribly. If not for Emil's interference and Peter's rescue, she would not still retain her innocence.

"She's only twelve years old," Solange said and there was quiet in the room. Older than any of them believed at first sight. No child—no matter their age—should be set upon by an adult, especially not in her own home. A child had the right to be a child.

"How could you keep your plans from me?" Amara asked Peter angrily once Solange had taken the girl from the room. "I certainly am glad Bernadette was spared, but if you had asked me beforehand, I would have told you why there wasn't a chance of Zeke helping us."

Peter's blue and bruised right hand contorted against his side. "What would your word be worth now, when you've done everything I told you not to?"

"Peter, perhaps we should—" Josie attempted to cut in, reaching for him, but he sidestepped her.

"We could have avoided all of this, Amara, if you had simply done what I asked. Instead, you married someone German-born then left America where you both would have been safe."

She wanted to shove him away and run from the room, but what good would that accomplish? It certainly wouldn't bring Emil home. Her brother's hard head needed some sense and if she couldn't impose it on him, likely no one could. "There was nothing safe about where I was!" she shouted at him. "There's nothing safe about any situation you've dragged me into. From the day you handed me that rail ticket to St. Louis, it's been nothing but secrets and lies between us. You said *Fides et Spes* doesn't take sides, except you have been, and I'm starting to wonder if you ever once chose mine."

He snorted. "Eventually you have to choose a side, or you'll be like Belgium. Overrun." He marched out of the room, his boots clomping *shuffle-step* down the hall, followed by the creak of the second bedroom door opening. Amara and Josie cast each other a concerned glance and followed. Amara's traveling case lay open on the bed.

Josie hurried over to Peter. "What are you doing?"

He opened the chest of drawers, scooping all of Amara's neatly folded things into his arms. "Packing. My sister's going home."

Amara watched him drop her belongings into the suitcase and turn back for more. *Home?* Did he mean America or "home" to Germany with their parents? Either way, she wasn't leaving France without Emil beside her or proof of his passing.

Peter tossed a second load of her clothes onto the first. He yanked open the second drawer, Emil's trousers and shirts staring back at him accusingly. He snatched them up and pushed them into a second traveling case, secured the ribbon ties over the entire bundle, and slammed both case lids closed. "This was too risky, allowing you to stay. You're leaving with Quentin as soon as I can hitch up the horses."

"No, I am not." She strode over and flipped the traveling case latches back open. The overstuffed lid popped up immediately. "I may be six years younger than you, but I'm not a child you can order around. I found a husband when you asked me to. Maybe he doesn't meet all your requirements, but he does love me and doesn't beat me like Zeke did."

Peter fumbled, his face registering the shock she expected it would. His lips parted a full half inch before he said, "Zeke did *what*?"

"Hit me," she clarified. "Almost every day we lived in Iowa. I hid the truth out of fear that you would send me away for my safety. I didn't want us to be separated, even if it meant drawing his abuse. But you still sent me away, didn't you? You said *Fides et Spes* has a duty to keep families together whatever the cost. Emil's my family. *You* are my family. Is that not more important than some stranger's letters?" She lowered herself to the edge of the bed, suddenly overcome with the effort of restraining her worst emotion. She peered up at her brother through eyes threatening to cascade over. "Please, Peter, we have to try to save him."

Peter clenched his gnarled fingers, flexing them over and over again, decisions warring behind his blue irises. Offering him more ammunition for his personal guilt wasn't what she wanted, but how could she begin to save Emil without her brother? Even with his deceit and leading her husband to be captured, her anger could only take her so far.

"At ease, all of you."

They turned to find Bill watching them from the doorway, Solange directly behind. He stood with his thumbs hooked in his waistband, meeting Amara's eyes with a sympathetic frown. He felt her pain, her desperation, she could tell. If the tables were turned and that was his wife out there, he would have wanted to immediately rush off on a rescue mission. Except Bill wasn't married. He could sympathize, but he could never fully understand, and therefore could make the decision easier than any of them.

"We're not soldiers, Amara," he said. "We don't have the ability or the resources to mobilize an army to extract him. Even if we rode to the nearest casualty clearing station, they would send us round again, especially since our organization flies in the face of every censorship law. We deliver letters and that's all we do. Peter and Emil broke that rule and they knew the risks of breaking it. It's unfortunate what's happened, but if we attempt a rescue mission on our own, we will fail." There were solemn nods all around.

"What will they do to him?" Josie asked the question Amara wanted to, but couldn't find the words to ask.

"Once the Jerries realize he's not one of them," Bill explained, "they'll assume him a spy. Interrogation is usually the next step. Possibly torture. They'll want to find out who he's working for and how to infiltrate their defenses. If they can convince him to turn traitor for Germany, he'll likely be rewarded."

"And if he doesn't?"

"I suppose they'll have no further use for him."

Solange stepped fully into the room, a sleeping Remy nestled against her chest. How the child could sleep happily through their racket was a wonder, as was the continued wonderment of how similar his appearance was to Emil's. Amara stared at her bitten fingernails.

"They'll send him East then, like Simon?" Solange asked. "Perhaps we can intervene when they are on the road with a smaller guard?"

Bill looked to Peter, wanting him to say it, but his friend turned to stare out the window. "Remember Mata Hari?" Bill said. "Spies are traitors. Traitors get a bullet in their brain."

His words caused Solange to gasp and at that small whisper of a motion, Remy woke and began to cry in earnest. His wails sliced through the room, threatening to rattle the walls and topple them around Amara's now crumpled desperation.

Solange soothed him as best she could, but still he kicked and screamed like a banshee. When she finally let him down, he looked around the group and apparently not seeing what he wanted, clenched two chubby fists at his sides, lifted his chin, and screamed again. Cheeks flushed with embarrassment, Solange gripped him around the middle, hefting his struggling body back against her shoulder, and circled a palm against his back.

"My suggestion," Bill continued over Remy's cries, "would be for us to take a day's rest, then return to London. Our position in Le Clé has been compromised. There's little reason for us to remain. Solange, I would encourage you to consider joining us."

"What about the farm?" Solange's voice rose to be heard over Remy's fits. "Simon may still return."

"He may, yes, but not before the war ends. The choice is yours; however, we should plan to depart for Brindille post-breakfast." With those words and an apologetic glance, he left them. After another moment's hesitation, Solange followed, Remy's cries echoing the sentiments they all felt. Lucien and Maël's voices were heard soon after from the kitchen.

Outside the bedroom window, snow began to fall, tiny whispers of white floating down to wet the panes. Individual drops trailed slow paths across the glass and Peter finally turned. His expression held even less than Bill's had. "I suppose I should pack then. I'll move back into the house for tonight. Too cold in the barn with the snow."

Amara knew that wasn't the reason. He wanted to keep an eye on her, to make sure she didn't chase after her husband like she had chased Peter to France. But he departed the room then and she was too exhausted to make mention of it.

She dropped her head into her hands, letting her eyelids close. "Oh, Emil, my husband, why did you do this?"

"I think you know why." Josie sank to the bed and wrapped an arm around her friend. Amara rested her head against Josie's arm. "He did it to save Peter from going alone. He did it because he loves you."

"Because he loves me."

Even in her and Emil's darkest days, in the midst of the greatest misunderstanding and betrayal of their relationship, even then he had done everything to protect her. He had traveled to New York then London then France and finally to his imprisonment all for her.

Tomorrow they expected her to leave this place. How could she though? How could she step one foot in front of the other and keep stepping without knowing what had become of her husband? She would have to face his parents and see the accusation in their eyes, knowing she was responsible for the loss of their second son.

All she could do now was pray, but would God grant her a miracle by morning? Would He grant it at all? Or was He pushing her to accept the challenge herself as He had so often done before? To forge a path where there was none. How could He expect her to take on such an impossible mission though? Her, the frightened German-American girl whom everyone, at one point or another, considered insignificant.

Except for Emil. He never saw you that way. He always believed you were beautiful. He always believed you were brave.

"What can I do?" she whispered, not certain who she expected to answer. Josie didn't, nor did she hear angels singing. No burning bush erupted out of the floorboards to show her the way.

Snow fell silently, covering the farmyard. Just as silently, Amara took her coat from the rack and buttoned each button, one by one by one. She nestled her woolen cap upon her head and slid her hands into her gloves one finger at a time. She walked out the front door and no one tried to stop her or ask where she was headed.

The snow landed in heavy flakes but gently, seeming to fall at half the speed they should. She felt them upon her shoulders, her face, and cling to her eyelashes as she blinked away tears lest they freeze.

She walked past the barn, past the barren crop fields, hiked up her skirts and tramped across fallen shriveled wildflowers to the edge of the forest. She knew the way to the creek; Peter had shown her.

There she stood, watching the water trip over rocks and slip under fallen branches. Its minuscule gurgle fought through the ice at its edges, practically shouting through the stillness of the snow.

Amara had always considered snow a sign of hope, that no matter how bad today was, tomorrow would be better. But what hope was there now? Her husband had fallen into the enemy's hands and she was left with no clues for how to find him. No skills for subterfuge and no one to help her. Four days had already passed. By now, he was probably dead anyway.

Emil Kisch, her husband, was *dead*.

That meant all her dreams were dead too. She had no one to blame but herself.

Amara fell to her knees in the mud beside the Clermonts' creek, lifted her chin to the bleary sky, and wept.

THIRTY - SEVEN

December 30, 1917 –
Le Clé, France

THEY IMPRISONED EMIL IN the same cellar where he arrived with no indication of how long he would remain there. They wore him down with ever more severe abuses, promising each time to end the torture, if only Emil would tell them what they wished to know. Sometimes he wondered how he managed to hold to his original story of being in Lieutenant Rohrbaugh's command when he knew no one believed it. He had demanded Zeke's presence repeatedly, although he had no idea if he ever arrived. Emil wasn't privy to the names of anyone who visited his cellar. He studied their faces and wondered which one, if any of them, was Amara and Peter's cousin. Was it the man who punched his face the first time? Maybe the one who slammed him up against the wall. Or the one who drew a trench knife from Emil's elbow to wrist before calling the doctor to stitch him up.

He may have been down in that cellar mere hours or it could have been days. There were no windows and lanterns were only brought during meals and interrogations. The rest of the time, the room remained dark and damp and he heard things scurrying along the walls. They brought him two meals daily but whether those were breakfast, luncheon, or dinner, he couldn't tell. The stale food was always the same. The pitch black always the same. He thought he had known every foul word from his time on the morality squad, listening to arrestees curse his name, but German profanity was an entirely different experience. No one here spoke English and little by little he felt like he was going mad.

Blindly following the wall, he found a corner and sank into it, folding his hands into his underarms. Everything in him hurt. They had been particularly vicious to his legs, probably to slow him down if somehow he managed to escape. He folded his forehead to his knees and felt tears welling.

No help was coming. His parents would only have one son left. Amara would be a widow. At least he still wore his wedding band. He had no reasonable explanation why they left him that when they had confiscated everything else except his clothes.

He thought about the last time he was with his older brother, the day before his family left for America. Charles had remained behind to finalize the sale of their home and planned to follow later. If not for *Titanic's* sinking, he would have. He asked Emil if he was nervous to sail. Not scared or afraid but nervous. Emil had laughed it off as he always did. That was the last time they saw one another.

Are you nervous, Emil?

No, Charles, I'm terrified.

It hurt to cry. He had two black eyes; he was certain of it. So, he stopped himself from letting the tears flow by scrunching his facial muscles, which proved to be a worse idea. He leaned his head back against the wall and let the dark seep over him. He let his mind go as blank as the world he sat in.

The cellar door opened, sending a glowing lane across the cellar. Emil squinted against the sudden brightness and his head ached with the movement. Gripping the nearby wooden shelves, he managed to pull himself to standing and slowly made his way towards his latest meal.

The soldier who entered wasn't the one who normally brought him food. He hadn't met this man yet. He was young, easily no older than Emil's almost twenty-two years. He had the same close-cropped hair as the other soldiers, but with an unexpected pleasant set to his features. When he placed the tray and lantern on the floor, he actually smiled. "Brought you some breakfast."

Ah, Emil thought, *so it was morning.*

The soldier backed away, blocking the doorway with his slender body, one hand on his rifle as he had been no doubt instructed. This kid didn't seem that intimidating; Emil figured he could probably knock him down with the food tray and rush out. Except this kid was also the first German who had shown him any ounce of mercy since he arrived. He was probably just fulfilling his orders, fighting to make his father proud, the same as Amara's father had asked of Peter.

Emil sat before the tray, tearing a piece off the hard wad of war bread. There was some sort of slop beside it and a cup of murky water. At least they were still feeding him.

"What's your name?" he asked the boy soldier.

"Lengfeld Rosch."

"How long have you been in, Herr Rosch?"

"Six months. I enlisted the first chance I could." Then he was younger than Emil assumed. He slowly chewed his war bread, thinking about Winnie and how she had joined even younger.

"What'd you do to get thrown down here?" the boy asked.

"Followed my convictions." There, that should cover it without giving anything away.

"The soldiers say you're an Allied spy."

Emil shrugged which hurt both his shoulders. "Well, if that's what they say ..."

"It's true then!" The boy's eyes widened. He abandoned his post and dropped to the floor in front of Emil, legs crossed under him, rifle across his lap. The motion made him appear so much like an excited child, so much like Solange's sons. Probably a bit like Emil's own son might have been.

I might really have been a decent father, he thought. Given the chance, he bet he could have done a fair job at it. He would have told his children war stories and adventures of his time on the morality squad. There would have been no bedtime stories like Emil Kisch's bedtime stories.

Lengfeld set his rifle on the floor beside him, easily within Emil's reach if he wanted to grab it. This boy wasn't made for the *Deutsches Heer*. He wasn't even made to bring a prisoner his breakfast. The reality was he probably wouldn't make it through this war alive. He would be another casualty, another faceless name on a list, a number in the paper. *"12,000 more reported dead."* There would be a letter sent to his parents with an apology. Then nothing. Just memories.

Emil understood what that sort of grief felt like first hand. He witnessed it on his parents' faces when Charles died. For five years, he drowned in it. Even now a pin pricked his heart every time he thought his brother's name. The pain had lessened, but it never fully went away.

"Why did you become a spy?" Lengfeld asked. "Is it as exciting as it sounds?"

Emil remained silent, slurping up gruel straight from the tray since there were no utensils. How interesting it was that he and Amara fled St. Louis under accusation of spying and now he actually had become one. And a lousy one at that. He simply shrugged again.

"They plan to kill you, you know."

"Why don't they kill me now? You wouldn't bother having to feed me anymore."

"I won't be feeding you again anyway. Tomorrow, I'm headed back to the front." The boy pulled his knees up, wrapping his arms around them. Emil hadn't noticed the damp chill since his first day in the cellar, but likely Lengfeld now grew cold from it. Or from the thought of returning to the trenches.

"Do you think you could help me with something, Herr Rosch?"

"Sorry, sir, but I cannot help you escape."

"No, not that. I won't get you into trouble." The boy would face execution if Emil escaped on his watch. "I need you to take a message to the village priest, Father Ferdinand. Do you know him?"

"No. I think I could locate him though. What do you need me to tell him?"

"If I'm going to die, I need one last confession."

THIRTY - EIGHT

December 31, 1917 –
Clermont Farm, France

PETER CLOSED THE SECRET WEAPONS compartment for the last time, the remains of their meager arsenal laid out across the barn floor before him. He would leave the rifles for Solange's safety; he and Bill would take the others. Slipping the C96 into his side holster, he lifted the remaining Browning in his right hand, his busted finger threading awkwardly through the trigger point. Before the air raid, that same finger had been the one to take down over a dozen Allied soldiers. Would it have been any different if he stayed in America only to be drafted in Wilson's army? He still would have been required to kill and he would have done it to protect his country.

War made murderers of them all. Patriotic justified murderers, but murderers all the same.

Would leaving Emil imprisoned be viewed the same? Peter felt the stab of guilt more clearly now than ever, but he didn't see any other way around it. Le Clé would be on high alert now that the Germans knew about their presence. Exchanging letters would be nearly impossible. They could attempt to petition Zeke as originally planned, but what if his plan backfired again and his cousin didn't listen? Or what if Zeke agreed to help, but he didn't have the authority or the know-how to initiate a release? What if Emil was already dead?

Clenching the Browning beneath white knuckles, Peter stormed from the barn, sprinting towards the creek as fast as his limp and the snow would allow. He crossed the rocks and out of the trees on the other side into one of the Clermonts' fields. Finding himself alone, he raised the pistol and fired all six rounds across the mile-wide clearing. If he had taken the time to pause and consider, he would have probably realized how outright foolish the action was, but frustration had taken hold and he no longer carried the strength to calm it.

He hated what war had done to him, who it made him become. He hated the actions he had performed with the trigger beneath his finger. He wanted to shoot all the pain inside of him like he had killed those fourteen men.

He flung the Browning to the ground and yanked the C96 from his holster to continue firing. Every shot echoed across the emptiness, striking the snow yards away with malice. He felt the force of each blast beneath his ribcage, straight to his core, and when he finally finished, his ears were ringing.

He dropped the second pistol into the snow. "Was it so much to ask for, Lord?" he shouted. "To help me do at least one thing right?"

"All He ever wanted was for you to ask, Peter."

Peter spun, his right knee protesting with the movement. He struck out an arm to steady himself and found Father Ferdinand's hand bracing his shoulder. The priest appeared exhausted and near frozen, his cheeks and nose rosy, and lips cracked from the wind. Even so, beneath his woolen cap, his eyes sparkled.

"Yes, it is me." The priest smiled. Certain Peter was steady, he released his shoulder.

"Father Ferdinand?" Peter gaped. "What are you doing here?"

"I've come with glad tidings and good news."

Peter always thought he would feel overjoyed when he finally managed to free Father Ferdinand from the Germans' clutches, but the priest's words of "glad tidings" only intensified his frustration. "Christmas is over," he seethed. "The angels have all gone and taken their good news with them." He bent to retrieve the empty pistols. Replacing the C96 in his holster, he held the other with his good hand. "We're to leave for Brindille this morning. You may join us if you wish."

"I do have several letters in need of transport, but I believe you will want to delay your deliveries."

"We aren't going to Brindille for a delivery, Father. Deliveries are done. *Fides et Spes* has failed ... or this line has at least. We're leaving for London. As I said, you're welcome to join us if you wish."

"I can't leave, Peter. I told you that from the beginning. My children still need me."

"Then what are you *doing* here?" Peter should feel ashamed practically screaming at a man of God, but the action was so much less than anything else he had done, it barely blipped his radar. "I've been trying to convince you to leave Le Clé for months. You are the reason I came back to this filthy mudhole in the first place! You saved my life. Why won't you let me save yours?"

"Because it was never my life which needed saving." The priest smiled again, warm and caring, and Peter turned away.

"Excuse me, Father. I need to hitch up the wagon. Come with us or don't. It makes no difference anymore."

He limped back into the trees, across the creek, and up the hill towards the farm. As soon as he reached the top, he saw Bill running towards him from the barn, pistol in hand. He looked over his shoulder repeatedly as he ran, then grabbed Peter's arm, pulling him back towards the house. He dragged him at a clip Peter couldn't manage and he stumbled, falling onto his side in the snow.

Bill reached down to pull him up. "Hurry!" he gasped. "Did you hear all those gunshots? We could be under siege."

Peter shoved him away. "We're not under attack. That was me shooting."

Bill paused, his expression crinkling in confusion. "You? What were you shooting at?"

"Nothing. I just needed to shoot." Slapping the empty Browning into Bill's hand, Peter stepped around him and marched towards the house. He flipped his next words behind him. "Oh, I also found Father Ferdinand while I was out there. Mission accomplished. Now we can go home."

The farmhouse door opened before he reached it, Josie rushing out to throw her arms around him. He stumbled again with her added weight, but something about her frantic embrace made him melt against her. His cheek pressed upon her hair and he stared up into the morning sky, blinking away moisture in his eyes. The clouds were grey again, like everything about him and his life. There were no more easy decisions, no more black or white, and certainly very few days that held much color. Josie was all the color he had left.

She pulled away, scanning him up and down. "Are you all right? I assumed it was safe when you and Bill decided to speak out in the open, but we were so worried. We heard gunfire and thought ... It's no matter. You're fine." She glanced again at his chest, as though she had missed a critical gunshot wound on her first pass. Then slowly, her eyes raised back to his. "Aren't you?"

"Yes. Is everyone ready to leave?"

"Is that Father Ferdinand?" She stared past him to where Bill was speaking to the priest in hushed tones. Peter nodded and Josie's face lit up with excitement. "How wonderful! All this time you've been trying to save him and here he is." She turned back, running for the house, shouting for Amara. "Come quick! All is well! The priest is here!"

"Josie, wait!" Peter gave chase, cringing as he overextended his defeated leg, but still managed to catch her as she reached the door. Amara stepped outside at the same moment, buttoning her overcoat, her eyes frantically searching the farmyard. It wasn't difficult for her to spot the priest, however, given that he and Bill were already headed in their direction.

"Father Ferdinand?" Amara asked as he approached. When he nodded, tears began to stream from her eyes. She buried her face in her hands, releasing such sobs that Peter felt his own emotions start to crumble. He had been furious with the priest, with their situation, with the whole of his life, but he hadn't stopped to consider how much his sister was grieving her own.

How would he feel if Josie had been the one captured? He would have been beside himself as well.

Stepping forward, he drew Amara to him, letting her weep into his chest while he held her close. Solange appeared in the farmhouse doorway, Bernadette at her side, the young girl appearing more frightened than ever. Living in Le Clé, she had probably become used to hearing gunshots and screams, but even if one was used to such things, did it ever become less frightening? He had become plenty used to gunfire in the trenches and it still terrified him every time.

This time, however, he had been the cause of the frightening.

"We should take this conversation inside," he told them. "It's cold and if the French come to investigate, we don't want to be out here appearing guilty." Even though he was.

He shuffle-stepped right past their concerned expressions into the house, stamping snow from his boots with Amara still tight beneath his arm. Her sobs had lessened and she wiped her eyes upon her sleeve as Peter directed her down onto the sofa. Surprisingly, Bernadette climbed up onto the seat beside him, nestling herself beneath his opposite arm. She reached out a hand to pat Amara's arm as though she were a toddler comforting someone without truly knowing why they needed solace.

For the first time, he really looked at Bernadette, at her thin form and the years that inadequate rations had stolen from her features. She was twelve, but had known nothing except this life since she was nine. It was then that she lost her parents, her childhood, and all she held dear. Trapped in a nightmare until Peter offered her a way to escape. He was sorry that they lost Emil and compromised their organization, but he would never be sorry that he saved Bernadette.

Perhaps he had done one thing right after all.

He took a deep breath, preparing himself for whatever happened next. He would rather stay here in this moment, but he was still a soldier, a letter carrier, and a spy. Their key contact in Le Clé was standing across the room from him; they could not let that opportunity pass them by.

"Father," he addressed the priest. "I would like to apologize for my poor behavior earlier. I was in a foul mood and your appearance took me by surprise." He offered him what he could muster of a smile. "It is good to see you finally out of Le Clé."

The priest did not return his smile. He folded his hands over his middle and tilted his chin towards the window. "I thank you for your apologies; however, as I said, I did not come to leave Le Clé."

"I know. You said that you came with good news." Peter glanced down at Amara, mentally preparing himself for her reaction. "You came to tell us where Emil is."

The air stilled, every breath held in wait for the nod that followed. "Yes," the priest confirmed. "I know where they're keeping your friend."

Amara released a quick sob and Peter held both her and Bernadette tighter, trying to rein in the brittle pieces of his emotions. Until this very moment, he honestly hadn't believed they would ever hear tell of Emil again.

"Where is he?" Amara begged the priest. "How is he? Please, tell us, so we can find him."

Father Ferdinand gifted her with that same warm smile and Peter wondered if there was anything in this life with the ability to bring the man to despair. Not once had he ever heard him raise his voice or discuss the war's havoc as something dismal. He spoke in parables and proverbs and reflected on hope while Peter wandered the desert of his soul. He wished he could be more like that.

"They're holding your friend in a cellar," the priest said. "He has been masquerading as one of Lieutenant Rohrbaugh's men, but they know this story to be false. He has agreed to speak only if they allow him a private audience with the lieutenant, which so far, they have refused. They've tortured him and I will admit to you, it is not a welcome sight to behold. I do not know how many more days he can bear it before he breaks."

"He won't tell them anything," Amara whispered. "He won't betray us."

"I believe you. He called for me only to request last rites and a final confession and not once asked for rescue. I was surprised they allowed it." For the first time, the priest's smile wavered, his eyes turned serious. *So,* thought Peter, *there* is *darkness there.* Father Ferdinand could feel the weight of this invasion even if he didn't always show it.

To ask for last rites, Emil must believe that his execution was certain and close at hand. If he believed that, then he hadn't disclosed anything about their organization. Peter should have trusted him from the beginning.

"You have a chance to save your friend," Father Ferdinand said. "Would you not take the opportunity God has offered you?"

"Do you really believe it's God who brought you here?" Peter returned. He wasn't scoffing the question. He honestly didn't know the answer.

"Peter, I am a priest. You know what my answer will be. The question is not, do I believe? The question is, do you?"

"I do," Amara reached up to take her brother's hand, still wrapped around her shoulder. "Last night, I asked Him to show me what to do, to keep us here if there was still a chance. I don't think it's coincidence though that Father Ferdinand arrived today. I think this is the miracle we needed. Without Father's information, we had no chance of helping Emil, but now we do. We know he's alive. We know where they're holding him."

The way she said it, so calm, so certain, Peter recalled when they were children and she would still ask him to tuck her into bed. She would hold his hands and close her eyes and pray in that soft tiny voice of hers. The last time had been the night before he left for the United States, ready to build his own life and form a business with Siegfried.

Watch over my brother, she had asked in her determined twelve-year-old way. *Keep Peter from getting lost. Keep him out of trouble and keep him safe. I know he'll do well wherever You take him.* He had brushed her sentimentality off at the time, being eighteen and immature, but now...

Bill leapt from the sofa, pulling Peter up by the shoulders and releasing his arms from around Amara and Bernadette. "You're not considering this, are you? We already agreed to leave. We packed our bags. You were about to hitch up the horses, for blimey sakes! You don't honestly believe it's God's will for us to lead a rescue mission and die here, do you?"

He paused. "We knew that might happen anyway."

"Peter ..." Bill groaned. He slapped a hand against his thigh. "You're asking us to sneak past dozens of armed guards to a man, likely injured, and expect that no one will apprehend us. Especially after you wastefully unloaded half our ammunition? You've made this into a pointless task."

Peter shook his head. His frustration was being replaced with something he couldn't quite name. It felt a little like optimism, maybe hope? It had been so long since he felt either, he wasn't exactly sure. Would this mission mean their deaths? Possibly. Would it add to the war effort or help the Allies to win? Probably not. Emil was only one person, a statistic like any of the other men Peter had killed. His death likely wouldn't change the course of the war, but it would change the course of every person in this room.

"He's my brother-in-law, Bill. He's family." Peter offered Amara a pained smile. "We're *Fides et Spes*, faith and hope. We should try to keep families together no matter the cost."

"It's our lives," Bill argued. "That's the cost."

"Or it's his. You don't have to come with me. I won't ask it of any of you. I'll go alone. I owe it to what's left of my family." He held his busted hand out to Amara and she stood, entwining his fingers between hers. He exhaled through the resulting discomfort. "I'm sorry, Amara. Sorry for everything I've done. I made a mess of it all."

"Peter, you did what you thought was right. I don't blame you."

"That's kind to say, except that you do. You should. I'll make it right though. I know you don't trust Zeke, but—"

Amara pushed away from him, roughly breaking their embrace. Heat flushed her face. "You're going to beg Zeke for Emil's release?"

"Not beg, no. I'm going to do what I intended and convince him to join the side of right. When I explain how we're working to end the war, he'll see reason. He'll release Emil and walk us right out of Le Clé, no armed guards to contend with. He'll join us, you'll see."

Amara's lips parted in dismay. "How are you certain we can trust him?"

Do I trust him? Peter thought. *No.* Especially not after learning of Zeke's abuses towards his sister. But this was their *only* option. Anything else was certain failure. At least with Zeke they had a chance higher than nothing. Without Zeke, they may as well return to London and pretend Emil was nothing more than another unfortunate casualty of war.

"I'm not," he admitted. "However, you can trust me."

She nodded slowly. "I'll do whatever it takes to bring my husband back."

"I know, and we will." With a wry smile, he turned to Josie, seated on the sofa beside Solange. She had remained quiet through all of this and he wondered whether she approved. He wanted her to be on his side more than anyone else. Crossing the room, he reached for her hands, his heart beating so loudly, he feared it echoed to the rafters. He lifted her fingers to his lips and gently kissed them, inhaling the promise of everything he wanted for all time. Or only for today.

"Joselyn Harrington," he said. "Will you marry me now, today, before I go?"

The corner of her lip twitched in confusion. "Now?" and behind them Bill muttered, "Is now really the best time for this?"

"There's no better time," Peter said before addressing his fiancée again. "I want to marry you now, Josie, today, this afternoon before I leave to look for Emil. Father Ferdinand's here and this might be the only chance we have."

Her grip tightened around his knuckles. It caused his disfigured hand to throb in protest, but he didn't. He rushed on. "You traveled all this way to find me. You brought me my sister. I should have married you the second I saw you standing in this room. No—" He shook his head, clutching her fingers even tighter. "I should have married you before I ever left England. I'm going to fix everything. I'm going to marry you, and save Emil, and bring my cousin back to who he was."

"That's an awfully lofty goal, Peter. You might not be able to save everyone."

"I shot men out on the battlefield, men with families like mine. I saw their faces as I sent a bullet into their chests. I will never, never, be at peace with that. There's a chance I'll fail my next mission too. I might not save Emil. I might not make it back alive. So, please, let me do this one thing right before I go. Let me marry you."

Everyone stared. Bill tapped a toe, Amara and Solange held their breath, and Father Ferdinand folded his hands in his robes and eyed them like God Himself may descend upon Josie's answer. Slowly, her eyes slid to the floor and she released his hands. "I'm sorry, Peter. If you want to marry me, you need to come back alive."

"Oh," he said. "That's ... that's fine. Really. Maybe when I return then." With a kiss to her forehead, he turned and left the room. They heard his shuffle through the kitchen, followed by the back door, then deafening silence.

—

They were the most difficult words Josie had ever had to say. That she didn't want the person she longed for more than anything else in the world. Now alone in the back bedroom, she wrapped her arms around herself, blinking upward to stem the tears. Fresh flurries fell outside the window, laying white upon white, drifts growing higher against the barn walls.

A soft knock sounded at the door. "Josie?" Amara asked. "May I come in?"

"Yes." Josie sat back on the bed, drawing her knees up and folding the quilt over herself. It was cold away from the warmth of the sitting room fire.

Amara entered, closing the door behind her. She crossed the room, watching her friend with concern. It was no wonder. Josie had fled the room immediately after Peter left and spoken to no one.

"Father Ferdinand took one of the horses to Brindille. Its residents will celebrate Mass for the first time in two years."

"That is wonderful news for them."

Amara sat beside her. "Yes. Father will circle the village then return here on his way back to Le Clé. Peter wasn't pleased."

Josie shivered, even beneath the quilt. Of course, Peter would not be pleased. After all he had done and sacrificed to extract Father Ferdinand—how many times he placed his own life at risk—he would want to feel like those actions meant something. He would want the priest to remain safe.

"I love him," she whispered. "I do want to marry him."

"Then why did you say no? There is a chance he won't come back." Her voice remained surprisingly calm for talk of her brother's demise and Josie wondered if her friend was simply in as much shock as she was.

"Because I don't want him to take foolish chances. If he knows I'm waiting to marry him, hopefully he'll take this mission more cautiously than the others." She rested her cheek on her knee, focusing on the quilt's light blue stitching.

Without the war, she wouldn't have met Peter. He would have married a nice Iowa farm girl and Josie, a British man. Their fates would never have collided. She couldn't imagine a path without him there, but she also wouldn't run that path too quickly due to fear.

Outside the window, snow fluttered down, floating on the breeze like a bridal veil for the world. One day the war would end. They would all be different people when they got there. She couldn't let them lose themselves in the process.

"You never agreed to Peter's plan," she realized then. "You only said you would do whatever it took to bring your husband back."

Amara followed her movement to the window. The snow grew heavier. Full of possibility to become a full-fledged storm by nightfall. "Wouldn't you?" she asked Josie. "Wouldn't you do whatever it took to keep Peter alive?"

Josie nodded. "Of course, I would. That is why I came to France in the first place."

"Good, because there may still be a chance. But only if you do exactly as I say."

THIRTY-NINE

AMARA COLLECTED HER SMALL SACK of provisions, just enough food for her to make it to Le Clé and bring Emil back again. She tied the bundle into a tattered yellow hand towel she dug out of Solange's rag bag so it wouldn't be missed. Then into Emil's satchel it went. Next she rolled torn—and also stolen—rag strips in case one of them were injured in the process of escaping and needed bandaging. She hoped that wouldn't be the case, but who knew if they would be able to stay to the appointed paths. Only once before had she fled for her life, during the riot, and that night had been rather different. For the most part, those rioters ignored them as they fled and there had been no rescue to perform.

"Would you care to assist me?" she asked Bernadette. The French girl sat at the kitchen table with Remy on her lap while he banged a wooden spoon on a set of tin bowls. The result was a deafening cacophony, purposely orchestrated by Amara to keep everyone else out of the kitchen. So far it had worked perfectly. Everyone had vacated the room while Josie kept Peter at bay in the barn. Amara wondered if they would end up married today after all.

She held out a rag strip to Bernadette with a smile. "Help?" She demonstrated rolling the bandage, set it on the pile, and held up the next strip. Bernadette merely stared at her in bewilderment. "*Non,*" she said and turned her attention back to Remy. All she ever replied with when Solange wasn't in the room was "*Non,*" the French word for "No." Only Peter had been able to ease her shell open a crack. Although he knew no French, every morning he won her smile. She asked to sit beside him at every meal and sat next to him on the sofa each evening. After she fell asleep against his shoulder, he tucked her beneath a blanket, choosing to sleep again in the barn rather than move her. Then earlier today when she snuggled beside them and patted Amara's hand ... that small gesture had comforted her more than any other. Despite all the awfulness in their lives right now, it warmed her heart to witness her brother in such a tender state, rather than laced with constant scowls and dismal thoughts. She hoped the girl's devastation would not be too great when he returned home.

Increasing her urgency, Amara finished with the wrappings and included them in the satchel. She slid on her winter overcoat, secured her woolen cap and gloves, and finally raised the satchel over her head, flattening the strap across her chest. She was ready.

She *was* ready, wasn't she?

She had to be even if she wasn't.

She hadn't planned to say any goodbyes; however, Bernadette stared at her again with those innocent saucer-wide brown eyes, and Amara held out her arms. Surprisingly, the girl reached out and hugged her around the waist, Remy still on her lap. The little boy's clanging ceased and he wiggled between them, fussing his displeasure, but Bernadette didn't let go. She whispered something in French Amara wished she could translate. She offered Bernadette a smile, probably the last she would ever feel. She had no delusions that the mission ahead of her contained a dismal chance of success. If she was sent east to the workcamps, she would consider herself lucky. Chances were she would end up in a grave beside her husband, but at least they would be together.

A sob caught in her chest; however, she refused to release it in front of Bernadette. She swallowed instead, managing to maintain that pleasant painted-on smile. "*Au revoir,* Bernadette."

"Going somewhere?" Bill asked. He appeared in the sitting room doorway, one hand braced on either side of the frame. "I came from the barn. Peter's under the impression that you'll be here to see him off."

"I will be. I'm packing some supplies before he goes." That much was true. She had packed supplies, just not for her brother. As she spoke, Josie was feeding the same lie to Peter, ensuring he wouldn't pack his own bag. It would only delay him a short while, but it would be time enough to allow Amara to make her getaway. Although only if Bill would leave her to it.

He stepped into the room, both hands falling to his hips. Suspicion wrinkled his forehead. "You're going after Emil."

She released Bernadette and clung to the satchel, hoping he wouldn't wrench it away from her. She would leave with or without supplies, although without would be infinitely more difficult.

Thankfully, he stayed where he was, watching her with interest. "You won't make it far without a guide," he told her.

"I have a map." Josie had stolen Peter's, carefully marked with the most efficient ways in and out of Le Clé. After traveling across the line numerous times, he no longer needed to carry it on his person. The markings had been unfamiliar, but Amara thought she could follow it easily enough.

"What about a plan?" Bill asked. "Do you have one?"

"Of course, but what interest is it of yours? I thought you were against this 'course of action.'"

He stepped again towards her until they were only a foot apart. He placed a hand on the empty chair behind her and leaned in. "How do you plan to transport Emil back here? He could be beaten or injured. He could be unconscious. What if they cut off his legs? What will you do then?"

She couldn't help it. She gasped, both hands raising to cover the round "o" of her lips. The image of her handsome husband, beaten and bloody, dragging two stumps across a cellar floor was too much. It was too much.

Bernadette's stare shifted between them while nudging Remy's fingers away from tugging at her blouse. Although she couldn't understand English, she obviously understood the level of tension in the room. She lifted the toddler from her lap and ushered him into the sitting room with a final worried glance over her shoulder.

"This man, Zeke," Bill continued. "You've suffered by him under the best circumstances. These will be the worst. How can you be certain he will listen?"

"I can't. But if I don't try, my husband is lost to me forever. If I allow Peter to go in my place, I could lose him too." She stepped under Bill's arm, out of his reach, and gripped the back door knob. She turned it. "This is my place, beside my husband. This has always been my place. Unto death."

Her boots had made their first dainty tracks on the snow-covered porch when she heard Bill again behind her. His words were swept away with the wind, slightly louder than a murmur, almost hushed on the breeze. "Take a horse."

She half-turned, observing him over her shoulder. "A horse," he repeated. "If Emil's injured, you'll need a horse. Can you saddle one on your own?"

"Yes, my father taught me." Even when she was young, she could easily tack up a horse by herself with only a footstool and a little elbow grease. "But what of the risk?" she asked him. "Peter said to never take a horse over the line."

He offered her a sour grin. "Peter may be making foolish decisions, but he was right about one thing. We are still *Fides et Spes*. Without risk, we would have no mission." He nudged past her, head down against the wind. Flakes were beginning to fall again, not nearly as gentle as the last snowfall. "Give me five minutes to get Peter out of the barn. Then you ride like the wind."

FORTY

JOSIE HELD THE BLACKOUT CURTAINS ASIDE, watching fat white flakes land atop a snow-blanketed farmyard. She wasn't proud of what she had done nor what she permitted Bill and Solange to do. She had deceived her fiancé, then watched as he drank an innocent-looking herbal tea which sent him to sleep on the sitting room sofa. Solange told him it was an old family recipe for relaxation prior to trials. She said that her mother had often consumed it right before setting out on a sea voyage to calm her nerves. What she had not said was that it was best taken in pursuit of a good night's rest.

Six hours later, the sky darkened to the color of pitch. The snow still fell, bright against the ebony of night, forming a barrier between the farmhouse and the trail Amara blazed. She hoped her friend made it to town without issue. So much could go awry before she even made it to the village roads. Amara's mount could slip and break a leg and the endeavor would be over before it even began. Or she could fall from the saddle, her mare running off through the woods. In the dark, it would be near impossible to find her way back.

She would never come back, Josie thought. Amara would press forward towards Le Clé and her husband, even if she froze to death shuffling circles in the snow.

A fresh fire roared merrily in the Clermonts' hearth, the flamelight dancing off the Christmas tree ornaments and the worn lines of Peter's face. He had aged even in the short time since they were together at Olmsted Manor. He deserved to rest and to be free of all the worries he plagued upon himself.

"What do you say, should we wake him?" Bill asked. "Tell him what we've done and let him get all riled?" He sat on the sofa opposite Peter staring into the fire, his hands folded over his knee. It wasn't worry his expression held, but a wondering. Perhaps not knowing if what they had done was the proper course.

Because of *Fides et Spes* and this mission, they had all discovered that every time they delivered a letter, they risked much more than themselves. They risked their newfound family too. Despite the ache of loneliness, perhaps sometimes it was better to be alone.

She let the blackout curtain drop from her fingertips. "You weren't actually spurned by your love, were you, Bill? You let her go to spare her. Didn't you?"

His chin tipped in her direction, the firelight revealing surprise in his gaze. "How did you know?"

"Something you told me when I arrived. That being alone means having no one to risk but yourself. You would have rather let her go than place her at risk by association. You've always treated this like you were part of the Secret Service Bureau. Attempting to close your heart falls right in line."

He tapped a finger to the seat next to him and Josie joined him on the sofa. The fire's warmth lay too hot after the chill near the window. Outside the wind whistled, making sure they knew the storm had not yet vanished.

"Lucille did hand me a white feather," he told her. "That was her name: Lucille Cartwright. She made sure I received that feather in front of all our friends in the parlor of some very prominent people. She wanted me to know that she didn't want me and no one else should either. Her dismissal worked even better than I planned it." Reaching to the coffee table, he grabbed a cigarette from the pack there and lit it with ease, releasing his next breath in a rush. "I knew I was joining *Fides et Spes* and I knew I didn't want to stop there. I was reading the letters even before I recruited Peter. I couldn't tell any of that to Lucille though, now could I? I told her I received an exemption, but that I was glad I had. I told her I never wanted to enlist to begin with, that there were plenty of other men to fight." He drew another breath and eased the smoke out towards the fire. "When you're a spy, love isn't an option you can afford."

"But you did find love, didn't you?" Josie said. "You loved all of us and to make matters worse, we loved you back."

He gave a miserable chuckle, flicking ash in the fire. "Life's sure a rank old hag, isn't it?"

She joined in his laughter, muffling the sound with her hand, so neither Solange, the boys, nor Bernadette would wake. Unfortunately, Peter did.

He stirred, easing his muscles from the sedentary position they had taken for so long. He flexed his fingers with ginger motions before his eyes blinked open and traveled the room in confusion. He stared at them. "What's going on? Why is it dark?"

"You fell asleep," Bill said. "We thought it best not to wake you."

"What time is it?"

Bill strained to read the mantle clock. "A little after nine."

"Nine?" Peter leapt from the sofa, wincing with one hand to his right thigh. He glared at both of them. "How could you let me fall asleep? How could you let me stay asleep? I was supposed to be on the road hours ago!"

"It's too late to go after her," Bill told him. "It's been snowing like a bullwhip. Her tracks will be long gone."

"Her? Who's 'her'?"

Bill looked at his cigarette. "Your sister. She went after Emil."

Josie was glad he was the one to say it. She hadn't wanted to break that news to Peter even though she played as integral a role as anyone else in Amara's departure. This could very well mean the end of their relationship.

Peter stormed to the window with significant effort in his stride. He couldn't run after Amara like that and he had to sense that he couldn't. Especially not in a snow storm. He threw open the blackout curtains and stared at the still falling snow, dropping in ever larger flakes. With his back to her, she couldn't judge his full reaction. Juggling a cigarette from the pack in his breast pocket, he stuck it to his lips and flicked the lighter, only his hands trembled and it tumbled from his grasp. He left it where it lay on the floorboards, instead pressing his gnarled hand against the frosty window. His breath fogged the glass.

"What were you both thinking?" he seethed. "She'll be killed."

"She made the decision to save her husband." Josie said. "We did it to save you too."

"You shouldn't have. There are a thousand other lives that matter more than mine."

She rose then, moving to stand beside him, wanting so much to save him like he tried to save the world. "You're not responsible for every evil in this war," she said softly. "God has forgiven you for the lives you took. You have to forgive yourself."

"Amara doesn't know what it's like, feeling like you're to blame. She doesn't understand."

The pain in his voice broke her heart. Fairly shattered it, the pieces embedding themselves in every inch of her. This was what she had risked to be part of *Fides et Spes*. To be branded by irons, to risk love like she had never loved before.

She placed a gentle hand on his cheek. "I think she does understand, Peter. I think she understands exactly."

FORTY-ONE

December 31, 1917 –
Le Clé, France

THE MILES PASSED QUICKLY atop Amara's mount, easily leaping over fallen branches. She hadn't ridden in years, but being back in the saddle was like being back on her father's farm in Oberammergau. Easy. Freeing. Hopeful. Before she knew it, she was passing through the ravine on her map and clearing the barbed wire Peter and Bill had snipped away months ago. Twice, she thought she heard voices and paused on alert. The snow grew bolder, stinging white against her exposed skin, and she raised a gloved hand above her eyes in an attempt to stymie the driving moisture. Spinning the horse in a full circle, she peered through the empty branches, squinting against the failing light. Barren branches clicked together in the wind. As far as she could tell, she was alone.

Following Bill's instructions, she left the horse sheltered inside the abandoned church's Marian Chapel and offered the half-frozen animal a handful of feed from her satchel. She rubbed the mare's snout as it snuffed the grain from her palm. "I'm sorry, girl. I wish I didn't have to leave you here, but at least you're out of the wind." Snow swirled through the bombed-out sanctuary, the wind spreading drifts over the broken church pews. The Marian Chapel was one of the only remaining spaces with both walls and a ceiling. She prayed the mare would survive the cold until she could return. If she returned.

Darkened buildings cast ominous shadows as she hastened the last quarter mile through the silent town. Brick and mortar blocked much of the snow, the roads only lightly dusted in several parts. Perhaps she would find luck and the blizzard would sweep around Le Clé rather than through, assisting in their escape.

She leapt back as a truck rumbled around the next corner, her petite frame pressed into the shadows as she clutched her satchel against her chest. *Correction, Emil's satchel*, she thought. She would find him. She must.

From across the street, a Frenchman eyed her through a thin parting of blackout curtains. With her short stature, he likely thought her a wandering child, possibly another orphan of the war. He ducked back into darkness at the same time someone seized her arm, swinging her roughly against him.

She slammed into the man's broad chest, his polished uniform buttons the only part of him that reflected any light. She froze when he grabbed her other arm and asked in German, "Where have you been?" Her eyes rose with the sound for the man's voice was not Zeke's but a stranger, although still a stranger in military attire. Snow peppered his woolen overcoat as though he had been out wandering for some time. Probably searching for whomever he thought she was.

His assessment registered surprise, and Amara remained silent, for what else could she do? He likely thought her to be a French woman and assumed her not to speak German. The truth, however, would surely end her mission in its tracks. After all, what would an American woman be doing in a French village if not spying?

She decided to use the only story she could easily remember.

"I was sent for Lieutenant Rohrbaugh," she explained in German. "A gift of congratulations on his promotion."

The soldier's grip remained fierce. "Why are you unescorted?"

"The transport was late for his next post. He shoved me off with little regard; I only hope the lieutenant will not be displeased."

"What is in the pack?" He reached for her satchel and she swung it away behind her back.

"Please, sir. It is of a most delicate nature." Widening her eyes, she thought of the ladies she had seen back in New York, the ones who lingered too long outside the nicest hotels. It was their coy pouts she tried to replicate now. She hated the implication, however, it worked.

His expression softened into a curious smile which, under other circumstances, she might have thought almost handsome. At least until he opened his mouth again.

"Come. I will take you to the lieutenant." He released her arm to offer his. "Then perhaps when you have finished with him, you might indulge me as well? I'm afraid my own French madam has run off and hidden."

Amara's chin quirked up, disgusted. "Is that so?"

He patted her hand, although his sights remained ahead. "Not to worry. I will track her down soon enough. She will be sorry she made me wait."

Flurries continued to fall, now growing lighter while her heart sped with every step they took. They passed a bar, lantern light and New Year's Eve revelry filtering under the entrance door. She and Emil had met on New Year's Eve, only one year ago. Snow had covered the ground then similar to that which surrounded her now. He had been tending bar, and she was brand new to the city. He had come so close to ruining everything before their romance even began.

"Rohrbaugh!" The soldier banged on the front door of a two-story home several establishments father down. He held her arm tighter and laughed. "Come out, Rohrbaugh, or I will claim your lovely gift for myself!"

She stepped back with nowhere to go. The soldier gripped her arm as fiercely as Zeke ever had and laughed again at her discomfort. *Please be home*, she prayed. Although it brought her no pleasure to be with him, she could not be taken by this man and could not flee without Emil.

Heavy footfalls hustled downstairs, crossed two paces to the door, and the lock clicked over. Zeke's movements pounded out every beat of her heart, drumming with a fury in her chest. How could she face the man who battered her ribs and bruised her arms, knocked her knee into a kitchen table, and pushed her against the walls? Who flung more insults at her than there were stars in the sky. The man who claimed she ruined his life. The man who tried to ruin hers.

The same man who was now her husband's only hope.

All this flew through her mind in a minute. A single minute where all that separated her from her former fiancé was a wooden door. The longest minute she would ever live. Then the door opened and there he was.

A wide grin split Zeke's face as he noticed his fellow soldier come to visit. His sandy-blond hair lay perfectly greased, his boots immaculately polished, appearing as though he need only slip his jacket on to model for the ideal poster of German loyalty. He was still handsome, she thought. He always had been. It had only been his behavior which made him ugly.

His smile died when he caught sight of her and his eyes glazed, clearly unable to comprehend what he was seeing. She wasn't supposed to be here. There was no conceivable reason why she would be.

"Your lovely German mistress!" the soldier declared. "Someone must like you indeed to send such beauty." He shoved Amara forward and she tripped directly into Zeke's chest. Her palms pressed upon his stomach, her legs trembling beneath her skirts, while he stared down at her with that same bewildered expression.

"You were sent for me?" he asked.

She only nodded. He waited for further explanation, but she offered none.

"Then, I suppose you should come in." Lifting her off him by the arms, he set her to her feet and stood back. He extended an arm into the house and Amara caught his friend's wink as the door closed behind her.

Trapped.

He stood mere feet away, blocking the door with his back, the stairs rising up behind hers. Lamplight filled the entryway in stark contrast to the inky somber of the outdoors. After her cold ride, the space would feel warm and almost pleasant, if she could only forget why she was there to begin with.

Pretend we're in Oberammergau, she ordered herself. *Pretend Siegfried has returned home for a visit. You're still in his good graces and he's willing to provide anything you ask.*

Some acts, however, were easier to pretend than others.

"Are we able to speak in private?" she asked him.

"No need. The housekeeper will not return until morning and Lieutenant Scholz is at the bar for the holiday."

"Why aren't you there?"

"I never cared for a room full of drunkards. You know that."

"I did, but much has happened since then. I doubt we know each other well anymore."

"It seems we need some reacquainting then." He surprised her then by taking her coat. Slipping it gently from her shoulders, he hung it on the rack near the door. When he reached for her pack, however, she stopped him, holding it to her chest.

"No thank you. I'll keep this with me."

He nodded, extending an arm into the sitting room where two armchairs and a sofa surrounded a crackling fire. Every blackout curtain was strung and every gas lamp gleamed, bathing a soft light over delicate peach fabrics and ornamental paintings. This home was clearly more well-to-do than the Clermonts'. It was no wonder the Germans requisitioned it for their officers.

"Coffee?" Zeke asked. He followed her into the room, his boots moving silently across the throw rug until he stood beside her. When his palm cupped her elbow, she flinched out of reflex, but his touch contained none of its usual aggression. She wondered how that could be. She had expected him to strike her the moment she entered the room.

"Or would you prefer tea?" he offered. "We received a shipment before Christmas that reminds me of the kind you brewed back in Iowa."

Why would he mention that? Every time she brewed tea in Iowa, he had complained. It was either too hot, too cold, too bitter, too sweet. Had war been so vile that he preferred her inadequacies to battle's miseries? She would doubt it except she had seen how battle transformed Peter. He had returned a different man. Was it possible Zeke underwent a similar transformation?

She would not lower her guard so quickly. Minutes of kindness did not erase years of abuse in an instant.

"How is it that you have such luxuries as tea and coffee when the French people struggle for them?" she asked.

His lip curled, hiding a smile. "German soldiers are afforded certain privileges. It comes as part of being the dominant people."

The dominant people? ... No, she would certainly not lower her guard just yet.

"Tea sounds wonderful. Thank you."

He stepped from the room and she listened to his heavy boots march across the adjoining kitchen floor. She wandered to a side table nestled beneath the front window. Its smooth top was arranged with a number of porcelain figurines, provincial Frenchmen and women dancing together. Similar to the night she danced with Emil in Wood-Smith Castle before they were engaged. That was the night they poured out all their innermost secrets to one another. Looking back, she was certain it was also the moment they fell in love.

She peeled back the edge of one blackout curtain, its cloth rough against her fingers. The street remained as deserted as ever. Even the last flurries had finally stilled.

"Where are they?" she asked Zeke when he returned. "The family who lives here?"

He stood beside her, choosing one of the figurines of a young girl in a pink dress holding a batch of wildflowers. He passed it from hand to hand then set it back on the table. "Who *lived* here," he corrected, "and I have no idea. They were displaced before I arrived."

"Oh. I see."

He lifted her hand from the draperies, causing the blackout curtain to swing back into place. He rubbed her fingers, his touch almost tender in its motions. She examined them to make sure they were still the same ones who used to strike her. Each digit was lightly stained with tobacco. Yes, those were the hands she remembered.

"Why are you here, Amara?" he asked. "How are you here? I thought Peter sent you to St. Louis."

"He did. I was there for a while."

"Then how did you end up in France? I assume you're not actually here to be my mistress. Are you serving in the war?"

How to answer that question? She was serving the war in a manner of speaking, but her conscience warned her not to share too much too soon. It would be beneficial if she could convince Zeke to switch sides as Peter had so hoped, but whether he would or not remained to be seen. Her most urgent mission was to free Emil. Until she succeeded in that, talk of anything else related to *Fides et Spes* remained inconsequential.

"I'm doing my part, yes. All the women have been asked to contribute."

He frowned. "I was unaware Berlin planned to send civilian volunteers into occupied areas. Why didn't you send word with my parents' last letter?"

It took all her strength to keep her expression void. She removed her hand from his lest he notice it shaking. "I didn't know I would be here. I thought it best to keep it a surprise."

He grinned. "That it was. If you are interested, I would be willing to have you as my mistress. There wasn't a woman to be found in the trenches."

"I wouldn't be worth having. You always claimed I was damaged goods, or do you not remember?" She turned away before she could see his reaction, not wanting him to smirk or nod in agreement. She had heard and seen it all before; it was frozen in her mind's eye. It sickened her now to imagine there was a time she actually wanted to share his bed.

The tea kettle whistled then and he left the room to fetch it. She thought about fleeing the house and locating Emil on her own. Father Ferdinand said he was being held only one building over. Perhaps she could find another way to free him.

The wind howled in response, rattling the window panes. Heading out alone in this weather would be fruitless, especially if Emil lacked a proper winter wardrobe. She couldn't set him on a horse and expect him to not succumb to the elements. Assuming, of course, that her mare had not already succumbed before she returned. They would need to find a place to hide until the storm died down. Father Ferdinand's safe house seemed too far and too obvious. Emil had mentioned a bartender who was sympathetic to their cause. Perhaps they could hide with him?

Zeke returned with a carved wooden tea tray and after placing it on the coffee table, rounded the sofa to take her elbow. He drew her away from the porcelain figurines, settling her on one end of the sofa before claiming the other. He poured two teacups and handed her one. Steam billowed from each rim. "Now tell me, what work has Berlin assigned you?"

This was where it all rested, on her next words, whether Emil lived or died. She couldn't hold her teacup, her hands were shaking so badly. Even when she set it on her lap, the china rattled in the saucer.

Emil, she thought. *You have to help Emil.*

"Not ... not Berlin." Her voice quavered and she cleared her throat, but it did no good. It continued to warble. "I'm he-here to app-appeal—" She paused again and swallowed. Somehow, she managed to settle her hands enough to place the teacup and saucer back on the coffee table. "I'm here to appeal to you as fa...family."

"Family?" For a moment, he appeared genuinely confused, then his lip lifted in a half-smile. "Ah, so, Peter wrote you then? I figured he would. When I saw him, he ran from me like he thought I was going to shoot him on the spot."

"Per-perhaps then you shouldn't have chased him like you were about to."

"Hmm, perhaps." Zeke blew across his tea, but didn't drink it. He watched her from the cup's rim with cold calculation, biding his time because he knew he held all the time she had. Those hands that now held hand-painted china once pushed Peter in front of a passing motorcar. They left her bruised from early 1912 to the end of '16. If he wanted, he could silence her with a swift stroke of his fist. He could bury her in the cellar and no one would be the wiser.

Ask him about Emil, she ordered herself. *Tell him about Emil! Beg him if you have to!*

She opened her mouth, but no sound emerged. She had to say something. Despite his many aggressive faults, Zeke wasn't an idiot. She knew what would happen if she remained silent. She also knew what could happen if she spoke. Never before had she confronted him and won.

That's because you're pitiful, he would say. *Pitiful and worthless. Incapable.*

Noticing that the fire dimmed, Zeke rose and settled another few logs in the hearth. He swiped his palms together to remove the wood dust and turned, his thumbs finding the edge of his belt. "Our entire regiment was told Peter died in that air raid," he told her. "We had a memorial speech and sent his belongings back to your parents. Now I learn that he actually deserted."

She hesitated again. How much more to tell him? How much to trust? Peter thought that if presented with a solid argument, Zeke would defect to their side, but she had never been certain.

"Has Peter joined the French now?" he continued. "Good luck to him when he can't speak the language. Leave it to your brother to make one stupid decision after another. He really would have been much better off in Iowa hiding in the horse feed."

"Wouldn't we all?" she finally managed. "Do you ever consider if we shouldn't have ignored our fathers' requests and stayed away?"

"Not at all. Your existence may be dismal, but I've had a perfect time without you and Peter. After the air raid, they promoted me to Lieutenant and offered me the best house in Le Clé. I have to share it with Scholz, but it's not a bad deal. I was granted an entire month here before I go back to the front. All I have to do is interrogate a few French citizens, oversee some deliveries, and perform an execution."

"Execution?" She grasped the seat cushions to keep from falling off the edge.

Zeke didn't seem to notice. "We captured a man who struck one of my soldiers in a failed attempt to help a French girl. He continues to claim he's in my regiment, however, is not on any home census or military transfer records. Therefore, we've concluded he's an enemy spy."

Heat burned up Amara's neck and across her shoulders. The time for delay was over.

She shook her head. "Your prisoner is an American. I'm here to negotiate his release."

Zeke actually laughed then, full on bellowing. He plopped himself down on the sofa beside her, resting one ankle over his knee. "Be serious. No government would send someone like you to rescue a prisoner."

"They didn't. The man you hold is an American civilian, not even a soldier."

His laughter died then. "Civilian or no, he's clearly an imposter. He hasn't spoken a word to defend his actions, so tell me why should I care whether I end his life? Why should you? The best compromise the Americans can hope for is a workcamp sentence."

She quieted again, knowing he wouldn't like her answer. How could she possibly spin this to her advantage? Everything seemed to be unraveling exactly like a knit cap for the orphans. The orphans ... would she ever adopt one? Not if she couldn't free her husband.

Zeke's palm struck her cheek so fast that she had no time to avoid it. She stared into the fire's flames, its crackle like an auditory representation of the cruel sting upon her skin.

"Do you know that I've always wanted to do that?" he said. "Never could though. Peter would have lockjawed me." He stood, moving to stand between her and the fire. He folded his arms over his pale green dress shirt, the firelight silhouetting his figure. "Now answer my question. Convince me not to walk next door and shoot him right now."

She looked away, tears breaking free. She didn't want to give him any more power than he already possessed, but once they started to fall, she couldn't stop. The room was a blur. "Please," she sobbed. "He's my husband."

"Your husband?"

"Yes. We married in June."

She wiped damp palms across her eyes until Zeke's form came back into focus. She remembered a time when that cold gaze held such affection. She remembered walking the railroad tracks together as children. Her thirteenth summer, he kissed her so quickly she barely felt it. She spent years longing for his next kiss, while he spent those years transforming himself into a stranger.

Had he planned it? she wondered. Had he even realized what became of him or was the change from Siegfried to Zeke so slow he didn't even notice? One breath at a time—one whisper—until he forgot he was ever anyone else? Peter never understood that there was a darker side to their cousin. He had lived Amara's worst years in blissful ignorance.

This time when Zeke's slap struck, she felt it less. When he grabbed her chin and tilted her face to the side, she peered past him and thought of the family who once lived here. They were gone now, more likely murdered than sentenced to hard labor. Where had their bodies been taken? Who had buried them? A simple carved wooden crucifix hung over the fireplace. Did their Joseph of Arimathea come forward to lay them to rest in his tomb?

"What lie did you tell to make him marry you?" Zeke sneered. "Worthless, *childless* you? You have nothing of value to offer any man."

You're not worthless though, she heard a voice say. *You may be childless, but you're not insignificant and you never were.*

This time when he grabbed her shoulders, she didn't even flinch. She met his eyes and stood tall, as tall and strong and confident as she should have always been. She wasn't afraid of him anymore. Let him cut her down, let him tear her apart. Blow by blow she would stand tall. Blow by blow, she would return each one.

"I had everything to give him," she countered. "Everything I would have given you. You were what I set my clock to, what I once set my life and every plan upon. Until my husband, I never wanted anyone else. Why couldn't I be that for you too?"

"Because you're a liar! I wasted years believing you cared when all you wanted was free passage to America."

"That's not true and I think you've always known it."

His tobacco-stained fingernails dug into her shoulders and still she didn't cower. She knew that was what he desired, to see the girl she used to be cringe and falter and flee. The problem was that he wasn't the only one who had changed. His abuses, her infertility, and a war-torn world had transformed her from child to woman. She couldn't hide from that woman any more than she had ever been able to hide from his cruel words.

"I loved you," she said softly. "Why wasn't that enough? Just me without anything else?"

Despite the nightmares, many a daydream had she spent on picturing how he would apologize, when and where and why. She wished right there in that French house was the moment it happened, but she would have been making another empty wish. German lieutenants didn't apologize with sincerity and they certainly never admitted wrongdoing. That was why her birthplace was currently the world's leading military power; they lacked emotional weakness.

"It isn't too late to set things right," she told him. "I know where Peter is. You could leave the *Deutsches Heer* and join the Allies. The war is turning in their favor. When they win, they'll pardon you for your assistance, I'm certain of it." She lifted one hand to his cheek, caressing the slight stubble in hopeless appeal, praying ... praying ... praying. *Oh please, Lord, please.*

"Please, Siegfried, release my husband. Come home to America and be a hero."

He paused at the sound of his true name and she prayed all the harder, hoping he might actually be considering her offer.

Then he shoved her to the side and marched from the house, leaving a flurry of snow behind him.

FORTY-TWO

December 31, 1917 –
Le Clé, France

BEFORE MEETING AMARA, Emil always imagined he would die old and in bed—or young and very drunk. He certainly never expected to be taken down in a French cellar, murdered by his wife's former fiancé.

From the cellar's dirt floor, he looked up at Zeke's blue eyes and sandy-blond hair, at that smooth smirk and the hatred in his gaze. He felt Zeke's fist slam down again, felt the room spin momentarily, and warm liquid rolled down his cheek to pool in the ridge of his ear. He didn't need to touch it to know his fingers would come back in sticky crimson, the same as the floor now spattered with his blood. Maybe he should have accepted more combat training from Bill and Peter, but he doubted it would have done any good. No amount of training could have prepared him for Zeke's wrath.

"What are you waiting for?" he gasped in German, determined to maintain his soldier's facade to the bitter end. "Take out your pistol and shoot me."

"It's not nearly as enjoyable as watching you suffer." Rather than strike him again though, Zeke removed a clean white handkerchief from his shirt pocket, dabbing it gently against his bloody knuckles. He returned it folded to his pocket. "Besides, I can't kill you yet. You haven't told me anything."

Emil stared at the evenly spaced floor joists above him. "I'm not going to tell you anything, so you may as well get it over and done with. I'm sure your superiors would understand if you accidentally killed me in the heat of interrogation." He lifted one finger to his pounding temple. "Slam the butt of your pistol into my skull right here. It'll kill me with less mess than if you shoot me outright. Brain spatter's a nightmare to clean."

"How would you know that?"

"Used to be a police detective. Arrested dozens of folks in my time." The ceiling flickered above him. He couldn't tell if it was from the lantern light or if his vision was failing. It wasn't as though he would need to see anything anyway. Trying to escape was out of the question. In the shape he was in, he wouldn't even make it up the stairs.

Zeke gave a dry chuckle. "So, you thought that made you capable of becoming a spy? You're a pretty poor one at that. A spy should never make his business personal; wouldn't you agree?" He leveled his prisoner with a long glance to which Emil didn't respond. "Ah, it seems not. I would wager you told Amara everything."

Emil froze. Every muscle in his body tensed with incredible pain, his heart pounding like it would drive him to death this very moment. How could Zeke know he had any relation to Amara? He hadn't said. Had Peter tried to rescue him and been captured himself?

"She was supposed to marry me once," Zeke continued. "I'm sure she told you. She couldn't have children so I declined. But I never thought she'd choose some spying filth instead."

Emil's heart began to pound at a dangerous level. He breathed heavy with fear. Zeke did know. He didn't know how he knew, but he supposed there was no use pretending otherwise. If he was going to die, thankfully he could die fully himself.

He switched to English and said, "I don't care if we never have children. That wasn't why I married her."

"*Gut*. Because you never will." In a swift movement, Zeke unholstered his pistol and swung it at Emil like a club. He rolled and the pistol snapped him across the ribs, sending an electric shock down his side. He tried to push himself to his knees, but a black boot collided with his shoulder, knocking him back flat.

In the flickering lantern light, Zeke's murderous glare came at him again, horrific shadows sweeping back and forth across his skin. Emil nearly heaved as a uniform-clad knee jabbed into his stomach, pinning him into the dirt. Five fingers laced his jaw, wrenching his chin up to meet his assailant's eyes.

"I can't stand a *liar*." Zeke spat the word full force. "Almost as much as I can't stand a spy, and you're the worst sort of both. You're the kind who lies to himself. Every man wants a son, every grandfather a continuation to his lineage. Do you not realize that marrying Amara ended your family line?"

"So?" Emil croaked. "No woman should live without simply because life threw her a bad hand."

"And a man? I am my father's only son; should I have lived in disgrace because of someone else's inadequacy?"

"You're pretty disgraceful now though, aren't you?" Emil gasped as Zeke's knee pressed harder against his ribcage, unable to draw a full breath.

The lieutenant bent nearer. "Are those really what you want your last words to be?"

Emil shook his head and thankfully Zeke released him. He lifted his knee from Emil's stomach and stood, leaving him on his side gasping for air. It took a full minute before he could formulate a conscious thought.

His left hand stretched out limp in the dirt, the gold wedding band on his fourth finger slick with blood. He remembered the day Amara placed it on him, only six months ago. He could recall her smile and how remarkable she looked in her blue gown. Carrying her over the threshold of their rented room and every passionate detail thereafter. He remembered holding her hands the next morning and promising that he wouldn't let the war separate them for anything.

It would never happen now. The life they vowed to share, a home and a family of their own. He hoped somehow, someway, someone would tell his wife how he thought of her at the last, how he died with honor loving her and loving his country. Fighting for America. His blood may be German, but blood wasn't everything. Often, it wasn't even anything.

"I forgive you, Lieutenant," he said then. Words he had never expected to say.

"You forgive me when I feel no remorse?" Zeke scoffed. His voice muffled within Emil's blood-stained ears. "You're not only a spy, but an idiot. I won't be sorry to see a bullet in your head."

"I'm sure you won't. But if I'm about to meet my Maker, I want to do so with a clear conscience." And one that would lead him to the same place Charles was. If he had to die, he didn't want to spend eternity without his brother. Living without him these past five years had been difficult enough. "I forgive you, Zeke. For how you treated Amara, for every time you struck her, and every insult you flung in her face. I forgive you for everything I've endured here and for the hatred you feel for someone you don't even know. I have to forgive you."

"You don't have to do any such thing. I don't forgive you, so don't feel obligated to return the favor."

"Amara would want it, and I want to be the man she chose, even at the last. Even if she never knows," he finished quietly. He looked once more at his wedding ring then up at Zeke through heavy eyes. "This is war, Lieutenant. We do what we have to do. So, do what you have to do and know that I don't hold it against you. Not anymore."

Zeke stared at him, nothing changing about that incensed expression. Then he turned his face to the door and bellowed, "Eidmann!"

Boots tapped down the cellar stairs followed by the door opening and with it, the room grew lighter. A pregnant pause followed, likely from the soldier's observation of Emil's battered body and the blood-stained floor. Like a dutiful soldier, however, he made no comment. "Yes, Lieutenant?"

"There is a woman waiting in my quarters. Please bring her to me immediately. At gunpoint if she refuses."

"Yes, Lieutenant." The door closed, darkening the room once more to flickering lantern light. Emil closed his eyes and let his mind be taken.

FORTY-THREE

December 31, 1917 –
Le Clé, France

SCREAMS EMERGED FROM THE DARKNESS. Emil couldn't will his eyes to open though. He felt … strange. Not quite right. It hurt. He hurt. Everything hurt.

Someone's slight palm pressed against his forehead, smoothing from his brow down to his cheek. Another shook him by the shoulder, shouting … something. Were they going to wash the blood away? He must be drenched in it by this point. Reaching a hand to his scalp, he found hair plastered to his forehead. He managed to open his eyes a sliver. His fingers were red. He wondered with a dim humor whether he appeared fetching as a fiery redhead.

The slight hand grabbed his. "Emil!" a woman cried. Her voice seemed familiar.

He forced his eyes towards her. Even that took too much effort. How had that lousy Zeke managed to bruise his eye muscles too? That took a talent beyond all reckoning.

Those hands were back on his face. They were warm. He liked the feeling.

"Emil, wake up! Look at me!" Her voice turned away. "How could you do this to him?"

He opened his eyes a bit wider, noticed ashen-brown hair, the familiar curve of a face, then those blue eyes. He had fallen in love with those eyes before he fell in love with her.

At first, Emil wondered whether he was dreaming or hallucinating.

Amara couldn't be here. Then he realized in waking horror that she must have come to rescue him. When he had sent for Father Ferdinand, he had no delusions of being rescued and didn't want anyone in *Fides et Spes* to risk their lives for him, especially not his wife. He had received last rites, a final confession, and sent the priest away with a clear conscience.

"What're you doing here?" He had meant to expel the words with force, but they came out in a murmur. He gripped her hand with blood-stained fingers. This wasn't what he wanted. She wasn't safe here. "You have to go," he managed.

She shook her head. "I can't."

He searched for Zeke and found him not far off, watching their exchange. His fingers gripped his pistol holster with murderous intent. "Let her leave," Emil told him. "Please. I'll admit to being a spy, but she isn't involved."

"No!" Amara cried. She wrapped her petite arms around his chest and clung to him, his blood soaking into her coat and the hem of her dress beneath it. "No, Emil. Without you, it's like I've lost half my body. We should have done this together, together or not at all."

Boots marched across the floor and then she was yanked to her feet. Blood covered her front from where she had held him. "Don't you know that staying here means you meet the same fate?" Zeke demanded. "That's death, Amara! You stay here and you will die."

Emil knew she must be terrified, but she didn't cower. "Then that's what I choose."

"Think of your parents, Amara," Zeke argued. "Think of Peter. What will they do when they learn you've perished?"

"What will they do when they learn it happened under your watch? That you stepped back and did nothing to stop it?" She paused and her voice grew softer then. "You loved me once, Siegfried. I know you did, even if you've forgotten. Every time you struck me, I remembered." She raised her free hand and placed it palm-splayed over his heart, directly atop the military pin on his breast pocket. "I miss the man you were back then. I often wonder what happened to him."

His fingers gripped her arm, his scowl refusing to release even

299

minutely, with no indication if her words had any effect whatsoever. Then his eyes slid to his prisoner and Emil had never been so afraid.

"Say goodbye to your husband, Amara."

"No!" Emil moaned, but he was helpless to stop it. He dragged himself to his hands and knees, but the motion felt like wading through waist deep water. His fingers brushed Amara's coat as Zeke yanked her away, and he pitched forward, palms slapping the floor painfully. She struggled back towards him, attempting to pry Zeke's fierce grip from around her waist as he hauled her towards the door. He lifted her clear off the floor, her legs flailing against him.

"Zeke, no, no, please!" she pleaded. Her slipping fingers grasped at the doorway. "Don't do this! Don't do this! Leave me with him! Emil!"

Emil's eyes met hers, blue to blue, heart to heart, then she lost her grip. The door slammed.

He heard her cries echo all the way up the stairwell.

Then he heard no more.

—

Despite the magnitude of Amara's screams, every blackout curtain remained secured. The French would not dare defy curfew and any German lookouts retained their posts without a word. When she saw the enclosed military-issue supply wagon, she knew where he must be taking her. He was sending her back into Germany, to a prison or a work camp. Or to her death.

"No!" She screamed again, "No!" but her cries fell on deaf ears.

Hauling open the wagon's back door, he shoved her inside. "The German army thanks you to remain silent, *Frau.*" Then he slammed the door and barred it.

FORTY-FOUR

EMIL LAY IN THAT FRIGID MISERABLE cellar for hours—or maybe it was days—without any hint of what tomorrow would bring or where they had taken his wife. Every time he heard footsteps or voices, he would yell out, "Where is she? What did you do with her?" but he remained in isolation with no indication that anyone would ever return. The torture of not knowing was worse than all the beatings he had been inflicted.

Eventually, he succumbed to exhaustion, only to be startled awake by the rattle of a food tray sliding across the floor. Ignoring the protest of his battered limbs, he shoved himself to his feet and limped for the door, hands outstretched, determined to barrel through it and escape. But the guard slammed the door closed and his wrists bent back against the metal, sending sharp pains through his forearms. Tears streamed his face, already so bruised, and he sank to the floor, hands curled into his stomach while he wept.

He had lost his wife and the best he could hope for was that she would be taken to a work camp and not to the firing squad. At least if they sent her to Germany, she knew enough of the country to survive. If the Allies won the war, the camps would be liberated and she could go home to her parents.

To his surprise, a military doctor arrived to examine him that evening and each of several evenings after. He offered no pain medication, however, made certain that his wounds were not too

301

severe. On the second day, he even brought a wash bowl to rinse the blood from Emil's face and hair.

"Why would they nurse me back to health only to kill me?" Emil asked as the doctor ran chilled fingers over his ribcage.

"It is part of the process," he replied without looking up from his work. He pressed two fingers against a single rib and Emil winced. The doctor nodded and lowered his patient's shirt. Still he didn't meet Emil's questioning gaze. "Severe bruising, though not broken. You will heal."

"But why bother?" Emil asked again. "I'm set for execution. They told me I was. What does it matter if I look like hell personified?"

The doctor lifted his black bag from the floor and snapped it closed. "Officers are arriving from the front to witness," he finally explained. "Perhaps from Berlin as well, I do not know. You must appear presentable."

So, that was the reason. Zeke didn't want his superiors to know how harsh his interrogation tactics had been and yet produced so few results. He wanted to make certain Emil could walk tall to his death. This way, when word was received by the Allies that one of their spies had eaten a bullet, they wouldn't know how poorly he had been treated prior.

"Have you heard anything about my wife?" Emil asked. "She was taken from here recently. Petite, ashen-brown hair, blue eyes. Have you seen her?"

The man rapped on the door for a soldier to release him. He didn't turn. "I've seen no such woman." The door closed behind him in a thrum of metal. Every visit after, no amount of Emil's questioning elicited a response. Not until the sixth evening would the doctor speak again.

On that day, after performing his examination, he nodded, lifted his medical bag as usual, and finally met his patient's eyes. "This is to be the last time I come."

Emil released a falsely optimistic chuckle. "Because I am being released?"

"No." The doctor collected his things and left.

So, tomorrow he would die. At least he could stop wondering. It was better to know.

He ate his final meal alone and in silence. When Zeke opened the cellar door, he went willingly.

The doctor had done his job well. After almost a week, most of Emil's bruises had lessened to a manageable level and he could easily rise up the cellar staircase without trouble. His ribs still hurt, but he was able to breathe easier than he had in days, if not for the stone of defeat bearing down upon his chest.

They encountered no one as they moved through the house's darkened main floor nor when Zeke grasped his arm and directed him out onto the street. The hour was still early as they made their way down the snow-covered walk, the sky midnight blue with a bright smattering of stars. Snow crunched underfoot through the strange sort of silence that only a winter night can leave, as though the world itself held its breath. Emil placed one foot in front of the next with only the occasional glance at Zeke's emotionless expression. He wouldn't garner any sympathy there. To think, he had once felt threatened by this man's mere memory. He supposed he had ultimately been right.

Zeke led him down one street then another. His pistol glinted in his opposite hand, the safety released and ready to fire. Emil could probably knock him down, but his few second head start wouldn't be enough for a soldier at the ready. He would simply end up with a bullet in his back rather than his skull. The conclusion would be the same. So instead, he allowed Zeke to lead him on, his eyes on the night sky rather than his destination and thoughts on the brother who would be waiting on the other side. At least he had someone to guide him home to Heaven. He could meet Reuben's family too and his grandparents. That would be nice. He only wished his parents didn't have to lose another son ...

After this terrible war ended, he hoped—no, he prayed—that his brother, Friedrich, would become the son their parents needed. If not, at least they had Winnie—assuming she survived the war. Emil had no doubt his sister would make sure to leave her mark on the world, whether or not she carried the Kisch name.

For the first time in a while, he was quite glad he didn't have any children to leave behind who would know only of their father through stories. Children who wouldn't understand.

Zeke led him towards a dilapidated house, the eastern wall left in ruins while the opposite side remained intact. It seemed an odd place to perform an execution, but who was he to judge the *Deutsches Heer*'s methods? The door hung lopsided on two hinges, revealing a sitting room covered in a thick layer of stone and plaster sediment. A dune of snow swelled down into the room from atop the rubble of the eastern wall.

An unexpected shove to his back followed by a swift boot kick to his rear sent Emil stumbling through the entry and against a ruined sofa. Dust billowed from its cushions, filling Emil's airways as Zeke strode again towards him with pistol drawn. Coughing, he stumbled backwards, knocking against a side table and sending knick-knacks crashing to the ground. He knew he had nowhere to go, still self-preservation had him running scared. He spun around the table with both hands raised, the metallic glitter of death drawing ever nearer.

"Wait," he choked. "Siegfried, please. Think about what you're doing." Stepping back blindly, he didn't notice the pile of debris until he tripped over it, frigid water soaking his trousers when he landed in the mounded snow. Above him the destruction of war opened into the deep black nothingness of midnight and Zeke's pistol pressed painfully against Emil's sternum. He was on the verge of begging even though his inner self wanted to make some clever remark and die with honor. Zeke glared at him, his finger poised above the trigger.

He squeezed his eyes closed and waited for the blow. He didn't want to watch it happen. "Think of Amara," he ordered himself.

"I am," came the disgruntled reply and the pistol's weight disappeared from his chest. Had he been shot? He thought it would hurt more.

He opened his eyes to find Zeke holding the pistol out to him, the barrel between his fingers rather than the grip. His expression hadn't changed, only his stance. "Take this. You'll need it to escape."

Emil remained silent, breathing heavy with uncertainty. What sort of trick was this? Was Zeke provoking Emil into shooting him? For what possible reason?

Zeke shook the weapon. "Take it, you fool," he growled, "or I will shoot you and be done with it. It's certainly what I would prefer to do."

Emil accepted the weapon with shaking hands. "You're releasing me?"

"Yes." Stalking to the far side of the room, Zeke bent to extract a rumpled haversack from within the ashes of the fireplace, then returned to where Emil still sat rooted in the snow drift. He removed a grey-green German army uniform from inside the bag and thrust it at him. "Put that on and be quick about it. We might not have much time."

Scrambling to his feet, Emil set the pistol on the side table and began yanking his soiled and bloodied clothes off in a manner he would have considered indecent in any other situation. Cold air bit his bare skin while he tugged on each piece of the German uniform and forced himself to not audibly question this change of events. Zeke was releasing him. Who bloomin' cared why?

Situating the cap low against his ears, he slid into the military-issued overcoat Zeke handed him. Once it was across his shoulders, he released an involuntary sigh of warmth and slipped on the included leather gloves. The coat hung several inches too short for his six-foot-two-inch frame, but he hoped that in the darkness no one would notice an unfashionably high hem.

Zeke slapped the haversack to release some of the ash and soil. "This has provisions for the next few days, a blanket, and fifteen francs should you need to pay off someone's silence. You have about five miles to the front line. Don't stop anywhere along the way. Sleep in the woods. If you run out of food, steal or kill more."

He slipped a folded parchment from his jacket pocket and directed Emil into the dim moonlight from the fallen wall. Unfolding the document, he revealed a map of the area with certain places circled. "This—" He pointed to the first marking. "—is where we are. I've lined the roads you should take, and here—" He pointed to another mark a few miles from the first one, quite near the Brindille Bridge. "—is where you need to change clothes. There's a French uniform in the bag. Its owner donated it to your cause two days past."

Emil said a silent prayer of gratitude to the deceased Frenchman and pushed any excess grief from his mind. There would be time enough to dwell over that if he made it out alive.

"What do I do if someone sees me before I get to the front line?" he asked.

"Lie your way out. Don't let them bring you back here."

"And if they see right through the lie?"

Zeke tipped his chin in the direction of the uniform Emil wore. "You're in the army now. Figure it out."

Emil swallowed hard as he examined the map. Was it a trick? He had to trust that it wasn't. This was his only chance to escape; if he remained in Le Clé, he was certainly dead. The circle beside the Brindille Bridge shone up at him like a beacon calling him home. He had to get back to the Clermonts', back to Peter and Bill. Together, they could devise a plan to find Amara. Peter would guide him across the bloomin' Alps and through the whole of Germany if need be. They wouldn't rest until they found her. Assuming she wasn't already dead.

"What happened to her?" he demanded. He knew Zeke understood who he meant. "Did you ..." He almost couldn't speak the words. "Did you kill her?"

Please, just give me a word, he begged. *An indication that she's all right. Any word besides, "Yes."*

Zeke cinched the haversack and offered it into Emil's care. Thankfully, he didn't say, "Yes." He didn't have a chance to say anything.

A shout rose in the distance followed by another nearer then another still closer—a message being relayed through the streets. Zeke retrieved another pistol from beneath his coat while shoving the first into Emil's hands. He narrowed his eyes on the battered doorway as the commotion outside increased. "They've discovered you're missing. Time to leave."

Emil folded the map into his pocket, shouldered the haversack, and raced out the front door on Zeke's heels. They wove between buildings, Emil struggling to keep pace. Holding the pistol stiffly in his right hand, he draped his left around his stomach to clutch his bruised ribs, all while somehow managing to keep the haversack upon his shoulder. It bounced against his back with every step. If not for its role to save his life, he would have chucked it to lighten the load.

"Only two more blocks to the gate!" Zeke whisper-yelled over his shoulder. He didn't look back to make sure Emil followed. "Maybe we can steal a truck. It can get you to Brindille."

"Do you mean to come with me then?"

"I wasn't planning to." Zeke skidded to a halt, throwing out a hand to keep Emil at bay. He shoved him back against the nearest building and leaned around the corner. About thirty feet away was a barricade, two beams of constructed steel blocking the path into or out of Le Clé. Two guards stood at the ready, rifles in position while their eyes scanned the street. Zeke shoved Emil back again as more boots clomped past them, joining their fellows at the gate.

"The Allied spy!" one shouted. "He has escaped."

"How?" came another man's return. He cursed in several short bursts. "The lieutenant will have us all shot for this."

"Stay at the gate," sneered a third. "We've sent men to scan the borders. We'll be ready whichever way he chooses to leave. If he remains hidden, we'll burn the village house by house until we find him."

They would burn an entire village for one man? Emil shuddered. He couldn't be responsible for a thousand innocents meeting their end. He tried to shrug Zeke off and move around him, but the lieutenant turned to elbow him back against the wall. "Where do you think you're going?" he hissed. "You heard them; they're patrolling the borders. You'll have to wait in the ruins until morning."

"By morning, the entire town could be ablaze! I appreciate what you've done for me, but my life isn't worth all of theirs."

"You would turn yourself in?"

"Yes. I was prepared to die when you came for me an hour ago. Now shouldn't be any different."

Zeke studied him another minute, perhaps two, while additional shouts filled the air and boots filed through the streets. "You really are who she said you are," he said slowly. "She was right."

"Amara?" Emil cried. He grabbed Zeke's coat sleeve. "Where is she? Tell me!"

Zeke checked his pistol, made sure it was loaded. He shrugged Emil away and peered around the corner again. "You need to run now and don't look back. Whatever happens, keep going."

"You didn't answer my question!"

"And I'm not going to. Now, run."

Zeke leaned once more around the brick building, took sight of the gate guards, lifted his pistol, and fired. The bullet flew through the first guard's chest and at the same time he crumpled to the ground, his rifle fell from his hands. The other three guards barely had time to notice their fallen soldier when Zeke's second shot pierced the next man, sending him on top of the first.

The other two raised their rifles, searching for the gunman, but Zeke had the advantage of surprise. The third man fell with a shout on his lips and the fourth swung his rifle back and forth, eyes wide. "Hurry!" the man shouted towards an area of the street outside Emil's sights. "They're here!" More boot clomps, more squelches of snow underfoot.

It was then that Emil recognized the very noticeable flaw in Zeke's plan. As soon as he cleared the gate, they would see his tracks in the snow. They would be able to follow wherever he went.

"I gave you an order!" Zeke yelled at him. "You wanted to be in my regiment, so listen!" He yanked Emil around by the coat sleeve, spinning him out into the open where he was exposed to every guard. A contingent of five men hustled down the street, approaching rapidly with rifles at the ready. The last remaining gate guard directed his own at Emil a second before Zeke's shot sent him to the ground.

That was when Emil finally ran.

He tore across the open street, slipping in the snow, nearly falling more than once. A shot rang out over his head and he realized he had ducked at exactly the right moment. He pushed off from the snow with his free hand and pivoted again towards the gate. Blood peppered the slush and puddled where the departed guards lay silent. He hurdled the steel gate as a bullet pinged off its edge, the sound ringing in his ears. Another bullet whizzed into the snowy earth beside him. Their aim appeared to be improving.

Zeke vaulted the steel gate after him, cursing in all varieties of

German. He let another shot off behind him without judging where the bullet landed. In the street, two more soldiers lay unmoving, similar crimson circles drawing outward, the liquid almost black in the moonlight.

"Go, you idiot!" Zeke shouted. His fingers clenched Emil's overcoat. "Run. Tell Amara—"

In the sound of another rifle shot, blood splattered Emil's chest, his face, into his hair and across the snow. The lieutenant still gripped Emil's coat sleeve as he crumpled to the ground, forcing Emil to his knees beside him. Zeke's unseeing eyes stared straight at the sky and his hand finally dropped into the blood-spattered snow, unmoving.

"Zeke!" Emil yelled. He pressed both hands to the hole in Zeke's chest, blood pouring over his fingers. The sleeves of his once pristine German uniform soaked it up like a kitchen sponge. "Zeke!" Those blue eyes still stared. Blue eyes, like Amara's.

A bullet whizzed by, burying itself in the soil by Emil's knee, followed by another near his ankle. He surged forward and ripped Zeke's metal identification tag from his neck, shoving it into his coat pocket. Snatching up both of their pistols from the ground, he grabbed the haversack and ran off the road towards the forest, slapping through the trees. Bullets pelted the air behind him and incomprehensible shouts, but it was Zeke's last words which he now remembered.

Tell Amara—

Emil might not know much right now, but he did know one thing with certainty. If Amara was dead, Zeke wouldn't have had anything else to tell her.

FORTY~FIVE

December 31, 1917 – One Week Prior
The French Countryside

AMARA HAD TUMBLED ABOUT IN the back of the empty military wagon, bracing her feet against the corners to keep from knocking against the wall with every turn. There was nothing else she could grab ahold of except for her satchel, which Zeke had mercifully allowed her to keep. Perhaps he hadn't realized she still carried it.

When next they stopped, she dug through the bag searching for anything she might be able to use as a weapon. Unfortunately, she had been clever enough to bring food and medical supplies, but didn't think to bring a pistol or even so much as a butter knife. Her fingernails, bitten short again, were too blunt to prove resourceful.

No matter where her current location may be, she had to find a way to escape. Once they crossed the border into Germany, it would be more difficult to flee, if she was ever able to. Her chances were better out in the French countryside with only Zeke to contend with. After seeing what he did to Emil, the way he bloodied the man she loved, she could be compelled to batter back any amount of force he might send her way.

At least she had saved her brother from meeting the same fate. Or so she hoped.

The door flapped open, sending a gust of snow through the back of the wagon and underneath Amara's skirts. Zeke's outline appeared in the rectangle of the open doors, a flashlight in one hand, the same sort Bill had stolen. "We're here," he snipped. "Gather your things and get out."

She lifted the satchel strap over her head and crawled towards the doors, peering out. "Where's here?" All she could see was a dark road and little moon.

"The Brindille Bridge. I will speak with the guards while you cross the bridge. Follow the road into town. Find shelter there and in the morning, return to wherever you came from."

The Brindille Bridge? Ducking under his arm, she jumped from the wagon and peered around the open door. Winter wind slapped loose hairs against her face and neck, combining with the sting of snow. She raised her hand to see through the white swirl. A dim lantern sat inside the guard shack window and past it, the wagon's headlamps shone across the Brindille Bridge. Wheel ruts ended before reaching the bridge's wooden planks, several making wide circles to return the way they came. No one was allowed into unoccupied territory without the proper passes and few were awarded them.

She stepped back behind the wagon door to block the wind. "Do you think I would leave without my husband?" she asked Zeke. "I won't."

Zeke clenched his jaw then unclenched it. The flashlight beam swung to her shoes then back to her face. His overcoat hem snapped in the wind. "I'm giving you a free pass to safety. Why won't you take it?"

"Because a free life at the price of my husband's is no life at all." She turned in the direction they came from, head down against the wind. Once again, she thought she heard voices cautioning her. Once again, she ignored them. "I'm going back. I'm not leaving without him."

"In this weather?" He strode after her, catching her arm. The snow swirled, seeming to ever increase in magnitude. Already her toes were numb and her lips chapped. Brindille was only a straight mile's walk, while Le Clé nearly four and she did not know this particular route. She wouldn't survive out here alone and he knew it.

Still, she yanked her arm away. "I'll do what it takes."

They stared at one another for a hard moment. She wouldn't leave without Emil. She had every intention of staying in that cellar to die with him. To stop her, Zeke would need to either drive her back or shoot her right here. She still wasn't sure why he hesitated to do so.

Finally, he grunted. "Fine. I will bring your husband to you."

"That's a bundle of lies if I ever heard one."

"Would you rather he died? Before he can travel, he needs to recover from his wounds. I will order our doctor to treat him, then spread a story about delaying the execution until elite officers arrive from Berlin. My men won't question me and risk insubordination. I can take your husband as far as Brindille. After that he's on his own. You have my word."

"Your word isn't worth much to me anymore."

"Then walk back on your own." He punched a fist towards the darkness leading to Le Clé. "Die in the snow or be imprisoned. Even if you could free him, your husband's wounds are too severe to travel far. You'll both be shot before you reach the gate."

She knew he wasn't lying about that. She had seen Emil in the cellar, held him in her arms. His blood covered her coat, her dress, and her hands. His swollen eyes, barely able to look at her. She couldn't rescue him in such a condition, at least not alone. "I don't understand. Why would you help us?"

Zeke pulled off his cap and slapped it against his palm. He sat on the edge of the wagon's bed between the open doors. The hat spun between his hands. "Because you remembered who I used to be. You never forgot. I forgot. All those years ago, after you told me you couldn't have children, I was so angry I forgot I was supposed to love you. You never stopped loving me though, did you?"

Had she? She certainly didn't feel for him now what she did those many years ago and her feelings could never compare to the love she held for Emil. Yet, she knew there were other kinds of love, like the kind you felt for your enemies. Wanting them to possess a piece of goodness even when they only showed the worst to you.

She sat beside him and covered his hand with her own. Here they were sheltered from the worst of the wind. "No," she admitted. "I don't think I ever did. All I wanted was to understand why you never loved me like Emil does. He cares about every part of me, even the broken ones. Especially the broken ones. He's the best man I've ever known."

Zeke remained silent. His fingers moved to wrap hers and held them gently.

She wanted to remember this. This time, this gesture. He gave her a sad smile and for a single glimmering moment, she recognized that seventeen-year-old boy who kissed her on the railroad tracks in Bayern. She wanted him to still be there, but knew he never would be again.

She released his hand. "Goodbye, Siegfried."

"Goodbye, Amara."

She rushed towards the bridge and Siegfried let her go. She prayed he would play his part as promised.

—

January 1, 1917 – The Next Day
Clermont Farm, France

It was the most difficult decision Peter had ever made, not to immediately saddle his horse and chase after his sister. Although he would have gladly given his life to save hers, he knew that his current physical condition would have made him more of a liability than a savior. Even if his leg gave out entirely, Amara would never have left him behind. They would all have been lost because of his stubbornness.

So he decided to let her fight this battle on her own and pray that God's plan for her life didn't end there. He didn't know if it was the right decision, but too often there were no obvious decisions. Sometimes you simply had to hope for the best.

"Peter!"

At the sound of her voice, he limped from the barn, wondering if he had imagined it. Her hair flew about her shoulders as she sprinted towards him, her coat covered in blood. *Blood?* How could she have so much blood on her and be able to run so well? That meant it was someone else's blood. Emil's? Or Zeke's? Neither was with her.

Had the mission failed completely?

Then her arms were around him and he swallowed her up, both of them crying in harmony. In that moment, he couldn't think about Zeke or *Fides et Spes* or what had become of Emil. At that moment, all he could do was close his eyes and thank God.

FORTY-SIX

January 6, 1917 – Five days later
The French Countryside

EMIL TRUDGED THROUGH THE frozen forest until he thought he could go no farther. He tumbled down an embankment and his bruised shoulder landed against a rock, causing him to cry out involuntarily.

He didn't know how long he ran before the rifle shots disappeared. Not as long as it took to lose the hostile shouts tracking him through the trees. As soon as he was able, he ditched the bloody German uniform for the French one and thankfully encountered no one after. His muscles grew stiff with the cold, and all the pain he endured in that cellar felt like it was returning to crush him. He checked the map and shivered violently. Only another few miles.

He could make it.

He had to.

FORTY-SEVEN

January 9, 1918 – Three Days Later
Clermont Farm, France

AMARA HAD NEVER BEEN SO RELIEVED—and frightened—to see anyone as when Emil stumbled into the Clermonts' farmhouse that afternoon. His filthy haversack dropped shortly before he did, cushioning his fall against the hard floorboards. Amara sprinted to him, easing his head and shoulders back onto her lap, her eyes and hands examining him for wounds. Siegfried had kept his promise.

"What can we do?" Josie asked, kneeling beside her.

"Bill, fetch my brother from the barn!" Amara ordered, but he was already three steps ahead. The front door closed without reply. She craned her neck to look for Solange and saw that the French woman was already scooping Remy up and ushering the other children from the room.

Amara held Emil, wiping bloody hair away from his face as she and Josie searched him over for wounds. He was wearing a French uniform; where had he gotten that from? Did he steal it? Kill someone for it? Perhaps the blood was his, leftover from the cellar.

"Emil!" she cried. "What happened? Are you hurt?"

Emil shook his head and closed his eyes.

"Emil," she cried again, starting to feel hysterical. He couldn't make it all the way back to her only to leave her now. "Stay with me."

"From now on," he whispered. He reached into his jacket pocket and removed a piece of metal, its surface tacky with dried blood and

316

pocket fibers. He pressed it into her hand. "Your cousin saved me."

Emil passed out after that, leaving Bill and Peter to half-carry, half-drag him to the back bedroom. Upon a quick examination, Bill declared his patient in no imminent danger and thought it best to let him rest. Only then had Amara gone to the water pump and scrubbed the metal's surface clean.

It was nothing more than a simple piece of tin on a leather cord, cut into an oval and stamped with Siegfried's personal details. Several numbers and abbreviations followed which she supposed were related to his specific regiment. A hyphenated line cut across the center, a mirror image of the words stamped again beneath it.

Sieg. Rohrbaugh, the tag read. *26.11.1891, Oberammergau.*

Dead at barely twenty-six years old.

From the straight wooden chair beside her husband's bed, she now studied the edge of each letter and wondered how many times Emil also read them during his journey back. It shouldn't have ended like this. Not for Siegfried. Not for any of them.

Emil's eyelids fluttered open then, his robin's egg blue irises immediately locked with hers. Portions of his face were still bruised and other parts contained cuts now scabbed over, but thankfully he was healing. That night in the cellar had been one of the worst of her life, seeing him so abused and believing it was the last time she would ever see him at all. To have that be her final memory would have haunted her nightmares even more than it already did. She shook the image from her mind; she didn't want to dwell on such horrors now that he was finally back beside her.

Instead, she allowed her mind to fill with all her favorite memories. The tender warmth of his childhood story about saving two hurt turtledoves. How his hand lay on her waist when they danced. The sound of his laughter through his whispered jokes. When he pulled out her chair the night they met because no man ever had. The sweet pull of his kisses, such perfect beautiful kisses. His promises to love her no matter what. For now, she didn't need to know anything past the two of them in this room. He was alive and so was she.

"You're back," she said with a smile.

He nodded. "What day is it?"

"The ninth of January."

"The ninth?"

"All day long."

He gave a weak smile. "Not my birthday then?"

"Not for another three days."

"It's funny how recently I didn't think I'd live to see twenty-two." He extended his hand to her atop the quilt, palm up, silently requesting her to take it. She realized then that she still held Siegfried's identification tag. Quickly, she laid it on the bedside table.

His gaze swept to the tag then back again. "You're allowed to grieve him, you know. He was still your cousin and more. I can't expect you to erase that part of your heart completely."

"I feel like I should though. For years, he was horrible to me. He abused me, then he tried to kill you—"

"He also saved me. He gave his life for us in the end." Emil swallowed hard, his eyes rolling to stare at the ceiling. His voice came low and forced, stuck somewhere inside. "Zeke was helping me escape, providing us with cover fire. We made it to the gate when ..." He paused, took a breath. "They shot him. His own men. I tried to save him. I covered the wound with my hands, but he ... he was already gone."

Amara focused on the hand gripping hers. The space under his fingernails was still stained red. She did despair for Siegfried. She did love him, as much as she was able after all he had done. He had finally found the lost pieces of his humanity—at least a small part of who he was before—and then he was simply ... gone. No more chances to make the most of what he had left. He had been her aunt and uncle's only child. Once they received the *Deutsches Heer*'s version of his death, their memory of him would forever be tainted by dishonor.

"I love you for what you tried to do," she said at last.

He squeezed her hand. "As long as you still love me."

"Always." She wanted to speak about something else. Anything else except death. "Would you like to wash up?" she asked.

"I'd like nothing more." He tried to sit up and grimaced, falling back to the pillow. "I don't think I have the strength to get to the wash tub."

She brushed his tangled and gritty blond locks away in order to place a gentle kiss to his forehead. "Wait here. I'll be right back." Ten minutes later, she returned with a bowl of water warmed on the fire and several wash rags.

She wiped his face with tender motions, then across his palms, and finally picked dried blood from beneath each fingernail, rinsing the rag after each step. His once-platinum hair, now tan, she smoothed back with the washrag, holding the bowl up to catch the dirty rinse water. When the liquid turned a murky copper, she left to cast it out the kitchen door and refill the bowl with fresh.

Returning to the bedroom, she helped ease him up and out of the French infantry jacket, then eased his soiled undershirt over his head, watching him silently protest every movement. She stifled a gasp. Mottled bruises covered nearly every inch of him in a garish array of blue, green, and purple, the largest section of damage filling the entire side of his right rib cage. From his left wrist to directly below the elbow, haphazard black stitches sealed a jagged wound. She traced the line with her finger. Her beautiful husband, reduced to such colorful misery on her account.

"Don't look that way," he said. She met those vivid blue eyes, so full of similar hurts. "Don't blame yourself for this. I don't regret any of it. I did it for you."

"How can I not feel regret?" She wrung the washrag between her hands, water dripping onto his stomach. "I had to wait a week to know if Siegfried would keep his promise. A week wondering if I was a widow. I thought about where I would be if you never returned. If you had sacrificed your life for me and my brother, it would have been honorable. You would have been a hero, but it would have still been my doing."

"I didn't do it to be a hero. I did it because—"

"Because you love me."

"Yes." He held her gaze. "You and Peter. And I would do it again."

He lifted her hand, still clutching the washrag, to his chest and she obliged, wiping the skin clean with the same careful strokes. He leaned into the pillows and closed his eyes. After a minute, his breathing slowed and she wondered if he had fallen asleep. Walking so many miles with so many injuries … it was amazing he made it back to her at all.

When the water again turned as brown as the Mississippi River, she placed the washrag in the bowl and rose.

"Leave it for now." He reached for her, one palm flat against her stomach. His long fingers splayed against the place where most men at one time or another would feel their baby's movements. Not her husband though.

"Come lie beside me," he offered. "I've missed being near you."

Placing the bowl on the bedside table, she slid beneath the bedcovers, allowing his arms to encircle her even though the effort must pain him. She rested her cheek upon his damp chest, glad to have his warmth so near. There was safety in it, the same safety she found when she married him. The same safety which despite any conflict they might encounter, would do his best to be there. For better or worse. They had certainly endured much of the worse. She was ready for the better.

She slipped one arm from around his waist, lifting her fingertips to light over the supple blond beard upon his jaw. "Emil, will you forgive me?" she whispered.

"I already told you that I don't blame you for what happened."

"Yes, but I still caused a distance between us before we ever left for France. I need you to forgive me for holding your past captive and inflicting mine upon you. For not trusting you completely with my heart when I should have known it was already yours."

Emil took a deep breath. He didn't answer right away and she wondered if she had said something wrong. Here she was, pouring her heart out and he—

"You were the last person he thought of."

"Who?" she asked, but he remained silent. How many *hes* could there really be to choose from? "Siegfried?"

Emil ran a slow palm up and down her back, sending chills up her spine and across her shoulders. "Right before he died. He wanted me to tell you something, but I never found out what it was. I believe he loved you too … whatever small amount he could. At least enough to set me free."

She knew it probably agonized him to admit to another man loving her, especially one as rough and vile as Zeke had been. Had the situation been reversed, she doubted she would have the courage to admit it. She would be too afraid to have his heart divided. It would likely be a struggle for her even as the years wore on, to trust that someone could love her so completely, brokenness and all.

"You're forgiven," he said then. "Being here was exactly the cure I needed to understand where your heart lies and where mine always will." The sincerity with which he spoke instantly lightened her heart and when he smiled, all else melted away.

She raised her lips to her husband's, allowing them to roam upon his skin, while praising every piece of God's great goodness that she had been given another day to do so.

"Do you think anyone would notice if we lingered here all day?" he mumbled. "I trust you to be gentle with me." He tugged at the buttons on her day dress at the same time a knock sounded at the bedroom door. He groaned. "The timing of some people is utterly ridiculous."

She kissed him lightly. "Don't worry, there's always tonight." She slid off the bed, releasing his fingers last.

"That's too far away," he called as she opened the door.

"What's too far away?" Peter asked as he and Josie stepped into the room. Solange and her older boys stood right behind with Remy on her hip. Bill propped himself up in the doorway, his hip against the frame.

"A good night's rest." Emil pushed himself up to sitting, managing to stifle a full-on grimace. Amara hurried to adjust the pillows behind his back, then helped him maneuver a sweater over his still-bare chest. The last thing he needed was to catch a cold after surviving all else.

Once he was situated, Solange ushered the boys forward. They actually seemed shy for once, remaining a full foot away from the bed as though Emil would reach out and grab them. Amara supposed she could understand their hesitation; between all the bruises and scabs, he did appear somewhat frightful. First Lucien then Maël murmured something in French to which Emil replied, *"Merci,"* and smiled.

With a nod from their mother, they scampered from the room and Solange placed Remy down beside the bed.

"Remy, *non, non,*" she said when the child attempted to climb onto the mattress. He looked back at his aunt then squeezed a hug to Emil's arm instead. Solange smiled. "*Très bien,* Remy." With a light pat to his bum, she sent him toddling after his cousins.

"The boys are so pleased that you're well," she told Emil. Relief flooded her features. "As are we all. As much as I have enjoyed your friendship, please tell me you do not plan to continue here."

Ten eyes all swept onto Emil, the room waiting on his reflection.

"No," he said immediately. "I think it would be incredibly foolish for us to remain after all that has happened. There is certainly more to be done to support the war, but it might be time to find another way to serve." He reached for Amara's hand and tugged her to sit on the quilt beside him. He lightly ran her knuckles across his lips. "I think we should do what we planned all along. Go home and adopt a baby."

She hardly dared to believe it. Her dream—their dream—at long last coming true. After all they had endured, after seeing the misery the war had wrought, she had questioned if Emil would still agree to her spontaneous request. It wasn't wise. But it was what she wanted.

All she said was, "Where is home?"

He kissed her hand again and exhaled. "I think St. Louis if you are willing. I'm tired of running and tired of hiding. Any day might be our last. I'd rather spend our last with my family."

"What if Earhart decides to turn us in as spies?"

"It's been seven months since he threatened us. I have to believe if he was going to turn us in, he would have done so by now."

To go home, she thought. To their actual home, not somewhere they were forced to make home by circumstance or necessity. To create a life and a family beside his family was a wonderful notion.

"Would you come with us?" she asked Peter. He leaned against the chest of drawers, one arm around Josie's waist, observing them in silence. It pained Amara to think of losing her brother now. Worse, to hear he would remain in such hazardous circumstances.

"Someone has to continue to serve Le Clé," he told her.

322

"Peter, no." Josie moved out of his embrace to face him. "It's too dangerous. They know what you look like."

"I'll stay then," Bill said. He shrugged at the resulting stares and tugged a bit of string from his cuff. "I can change my mind, can't I? There's still a farm to tend and letters to deliver. I'll find another man or two in Brindille willing to help share the load."

"You can't possibly mean to go back into Le Clé?" Josie astounded.

"Why not? It's more than I was ever doing at the manor, isn't it?"

"Bill," Peter began. "You can't stay if I go. Coming to France was my idea."

Bill's expression eased, although he folded his arms and Amara knew further argument would be wasted breath. "I think you've completed the mission you set out to. Don't you think it's time for you to begin a new one elsewhere?" He looked to Josie. "Perhaps with someone else?"

A moment of silence followed where Amara could see the indecision on her brother's face. "It took me a long time too," she told him, "to believe I deserved happiness. Perhaps it's time for us both to accept we do."

He blinked. "Perhaps." A pause. A nod. "Perhaps we do." He reached for Josie's hand, securing it between both of his, laying his worn and beaten left fingers on top of her blue string ring. He dropped to his good knee with only a slight stumble. "Joselyn Harrington, can you forgive me for everything I put us through? Will you marry me and move to Missouri—of course, only if you wouldn't miss London too much."

Josie shook her head with a smile, her light curls bouncing against her shoulders. "I'll miss London because it was where my father was. But he isn't there anymore. He's buried in the Somme, and I'm ready for something new ... with someone new." Lifting his hands, she eased him back to his feet and lifted her lips to kiss him. "Perhaps someday with more than only the two of us."

He grinned before kissing her again. "I would like that."

Solange chuckled. "You may be granted that wish sooner than you think. That is if you are willing." She swept past Bill and led a very timid Bernadette in from the other room, her new evergreen dress stitched from one of Solange's old ones. Its creation had filled Amara with her only joy during Emil's imprisonment.

Solange eased the girl forward, encouraging her in enthusiastic French. Bernadette crept along until she stood between Josie and Peter. Glancing from one to the other, she mumbled a quiet batch of French. Amara looked to Emil for translation, but he shook his head. Even he hadn't been able to make it out.

Solange, however, replied reassuringly to Bernadette before switching to English. "Josie, Peter, she has a request for you."

Eyes downcast, the child repeated her statement and this time Amara felt Emil's hand tense against hers. To answer her questioning look, however, he only provided a quick shake of his head. Either he felt it wasn't his place to translate or he didn't want to.

Solange rested both her hands on the girl's shoulders and smiled. "She asks if she may come with you to America. She says she has no one else and wonders if there might be room within your family."

"*Our* family?" Peter gasped. Bernadette stared at them expectantly. He turned to Josie who also appeared dumbstruck. "Neither of us know French," he stammered. "How can we take in a child when we don't speak the same language?"

Although she could not translate, Bernadette took a step back from his tone and Solange didn't bother translating. She stepped up behind the girl and laid a hand on either of her shoulders. The child wrung her hands in her skirts, although her attention was ever on Peter. "Did you know English when you moved to America?" Solange asked.

Peter shook his head.

"Then she will learn too. She has told me how she adores you and I have seen the same sentiment from you. She trusts you because you saved her."

Bernadette's pretty wide eyes grew wider. She had no idea what they spoke of or if it would end in her favor. She likely worried that they didn't want her, that she was nothing but a bother and shouldn't have asked. Amara understood feeling unwanted and unsure. Wondering what your meaning was in life. It amazed her how it had taken matters of life and death for her to see that she held the answer to her uncertainty all along. She only had to have the faith to find it.

It was Emil, however, who spoke. "You have a heart, Peter, and it's still beating. That's all she's asking for."

"He's right," Josie said. She held her right hand out and Peter placed his mangled one inside it. "Six months ago, every day was the same. I would ride my bike through London, deliver letters, and try to survive the air raids. Marriage wasn't in my future, nor was being a mother. It wasn't in yours either. Now we're here with this brilliant opportunity. To not only be happy, but to also help an innocent. Wasn't that what we came for?" She placed a hand over her stomach. "I'm so nervous, I could be sick, but I'm so excited, I could burst."

Peter gave a low chuckle. "Like you've eaten an army of fire ants?"

Josie laughed. "Yes, and they're dancing to a ragtime beat."

"Then I suppose it's decided. Solange, how do you say, 'Welcome, daughter'?"

"That one is easy. *Bienvenue, ma fille.*"

Peter smiled at Bernadette who finally managed a lopsided smile in return. "*Bienvenue, ma fille.* My family is yours." He extended his arms and with a peal of laughter, she ran into them, wrapping herself around his waist. Josie knelt to lace her own arms around her new daughter and together, the three of them laughed and cried and laughed some more. Even stoic Bill hid a grin from where he remained propped in the doorway.

Amara watched the grin on her brother's face broaden until it seemed like it could light the room without lanterns. With her dark wavy hair and soft features, Bernadette could easily pass as Peter and Josie's kin. She deserved a life far away from the childhood war had stolen from her, and Amara had no doubt that her brother would provide it. For the very first time since learning she could never bear children, she finally felt at peace.

"Are you all right with this?" Emil said softly, low enough so no one else paid any mind. "What if our adoption isn't approved and a child never comes?"

Pressing her lips to her husband's, she said one more prayer of thanks for the life she never imagined would be. "Then I will live and die knowing I had exactly the life *I* needed." Amara smiled. "You."

FORTY~EIGHT

June 1918 – Five Months Later
St. Louis, Missouri

EMIL WOKE TO THE SUMMER SUN streaming across the foot of their full-size bed. A gentle breeze filtered through the open window, leaving his bare skin sticky with the promise of another humid St. Louis day.

Nearly four months had passed since they returned home to Missouri along with newlyweds Peter and Josie and their new daughter, Bernadette. Despite her parents' initial hesitation, it hadn't taken long for Bernadette to wind her way into their hearts. You could see the joy she brought every time her mother or father looked her way.

For four months, Emil and Amara had lived and worked and celebrated without intrusion from either Earhart or the St. Louis Police Department. Sunday evenings were spent around Karl and Elsa Kisch's dining room table, laughing and talking of anything and everything—except the war. They knew it was still there; they received letters regularly from Bill, Solange, and sometimes even Winnie, but they decided there was more to focus on than destruction. As Father Ferdinand's most recent letter said, it was time to hope for the future.

Of course, nothing had been simple to this point; why should he assume it would be simple now? There was still risk that their happiness would be upended again; but, come what may, it was a risk they had decided to take together. This was their family, their country, their home. They had left them once. They would not abandon them again. Even after the white flag flew, they would continue to fight. After all, there would always be another person, another country, another idea that would try to take them down. He was a father now. He had to make sure his children inherited a world worth living in.

Beside him, Amara slept soundly, her ashen-brown hair splayed across her pillow and their handsome son, Charles Lengfeld, snuggled close to her side. The infant's eyelids were tucked closed, lashes whispering his cheeks like tiny feathers. When Emil laid a hand to his chest, it rose and fell without a care.

Emil never found out what happened to the boy soldier who helped him and probably would never know; but they named their son after him all the same. In the two months since adopting the precocious ten-month-old, Charlie had put on weight, his chubby cheeks filling out and a bit more pudge lining his little legs. He had no problems toddling around the little apartment above the family tobacconist and no qualms with tossing his dinner on the floor and throwing his toys in a tantrum. His slobbery baby kisses and gentle nighttime snuggles made it all worth it though. Amara had her dream and in turn Emil had his. Charlie wasn't theirs by blood, but with his light hair and blue eyes, he looked like he could be. Their plans had never gone the way they wanted, yet in the end, they always went the way they should.

Emil kissed his sleeping wife, her bare shoulder peeking out from under the blankets, then eased from the bed to quietly dress and tiptoe downstairs. He slipped out the front door onto the sidewalk where the beautiful sunshine awaited him. The steeple of St. Francis de Sales rose above the rooftops, waiting against a pink and gold-tinged morning sky. He would have to get to work soon enough, but first he could have a few moments of solitude to thank God for everything he had been given.

After that, he had letters to deliver.

AUTHOR'S NOTE

LIKE THE CHARACTERS IN *Unsettled Shores*, domestic abuse, infertility, and post-traumatic stress disorder (PTSD) affect millions of people worldwide every day. If you, or someone you know, live with these conditions, you are not alone. Hope is only a call or click away.

Substance Abuse and Mental Health Services Administration
1-800-662-HELP (4357)
https://samhsa.gov/find-help/national-helpline

National Domestic Violence Hotline
1-800-799-7233
https://thehotline.org

National Center for Women's Health and
NaProTechnology Education
https://www.naprotechnology.com/
https://popepaulvi.com/

National Center for PTSD
1-800-273-8255 (Press #1 for veteran-specific assistance.)
https://www.ptsd.va.gov/

There are many additional resources available in addition to those listed. While the organizations listed above are United States based, similar organizations are available in other countries.

You are strong. You are beautiful. You are brave.
Life isn't finished with you yet.

HISTORICAL NOTES

AFTER WRITING ABOUT THE GREAT WAR from the American home front in *Broken Lines*, I enjoyed the opportunity to examine the home front from the English and French perspectives. All three were different, yet their experiences were made of the same emotions, the same fears, and the same heartache. The very first chapter I wrote actually came about in the midst of writing *Broken Lines* and was the scene where Siegfried helps Emil escape. From then on, I knew I wanted this story to focus on redemption, forgiveness, and overcoming the battles we fight within ourselves.

It's important to note that while *Unsettled Shores* is a story that takes place during a war, it is not strictly a war story. Historical accuracy was important, but several liberties were taken for purposes of the story. For instance, the front line's location was rather fluid with both sides making gains and retreats. Likely the Clermonts' farm and the town of Brindille would have become occupied at some point due to their proximity to the front line. Brindille and Le Clé are both fictional, although their inspiration draws from many actual French towns, including the German-occupied city of Saint Quentin, for whom the character of Quentin Thoreau is named.

The basis for the fictional organization, *Fides et Spes*, began with one small piece of information I found about the underground letter delivery organizations, *Mot du Soldat* (Word of the Soldier) and *Poste des Alliés* (Postal service of the Allies). These two organizations delivered letters between French and Belgian soldiers and their families in occupied territories. As Josie mentions, all letters sent by usual means were subject to censorship and any information considered classified was blacked out before delivery. I liked the idea of an organization completely focused on serving the innocents without any other selfish expectations. Of course, as the characters discover, it's impossible to fight a war while living in shades of grey. I could find no indication that either of these organizations engaged in spy work, but the beauty of historical fiction is asking, "What if?"

Creating an underground organization also meant developing a set of rules to follow. As a Catholic, I immediately wanted to find a way to incorporate my faith. Although Mass is now typically said in each country's vernacular, Latin would have been the only language used in 1917. Outside of Catholicism, Latin would not have been as common, making it ideal for code phrases. As for the churches mentioned, all except for St. Sebastian's can be visited today. Built in 1250, St. Etheldreda's is the oldest Roman Catholic church in London and attracts many American soldiers, due to its similarity to the Catholic Chapel of America's West Point Military Academy. A virtual tour is available online and modern photographs are available of the crypt which is currently being used as an events space. Unfortunately, there are no surviving photographs of either interior prior to World War II.

As for the priests in *Unsettled Shores*, they are all named for French war saints. Father Ferdinand honors St. Ferdinand III, King of Castille; Father Ignatius honors St. Ignatius of Loyola; and Father Jean, who leaves Brindille for enlistment, honors St. Joan of Arc, the patroness of French soldiers.

From the *International Encyclopedia of the First World War*: "Between June 1917 and May 1918, Gotha bombers joined by the massive R-type Staaken "Giants" (Riesenflugzeug) attacked London on seventeen occasions and also bombed many south-eastern coastal towns." Citizens were warned with air raid whistles, "take cover" shouts, and rockets flares. These attacks originally took place in broad daylight, but by September 1917, the Germans had moved to nighttime raids, including the three-day raid Josie and Peter experience in the story. The June 13 raid when 18 children died in the Upper North Street School is also factual. While there was not an attack on November 19, 1917, as shown in the story, the raid Amara and Emil are in is based on real events.

The Battle of the Somme, fought from July to November 1916, was the bloodiest battle of The Great War, with over one million killed collectively. Like Josie's father, many soldiers' bodies were never recovered; often identification tags weren't even found. In 1932, the Thiepval Memorial to the Missing opened, a memorial to more than 72,000 Allied soldiers who remain buried in the Somme battlefields. This is where Hunter Harrington would have been commemorated. There are other similar memorials spread throughout Europe dedicated to those missing in WWI battles, both from the Allies and Central Powers.

For those soldiers who did return home, a large portion found themselves with a new addition—cigarette smoking. Since the health effects and addictive properties of cigarettes were not well known at the time, it was common for World War I soldiers to begin smoking while overseas, often for the reasons Peter mentions doing so. Cigarettes were even included in every soldier's ration pack as governments considered them a necessarily kindness to ease the toils of war.

The young German soldier, Lengfeld Rosch, who helps Emil when he's imprisoned is based on two real-life German soldiers during World War II. Friedrich Lengfeld (aged 23) who lost his life attempting to save a wounded American soldier and Karl-Heinz Rosch (aged 18) who saved two Dutch children while the Germans occupied their village. Both have monuments erected to them, although it took years. The last line of Karl-Heinz's monument reads, "This statue is a tribute to him and all who do good in evil times." Friedrich's monument also contains two particularly fitting lines: "No man hath greater love than he who layeth down his life for his enemy." And, "Deeds not words." While neither of these real-life soldiers survived, it is my hope that my character, Lengfeld Rosch, was able to return to his family in the end.

"Do not be overcome by evil, but overcome evil with good."
(Romans 12:21)

—

I would like to thank my always wonderful support team who helped bring *Unsettled Shores* to life.

As always, a most massive thank you to all my readers for continuing the Hope or High Water journey, especially my amazing family. God has blessed me seven-fold!

To my husband, Scott, and our children. You make every day beautiful, even in the midst of a pandemic. Thank you for standing beside me every step of the way. Together, we have it all!

To my fellow authors and critique partners, Jennifer Q. Hunt, Susan Laspe, and Tanya E. Williams. Not only for your writing advice and review, but for your sincere friendship. 2020 was a rough road. Thank you for riding it with me!

To my additional beta readers: Ann, Diana, Katherine, Ken, Mary, Ruth, and Sharon. For your many comments, suggestions, edits, and hours of discussion and debate. You find all the missing pieces!

To Patrick T. for providing my Latin translations and Katherine L. for checking my French internet translations. Thanks for steering me right!

To my advance reader team and the wonderful bookstagram community. Thank you for your reviews, posts, interviews, and well wishes!

To the many organizations that helped make my WW1 information accurate and believable, especially Soldier's Memorial of St. Louis, National World War 1 Museum and Memorial (Kansas City), Somme Tourism, St. Etheldreda's Catholic Church, and the "1914-1918-online" International Encyclopedia of the First World War project.

To all the incredible authors whose own fiction I pored over for war-time inspiration including Kate Breslin, Jennifer Q. Hunt, Pam Jennings, Jenny Knipfer, Julie Lessman, Liz Costanzo, Kate Quinn, Rosanna M. White, Beatriz Williams, and Tanya E. Williams.

And most importantly, to my Lord and creator, Jesus Christ. Without Him, none of this could be.

ABOUT THE AUTHOR

Photo by Valerie Boaz

BORN AND RAISED IN ST. LOUIS, Missouri, Kelsey Gietl grew up with a love of books and excessive use of her library card. She earned a Bachelor of Fine Arts in Theatre Design and Graphic Design from Stephens College in Columbia, Missouri, and has made a career in fields from event planning and proposal writing to product management and communications.

In her free time—when she's not writing, reading, or researching—she enjoys yoga, musical theatre, beach vacations, and gallivanting around St. Louis with her amazing husband and two beautiful children.

You can connect with her online at:
kelseygietl.com

www.ingramcontent.com/pod-product-compliance
Lightning Source LLC
Chambersburg PA
CBHW051331250626
47155CB00007B/2558